# HAZARD

# HAZARD

Gardiner Harris

Minotaur Books ⚏ New York

HAZARD. Copyright © 2010 by Gardiner Harris. All rights reserved. Printed in the United States of America. For information, address St. Martin's Press, 175 Fifth Avenue, New York, N.Y. 10010.

www.minotaurbooks.com

Library of Congress Cataloging-in-Publication Data

Harris, Gardiner.
    Hazard / Gardiner Harris.—1st ed.
        p.   cm.
    ISBN 978-0-312-57016-3
    1. Coal mines and mining—Kentucky—Fiction.   2. Mine accidents—Fiction.   3. Accident investigation—Fiction.   4. Brothers—Fiction.
5. Family secrets—Fiction.   I. Title
    PS3608.A78285H39   2010
    813'.6—dc22                                                                 2009041128

First Edition: March 2010

10   9   8   7   6   5   4   3   2   1

To T George Harris, whose passionate embrace
of ideas has always inspired me

# ACKNOWLEDGMENTS

First, I'm grateful for the patience of my wife. Writing this book increased the burdens on her, and I couldn't have done it without her support. The book also results from my years writing from Hazard, and I wouldn't have been much of a reporter if not for the help of many. Among them are Hunt Helm, who got me ready to go to Hazard; David Hawpe, who sent me there; and Lee Mueller, Ken Ward, Jr., and Paul Nyden, who made me a better reporter while I was there.

# HAZARD

# CHAPTER ONE

In a space less than five feet high, Amos Blevins rode a shrieking, convulsing mining machine that clawed coal out of a worked-out vein more than fifteen stories underground. The walls left behind barely supported the roof.

A mountain of rock hung suspended above him as he tunneled away at its base. The mine was murky, dense with black dust and barely lit by a few lights and headlamps. To reduce the risk of coal-dust explosions, the walls were coated in chalky limestone, making them look frozen—like a black-and-white photo of an arctic night.

Ears covered, Amos felt the machine's roar more than heard it. Sound waves bathed him from every direction. They made a drum of his sternum, massaged his organs and fought the very rhythm of his heart—on occasion, making him gasp.

And always there was the dust. It could swallow him up and nearly drown him. Like most miner men, he couldn't work with a mask or respirator because it clogged far too often. He hated the dust that filled his mouth, clogged his breath, and hardened his snot.

But sometimes, being enveloped by the dust made him feel as if he'd joined the mountain in some intermediate stage between existence and oblivion. The feeling brought a blend of sadness and wonder, the way he sometimes felt standing over a dying buck.

The mountain seemed to wake up, struggle, and surrender its black soul.

He backed the machine's studded drum away from the coal, and the effect was broken. He figured he'd cut forty feet from the last crosscut, twice what the law allowed. He pulled the giant machine away from the wall and, as always, did it a little too quickly.

He knew that he was no more likely to get crushed in a roof fall while backing out than while digging ahead. But he'd known a guy who was killed while in reverse. The men with him had said that, with just a few more seconds, he would have lived. Amos didn't want to die like that. He wanted to be fully into the mountain when it gave way so there'd be no doubt, no what-ifs for Glenda.

Coal mine roofs stay up in part because miners leave behind columns of coal as supports, making the mine a series of tunnels and cross tunnels that, when mapped, look like city blocks. More support comes when men on roof-bolting machines drill yard-long screws into the ceiling, cementing several layers of overhead rock together.

Amos sat in the small operator's chair stuck under a canopy on the side of the machine, which was the shape of a huge brick with a studded roll on its front. Barrel-chested, he wore black coveralls, a miner's helmet, headlamp, and a coat of grime that blacked out the gray in his shoulder-length hair and full beard. The whites and shiny wetness of his eyes were the only contrast to the dull black that enveloped him and erased the creases from his fifty-year-old face.

Amos knew he didn't have to worry about backing into his helper. The kid stayed well behind him, never venturing under unbolted roof. Made the job harder for Amos. He didn't have anyone just over his shoulder to guide him. The kid was jumpy as a cat. Amos had heard that his girlfriend had just given birth to a son.

No man can work every day in terror. Either the kid would quit or he'd give himself up to the mountain. Amos wished that he'd get on with doing one or the other.

Amos backed the miner left into the crosscut. Steaming, the drum smelled of battery acid and barbecue. He put the miner into forward and headed right, across the face of the coal.

Amos glanced behind him and saw Rob Crane drive up on a wide, low-slung cart. Rob was one of several scoop operators in the mine who ferried coal from Amos's machine back to the mine's conveyor belt.

Amos signaled with his hand that he was continuing on, and Rob nodded and then broke into a wide grin. Amos raised his hands in question. Rob pointed at the kid and then laughed. Amos shrugged.

It was a running joke in the mine. Amos often brought game for dinner, which turned the kid's stomach. Today, he had packed the grilled half-carcass of a possum, an animal akin to a huge rat. At dinner, he had cut away portions of the eighteen-inch stalk of bone and meat with a pocket knife, blood and grease dripping into his beard.

As usual, the kid had stared at Amos with a mixture of fascination and horror. The rest of the crew had watched in silence, waiting. Finally, the kid said, "Jesus," and crawled off to eat his dinner elsewhere. Several crew members had chuckled, but Rob had hooted with laughter that kept on bubbling out of him.

His laughter wasn't the only thing that set Rob apart. Rob was black, a rarity in Appalachian coal mines.

Amos watched Rob's mouth appear and disappear as he laughed, and Amos smiled despite himself. Amos turned the machine into the coal face to continue mining. He looked around again. No sign of their foreman, Mike Barnes. Wondering what Mike did all day, Amos started the machine's drum spinning and edged the miner forward into the coal. The roar began again.

Amos began at floor level and gradually moved the drum up five feet to the roof. When the teeth started to spark on the rock layer above the coal, Amos eased the drum back down and moved the miner machine forward. Rob edged his scoop forward and coupled with the miner so that Amos's machine would disgorge its coal.

Amos made it about twenty feet into his cut when a block of coal about the size of a stove shot out of the wall and grazed the miner's canopy before it crashed into the machine's tail and rolled on toward Rob.

Amos turned to see where the block had gone. He saw the rock first and then Rob, somewhat to the side and underneath it, slapping it with his left forearm.

And behind the scoop he saw the kid, pinned to a mine rib by a column of water. Amos realized that water was pouring out of a hole in the mine wall, pushing him back against the canopy's supports. Amos fought against the pressure but couldn't get out. He put both hands on the canopy support before him and pulled against the force of the water. He slid his left leg out of the seat, ducked his head out from under the canopy, and was immediately swept back.

He slammed feet-first into Rob's scoop and was lifted up onto its side. Amos righted himself and edged along the machine to Rob, who had stopped pounding on the block and sat staring at it.

Amos braced his legs against the nearby rib and pushed on the block. Nothing. He grabbed Rob under the arms and pulled. Rob looked up at Amos, surprise on his face. Amos stopped and looked down.

Rob's coveralls were torn at the waist, and Amos could see that his legs were beginning to tear away. As their helmet lights lit up the gash, Amos saw a tangle of yellow, white, and red gristle.

He put a hand on one of Rob's shoulders and then moved, hand over hand, back toward the kid. At the end of the machine, Amos crossed to the wall of the mine, clawing at the coal to brace himself. Crouched under the low ceiling, he edged along the wall and raised his arms to shield his face from the spray. Soon, he could barely make headway against the force of the water. He finally reached the kid's hand and pulled. It wasn't enough. Amos edged closer and brought his left arm across his body and grabbed under the kid's left armpit.

Without an arm in front of his face, the water hit Amos with its full force. He couldn't breathe. He figured he had one chance to pull the kid free before they both drowned.

# CHAPTER TWO

It was like having a fire hose right on my chest, sir," the kid said. Will Murphy looked down at the chart he'd picked up from the basket outside the hospital room. James Earl Benedetto really was a kid, just eighteen. "Only it was the biggest damn fire hose you ever seen."

"How'd you breathe?" asked Sergeant Detective Gene Freeman of the Kentucky State Police.

With eight men presumed dead, the state police had some claim to running the investigation. So Will, a special investigator for MSHA, the federal Mine Safety and Health Administration, suggested that they all interview the kid together. That way, the state police could declare it an accident, conclude nothing criminal had happened, and Will could take it from there.

Will didn't bother to point out that if anything criminal did happen at a mine site, the FBI would have jurisdiction, not the state police. No need to piss these state boys off for a case that was gonna go nowhere.

Will folded his arms and listened to the interview. Once considered handsome, Will had blue eyes that sparkled like the Caribbean in hurricane season.

"I barely could," the kid said. "I had to, ya know, stretch my neck up."

The kid had been fished out of the mine with five of his coworkers just four hours earlier. They brought him to Hazard Community Hospital suffering from two broken ribs and hypothermia. There were four lawmen packed into the hospital room—two state police detectives, a state mining inspector, and Will. The sergeant detective had pulled up a chair. The rest were standing in a semicircle around the bed.

Will stood between the police detective and the state mining guy, who seemed even less interested in the interview than Will. A young nurse stood on the other side of the bed. A small TV was bolted to the wall near the bed, and it was on. In fact, every TV in the hospital seemed to be on.

The kid was watching *Hollywood Squares*, but the show had been replaced by a vacuum cleaner commercial, which held the kid's attention better than talk with the detectives.

"So then what happened, Mr. Benedetto?" Detective Freeman asked. The kid tore his eyes away from the TV.

"Oh, well, Amos come over and got me. He had to yank pretty hard. Nearly tore my arm off, but h'it done the job," the kid said, nodding his head. "That Amos is something hairy. I thought he's a freak. He'd eat animals—I mean the whole dern thing—for dinner. Just sit there carving off pieces."

The kid was now shaking his head at the memory. His eyes drifted back to the TV like iron filings to a magnet. The show came back on, and he turned up the sound. The lawmen all turned their eyes to the set. The show's host, John Davidson, asked which had more calories, a salad with blue cheese dressing or angel food cake with chocolate sauce.

"Got to be the cake," Will said.

"My wife's been cookin' nothin' but angel food for the last year 'cause she says it's low-fat," the state mining inspector argued. "I'm goin' for the salad."

"I seen this show already," the kid said. "It's the salad."

"You've already seen this?" Sergeant Freeman asked in an irritated voice.

The kid glanced over, a blank look on his face. He turned back. Charles Nelson Reilly advised picking the dessert "because if chocolate-covered cake was better for you than salad, hm hm, I'd eat it for breakfast." The guest agreed.

"No, sorry. It's the salad," John Davidson said.

"Think he's a fairy?" one of the lawmen asked.

"Charles Nelson Reilly?" the kid asked in a shocked voice.

"Nah, everybody I know wears an ascot," Will said.

"A what?" the kid asked.

Another commercial came on.

"Mr. Benedetto, what happened after this Amos fellow pulled you out of the water?" the detective persisted.

"Well, we wasn't out of the water. Not yet, anyways," he said, this time without moving his eyes back to the sergeant. "There was probably foot 'n' a half, two foot of water already at the face. And the roof's only five foot. So Amos, he picked me up by my miner belt and drug me down the fresh air."

"The fresh air?" the detective asked.

"A tunnel leading to the shaft that draws clean air into the mine," Will said quickly.

"Yeah," the kid said. "Amos drug me about twenty breaks. He finally put me down and asked if I could crawl on my own. I told him I thought I could. I's damn sure ready to try."

The kid looked at Will. "Ya know, I don't know if my ribs broke from that water pinnin' me or from Amos carrying me. He 'bout killed me. But I don't know how he done it. Twenty breaks."

"What's twenty breaks?" asked the detective.

"Sixty-foot centers?" Will asked the kid.

"Yes, sir," the kid answered.

"So twenty breaks is about twelve hundred feet," Will said, looking at the kid. "Carrying someone that far stooping under a five-foot roof is a helluva thing."

"Yeah, it were," the kid said. "Amos tol' me he was gonna go back and see 'bout the others. Then he left. I didn't think I'd see him again. Water was pouring in. I started crawling. I had about fifty breaks to go. Tore up my knees and hands getting there," the kid said, using bandaged hands to point to bandaged knees.

"The foreman, Mike Barnes, was already there and so was two other guys, Darrell and the really short guy on the scoop, uh, Coot. The elevator was shorted out and they was shouting for the up man. I just lay there till the water started coming up. Then I stood and waited. Seem like we was there for hours. Then Amos showed up with Carl. He left to go t'other section, but he come back pretty soon. Couldn't get through."

The show started again, and the kid went back to looking at the TV.

"Just to be clear, Mr. Benedetto," Will said, uncrossing his arms and putting a pen from one hand against a small pad that had been hidden in the other, "the last time you saw Rob Crane, the scoop operator, he was still on that piece of equipment, right? In the fresh-air tunnel?"

"Yes, sir," the kid said.

Will looked down. Without raising his eyes, Will asked, "You think there's any chance he made it?"

"Who?"

"Rob."

The kid shook his head.

Will nodded sadly.

"And you don't know what happened to Crandall Morton, the roof-bolt operator?" Will asked.

"No, sir. I never seen him after the water come in."

"And the men from the other section?"

"Never seen them, neither."

Will clicked his pen and closed his notebook. "I think I'm done here, fellas," he said to the other lawmen. "Thank you, Mr. Benedetto."

The kid reached for the TV remote to turn up the sound but the detective stopped him.

"What d'ya think happened, Mr. Benedetto? You hit a well?" asked the detective.

"Sir?" asked the kid, his brow furrowed to show his annoyance that he was still required to answer questions.

"Why'd the water pour in? A well? A spring?"

The kid glanced at Will, who raised his eyebrows. "No, sir. We cut into the old works. Least ways, that's what I'm thinking happened. We knew they was old works around. We just didn't know they was so close," the kid said.

"I think we've bothered Mr. Benedetto enough, don't you think, nurse?" said Will.

Startled, the nurse pushed herself off the wall and stepped toward the foot of the kid's bed.

"Yes, Mr. Benedetto needs his rest. Y'all can come back tomorrow," she said, motioning toward the door.

Detective Freeman stood up silently and stepped toward the door.

"Oh, thanks for your cooperation, Mr. Benedetto," the detective said on his way out. The kid nodded absently.

Outside, the detective turned on Will.

"What was that all about? What are old works?" he asked.

The state mining inspector didn't stop to hear the answer. He walked down the hallway and out some double doors. The other state police detective looked at the floor. They were standing near a high desk, probably a nurse's station. The grill on the fluorescent light above was hanging loose. They were bathed in a harsh light.

"You're not from around here, are you, Detective?" Will asked with a slight smile.

"No," the detective sergeant said in a flat voice. The other detective was now inspecting his fingernails with intense interest. "I'm from Louisville."

Will nodded.

"These mountains are pockmarked with old mines," Will said. "Whole houses sometimes disappear into them. Hills will suddenly slide into creeks because of 'em. And about every year, a kid gets killed playing in one of 'em. Parents tell 'em to stay out, but you know kids."

Will looked away.

"The worst is when miners cut into these old mines. They call 'em old works. When it happens, miners die. Sometimes the air inside doesn't have oxygen, and miners die gasping for breath. Sometimes the air is poisonous or filled with methane that blows up with any spark. And sometimes the old mines fill up with water. Cut into them, and you drown in millions of gallons of water."

"Jesus," Detective Freeman said. He glanced at the other detective, who finally looked at him. "What the hell are miners supposed to do? How do they prevent this?"

"Well, they're supposed to have maps of the old mines to make sure they don't get too close. They're supposed to drill bore holes ahead of their mining to make sure the maps are right. They're supposed to follow rules about distances between new mining and old.

"But even when they follow the rules—which they probably did here—accidents can happen." Will emphasized the word "accidents."

"Who's supposed to make sure all these rules are followed?" the detective asked. "Wait, that'd be you, right?"

"Me and a few others," Will said.

The detective sighed.

"In your experience, Mr. Murphy, there's no chance somebody would purposefully want to cut into old works, right?"

A bored tone bled from his words.

Will shook his head. "Can't think of a reason any of these guys'd want to die."

"Well, that's that. Come on, Pete. Let's go."

Detective Freeman walked briskly down the hallway, followed by the other detective. Will watched them go. The state police had trouble filling slots in its eastern Kentucky posts, so newly minted sergeants and lieutenants from Lexington and Louisville often did turns in the Hazard and Harlan posts. Problem was, they knew nothing about hillbillies.

Will looked down and noticed that he was still holding the clipboard with the kid's medical information. He reached over and put it in the clear plastic holder outside the kid's room and turned to go. He followed the others down the hallway, stopped, smiled, and headed back, deeper into the hospital.

Down a set of stairs, he came out in front of a door with "Mountain Dialysis Center" stenciled onto a glass pane. He entered, waved at a nurse, and headed for an elderly man quietly snoozing in a comfortable chair beside one of the machines.

Will pulled up a technician's stool and sat beside the old man. His snow white hair was cut short, his face deeply creased. With a bushy mustache and glasses, he looked a bit like an oatmeal pitchman. Will smiled sadly and then patted him on the thigh. The old man's eyes opened.

"Hey, Uncle Elliott," Will said.

# CHAPTER THREE

S orry to wake you."
    The old man shook his head slowly.

"Glad you did. I can sleep anytime."

They'd had this same exchange many times before. When Uncle Elliott's kidneys first failed, a nurse had told Will that dialysis patients often become depressed, even suicidal, in their first weeks of treatment. So Will had tried to visit him during treatment at least once a week in that first year.

"What brought you?"

Will thought briefly about claiming that he'd come to the hospital just to see his uncle, but it had been some time since he'd done that.

"An inundation case."

"The one at Blue Gem?"

"Yup."

The old man whistled softly. Blue Gem was a family company—Will's family. It had been owned by Will's father and was now run by Will's brother, Paul. Will had once worked at the company, too, but there had been a blowup.

"You and Paul gettin' along any better nowadays?" Uncle Elliott asked.

"Same as ever."

The old man shook his head.

"Just like your old man and me," he said.

Will licked his lips. "It's worse than that, Uncle El. Rob Crane was in the mine when it flooded. Ain't been seen since."

"Oh Lord, forgot about that. Black fella, right? You and him were best friends, right? I mean for years."

"Sure," Will said.

"Any chance he's all right?" Uncle Elliott asked.

"Not much o' one."

"Rough," Uncle Elliott said. He touched the needles going into his left arm. Without looking up at Will, he asked, "You think Paul did some'm he shouldn't oughta?"

Will raised his eyebrows in surprise. "Not that I know of. I mean, I got no idea. Yet, anyways."

Uncle Elliott pursed his lips and raised his eyes back to Will's.

"You know, Paul give me a job year or two ago, after your dad's health took a turn for the worse and Paul knew he wouldn't care. I hire his miners and make up some o' the crews," Uncle Elliott said.

"Yeah, you told me. I think that's great," Will said.

The old man looked at Will for a moment. "It'll turn out, son. It'll turn out."

Will smiled and patted Uncle Elliott on his unencumbered arm. A nurse came over.

"How we doin' here?" she asked and looked at Will.

Will smiled and nodded and then realized the woman was looking at his stool. "Oops, sorry," he said and got up. She sat down beside Uncle Elliott.

"All right, now. Looks like we all done," she said and began pulling needles out of him. Once freed of the machine, Uncle Elliott tried to get up. He stopped and shook his head gently. Will sprang to his side and helped the old man to his feet.

"That takes some'm outta me," Uncle Elliott said.

"I think it takes just about everything outta you, Uncle Elliott. That's the point," Will said.

Uncle Elliott smiled. "Buy you a cup of coffee?" the old man asked.

"Uhm." Will hesitated then shrugged. "Sure."

"Hey, it's Valentine's Day. You probably got some'm with Tessy. You go on. Don't let me keep you," the old man said.

"No, it's all right, Uncle El. I don't have anything else."

"Sure?"

"Yeah . . . This was Jeff's birthday," Will said, looking down at the floor.

The old man frowned. He patted Will on the back.

"You're never gonna let that go, are you?" Uncle Elliott asked.

"No."

"Come on," the old man said.

The old man walked out of the unit door and turned left. Will followed him and stopped outside the door.

"I'll meet you there," Will said and took a step the other way.

"Will," Uncle Elliott said. "This the fastest way. Time you started walking it."

Will looked at the old man, shrugged, and followed him.

It was the usual institutional hallway. Strips of molding about four feet off the ground, now painted off-white along with the rest of the walls, ran like lane lines along the walls. Speckled linoleum covered the floor. There were framed, pastel pictures of flowerpots and mountains between doorways into dark rooms.

Then the hallway widened, and the two men entered what was obviously an older part of the building. There was wooden wainscoting on the lower part of the walls, plaster above it, and a ceiling with wooden, exposed beams. A wooden double door with a cross above it—obviously a chapel—was on the left. To the right, carved lettering read, "The United Mine Workers of America." Under the lettering was a series of bronze plaques nestled into the wainscoting.

Will took a deep breath and looked at the first plaque. "The Farmington Mine Disaster," it said at the top. There was some writing and then an odd picture in the bronze of an elderly miner with a beard. The next plaque was titled, "The Hurricane Creek Mine disaster."

More plaques and disasters followed. The last three were framed newspaper articles—no bronze. They were a bit higher than the others because no one had bothered to rebuild the wainscoting around them. Will clenched his jaw and walked up to the middle one.

"Disaster at Blue Dog!" blared the headline. "Hazard, Ky—An explosion in the Blue Dog mine Sunday killed at least one miner and badly wounded two more. The men were part of a Sunday maintenance shift and were getting the mine ready for full production on Monday.

"Jeff Murphy, 25, was killed immediately, according to officials. His brother, Will Murphy, 28, sustained third degree burns over 60 percent of his body and was listed in critical condition at Hazard Regional Medical Center. Another miner, Rob Crane, was also hospitalized, but his injuries were not considered life-threatening, a hospital spokeswoman said.

"Lucius Haverman, district director for the U.S. Mine Safety and Health Administration, said the cause of the blast was still under investigation, but an official with knowledge of the investigation said that a pack of cigarettes had been found near one of the injured men.

"Blue Dog is a family-owned mining company, with Paul Murphy Sr. of Fleming-Neon serving as the company's president and Paul Murphy Jr. as a mine superintendent. Paul Murphy Jr. was outside of the mine at the time of the blast and called emergency officials. Paul Murphy Jr. sustained some burns trying to reach his brothers but refused medical treatment.

"'That's my family down there,' Paul Murphy Jr. said hours before one of his brothers was rescued."

"Will."

The sound made Will jump. He had forgotten about Uncle Elliott, the hospital alcove, the inundation of Blue Gem—hell, even his wife and daughter.

"Can't smoke in here," Uncle Elliott said, smiling sadly. "This a hospital."

Will pulled the cigarette out of his mouth and looked at it. He hadn't even realized that he'd lit up. Seemed appropriate, though. Those cigarettes in the mine had been his. He was the one who'd caused the blast, killed his little brother, wounded his best friend, nearly destroyed his family's mining company, lost the love of his father, forever changed his mother. The list of pains went on and on.

"Yeah," Will said and took another drag.

He'd never seen this newspaper clipping. There was a picture of the mine, just as it had been. Seemed fine. No smoke, no debris. And then there was Jeff's high school graduation picture. Jeff had been so serious in that photo. No sign of the laughter that always seemed to bubble out of him. Will remembered asking Jeff if he'd had food in his teeth when it was shot. Jeff had just laughed.

"Come on, son," Uncle Elliott said. The old man grabbed Will's elbow, and Will allowed himself to be led away. "Coffee's this way."

They walked in silence, Will's footsteps plodding. He vaguely thought that he should be helping Uncle Elliott to walk through the hospital, not the other way around.

"You sit down, I'll get this," Uncle Elliott said.

The cafeteria was an odd, triangular shape with floor-to-ceiling windows on the right and white-topped tables scattered haphazardly. Will sat at the farthest end of the cafeteria, a triangular wedge between the wall and window. The only other customers were two large women wearing the light purple scrubs that identified them as janitorial staff.

Uncle Elliott got two large cups of coffee and walked toward Will. As he arrived, one of the women in purple lumbered over. "Sir? You can't smoke in here. Not no more."

Will raised a hand in surrender and carefully stubbed out the cigarette on the side of the table. "Made it more'n halfway," he whispered to the old man, who smiled slightly.

"Sorry, Will," Uncle Elliott said. "Shouldn't have made you walk by there. Just thought, you know, it was time. You made a mistake. You nearly died in that mine, too."

"Yeah. Nearly," Will said, dragging the word across his vocal cords like a dead dog over gravel.

"Long time ago now," the old man said.

"Doesn't seem all that long ago, Uncle El," Will said. "Seem like I was just talkin' to Jeff. You don't know what it feels like."

The old man pursed his lips. "You can't say that no more."

"No. Guess I can't. But since Dad's death last week, it ain't the same," Will said.

"I know, son."

The old man looked out the window. Will followed his eyes. It was full dark. The parking lot was bathed in white fluorescent light and beyond that Hazard's shuttered downtown gave off a dull glow.

Will took a sip of his coffee. "I went to work for MSHA because Daddy said it'd be good for me. I went along hopin' he'd forgive me. But seem like it only got worse over the years."

"Your father was a hard man to please."

They both stared out the window.

"Why're you the one investigatin' this flood when your brother owns the mine?" Uncle Elliott asked and then turned to Will.

Will raised his eyebrows. "Well, that's a good question. I was a little surprised at that myself. But it's my district and I guess the guy from Pikeville is busy and the guy from Middlesboro is out on sick leave. And, to be honest, I don't think they see it as all that complicated."

"'Cause it's just an accident?"

Will shrugged. "You know, it's an inundation. There's not gonna be much left to investigate 'cause all that water means you'll never be able to reconstruct the scene. I mean, we'll go over the maps and figure out if they left the right buffer between the old works and the new ones. But that takes all of five minutes. And Paul hired Singleton Drilling for his bore holes, and those guys are pretty much the best outfit in the state.

"I mean, these things is always accidents. Nobody drowns theirselves on purpose," Will said almost apologetically.

"Hm," Uncle Elliott said.

"What?" Will asked.

"Nothing."

Will looked at the old man quizzically.

"You'll do a good job, son. I know it."

Will nodded, a puzzled expression on his face.

"Well, I better go," Will said.

"I'll walk out with you."

# CHAPTER FOUR

At dawn the next day, Amos squatted near the top of Pine Mountain and looked out over the Letcher County hills stretched out before him. Strip mines scarred almost every outcropping.

Pine Mountain is a high ridgeline that runs southwest from Virginia to Tennessee. Less a mountain than a geologic wave, it's the corner bracket to southeastern Kentucky. And though it has been mined extensively, its enormous mass has remained largely intact.

It was Amos's favorite place. Two of his best-producing marijuana patches grew on the mountain, each about a twenty-minute walk from this overlook. At first, Amos had used the outlook to check for cops. Then, as he grew more confident, he began to enjoy the place for its own sake. Now he even came out of season to stare and think.

He could also see his hollow from this overlook, although not his trailer. He could see his high school. He could even pick out the entrance to a mine he had once worked.

"How was your day?" Glenda had asked when he'd gotten home the evening before.

For a split second, he had thought the question was an uncharacteristic joke, but her face had shown no hint of humor or grief. Amos had realized with a shock that she must have heard nothing about the flooding in the mine.

He had expected frantic. She had seemed happy and more.

There was the flower-print dress; the smell of fried chicken; clear eyes; a knowing smile. Each had been a surprise. Together, they roused a rush of passion for his wife. An image of a naked and delighted Glenda moving underneath him flooded his brain. It was replaced almost immediately by the day's memory of a headless body. A cloud passed over Amos's face. Glenda's smile faltered.

He faced a decision. On the one hand, he could tell her the truth. "Well, honey, the mine flooded. Rob Crane, the scoop operator—you remember him? The black, funny guy I told you about? He got crushed and drowned. And the roof bolter, Crandall Morton? You never met, but you know his sister-in-law, Doris. He got his head blowed off. And . . ."

He had long ago abandoned the urge to tell Glenda the full truth. And she didn't seem to mind. She'd never asked where he got his money when he'd purchased one of those projection TVs as a Christmas present.

"Fried chicken?" he asked.

Glenda's smile returned.

"And peach apple pie," she added.

His favorite dessert, the final proof that she had definite plans for the evening.

She asked about the scratches on his arms, but Amos just shrugged. Such injuries weren't unusual in mining, so she let it go. As they kissed, he briefly worried that she would later feel that he was taking advantage. He didn't think this was true. He was doing this for her.

Worst come to worst, he could say that he was so rattled after nearly dying that he'd wanted and needed warm comfort, which she could best give not knowing what had happened. Satisfied, Amos let the thought go.

"And how was your day, honey?" he asked.

It was all she needed. She had worked hard to make the perfect evening. She had probably even imagined a few words of their talks. Amos needed only play his part, for which she generally wrote few lines in her imagined dialogue. This time, he was unusually grateful that she upstaged him.

In the morning, Amos crept out of the house and drove away. He was doing what was best for her. Glenda needed her rest. She was not at her best in the mornings. There was little chance that she would wake up right away and somehow hear about the flooding before he got back.

If that happened, he was in trouble. But before he left he'd carried the radio to the porch, so he thought it unlikely she'd hear the news. Now, he had to come up with the courage to tell her about the inundation. The truth still beckoned.

"The Lord giveth, the Lord taketh away, and sometimes He kicketh your ass," Amos mumbled. He chuckled.

Not a line that would work with Glenda.

She would cry. She would curse mining. She would talk about the death of their son, Lee.

That was all fine.

But he worried that worse would follow, that as her worries built, she would begin to pick at herself—turning her fingernails bloody and her eyes bare of lashes. She would go back to a select number of doctors in the area with packed waiting rooms and genial prescription pads.

He tried to envision his life without mining. His pot business was growing nicely and they could probably survive on it. But he thought of himself as a coal miner trying to make ends meet, not a full-time marijuana farmer. And he didn't like the idea that, if one of his patches was discovered, his family would face hardship. Might lead him to take risks he shouldn't.

What would his father think? He'd say there were other jobs. Lord knows his old man did every one—coal hauler, mule skinner, tobacco spiker, and anything else to support the family. Amos remembered fingering the stump that had been one of his father's thumbs.

"Being a man ain't always easy, son," he'd said.

There was long-haul trucking. It was a sensible option—maybe one his father would have taken. But Amos dismissed the thought. It would mean being on the road for the rest of his life, and Amos had never left Appalachia. He was mildly curious about the rest of the country but had no real interest in spending much more than a few days there.

He was too old to become a cop and didn't want to go back to school to become a nurse or data-entry jockey or any of those other jobs that, anyway, were women's work.

"Might as well start wearing a dress," he mumbled to himself, and chuckled again through his thick beard. It was another line that had failed in the past with Glenda.

He could try again to get a job at the lumber plant in Hazard. Amos had heard that jobs there were going only to people with training in forestry, but talking about it might help soothe Glenda. Blue Gem would probably give him a couple weeks off because of the accident. Might as well spend it looking for something else.

He'd tell her that straight off.

Still, she'd want to know what happened during the inundation. He had to figure out what to tell her.

"End the telling with getting the kid out," he told himself.

After dropping the kid, Amos hadn't been sure he could make it back to the face. His lower back was screaming. He'd scraped past so many roof bolts that he could feel blood running between his shoulder blades.

But he had no choice. After his son Lee's death, he'd sworn that he would never leave a disaster without trying to rescue anyone who could be saved. He had to go back for Rob. He had to look for the others.

He tried to spare his back by bending his knees and working his quadriceps. After two or three breaks, his legs began to buckle. He went back to stooping. The water once again rose above his knees, and for the first time he had to push against a fairly strong tide.

The mine was black. The only light came from his own helmet. He stumbled several times and pitched forward. Each time, he tried to keep his head up, worried that his headlamp would short out.

He figured that once the water reached the battery on his waist, he'd lose the light for sure. He consoled himself with the notion that until he reached the face there was nothing to see anyway. He plowed on.

His headlamp flickered over something odd. By the time Amos concentrated the light and his mind, it was nearly upon him. He lunged to the rib for safety.

A piece of the conveyor belt mechanism drifted past. Amos was shaken. It was almost impossible to imagine how such a heavy piece of machinery could get into the fresh-air tunnel. He pushed on and squinted a little harder into the gloom.

His light went out and the world went black. Amos put his arms out into the water in front of him, palms forward.

The utter blackness made him dizzy. He closed his eyes, and there was no change in the information going to his brain. He kept them closed until a wave of panic and nausea swept through him. He opened them again, and the panic subsided.

So he kept his eyes open.

The darkness meant that he would only be able to walk straight ahead. There was no chance for him to turn right into the other working section to check for survivors there. Made things simple. He didn't know the miners in the other section anyway.

The water got deep enough that he decided to pitch forward, hands out, head up and feet kicking behind him. His back stopped screaming.

A low roar grew. It sounded like an approaching waterfall. He had heard the sound before. The smell was new, though. Slightly sulfurous. He felt like he was sloshing around the belly of a dragon.

The roar got louder, the current furious. He touched metal.

He stopped, felt around, and recognized the scoop machine.

"Rob?" he yelled. "Rob!"

"Amos?"

The calm, natural voice no more than a yard away made Amos flinch.

"Hey, buddy, how ya doing?" he answered in what he hoped was a calm yell. He felt around the scoop toward Rob's voice.

"Amos, listen, you gotta tell Mary. The bank just give me a five-thousand-dollar life insurance policy, free. Got a letter in the mail, and I just signed up. She doesn't know."

"I can tell her that. Yeah," Amos answered.

His hand touched Rob's back, and his fingers moved around Rob's rib cage. The water was now near the top of Rob's neck. Amos pulled himself to Rob's side.

"Tell her the company has a survivor's benefit," Rob said in the same conversational tone.

"We need to get this rock off ya," Amos said, refusing to let Rob assume he was a goner.

He moved his hands from Rob to the boulder on Rob's lap. It was immobile, not loosened by the current.

Amos tried to get his feet under him. No luck. The current made his feet unsteady, and he could get no firm handhold on the rock. He let his feet drift behind him, caught them on the rib and straightened, straining against the boulder. No budge.

"Tell my kids that I'm proud of 'em. And tell Will, Will Murphy, that . . . Tell him . . ." He sputtered, spit water, and gasped.

Amos put his hand under Rob's armpit and pulled himself next to him. He cupped a hand around Rob's chin, trying to keep the water out but not being able to see how to get it done.

"Tell him," Rob gasped, and went under. "Not his fault," he said as he strained up.

He moved too much for Amos's cupping attempt to work.

Amos heard the water go into Rob's lungs in a horrible gurgling sound. He pulled up on Rob's armpits. Rob thrashed and Amos lost his purchase and was swept back. He caught the scoop and pulled himself back. Rob's body now felt calm, although not limp. He pulled on Rob's arm and pushed up his chin. Rob seemed to resist, and then his body went limp.

Amos let his feet drift back again. He caught the rib, put both his hands under Rob's left armpit, and straightened. Amos's head went under as he tried to push Rob up.

Nothing worked.

Amos stopped pushing and took his head out of the water. He held on to Rob's arm with both hands and let his feet drift behind him. He looked left toward a flicker of light. It flickered again. It was the only information coming to his eyes.

He surged off toward the light, half swimming. He briefly worried that he was imagining things but then realized the light was underwater. He reached out, caught it, and brought it to the surface. It was a miner's helmet. He turned the light to scan the mine.

Directly in front he saw the roof-bolting machine. He reached out and gripped the machine. Then he saw it: a headless body in the operator's seat. A cable snaked from the battery pack on the body to the helmet, which had kept the helmet alight and attached to the body.

The neck sprouted tissue and bones. The head was nowhere to be seen. There was little blood; the water had washed it clean. Amos saw all this in a flash and, terrified, lost his grip and was swept back. He breathed water, panicked, and struck a rock. Blackness overtook him.

# CHAPTER FIVE

Amos rolled over and over and over. Through instinct alone, his body managed to draw in air just as his mouth broke the surface. The air, fetid and rank, revived him. His heels dragged on the ground and his hand struck something solid. He grabbed it and stopped his drift. He recovered his feet, stood, and promptly struck his head on the roof. He'd lost his helmet. He cursed and rubbed his head.

"Calm down, Amos," he said to himself.

He saw the flashing again and, gritting his teeth to manage his revulsion, made it back to the roof bolter.

Amos caught the helmet, felt along the cable, and removed the battery from Crandall Morton's body. He felt gingerly inside the helmet, terrified of what he might find. It was empty so Amos put it on his head, although there was barely enough room to keep both the helmet and his mouth out of the water.

He had no idea why Crandall's light would work when his own wouldn't, but now he could see. He turned away from Crandall's body, scanned the face of the mine but saw nobody else.

Time to go.

With some relief, he released his grip on the roof bolter and let the water current take him away from the face. After several breaks, he saw the beginning of the conveyor belt. It was wrenched sideways. He focused his light and saw a body tangled in the wreckage.

He swam over, caught the coveralls, and pulled up the head. Carl Breathitt.

He put his hand on Carl's lips. They were warm. He shoved several fingers onto Carl's neck to feel for a pulse. Carl coughed.

Pulling Carl away from the wreckage, careful to hold the head out of the water, he swung around in front of the body and cradled the silent head in his own shoulder. He swam toward the fresh-air tunnel.

By midmorning the next day, the parking lot was crowded with police cruisers, mine-rescue vehicles, and white Jeep Cherokees favored by federal inspectors. Two black plastic pipes rose up from the mine shaft and fed into pumps, which belched a gray liquid. Some of the water backed up and came into the lot. The mine trailer was stranded in black water.

The door opened on one of the rescue vehicles—a black converted school bus—and a man in a black jumpsuit with yellow lettering on the back got out and sloshed toward the steep slope on one side of the mine. Rescue teams, Will Murphy thought. As Will picked his way across the lot, the man in black stopped at the slope and relieved himself.

Will tried to find a dry path to the trailer, gave up, and walked straight to the door. Cold water oozed into his socks.

He'd seen this trailer hundreds of times and been inside a dozen or more. Blue Gem's Red Fox mine was one of the few that could easily be seen from the highway. And it loomed large for Will. It was the first major mine opened by his brother and his father in which Will had played no role.

It was a door into a world where he no longer had a place.

Will opened the trailer door and climbed in. At the far end, two men were standing over a metal desk covered with maps. Several others were huddled in plastic chairs nearby but left the trailer about the time Will entered. The trailer was only slightly drier than the parking lot, with oily mud splattered over the floor. A thin coat of coal dust caked just about every surface.

"There ain't no reason to risk putting that bore hole any closer to the face than need be," said one of the two men, pointing to the map. "Let's put it over here on the return air, about three breaks back."

The man was tall with a gray beard, sandy hair pushed back from his forehead. He was wearing a checkered red and black flannel shirt and blue canvas pants. His name was Lucius Haverman, the longtime director of the U.S. Mine Safety and Health Administration's Hazard district, and he was in charge. Lucius looked up.

"Will," he said.

"Lucius," Will answered.

They shook hands, and Will felt the stump of Lucius's third finger dig into his palm.

Legend had it that Lucius had lost the finger in a roof fall when he was still a miner. A slab of rock fell beside him and crushed his hand. They say Lucius barely noticed and that he spent hours digging out a friend's body with his finger flapping uselessly. It was a heroic story that made Will almost proud to work for MSHA.

The other man stepped over and embraced Will. "Hey, little brother," he said.

"Paul," Will responded.

Paul Murphy was wiry, dark-haired, and of middling height. He wore engineer's glasses on his handsome face and had a pleasant smile. Will was taller and now outweighed Paul by a considerable margin, but no one who saw them together could fail to notice that Paul was the dominant brother.

"You all right?" Paul asked. "You look a little ragged."

"Yeah, I'm fine," Will said with the routine defensiveness of a drinker.

"Listen, Will. I told the lawyer to put off reading the will."

"All right. Makes sense," Will said. "I think I can wait to get the old man's dirty underwear, 'cause I'm figurin' that's all I'm gettin'."

Paul gave a tight smile.

"Mind if I butt into this little family reunion and ask if you learned anything from the kid?" Lucius asked.

"Salads can be fattening."

"What?"

"Sorry," Will said.

"Come on, Will," Paul said.

"Sorry, sorry. No, the kid didn't say nothing. He left Rob for dead in the right-most entrance, and never saw the roof bolter, and he didn't know shit about the other section," Will said. "Nothing we didn't already know from the miner man, Amos Blevins. Or at least you didn't already know, Lucius. I still ain't been able to talk to Blevins."

"He didn't stay," Lucius said. "Headed to the hospital with the others. I heard he left as soon as he arrived, though. I'm sure you'll get another chance. But listen, let me just give you a quick update."

Lucius glanced down at the table in front of them and pushed a map so that Will could see it better.

"As you saw, we snaked pumps down the shaft, but Paul tells us that the mine has a gradual descent from the shaft to the face, so we can't get all the water out that way," Lucius said, pointing to the map. "So we asked Dee Singleton to send one of his mobile drillers out, and we're gonna put a bore hole here and try to get the rest of the water."

Lucius pointed to a spot near the end, or face, of one of the mine's two active sections.

Will leaned over the desk.

"What about the other section?" Will asked, and pointed to an entirely different part of the map.

"We first gotta go where we think there might be survivors," Lucius said grimly. "This other section, it's lower. Nobody's come out a' there, and the water come in from behind 'em, not in front."

"Rob's in this'n," Paul said, pointing to Lucius's finger.

"We'll get a bore hole in the other section next," Lucius said.

Will peered more closely at the map. The mine looked like a city, a grid of coal blocks bounded on every side by tunnels. There were four circles with X's inside them in an arch just outside the grid at the far end of the mine.

"These the bore holes?" Will asked, pointing to blue X's on the map. "Can we use any of 'em for the pump? Might save us some time."

"Not in the right place," Paul said, shaking his head.

"All right, whatever y'all think," Will said. "You got a map of the old works?"

"Yeah, but it's not gonna help us," Paul said and fished out a large rolled-up piece of paper that had been set to one side. He unrolled it and pushed it open with his forearm. It showed another grid of coal and tunnels but far bigger and more elaborate than the first.

"Here's about where we ran into the old works," said Paul and used the back of a pen to circle an area well outside the grid pattern on the older mine. "The mine shouldn't have started for another four hundred yards at least."

Paul took his hands off the old map, which curled up. Will leaned over and spread it out again. It was titled "Bethlehem No. 11" and dated 1927.

"This the mine that starts over in Viper?" Will asked no one.

"Yeah," Paul responded.

"Not like Bethlehem to have one of their maps be so far wrong," Will said slowly and almost to himself.

"What are you edgin' at, little brother?" Paul asked, a tight smile on his face.

"Nothing, nothing," Will said and took his hands off the map, which curled up again. "Just, you know, weird."

Paul looked at Lucius and cleared his throat.

"Yeah, well, some'm you can look into later, Will," Lucius said. "We got a rescue to worry about now."

"Right. Sorry," Will said, nodding sheepishly. "What's the plan on that?"

"Well, even if we get the new bore hole done this evening, it's still gonna take all night and most of tomorrow getting all that water out. They's millions of gallons down there. I done told most of the rescue teams," Lucius jerked his thumb toward the parking lot, "that we won't need 'em till tomorrow at the earliest. Some of 'em left, but lots is still around."

Will looked up from the maps.

"Did you know Rob Crane, Lucius?" Will asked. Lucius shook his head.

"Well, a lot of those boys out there knew him. Probably the only black guy most of 'em ever worked with. His wife, Mary, she's standing on the road out there. I'm thinking some of them boys don't want to pass her by 'fore they've found her husband, or at least tried."

"Here's the driller," Paul said.

A truck that looked to be carrying a load of pipes had stopped along the highway above the mine. A man was walking through the parking lot toward the trailer. Paul walked past Will and left the trailer.

Will could see the two meet. Paul seemed to do all the talking. The man from the truck nodded. Paul pointed at the trailer and both men walked toward the door.

"You know Lucius Haverman and that's Will," Paul said, ushering the new man inside. Singleton shook hands with Lucius and said, "Good to see you." He turned to Will. "Been a long time," he said.

Singleton looked like someone in an Appalachian family album. He was medium height and rail thin with bulging eyes and an outsized Adam's apple. His hair was thin, short and sharply parted, and he wore a navy peacoat, brown pants, and heavy boots. Instead of leaning forward while he walked, he seemed to sway back and set his feet before him as if walking down a steep slope.

"Thanks for coming so soon after we called," said Lucius.

"More 'n glad to help," Singleton said in response.

"Paul tells us that you drilled his bore holes," Lucius said.

"Yessir, that's right," Singleton said, nodding.

"Good, 'cause we need one, and we was hoping you'd know right away just where to drill," Lucius said. "On the mine map, we want something right about here," Lucius said, pointing to the large map unfurled on the desk.

"But where that is on the topo," Lucius said, leaning far over the desk to sift through some of the rolled-up papers at the side, "we ain't exactly sure."

Lucius pulled out one of the maps and unrolled it. Instead of a grid, this one showed the wavy, organic lines of a topographical map. "We're thinking it'd be right about here," he said.

Singleton leaned over the desk and looked at the spot where Lucius was pointing, nodding his head. Then he picked up an edge of the topographical map to peer at the mine map underneath, still nodding. He flipped back and forth between the two maps, nodding all the while.

Paul broke the silence: "You don't have to memorize the goddamn thing. Can you drill the hole?"

Lucius added, "Should we get a surveyor?"

"There's a shelf up there that old Bad John Wright made when he first started to strip-mine with a dozer, Mr. Murphy. I reckon it'd be just above the Ames place," Singleton said, nodding. He kept nodding.

"And?" Paul said, visibly impatient.

"I reckon I can get my rig up 'ere," Singleton said.

"We'd be obliged, Dee," Lucius said. "You need anything from us? How do we communicate with you?"

Will's voice came out as a croak: "I'll go with him and take my radio," he said, and then cleared his throat.

"That'd be fine," Lucius said. "Let us know your progress."

Lucius put out his hand toward Singleton to let him know that the interview was over and it was time to get busy. Singleton shook.

"You think any of those boys are alive down there?" Singleton asked.

Lucius glanced at Will and then at Paul, who both looked down. "We sure hope so, Dee," Lucius said. "That's why we need that bore hole quick as we can."

Singleton nodded and headed toward the door. Will followed.

"Will," Paul said before they got outside. "Come here for a sec."

Will raised his eyebrows and walked back to the table. Paul motioned, and Will edged closer.

"Some'm you should know 'fore you go," Paul said and glanced at Lucius, who shrugged. In a voice quiet enough so that only Will and Lucius could hear, Paul said, "We found a couple of bricks of marijuana in the pump screen this morning."

"What?"

"Yeah. We're trying to keep it quiet. I called Captain Edwards at the Hazard state police post this mornin', and he agreed that we should let it go. Could be one of those miners down there was doin' some'm he ought'na. But till we know whether they're alive . . ."

Will puckered his lips into a silent whistle. Two men walked into the trailer, one of them wearing a tie. They waited for the huddle among Will, Paul, and Lucius to break.

"Any idea where it come from? I mean, where in the mine?" Will whispered.

Paul looked at Lucius, who shook his head.

"All right, well, good to know," Will said.

Paul raised his voice.

"Good to have a special investigator on this thing right at the beginning. Reduce misunderstandings later," Paul said with a strained formality.

"Mr. Beasley," Paul said and walked around Will to greet the new arrival, whom Will now recognized as a state senator.

Will realized that Paul was probably trying to downplay the brotherly connection. Paul was the owner; Will was the investigator. Everyone was a professional, and everything was on the up-and-up.

Right, Will thought.

"Well, I'm gonna . . ." Will said, motioning to the door. "I'll call in."

# CHAPTER SIX

Glenda had greeted Amos at the door when he came home a little before 9 a.m. She wondered what would bring him home that early.

The two lived in a tidy double-wide trailer in a hollow between Hazard and Whitesburg. The house was glistening white and set back about fifteen yards from the road. A short gravel driveway extended from the road to a narrow wooden front porch. From the back, hills rose on either side. A garden area was set off to one side.

Amos went inside and sat down. Glenda followed. He reached out and took her hand. But as he got started, her face tightened into an "I knew it" look and she pulled her hand away. She said nothing. Tears gathered at her chin. Amos stopped well short of the story's end.

The silence stretched.

They sat on the couch, part of a brown suede living room set gathered around the big TV. Crocheted antimacassars adorned the tops of the vertical cushions. A quilt lay on the arm of the easy chair. The coffee table was well waxed.

Even in her darkest periods, Glenda was a good housekeeper.

The dress from the night before was back in the closet. Glenda had pulled on tan khakis, a yellow blouse, and running shoes while Amos had been gathering his courage.

She was looking down, and Amos knew she wasn't thinking about him or the inundation the day before. Neither was he. But then, that wasn't anything new.

Lee.

Halfway through Amos's story, she had begun to pick at her cuticles. Amos glanced down at her hands, and she stopped. But she started again moments later, unconsciously.

He wondered how much she'd heard. He had told similar stories before. She had never asked for further details about his near misses, and she didn't this time.

He had mentioned the timber plant, but she had not reacted. She wasn't as angry as he thought she would be, and he realized that he was sorry for that.

The mines had taken her only son. They had nearly taken her husband several times. She hated coal, was dead set that he get out of the industry. But she had stopped talking that way some time ago.

Now he saw a resignation that he had never seen before. They sat in silence.

"Shoulda said I was gonna bust his ass," Will said to himself and then cackled. "That'd show 'em."

"Bust him? Mr. Murphy? Really?" Singleton asked.

"No, no, no. Never," Will said. "Just a joke."

They were sitting in the cab of the drilling rig. Singleton was driving, and another man sat silently in the backseat. Singleton had introduced him, but Will had promptly forgotten the man's name.

"I ain't seen you two together since the old Blue Dog days," Singleton said.

"Yeah."

"Mr. Murphy like you being an inspector, Will?" asked Singleton.

"Uhm. I don't know," Will said and thought, Mr. Murphy? That used to be what Singleton called their dad. Will wondered when he'd made the switch to calling his brother Mr. Murphy. Just in the week since his father's death?

"Well, Mr. Murphy sure has come a long way. Real long way," Singleton said.

Will just nodded this time. He'd heard this subtle rebuke before. He was just an MSHA inspector while his brother now ran one of the most successful independent coal companies in the state. Will could have been a part of that. Should have been.

Theirs had been a family operation. Blue Dog Mining. All three Murphy boys worked for it along with Rob Crane, their next-door neighbor and Will's best friend. Their father had inherited the tiny company, and it took off during the OPEC oil embargo when the price of coal soared. He recruited his sons to work mines that had been too small to be economical until the oil crisis.

Will spent his school years with dirt under his fingernails and dust in his ears. His brothers quit school well before finishing—Paul Jr. in tenth grade and Jeff in ninth. But Will and Rob Crane were the heart of their high school basketball squad, so they worked weekends and some evening shifts until they graduated, when they went underground full-time.

By then, the price of coal had fallen from its lofty heights, and safety standards in the family's three mines—never rigorous—slipped further. Will went along. He became a foreman, supervising Rob Crane. As their father's health began to fail, Paul Jr. increasingly ran the mines.

And then one Sunday, as Will, Jeff, and Rob Crane worked to ready a mine for the next day's shift, Will stopped for a smoke. He never smoked when coal was being actively mined since methane was far more likely to accumulate then, but he thought it safe to light up on a maintenance shift.

Will woke up in the hospital with more than half of his body charred. Jeff was dead and Rob injured. Will never forgave himself and neither did his father. Shunned, Will went to work for MSHA while Paul continued to build Blue Dog, soon merging it with Gem Mining to form Blue Gem.

The brothers fell out of touch. As Paul gained stature, Will lost it.

The same week Paul was given a prize from the Hazard Chamber of Commerce, Will crashed his truck into a tree, dead drunk.

Sitting next to Singleton in the driller rig, Will thought back to the days when he'd been a basketball star and Paul had merely been earnest. And then he thought of Jeff, the family cut-up and his mother's delight. Will felt his soul drain out.

"This investigation better not take too long," Will whispered to himself. He swallowed, his mouth dry.

They turned off the highway and headed up Hell-for-Certain Creek. The road was flat and serpentine. To the left ran the creek, and to the right was a small, tidy home with a garden. Sticks used to tie up tomato plants were standing in the garden, the shriveled vines still clinging to them. Everything in the garden was dead, but no one had yet taken the time to clean it up. There was no car in the driveway.

A short cement bridge squatted over the creek a little further up, and there was another house—this one bigger and browner—nestled on the other side. A pickup stood in its gravel drive. The house was two stories high, had a pitched roof and a six-foot TV satellite dish on the grass.

The land behind the house was wooded and rose steeply. The trees seemed to be mostly poplars and pines, though Will spotted one oak with a few dark brown leaves left.

More houses followed, most of them modest-sized and in pretty good shape. The creek was clean with only a few plastic bags fluttering on snags. It had been years since Will had been up this creek, and he was glad to see the community was still alive. Appalachia had been losing population for sixty years, and many once-thriving hollows were abandoned, with homes sprouting kudzu vines and creeks choked with rusty junk.

After almost a mile and more than a dozen homes, Singleton took a left onto a narrow road. The truck's tires chewed at both edges of the blacktop. They passed a couple of trailers. A dry creekbed ran by the side of the road.

The pavement ended and they dropped onto gravel. Singleton geared down; the truck slowed, then lurched forward.

They passed two more trailers parked on ledges scraped out of the mountainside. The driveway of the second was a twenty-foot strip of gravel on a steep grade. A Chevy Camaro sat in the drive, and Singleton had to slow almost to a crawl to get around its rear fender.

Will could see a small child—a girl, he guessed—holding aside a curtain and staring out a window near the trailer's door.

Singleton wheeled the truck to the right, and Will could see a dirt road leading steeply up the mountain. The truck stopped and drifted back down. Will's heart suddenly raced. The road—more like a trail—seemed far too small and steep to handle Singleton's good-sized rig.

Will snuck a look at Singleton, who was busily cranking the steering wheel and staring into his tall, rectangular sideview mirror. Will looked at the crewman behind, who was staring ahead, bored. Then Will looked out his window. The only road he could see was at least nine feet down.

"Want me to get out and watch the sides for ya?" Will asked.

Singleton was jamming a tall, floor-mounted gearshift forward, and the truck was complaining. "Only if'n you want to," Singleton said without looking at Will.

Before Will could say anything else, the truck lurched forward. Will grabbed at the dashboard to remain vertical with the world. Sweat pricked his back.

The truck bounced and lurched up the grade. Will looked ahead to see that a gulley was carved through the road and seemed to have taken out a large hole on its left-hand side. The front tire dropped into the gulley and the whole truck leaned left. Singleton kept going. The hole approached. Will leaned forward even further. His forehead was now almost touching the dashboard.

The hole disappeared under the truck and, to Will's surprise, the truck nimbly jumped it. He looked up the road and didn't see any more holes quite as big. He glanced at Singleton, who was resting comfortably in his seat. Will eased the small of his back into his seat but used his left elbow to lever the rest of his torso slightly forward.

The road dodged left, the grade eased a bit, and the mountain rose up along the right. Will looked through the spindly, bare trees. An abandoned appliance—a stove or washing machine—sat rusting in the middle of the slope. Will wondered idly how anyone had wrestled it up there.

Finally, the truck mounted a last, steep stretch and the road flattened out. They were on an old mining bench about thirty yards across. It ended in a sheer rock face of about twenty-five feet, after which the mountain climbed naturally for another thirty or forty feet. Trees topped the hill.

Singleton pushed the truck across a gravel clearing and then onto a track big enough for a four-wheeler. The truck's tires were well outside of both tracks, and Will could hear tall grass hissing underneath. Scrub trees rose sickly on either side.

The truck stopped. "I reckon it's about right here," Singleton said, and pulled back on the truck's emergency brake.

Stooping, Will unrolled the huge hose carefully, making sure to keep it straight. He realized that the hose probably would work fine even if he simply flung it along the bench, but he hadn't been a bit of help during the drilling so he wanted to do this right.

He made it to the edge of the bench and looked around for the right place for the nozzle. A wash seemed to start just a bit to his right, so he pulled at the hose to bring it in that direction and dropped the rest of it down the hill. The nozzle—actually a metal coupling—came to rest about five feet down the slope.

He walked back along the hose, checking for kinks.

Will stepped around the truck. Singleton, squatting beside the generator, looked up with a questioning expression. Will nodded.

Singleton looked down and frowned. He stabbed twice at the machine, and it roared to life. Singleton adjusted the throttle, and the pump motor's pitch rose slightly.

Will looked along the hose and waited. Soon the hose began to rustle, writhe, and stiffen. He walked back, lifting the hose in spots where it seemed to bend slightly. At the end, he saw with satisfaction a sizable cascade of black water.

Will strode back to the truck, walked around to the passenger side, stepped onto the runner, and reached into the window for his radio.

"Lucius," Will said, and waited.

"He's on the phone, over," came the answer. It was Paul.

"We got the pump going here," Will said.

"Roger, over," Paul answered.

Roger? Over? Will thought.

"Tell Lucius I'm staying here for a bit if he needs me," Will said.

"Roger, over."

Will rolled his eyes but said, "Out," because he knew Paul expected it. He sighed and put the radio on the hood of the truck.

Singleton and his crewman were sitting on their haunches about twenty feet from the pump, smoking. Will realized that this was routine for them. They'd just drilled a new well and were having a smoke. Except this time it was part of a rescue operation, and they were trying to get rid of the water instead of harness it.

Will went over to the two men and squatted. Singleton offered his pack and Will took a cigarette.

They sat in silence, all smoking.

Will was mildly interested in asking Singleton about his work for Paul. Will had only a vague idea about how big Blue Gem had become, and Singleton likely knew quite a bit about its operations. But the only question he knew to ask was about the accident.

"You drilled the bore holes for this here mine, right?"

"Yuh," Singleton said.

"Nothing unusual?"

"Nope."

"All dry?"

"Yuh."

"Can you get me those records?"

"Sure."

And that was that. Will took a long drag. He could ask a few more questions, but Singleton had basically ended his investigation before it started. And Will was a little worried that Paul might not want him questioning Singleton. By law, mine operators were entitled to be present during all phases of a mine investigation.

Better to stay quiet, Will thought. So he did.

There was an extraordinary trait among many Appalachians of

being able to sit quietly. Whether it was a form of patience, shyness, or calm, Will could never quite figure.

He'd heard that Indians had the same trait. Legends said that the Appalachian people were descended from escaped white, indentured servants who mixed with native Cherokee. So maybe the silent Indians were still present.

Some years back, Will had gone to Washington for an investigators' refresher course. One of the instructors had talked about the power of silence. He'd said that sitting silent can lead witnesses or suspects to say things they wouldn't normally say, just to fill the silence. Few people, the instructor said, can sit for long without talking.

Will had smiled. He had wanted to say, "Come back with me to Hazard."

So Will squatted wordlessly, curious to see how long these two men could hold their silence.

Dusk began to settle around them. The air grew colder, the light dimmer. Finally, Will shook his head and said, "You figure Kentucky's gonna beat Louisville?" He had surrendered.

"I reckon," Singleton said. His crewman's expression didn't change. Silence again.

Will settled in for another long spell of no talk.

"You think Hazard's girls is gonna get to the tournament?" Singleton asked.

So he speaks, Will thought.

"I reckon," Will answered with a smile. "I don't know. They sure got a lot of talent," he added in a thicker accent than he used normally. Will tended to speak with more of a backwoods accent when talking with folks with strong accents. Singleton's was thick.

"Now that we got your Helen, we do," Singleton said, nodding. "She's a damn good point guard. Just what we needed. You teach her?"

"No. No, I didn't," Will said. "Her mother did."

Will welcomed the enveloping silence this time.

"I think we got a real good chance this year, sure do," Singleton said, not letting go. "What we done to Fleming-Neon, now that was a sight. If'n we can get through Pikeville next week, I'm thinking the regionals'll be easy. Hell, we might could give Lexington Catholic a run in the tournament."

They all nodded. Will flicked his butt and, as it arched away, saw a figure emerge from the scrub. It was a large man wearing a baseball cap. He was carrying a gun, which he was pointing at Will.

"Turn that goddamn machine off."

# CHAPTER SEVEN

Will jumped to his feet. Singleton got up a bit more slowly. Will guessed that the man weighed about two hundred pounds. He looked sober and serious. Will had no interest in challenging him.

"Turn it off," he shouted again.

"Now, Virgil," Singleton said.

"Goddamnit," the man said and stalked toward the pump.

"Don't do that, buddy," Will said, his feet finally able to move. Holding his hands out in front of him, Will walked two steps closer to the pump.

Will couldn't take his eyes off the shotgun. It was a pump-action. Probably held ten or twelve shells—more than enough to handle the three of them.

"This is a rescue," Will said. "There are fellas trapped down there, and this thing will help us get 'em out."

"Those boys is long dead and you know it," the man said tightly. "And now you're taking away my water and everybody else's on this holler. It don't make no sense. Turn that machine off."

The man walked right up to the pump and poked it with the snout of his shotgun. Will took several more steps. The pump continued to clatter loudly.

"Mister, I got no idea what you're talking about. But if you touch that pump again, I'll have state police up here so fast you won't know what hit ya," Will said.

The man bent down, used a finger to ground the pump's spark plug wire, and it puttered out. Silence fell. By now, the light was almost gone. The man stood up again, breathing so hard that a fog enveloped his head. He looked at Will, Singleton, and his crewman. The shotgun now hung from one of his hands.

"Y'all are gonna make it so that we can't never live here no more," the man said, this time quietly.

"Virgil, that ain't true," Singleton said.

"It *is* true, Dee, and you know it," the man said. "You can't find no more water down here. You said so yourself."

More silence.

"What?" Will asked, looking between the two.

"He ain't told you?" the man said, looking at Singleton. Singleton didn't move. "All the houses here. All of the ones going up Hell-for-Certain creek, we's all lost our water 'cause of this thing. We was all tapped into the old works, but because those fellas cut into 'em, we lost our water."

The man waved the arm without the gun.

"The only way we'll ever get it back is if that water builds back up again. But if'n you pump it all out, that won't happen. Leastways, not for a long time. And I can't have that."

"Virgil, you know we got no choice," Singleton said. "Dead or alive, those fellas've got to be got out of there. You don't want those bodies in your water."

The man looked away. Will took another step toward the now-silent pump.

"Mister, I'm sorry about your water but this ain't the time. We got men down there, we got a rescue, and if we don't get that pump going again in the next two minutes, I'm calling the cops," Will said.

Nobody moved. Then Will turned around and headed for the rig.

"Dee," the man pleaded. "I already tried living without water that one time, and I can't do it again. It ain't no life."

Will made it to the truck and reached for his radio on the hood.

"Mister, I'm giving you fifteen seconds to put that shotgun down or I'm calling this in."

Winter silences in Appalachia rival those along the Arctic Circle. The bugs and cicadas are dead or in larvae stages. Cars are few and kids fewer, since the population is, on average, older than anywhere else in the United States. And there isn't a greater concentration of gun owners looking to shoot at anything that moves, so animals can get scarce.

The three men stood in utter silence. Eventually, a coal train's whistle pierced the night in a long, mournful howl. The sound seemed to break something in the man. He closed his eyes, tilted his face to the sky, and opened his mouth. He sobbed silently, raised the shotgun like a scepter, and held the stock to his forehead.

"Nooooo," he finally howled.

Quite suddenly, he swiveled the gun around and blew off the top half of his head. The shotgun slapped to the ground, and his body collapsed silently over the barrel.

"Jesus, Jesus, Jesus," Will said, and rushed to the fallen man. Will didn't know where to put his hands. The man's brains looked like fresh pasta. Will swallowed and put two fingers to the man's neck. There was a pulse. Will looked more closely at the broken head and saw a small rivulet of blood surging rhythmically onto the ground.

He ran back to the truck and scooped up the radio. "Lucius, Paul, anybody, pick up," he said. He looked back.

"Dee," Will said. Singleton's crewman was on his hands and knees, throwing up. Singleton himself had gone back to squatting, his eyes on the ground.

"Dee!" Will said again, and Singleton swung his head up.

"Turn the damn pump on," Will ordered.

The phone rang so many times that Amos unplugged it. He and Glenda were of the generation who answered telephones when they rang, as if fearing some sort of retribution should a neighbor be ignored. They did not own an answering machine. A call unanswered was a call lost.

If she had been herself, Glenda would have worried about the unanswered calls.

She had taken several long trips to the bathroom. After her second, she returned somewhat glassy-eyed. After the third, her eyes drooped noticeably.

Amos suggested that they go for a walk up on the mine bench. Glenda had shaken her head. Later he said with careful spur-of-the-moment cheerfulness that they should go to the Courthouse Café for lunch. Glenda had zoned out by then.

Amos tried to remember the last time she had taken pills. At least six months, he estimated. Not a record. When she started to sing to herself, he picked her up from the couch and took her into the bedroom. She looked at him reproachfully but said nothing.

He laid her on the bed, unfolded a blanket and spread it over her. She stared at the ceiling, humming. He lay beside her until she fell asleep. He rose and went back into the living room and retrieved his Bible.

It opened to First Corinthians.

" 'God is faithful and he will not let you be tempted beyond your strength, but with the temptation will also provide the way of escape, that you may be able to endure it,' " Amos read aloud in a low voice.

The passage in the middle of Paul's letter had never been featured in any sermon Amos had heard, but it had always seemed important to him. He wasn't sure if it spoke to him or to Glenda. He wasn't sure if her escape into pills was provided for or whether she was missing the route that God intended for her.

He was eager to pray for guidance, but he didn't want to leave Glenda alone.

He needed to clear his mind, so he turned to Mark, whose straightforward style had always comforted Amos. He had barely passed the story about the leper when he heard a vehicle pull up outside. Putting the Book down, he rose quickly, opened the door quietly, and slipped outside.

There was a brown Ford F-150 pickup in the drive.

As he walked toward the truck, Mike Barnes, the mine foreman, opened his door and got out.

"Amos, I come to see how you're doing," Mike said.

He reached out his hand, which Amos met with his. Mike brought up his other hand and gripped Amos's upper arm.

Amos blinked. He wasn't sure whether the accident, his rescue efforts, or something else had led Mike to make such an intimate gesture. They had never been friends. They had never talked about anything but mining, pot growing, and University of Kentucky basketball.

"Fine," Amos answered.

"How's Glenda?" Mike asked.

Amos paused. He was all but certain that he had never mentioned his wife's name to Mike. And it seemed unlikely that Mike cared enough to have learned the name in passing from anyone else. He just wasn't that kind of guy.

"Fine," Amos said and nodded. He wanted to get away from the house so as not to disturb Glenda. He walked several more steps away from the trailer, stopped, looked back at Mike and raised his eyebrows.

"Still ain't come to your church yet, but I'm thinking about it. Thanks for inviting me," Mike said and covered the distance between them in several tentative strides. "Listen, I gotta ask. There's no chance you still got a little supply left. You know, from last year's crop."

Amos looked back at the trailer for a moment. He shook his head.

"It would be really good if you did," Mike persisted.

Amos shrugged.

"Shit," Mike said.

Mike got out a cigarette, and Amos silently watched him light up.

Mike was about five-foot-six and slight, maybe 130 pounds. He was clean shaven and had closely cropped salt-and-pepper hair that had receded almost entirely from his forehead. He wore khakis, a button-up blue shirt, and an unzipped down jacket.

Amos wore only a T-shirt and jeans.

Amos had to admit that he owed Mike a lot. The foreman had persuaded him to try planting a few marijuana seeds in some of Amos's more remote hunting spots. He'd paid well for Amos's first meager harvest and had taught him how to improve his yield. He'd been the only buyer for Amos's pot, and Amos wouldn't know what to do without him.

Still, he'd never liked Mike mostly because he was a miserable foreman who never seemed to care about making sure equipment was in good repair. The crew would often waste hours because machinery that could have been fixed stood idle.

If he cared about productivity, Mike would have made sure everything was shipshape. He didn't, a waste Amos hated. He also disappeared during shifts. Amos suspected that he snuck off to smoke, something that endangered everyone. Amos often eyed him coldly when he returned from these disappearances.

But he'd offer no explanation and would often get mad for no reason. The day of the accident had been typical. As usual, the men had gathered at 6 a.m. at the mine office.

Amos had soon put on his coveralls, steel-toed boots, miner's belt, self-rescuer—a stainless steel box about the size of a paperback that provided emergency air—and his miner's cap. The other men had done the same, all in silence.

When he'd worked at Costain, the men had sat around joking. But that was a union mine, which paid men when they arrived. Blue Gem didn't start the clock until the men made it to the face of the mine, about a mile inside. So nobody wasted much time in the trailer, and everyone did their best to arrive on time so as not to hold up the others.

Dawn had been more than an hour away. Moon and stars were gone from the narrow sky. The air was still. The men's breath had clung to them like lint.

Mike had been the last of the crew to emerge from the trailer.

"Crandall, they still ain't fixed the five-twenty," Mike had said, still reading from a clipboard. He had glanced up to slide open the elevator door, and the rest of the crew shuffled onto the platform.

"You're gonna have to use the four hundred," Mike said.

"Shit," Crandall answered. It was among the last words Crandall would ever utter.

The door slid home and they descended. "They's fixed all the scoops, though," Mike said.

Later, at dinner, Mike had turned downright weird. As usual, there had been some comment about Amos's dinner. After the kid had crawled away, Mike had joined in the general laughter and then asked the obvious question: "Huntin' this weekend?"

"Hm. Up to Hell-for-Certain, just over by here," Amos had said, sticking a thumb over his shoulder in what he thought was the general direction of the creek.

"I heard it's pretty up there," Mike had said.

"Yeah. I seen a surveyor crew up 'ere last year, and I was thinkin' some kind of construction would happen," Amos had said. "Nothin' yet, though."

Mike's eyes had narrowed.

"You saw what?" the foreman had asked.

"Survey crew," Amos had said.

"That don't mean nothin'," Mike had said. "Could be they's just, you know, fixin' maps."

"Might be," Amos had said, nodding. "I grew up with one of the guys on the crew. Fella named Joe Fercal. Didn't say nothin' to him, but I know he works for contractors. Coal companies, too."

Mike had scowled.

"Companies is always surveying property. Don't mean nothin' . . . *nothin'*," he had repeated with some force.

Amos had simply stared. Mike soon crawled away toward the power station and made a show of checking the readout. The men had finished their dinners in a silence broken only by the rattle of lunch pails and Rob's giggles.

When they'd started running coal again, Mike had disappeared. Again.

And now he was here, looking for pot in the middle of winter.

"Thing is," Mike said after finishing half of his cigarette, "I was kinda countin' on the rest of the supply we had hid at the mine."

Amos looked away.

"Well, you're gonna have to wait till summer on that," Amos said.

"Yeah, well. I sort of already sold that stuff. Just hadn't delivered it yet."

Amos eyed him.

"Oh yeah?" the big miner said.

"I was gonna pay you when I delivered it. But now, now I got nothin' to give 'em. You didn't find nothin' down there, right?"

Amos shook his head.

"I heard one of the bricks showed up in the pump screens."

Amos sucked air through his teeth.

"Those fellas might get mad."

"Who? The cops?"

Mike looked at Amos sharply.

"The fellas what bought it."

"Well, just give 'em their money back."

"Yeah," Mike said and took another long drag. "I don't got it just now."

They both looked at the ground.

"I'll talk to 'em," the foreman said. "But we gotta hang together on this."

"We?"

"They know about you."

Amos clenched a fist.

"I'll handle it. Listen, this whole thing may turn out okay for us, better'n okay. But there's some other things we gotta talk about. I heard you found Crandall."

"Yeah."

"And that his head weren't there."

"Yeah."

"Shame."

"Yeah."

They pondered the shame.

"That four hundred, it was working good," Mike said.

Here we go, Amos thought.

"I'm just saying there ain't no point telling any inspectors about the four hundred not working proper because it was."

The 400, a roof-bolting machine, had not been working. Crandall had once said that the 400 had shocked him so hard that he felt as if someone had hit him in the head with a hammer. The water had likely found the flaw and delivered enough juice to Crandall to blow his head off.

MSHA was bound to consider the machine's history an important thing to know about.

"Ain't that right?" Mike asked.

Amos looked Mike squarely in the eye. A full day had not yet passed. Rob's and Crandall's bodies were still underground. The entire crew on the other section—six more men—were trapped or dead. And Mike was already working to get everybody's stories straight.

"'In the beginning was the Word, and the Word was with God, and the Word was God,'" Amos said, nodding.

"Amen," Mike said, nodding as well.

With anyone but Glenda, Amos quoted Scripture when at a loss for something to say. The Book of John seemed to work especially well because the meaning of the first chapter—so familiar, so beautiful— was lost on Amos and, he thought, just about everybody else.

"It's just that there's bound to be an investigation, Amos. And, you know, I figured you, me, Mr. Murphy, all of us suffered enough," Mike said, still nodding.

Me and Mr. Murphy? Amos thought. No wonder he got out here so quick.

"I mean, Mr. Murphy's just tore up about it. Not just losing his mine. His crews really mean some'm to him. I just think we need to stand together. Don't you?" Mike asked.

"'He was in the beginning with God; all things were made through Him, and without Him was not anything made that was made,'" Amos said and looked Mike straight in the eye.

"Amen," Mike answered.

They both nodded.

"I told Mr. Murphy he could count on you."

He patted Amos on the arm and reached into his coat.

"Here's last week's paycheck, and Mr. Murphy threw in next week's too."

Amos reached for the check, but Mike pulled it back.

"Now, don't go spending this here," Mike said in a lower tone. "Sorry to tell you this, Amos, but we may need ever' bit of this here and maybe some more, you know, to set things straight with the buyers."

Mike again held out the check. Amos took and pocketed it.

"Now, tomorrow, Mr. Murphy wants us to get together with a company lawyer. Just to go over how things was run at the mine, make sure we're all on the same page. Tomorrow at eight at the Blue Gem office outside of Hazard."

That would mean driving past where his coworkers were still entombed.

Mike nodded. He took a step toward his truck.

"This whole deal may turn out pretty good for us. Just, you know, gotta work some things out. See you tomorrow, Amos. And thanks again for saving Carl. You're a hero. And Mr. Murphy knows it."

Amos nodded. He made no move to accompany Mike back to his truck. Mike opened his door and waved as he stepped in. Amos refrained from waving since he knew Mike would be driving out past him.

Mike backed up, turned the pickup around, and waved again. This time Amos nodded curtly. The pickup disappeared down the road.

Amos had little doubt that this whole deal was going to turn out very badly for one or both of them. Mike was a guy who, it was obvious, had decided to screw his partners as well as his customers.

Amos thought about where Mike lived. There was a hill in front of Mike's house that would provide perfect cover for a shot at him.

# CHAPTER EIGHT

It was past midnight by the time Will drove back to Fleming-Neon. The streets were deserted. The Conoco was closed. Lights were out. It felt like a ghost town.

The Conoco used to stay open all night. And when Will first started working nights, he and Rob would stop by. They should have bolted home to get as much sleep as they could before school, but both boys loved listening to the men who stood around the counter inside the Conoco.

It was a fraternity of dust-covered brothers who swapped stories about the guts of the mines in which they worked, how the mountains felt and sounded. They got news of the night's high school or college basketball game from Gus, the Conoco's owner, who could give as good a play-by-play as anybody Will had ever known. They grieved when a miner was killed.

They ate pie and sipped coffee, and you'd see their lips appear from beneath the black. And sometimes, on a night after a near-miss or a mysterious roar, white crow's-feet would spring from the skin around their eyes as the men bubbled with relieved laughter.

The son of Paul Murphy Sr., Will was accorded a bit more respect than he'd earned. But it was his black face that bought him a ticket into that fraternity. For Rob, this ticket seemed even more precious. At the Conoco, his skin color was no different from anyone else's.

Those men, those nights, were everything Will had ever wanted from working.

Now the Conoco closed at 9 p.m. because not enough mines had second shifts anymore. With the union gone, most had shifts that went ten or twelve hours. Miners lucky enough to have jobs were too damned tired and too old to talk. They drove home, scrubbed up, ate, and crawled into bed.

And Will was no longer welcome anyway. Miners are as superstitious as sailors, and few wanted to hang around someone who'd caused an explosion. Fewer still were comfortable with an MSHA inspector.

His family, former coworkers, and, hell, even his wife—that one cigarette had cost him nearly everyone he knew. He groped around the passenger seat, found the pack, and shook out another.

Will drove on, past the tightly packed houses of the old company town. He slowed, took a right onto Baker Hollow and came upon a small home ablaze with Christmas lights. It was mid February but the DeMarcos had yet to take their lights down. Will stopped his car.

There was a full-sized sleigh with a set of life-sized reindeer, angels radiant in lighted glory, and a crèche. The entire house was outlined in twinkling colors, and strings of lights extended to trees on either side. This year, the family had added a Santa Claus who popped into and out of a chimney, driven by some sort of fan.

In years past, Will had liked the display. Tonight, it seemed ridiculous. More than half of the nation's electricity is delivered by coal-fired power plants. Eight miners had probably died the previous day digging coal out of the ground to fuel those plants. The life's work of those men was blazing away into the night sky in front of this house.

Will felt sick. He let his foot off the brake and drove the rest of the way up his hollow. He pulled into the short driveway, turned off his truck and sat for a moment. His mind drifted from the Christmas lights to the suicide he had witnessed. They had waited nearly two hours for the coroner, who'd been presiding over a viewing.

Dee Singleton had said that the dead man, Virgil Hogg, had worked for U.S. Steel and then Bethlehem for nearly twenty years but had been laid off. Bethlehem was one of the last big union operations in eastern Kentucky. It once had hundreds of miners working three shifts. The men shared bowling leagues, went hunting together. They ran a good mine. It had closed more than eight years before.

Will sighed, flicked his cigarette into the trees, put on his cap, picked up his mining belt, got out of the truck, and walked up his porch steps. He turned right and walked around to the back door. He stepped inside the house and, in the dark, dropped his belt in a bucket and let his cap fall on top of it. He sat in a worn wooden chair and took off his boots. Then he stood up, stepped out of his coveralls, and hung them on a peg next to the washer.

He walked through the dark kitchen, stopped at the refrigerator, took out a Bud and drained it. He stood for a moment in the wash of the refrigerator's light, got another beer, twisted off the top, and walked toward the hallway. He fumbled for a light. When it turned on, he was staring at his wedding picture. He knew it was there, but suddenly seeing Tessy's broad smile in the full light was a surprise. He toasted Tessy and took another long pull.

Singleton had said that Virgil's wife had grown tired of her husband always being underfoot, yelling at the TV. She'd been threatening for years to move to Lexington and take their children with her.

Will's eyes roamed over the wall before him. Tessy had filled every inch with family photos—mostly of Helen. There she was in her yellow school basketball uniform, a baby on a Florida beach, a toddler chasing after a basketball, a scrawny eleven-year-old holding her summer camp basketball trophy.

He finished the beer and put the empty on a small glass shelf filled with Tessy's glass bears. He walked back to the bedroom and pressed his left hand against his chest and concentrated on unbuttoning his shirt.

Tessy had bought him shirts with zippers, but Will wouldn't wear them. Zippered shirts, he felt, shouted cripple. You had to look hard to see Will's injuries when he was dressed, and a zipper, he thought, needlessly advertised his problem.

Will put his left wrist on the dresser to anchor the shirt and then pawed his cuff button open. He took his shirt off and, just because he was feeling blue, turned to look at his back in the mirror.

The hallway light washed into the room and showed the mottled sworls on his back.

He pulled off his underwear to see the full breadth of the scars. He reached his left hand across his neck and pressed hard at the skin on his right shoulder blade. He barely felt anything through the thick, regrown flesh.

After all these years, did Tessy finally get tired of seeing these burns every morning? They were ugly, Will knew. She would sometimes touch them curiously, feeling the hard ridges with the tips of her fingers. She never seemed disgusted, though. Sad, maybe, but not repulsed.

She said she wanted Helen to play for Hazard High School, which had a terrific girls' basketball program. She filed for divorce because if they'd just moved to Hazard out of the blue, Helen would have had to sit out a year before being allowed to play. The rules were designed to prevent high schools from recruiting star players from other teams. The rules were waived in urgent family circumstances like death and divorce. So some couples simply filed for divorce, and friendly judges sat on the pleading until the child graduated, when the divorce petition was withdrawn.

Will liked basketball as much as the next guy, but he didn't really believe that his wife should file for divorce so Helen could get on a better team. They had argued for weeks about it. The divorce wasn't real, she said, so why did he care? The fights had gotten so bad that when she finally did move out, Will felt like the divorce might as well have been real.

Will had to admit that she had plenty of reasons to leave. His drinking, for one. His driving, for another. And maybe even his scars.

At least she'd moved only as far as Hazard, taking a couple of bedrooms in Will's brother's overly large house. Will still got to see her and Helen—quite a lot, actually. If she'd moved to Lexington, Will wasn't sure what he would have done.

Will looked down and chuckled.

"Standing naked in front of the mirror with my undies around my ankles," he grumbled. "Jesus, I'm in trouble."

He pulled up his underwear, stepped into his slippers, and put on a bathrobe. He found a pack of cigarettes on his bureau and lit up. He went back to the kitchen and got another beer before heading to the bathroom, where he turned on the faucet.

"Leastways, I got water," Will said to the mirror as he put his hands under the flow.

Singleton had said that most of the houses on that tidy little hollow had lost their water either because of the mining or because of the accident. Singleton had spent much of the last year trying to drill new wells for families who'd seen their water disappear as the mine advanced. Those near the old works had a ready source of good water.

Singleton said he'd tested the water repeatedly, and it was clean—although he told folks to use filters. The Department of Health probably wouldn't give their say-so, but it worked for folks on Hell-for-Certain. And there was enough down there for everyone. Or at least there had been.

Teeth brushed, Will headed back into the bedroom and walked around to the left side of the bed, carrying his third beer.

Amos woke up around four in the morning and listened to the mountain. The chorus of summer sounds was long gone. Picking out different animals was now possible.

He rolled out of bed and crept to his bureau. He gingerly opened several drawers and piled the clothes on top, most of them camouflage. He brought the piles to the living room couch in two trips and then closed the bedroom door.

In the closet near the kitchen, he pulled out his pack and brought it to the couch. He unzipped a pocket and checked the string, compass, mini-flashlight, toothbrush, and range-finder all wrapped together in a small pouch. He carefully placed more items into the bag—camouflage pants and T-shirt, several pairs of socks, underwear, long underwear, and flip-flops.

He went to the gun cabinet and quietly opened the glass door.

He stood in front of the cabinet for a moment and then retrieved a

.22 rifle and a BB gun. Then came the shells—both rubber and real. He put each into a carrier that strapped to the sides of the bag.

He stood thinking again. After a moment, he took a 30.06 rifle out of the case, quickly broke it down, and put the components into the clothes part of the bag, along with the big cartridges.

He went into the kitchen and rifled through several cabinets. Into the bag he packed a mound of candy bars, several bananas and apples, packets of salt and pepper, and a bag of raisins.

Then he dressed—more camouflage—and put his hunting knife on his belt and laced it through the loops on his pants.

Opening the outside door, he set the bag on the small front porch and put on his boots. Amos came back inside and stood in thought for a moment. He went to a shelf, retrieved a pocket-sized New Testament, went back outside and put it in his pack, which he shouldered.

He walked off the porch and up the hill.


"What happened here could not have been predicted or prevented," Paul Murphy said to the crowd of reporters two days after the accident, and then paused. He looked down and spotted a tall young man with square glasses.

"You're from the *Louisville Courier-Journal*, aren't you?" Paul asked.

"Yes, sir," the man said.

"Son, any chance your editors are gonna see this for what it is? Can you take extra-careful notes so they'll learn there are good coal operators?" Paul said, and the young man, smiling slightly, went back to scribbling in his notebook.

Paul, Lucius Haverman of MSHA, a state mining official, a Kentucky State Police colonel, and a representative from Kentucky governor Bill Clendon's office were all standing on a stage inside a sizable room that had once served as the shuttered school's cafeteria and theater. A lectern had been brought in, and it bristled with microphones.

Beneath them stood a crush of almost fifty reporters, including representatives from all the networks, the *New York Times*, the *Wall Street Journal*, and even France's *Le Monde*.

Paul turned to the maps taped to the wall behind him.

"What we all agree happened here is that over the last eighty years or so, water from the Bethlehem mine," he pointed to the old Bethlehem map, "pushed its way through a flaw in the rock formations. And that water ended up here, nearly a thousand feet away," Paul said, shifting to the second map, which showed the Red Fox mine.

"How did the water make it that far? We don't know, but pressure and time seem the likely culprits," Paul said.

He turned away from the maps and looked out over the reporters.

"I run very safe mines, and I care deeply about my men," Paul said. "We are doing everything we can to rescue them. I'll take some questions."

He nodded at a well-coiffed man near the front.

"Bruce Heldon, CNN. If I understand the timeline, the flood occurred at eleven fifty-one a.m., but your company did not call federal mine officials until, ah, three seventeen p.m. Is that right, and if so, why did you delay so long in getting help?" the reporter asked.

"Well, sir," Paul said and sighed, "the inundation cut out all the electricity running into the mine. It shut off the mine phone. Nobody up top knew about it for a while because the crew underground couldn't call out."

"But aren't you supposed to have someone outside of the mine check on conditions below for precisely that reason?" the man asked.

"Yes, you're right. He should have done a better job, and we are working to make sure nothing like that happens again. People, there are risks in coal mining. And when accidents happen, no one regrets them more than me. But coal is the answer to this country's problems. We could walk away from the Middle East if we'd only mine more coal. We got more coal in these mountains than the Saudis have oil."

Paul smiled. More hands shot up. Paul pointed at another reporter.

It was a rare chance to eat breakfast with his family, one that foreman Mike Barnes squandered by reading the newspaper and checking to see if his trades on the Chicago Mercantile Exchange had recovered any of their value.

They hadn't.

Barnes sat chewing his thumb and wondering what to do. He would soon leave for his meeting at Blue Gem, and he needed a plan. How hard could he push?

He eventually got up, walked into the kitchen, and kissed his wife on the side of her head. Busy at the sink, she didn't take the time to look up. He tousled his twelve-year-old son's hair and smiled at his fifteen-year-old daughter.

He took his coat off the hook, opened the door, and gave one more look at his daughter, who watched him gently close the door and suddenly fall straight down the porch stairs. She screamed, "Daddy!" and jumped to her feet. Wife, son, and daughter rushed to the door. Barnes's wife pushed her children aside and made it to him first.

"Mike? Mike?" she screamed.

She pulled his upper arm, but Barnes didn't move. She tugged harder and only then noticed the pool of blood on the cement apron around the bottom of the porch.

"Oh Lord," she said. "Cassell, call an ambulance."

She walked around Barnes's body to look at his head more closely, now worried about moving him. She saw the nearly perfect hole near his left eyebrow.

"Oh," she said.

She placed both hands on his head and immediately felt the far larger hole in back. She pulled her hands away. Something gray spilled onto the pavement.

"Jesus, Jesus," she said.

# CHAPTER NINE

The men in the rescue teams had been pissing all morning in a corner of the mine area, but Will knew he couldn't pee in a crowd, never could. Couldn't even use public urinals. He'd often stand for minutes in front of a toilet in a closed stall in a public restroom waiting for the silence his muscles needed before they could relax enough to let the flow start.

So Will crossed the highway and tramped into the woods to find privacy. Cold and wind had stripped the leaves from the trees, so he walked quite a ways. When he tramped back, a woman was standing on the edge of the highway looking toward the mine. She wore blue jeans and a brown corduroy jacket that seemed too light for the weather.

He looked down the road toward the shuttered elementary school where the state police and MSHA had set up briefing rooms for families and the media. Eight or nine huge TV satellite trucks were parked along the side of the road and in the school parking lot.

On this side of the school, two women stood side by side with their arms folded, looking toward Will. They must have seen him walk into the woods, and one of them decided to waylay him. He wondered if they'd seen him pee. The thought bothered him.

As he approached, one of the women turned. She looked hollow-eyed.

"You gonna find my husband?"

"I'm sure gonna try."

"Why ain't you gone in there yet?"

"It ain't safe."

"Hell with safe. My husband's down there."

"Yes, ma'am," Will said and looked down. "I'm sorry for your, uh, situation."

She covered her face and started to cry. Will reached out but didn't touch her. "I gotta go," he said.

He walked away and didn't look back. A dark blue state police cruiser was parked next to one of the rescue vehicles. He walked into the office trailer. Two state troopers, standing with their backs to the door, turned to look at him.

One of them was the detective from the hospital. The other was a woman.

"Here he is," Lucius said. "Will, this here's Lieutenant Gail Northrup of the Kentucky State Police."

"Howdy," Will said and shook her hand.

"And this is . . ."

Will reached out and said, "Sergeant Freeman, right?"

"Right. At the hospital," the sergeant said and shook Will's hand.

"Good you two already know each other, Will, because the sergeant here is gonna join your rescue team."

Will paused.

"Uh, Sergeant, I don't think that's a good idea. We train a fair amount together, and if you do some'm wrong down there, things could turn out bad for all of us," Will said evenly.

"Sergeant Freeman has been through firefighter training. He knows how to handle himself on rescues," the woman said, her voice brittle and tight. Sergeant Freeman was quiet.

"That may be, ma'am, but this is a totally different kinda deal," Will said. "Lucius, you know how much we train together. You know what stupid moves could mean down there. This is not smart."

"It's already been decided. He's going with you," Lucius said.

"This about the drugs?" Will asked.

Lucius shook his head. "Worse. The foreman got shot this morning. Dead."

"We think he had something to do with the drugs, Mr. Murphy. He had a prior drug arrest," Lieutenant Northrup said.

They were quiet.

"All right, Sergeant," Will conceded, "but you gotta do exactly as I say. This ain't nothin' like you ever experienced."

The sergeant nodded. He didn't look any happier with the situation than did Will.


The bacon was cooked, drained, and cooling. Amos had mixed the egg, cream, and cheese in a small bowl, which stood near the stove. The potatoes were cooking, and he was nearly through squeezing the orange juice.

It was eight thirty in the morning. Amos had come back to cook her breakfast, but she was fixing to sleep through it. She slept a lot when taking pills, which normally was fine. But Amos wasn't quite sure how much time he had.

He figured no one would come looking for him until nine thirty at the earliest. That meant he should probably be out the door by nine twenty.

He decided it was time.

He spooned the potatoes onto a plate covered by paper towels and turned off the stove.

He walked quietly into the bedroom and lay down next to her. He picked up her hand and kissed it. She opened her eyes and looked at him blankly. She focused and a sad smile came to her.

She rolled over and put her face next to his thigh.

He patted her shoulder.

"Scrambled eggs?" he asked.

"Sure."

There was no enthusiasm in the assent. She could smell the meal he'd made. But she lost her appetite while on drugs and he wanted to get some food into her. He wasn't sure how long he'd be gone.

"I'm gonna start the eggs," he said. "Don't be too long."

"Hm," she said.

In the end, she didn't emerge. Amos fried his own eggs and ate most of the potatoes and bacon. He finally cooked her eggs, since he thought it unlikely that she would do so on her own, and he left a full plate warming in the oven.

It was nine twenty when he went outside and shouldered his pack. The note he'd left read, "Gone hunting." He walked back up the hill.

Will knew it wasn't the man's fault, but he couldn't resist feeling some satisfaction in Sergeant Freeman's growing horror.

"How long's it gonna take to build a ventilation wall?" Sergeant Freeman asked.

"Can't say for sure till we see the damage," Will said. "But rescues have been known to take a week or more. Turn around."

Will had given the sergeant one of the MSHA team's extra rescue packs—an alkaline air-filter system that looked like the jet pack from a Buck Rogers movie. Will checked the nozzles again and then, out of habit, tapped the tank. He swiveled the sergeant around.

"All right, you got about two and a half hours of air in there, and we're probably gonna be down there a lot longer than that," Will said. "We'll change out our packs, but we also don't want to waste air. When I lower you down, you're gonna keep your mask off. The air at the bottom of the shaft is fine."

"I just don't understand why we can't find those boys right away and just get out of there," Sergeant Freeman said.

" 'Cause that could get us all killed," Will said, and the two men looked at each other in silence. Angry at the sergeant's presence, Will had explained almost nothing about the upcoming operation.

"Look, we go running through the tunnels down there, we could stir up a pocket of methane and blow the whole place up. That wouldn't help us, those boys, or their wives," Will said.

He gestured to a shack at the edge of the parking lot.

"That over there is the mine fan. It's running again, but the first air that came out had methane levels around ten percent. That's about as dangerous as it comes. In the last couple of hours, those levels dropped below one percent—which is why we're going in now. That and the water's mostly gone. But it's doubtful every bit of that mine is getting ventilated. That means there's bound to be places with explosive levels of methane. You stumble into one without knowing it, and you go boom."

The sergeant nodded, and this time Will took no comfort in his obvious unease.

"All right, we gotta get going," Will said.

Will pulled the sergeant over to the shaft. One of the trucks was parked about five yards from the hole. A cable from a winch on the front of the truck was looped over the elevator supports. The cable was snaked back through a pulley that had been hastily added to the box of steel girders suspended over the mine.

Will put his hand on the girder to steady himself and reached out over the hole to grab the end of the cable. He pulled it to him and hooked it onto a ring secured by a strap across Sergeant Freeman's chest.

"I'm turning on your helmet light 'cause it's gonna be black down there," Will said. "You're gonna end up on top of the elevator. Unhook the cable there. There's a rope to help you down the rest of the way. Then wait. Sam and Alvin're already down there, and I'm coming right after you. Okay?"

"Yeah." Sergeant Freeman nodded. Will put his thumb up, and someone at the winch started it rolling. It pulled the sergeant up and over the hole. Bracing his right hand on the elevator supports, Will used his left hand to hold on to Sergeant Freeman's upper arm and steady him as he swung out.

"Okay?" Will asked again of the cop, who looked stricken.

Hugging the elevator cables hanging beside him, the sergeant nodded. Will let him go and etched a circle in the air. The winch reversed and the sergeant dropped. Will watched him disappear into the blackness.

Moments later, the cable wound back up. Will grabbed the hook, slapped it on his chest, and swung out over the hole. "Let's go," he shouted, circling again with his hand. He dropped into the shaft.

Will switched on his headlamp, and the beam focused on the sides of the shaft. Steel elevator guides were bolted into the rock on three sides, and Will could feel the elevator cables brush up against him. Outlines of the bore holes used to blast out the shaft were also clear.

He dropped through several layers of hard rock punctuated by seams of coal—at least two of them big enough to mine. There was a mountain of coal above the mine that had never been touched.

Will's headlamp seemed to grow brighter as the sunlight faded. He looked down and saw the elevator below him. He reached the top of it and the light of another headlamp washed over him.

"Okay, that's good," Alvin said. The winch stopped just before Will sat on the elevator. He stood up awkwardly, unhooked the cable, and walked to the edge. He thought briefly about jumping but decided to sit, grab the rope at hand, and slither down.

"Cable's all yours," Alvin said into the intercom.

The ground was muddy and there was a large puddle at the mine's entrance, but otherwise the walking was fine. Will stepped up to the three men, frowning to hide his exhilaration.

"Well, fellas, let's see how far we can go before the other team gets here."

# CHAPTER TEN

A tan pickup and a Mercedes sedan pulled up to Amos's trailer around noon, hours after Amos, who was hidden in a hunting blind up the hill, thought they'd show. Carl Breathitt, the guy Amos had saved in the mine, got out of the pickup; a guy in a dark suit—had to be the lawyer—got out of the Mercedes.

Carl walked to the trailer door and knocked while the lawyer hung back. There was no answer. He knocked again. He waited. Carl opened the storm door slightly and knocked on the inner door.

Amos's blind was well camouflaged but he couldn't quite see the front door from it. When Carl stood back and held the storm door wide open, Amos guessed that Glenda was standing in the doorway. Carl glanced up toward the hills. The lawyer stood there looking down. There was talking.

Carl let the storm door swing shut. He waved, turned, and walked down the front steps. The two men huddled between their vehicles. Carl gestured toward the hill, trailer, and sky. The lawyer leaned back against his car.

Eventually, the lawyer pushed himself erect and walked around to the driver's side of his muscle car. He gave a small wave to Carl and drove away.

One down, Amos thought.

Carl lit a cigarette and leaned against the bed of his truck. He waited and lit more cigarettes. Some time later, Carl pushed away from the truck and waved back at the trailer. He gestured.

Glenda came onto the porch, her arms crossed.

Carl shook his head.

Glenda's arms came down to her sides. Her fists were clenched. Amos could see that she was mad. Carl kept shaking his head. Glenda retreated from the open door. It looked like Carl was not going to leave until he could talk to Amos.

"But I saved your life," Amos mumbled to himself.

The first BB hit Carl on the back of his right hand. He jumped and dropped his cigarette. He looked at his hand and rubbed it with his left thumb while looking up the hill.

He took out another cigarette. In the midst of lighting it, Carl was hit with another BB on the palm. The cigarette dropped from his mouth, the matches disappeared. Carl turned and, holding his right hand in his left, shook them up and down angrily.

He pointed up the hill and yelled something that Amos couldn't make out.

Carl whirled at the trailer and gestured at the hill. Glenda emerged again and glanced back up the hill. The third BB hit him on his left calf where his jeans tightened. His leg buckled, and he bent down. The next hit him square in the ass. Glenda withdrew.

Carl lunged forward and crawled into the passenger side of his truck. He backed the truck up. When he stopped, his sideview mirror shattered. His tires spit gravel as his pickup slid onto the road and roared away.


When Will was a child, Glasscock's General Store was the best place in Hazard to buy toys. One year, Will's mother went there for some early Christmas shopping, and she sent Will and Rob outside to play while she bought presents. Rob's family lived next-door to Will's and, although the boys were a year apart, they were in the same first-grade class. They'd been best friends for as long as either could remember.

They must have been six and seven. Will had no memory of the reasons Jeff and Paul, his brothers, weren't there. Nor could he recall why his mother had charge of Rob that day. Still, Will remembered being delighted. He and Rob went behind the store and—he winced thinking about it—played on the railroad tracks.

"Ahm the law in these parts," Will said, straddling the rails and speaking in an exaggerated Western accent. "And I'm runnin' you in, you dirty dog."

"Not without a fight, you ain't," Rob answered, and the two boys—suppressing grins—reached for sticks shoved into their pockets.

"Blam blam," they both shouted. Will ran toward Rob, still pretending to shoot.

"I gotchu," Will shouted. "You're deader'n a doornail."

Rob clutched his chest and toppled over beside the tracks. Will gleefully jumped on top of him and the two wrestled, laughing.

The train whistle went through them like an electrical jolt. They both turned to see the behemoth bearing down upon them. The boys' eyes had gotten used to the darkening sky, so the headlamp blinded them. Rob ran. Will turned around and tucked his head between his knees. He would have been killed if Rob hadn't tackled him from the side and pushed him off the tracks.

Will never forgot the awful squeal of the train's brakes as it rushed past them less than a yard away. The wheels were huge, and the massive weight of the coal cars seemed to create an almost gravitational pull on the boys. The minutes needed for the train to pass seemed like years.

Only when the train was gone did Rob—who had lain on top of Will—roll away. There was a gentle slope covered by brush falling away from the tracks. Still panicked, Will leapt into it, tearing his clothes and ripping the flesh on his legs, arms, and torso.

Will leaned against the back of the store and sobbed. Then he looked up and saw Rob, who'd just picked his way through the brush, smiling at him like they'd gotten away with something. Which, Will realized, they had. They'd gotten away with their lives.

Will put his hands on his knees and started to laugh. Rob joined him. And the two boys laughed harder than they had ever laughed before. It would be days before the two of them could go more than an hour together without bursting into helpless giggling.

It was the crucial moment of their friendship. Up until that time, there had been a strange imbalance to their bond. They had grown up together on Nigger Hollow, a name given the place one hundred years earlier when Rob's great-grandfather settled there.

Although Will's family moved there long after Rob's, Rob had come into their house a supplicant. Rob's father had left and his mother worked, and he had no siblings. By contrast, Will's father came home every night, his mother stayed home, and Will had two brothers. The Murphy household was warm and active, and Rob was drawn to it like a moth to light.

As a result, Will ruled Rob. When Will demanded, Rob gave up the G.I. Joe he was playing with. When they played cowboys and Indians, Rob was the Indian. When they ate cereal together, Will always got the blue bowl.

After the train, they came to a new arrangement. Already close, they became inseparable. The difference in their race still mattered. There were some places they still couldn't go together, like churches, barbershops, and some parties. But between the two, their friendship was equal and almost perfect.

Devoid of light and color, the mine became a screen upon which Will projected memories. The deeper he went into the mine and the closer Will got to his old friend, the sharper the images seemed to become. Learning to swim together; fighting off older kids while trick-or-treating; winning and losing in basketball.

The richness of the memories contrasted with the monotony of the mine. Every tunnel looked the same. The only obvious differences were the numbers spray-painted on the metal doors built into the walls. They made it to twenty-seven, nearly eighteen hundred feet into the mine.

"Sam, Sergeant Freeman, drop the roll here," Will shouted. The two men put down their burden. "This is as far as we go. Retreat," Will shouted.

All but Sergeant Freeman turned to go.

"What? What about those men?" Sergeant Freeman asked.

Will looked at him for a moment.

"Sergeant," Will said. "You're gonna run out of air in about twenty minutes. We gotta go back."

Sergeant Freeman ripped off his mask and shouted, "Air's fine." Suddenly unmuffled, the sergeant's voice echoed around the mine, surprising them all.

"Sergeant Freeman, put your mask back on and turn around," Will said, trying to keep the anger out of his voice. Will pulled the sergeant's shoulders around and pushed him. "We'll get 'em, but this is the way we do these things."

The sergeant stood with his head down for a moment, breathing deeply. He put his mask back on.

They retraced their steps, this time pausing only occasionally to check the air and call in. Well before the end of the mine, the team saw flashes from other headlamps. Will's heart surged. He was surprised how happy he felt to see other men.

When he reached them, Will took off his mask, and the others followed him. It was an enormous relief to get that thing off. The straps had begun to dig into his face. He rubbed his cheeks and ears.

"We'll establish our fresh-air base here," said the man whom Will had greeted. "The Fremont team will take it from here. Why don't you boys sit down? We got water and some sandwiches. And we got replacement filters and oxygen."

"'Preciate it," Will said. "There's a roll of plastic at twenty-seven."

The man nodded. Will walked over to the coolers. Sergeant Freeman followed. They fished around inside the boxes and retrieved bottles and food.

Sergeant Freeman looked around for a place to sit. Mud covered the entire area. Holding a bottle of water and a sandwich, he squatted with his back to the mine wall.

"Get away from there," Will said.

"What?"

"Get away from that rib," Will said, and pointed to the wall. "It ain't safe. For any of us."

Sergeant Freeman sighed and slid forward a few feet. He dug his water bottle into the mud and took off his gloves to unwrap the cellophane around the sandwich.

The cop sucked his teeth.

"You know, I just don't understand why we can't run in, figure out if anyone's alive, and get on with the investigation."

Will was having trouble pulling the cellophane off his sandwich. He focused his headlamp and began to tear at the plastic. He finally bit into the sandwich and spit out a piece of bread mixed with plastic. He ripped off the rest of the plastic.

"Back there in Louisville, d'ya ever hear of Scotia?" Will asked.

"No."

"Well, it was a mine—not more than a few miles from here, actually," Will said. "Blew up in 1976. Terrible explosion. Trapped seventeen men. Everybody around here knew some of 'em. Fire burned for nearly two days. They finally got it under control, and they sent in a rescue team. Eleven men, most of 'em from MSHA. Folks were hoping some of those seventeen men were still alive. So the team went rushing in to find 'em.

"Nobody knows why, but the mine blew again. And this time, it wouldn't stop burning. They had to seal up the mine to put out the fire. Never retrieved the bodies."

Will took another bite of his sandwich and chewed for a moment.

"The worst part about it is that a lot of folks around here blame that MSHA team for the deaths of those seventeen men. They ain't even heroes. Nobody wants that again. So we got to make the mine safe as we go. Build ventilation walls to push the bad air out. Make sure the carbon monoxide and methane levels stay in the safe zone. It's slow, but it's the only way."

They both ate in silence.

"So what's next?" Sergeant Freeman finally asked.

"Well, the Fremont team'll probably make it another twenty-five or thirty breaks doing the same thing we did," Will said. "Then they'll probably send in another team. Then we might go again. The teams'll keep rotating in every two hours or so until the job's done."

"Wait a second, won't that next team find those boys?" the sergeant asked.

"Doubt it."

"Hey, Will," said Alvin, who was sitting nearby. "Look a here." He was pointing his headlamp at a lump on the ground in a nearby cross tunnel.

Will focused his own lamp on the object, which looked to be about the size of a body. Will got up, quickly followed by Sergeant Freeman.

Sure enough, it was a body, but a headless one. Will hesitated and then made himself stoop to get a closer look. Sergeant Freeman came up beside him.

"Can ya tell who it is?" Alvin asked, a few steps behind them.

"Gotta be the roof bolter," Will said. "That miner man, Amos Blevins, he told Lucius the roof bolter lost his head."

"How the hell did he get all the way back here?" Sergeant Freeman said and got down on his haunches.

"Water does funny things in coal mines," Will said.

The body seemed undamaged. Will put his headlamp on the stump, and they all saw a tangle of vessels and tubes, all in surprisingly rich colors. There was no blood.

"Jesus," Alvin said behind Will.

"Can't believe we walked right by it. It's not more'n ten feet from the main tunnel," Sergeant Freeman said.

"Let's look around for the head," Will said. The men swept the area with their headlamps, although none moved too far. Nothing.

"All right," Will said. "Alvin, you better call this'n in. And fellas, let's keep our eyes peeled for that head."

# CHAPTER ELEVEN

A large coon had waddled down the ridge. Amos had him in the sights of his .22, but he was pretty sure the coon would approach closer still, so he waited.

The dusk deepened.

The coon raised its head, its nose nudged the air, and its bandit eyes blinked. The wind was slightly behind Amos. No sense waiting anymore. He shot the coon in its right eye.

The sound echoed in the small valley, and Amos sat still for several minutes.

Nothing else moved, so Amos left his blind and picked the coon up by its tail. He went back to the blind, shouldered his pack, and walked down the hill to the trailer.

He dropped the coon in a basin behind the trailer, leaned his pack against the trailer's footers, and got out his knife. He skinned and gutted the coon. Cradling the carcass, he walked into the trailer, using his elbows to open the door.

"Honey, I'm back," he said.

He heard her come out of the bedroom as he walked toward the kitchen. He felt her eyes.

"What the hell was that all about?" she asked.

He dropped the coon on the counter and washed his hands in the sink.

"Amos?" Glenda asked with some insistence.

"Just a minute. Let me get the blood off," Amos answered quietly.

His back burned.

He left his hands wet and quickly opened a cabinet and took out a shallow basin. He put it on the counter and dropped the carcass inside. He rinsed his hands again and dried them on a dish towel.

He turned.

Glenda was standing with her arms crossed. Her hair was in a ponytail, brown and straight. She was wearing a gray sweatsuit and wool socks. Amos expected her to be delirious, but she was quite composed. Her face was tight, brow furrowed.

"That was Carl, the guy I saved," Amos said.

"You saved? But you just shot him."

"I hit him with a few BBs, Glenda. Shootin' him just outside our house wouldn't . . . well, wouldn'ta been smart."

"You reckon so? Amos, what the goddamned hell is going on?"

She said it just to bother him, Amos knew. She had angrily denounced God after Lee's death and had rarely entered a church since. Amos had turned even more religious. They tried not to talk about religion. Amos had grown up in a deeply religious household; Glenda had not.

On occasion, the differences would appear in their arguments. Amos would quote scripture, Glenda would cuss. Both were effective ways to annoy the other.

"Glenda, honey."

She considered him.

"This have to do with the flood?" she asked.

"Could be. They want me to talk to a federal investigator. I don't want to do that."

"Wait, I thought you said you already talked to the investigators, told them about Rob and . . . and . . ."

"Crandall."

"Yeah, Crandall."

"Baby, I said two or three quick things to some guy from the mine agency 'fore jumping into that ambulance. Then I hightailed outta the hospital 'fore they could question me again. This'd be different."

"I don't understand."

"All's I told that fella was who got stuck down there and who didn't. Rescue stuff. But the next thing they're gonna ask is gonna be about the mine and how it was run and that kinda stuff."

"So? Why not talk to 'em?"

He tried not to lie to Glenda, but he sometimes failed to tell her the full truth.

"A MSHA inspector is bound to ask questions I can't answer without lying, and I ain't gonna do that."

"Just tell him you don't know. He'll understand."

"But I do know."

She scowled at him.

"But you ain't even sure it's about the flood?"

He cocked his head at her.

"Is it about the new TV?" she asked, her eyes narrowing.

He considered her. "Could be."

"Like where you got the money from?"

"Glenda, there's some things that you don't want to know about."

They were about two yards apart. Amos was leaning up against the sink skirt and standing on linoleum. Glenda had her feet in deep brown shag.

"Honey, I think it'd be a good idea if you went to stay with Carla for a while."

Her mother was an addict, so he didn't want her staying there. Her sister, Carla, was against prescription drugs but was so righteous about it that Glenda and she barely spoke.

"This is my house as much as yourn."

"Glenda, honey, it ain't about that."

"What is it about?"

"This thing could take a while to settle out."

Glenda scowled.

"I don't understand why you can't talk to those fellers, figure out what they want and give it to 'em. We can get rid o' the TV."

"Honey." Amos shook his head.

He thought about saying, "Render therefore to Caesar the things that are Caesar's, and to God the things that are God's," but he knew that it would only make her mad. And he worried that to her the passage could mean the opposite of what he meant.

Better shut up.

"Well, I ain't leavin'," she said. "You can go if you want, but I'm staying right here."

Amos nodded and sighed.

"I gotcha a coon," he said in a low voice.

"Go on and wash up," she said and walked to the cabinet to get some potatoes.

"I might be doin' a lot o' huntin'."

"Suits me fine not to have you underfoot," Glenda said, her head still in the cabinet.

He smiled and walked to the bathroom.


Building yet another ventilation wall, Will remembered the last time he'd heard Rob's voice. Will had been about to enter his mother's hospital room when Rob's low rumble had stopped him. Will had almost turned to leave.

"You gotta help him, Rob," Will's mother said. "He's gonna kill himself, and someone's gotta stop him. He'll listen to you."

"I done tried, Mrs. Murphy. I done tried. Not gonna do it again."

"His drinkin's got so bad, so bad," she said, her voice breaking. "Tessy said he picked up Helen t'other day from basketball practice, and he was drunk. Everyone on the team knew. Poor little Helen didn't know what to do. She didn't want to get in the car, but what's she gonna say? He's her daddy. So she gets in and is scared to death the whole way home."

Will glanced around the hallway to see if he could light a cigarette. Too many nurses.

"Hm, hm," Rob said.

Something about hearing Rob cluck over him—the same way they both used to cluck over a neighborhood loser like Tickle Jenkins— made Will angry. He walked into the room.

It was a spacious private room with a sweeping view of the mountains, a clear sign of Paul's growing affluence. It was stuffed with flowers, many of them from mining-equipment and trucking companies. Will spotted his own bouquet by the window, now overwhelmed by larger displays.

Will had spent more than three months in this hospital recovering from his burns, but his own room had been far more modest. And he couldn't remember getting more than two bouquets.

Rob was sitting beside the bed holding his mother's hand.

"Oh," she said.

Rob followed her eyes.

"Hey," he said and got up. "Mrs. Murphy, you take care."

"No, sit," she said, pulling Rob back down. "Will, you sit over there," she said, motioning to a chair nearby.

Will hesitated and then did as he'd been told.

"Will, I was just telling Rob here," she said, patting Rob's arm, "that I got it all wrong. I used to think we took him in. Now I realize he took us in."

Rob looked down.

"Sure, Momma," Will said.

"You boys were so close. Like twins. I couldn't buy a jersey for one without buying one for t'other. Or lunches. Remember how I started makin' your lunches, Rob, so's you two wouldn't fight over 'em?"

Will looked out the window, remembering a day that his mother, who was given to crazy ideas, decided that the boys should eat their apples first, not last. She'd read something in the newspaper about how eating fruit first improved digestion.

Will had refused.

"Momma, fruit is dessert. Dessert goes last," Will had said.

"I know, honey. But I want you to eat it first from now on," she said.

"Momma, it don't make no sense," Will said.

"Will, I don't want you arguing with me," she said in growing exasperation.

Rob, who had arrived in the midst of this argument, put his arm around Will's shoulders.

"Don't worry, Mrs. Murphy. We'll eat the apples first, if'n you like," Rob had said and shot a look at Will. Surprised, Will quieted.

Will's mother looked at Will, who nodded.

"All right, thank you, boys," she said. "You'll see. It'll make you feel better."

Will silently allowed her to kiss him and went out with Rob.

"You gonna eat the dessert first?" Will asked at the bus stop.

"Heck no," Rob had said. "But she don't have to know."

And a light had gone off in Will's head. He could tell his mother one thing and do another. Will realized that Rob, whose mother was largely absent from his life, had probably learned that lesson years earlier.

It was not a memory he could share.

"How come you boys don't see each other no more?" Will's mother asked in the hospital room.

Both men were silent.

"When I'm better, I'm gonna have all y'all over to the house for supper. You and Will and Tessy and Mary and the kids and everyone. We haven't been together in forever."

Both men nodded, although Rob's face was set.

Will's mother went home the next week, but she never fully recovered from the stroke. The supper never happened. Will didn't see Rob again until the funeral for Will's father. Will fled the service before giving Rob a chance to approach.

Now stringing the plastic curtain on the wood frame he'd built for the ventilation wall, Will thought once again about Rob's clucking. Why had it bothered him so much? Lord knows he'd heard worse.

But when they were kids, Rob had always been the one needing help, even pity, what with his father gone and his mother working. And maybe there was something about him being black. Will was now the subject of pity from a black man. Something about that grated.

Will paused in his building. He was stringing a plastic curtain across a frame of two-by-fours to direct clean air into the mine just in front of them. He looked down the tunnel.

His headlamp wasn't strong enough to make the miner and scoop clear, but he could see dark hulks where he thought the machines must be. Rob was likely riding that scoop, dead. Will looked away and saw Sergeant Freeman, also peering down the tunnel.

It was like a horror movie. The shaky glimpses given by their headlamps only increased the tension. At one point, Will turned his head toward the tunnel's end and thought he saw a face. His heart leaped, and he looked again. Nothing.

The low ceiling made everything worse. It meant that the men generally only saw a few feet in front of them because, stooped as they were, they couldn't point their headlamps level with the ground unless they squatted.

The low ceiling also meant that the men battled claustrophobia the whole time. The weight above him seemed to push down upon Will's shoulders and was almost unbearable. Sometimes he would reach his hands to the roof and push in frustration—especially after catching his helmet on a roof bolt.

Worst of all, the mine rumbled and popped like ice on a pond. The first time they heard a pop, Sergeant Freeman took several worried steps back toward the mine's entrance. Will and the others only paused and then went back to work. Will felt badly for the cop. It was a horrible, frightening introduction to underground mining.

Another time, they heard a low rumble. Everybody stopped and looked around. Will slowly swept the roof with his headlamp and thought he saw a small wave pass through the rock. They all froze. Will finally glanced back at the others and nodded. They all went back to work except Sergeant Freeman, who briefly lifted his mask to throw up. The cop remained bent over for another moment and then joined the men again.

The headless body, of course, was on everyone's mind. They had not been able to remove it right away, so the men had built a small curtain to screen the area from view. And then they'd dragged the coolers a few more yards away.

In one of the only pieces of good news, a previous rescue team had discovered a working scoop. It was just right for hauling lumber and plastic. They finished their third wall and walked down the entry tunnel toward the next cross-tunnel, leaving the scoop behind. The water, which had been gradually getting deeper, rose to their knees.

Will measured the air levels and then stood stooped with his hands on his hips as Alvin read the numbers over the intercom.

"Fellas, we ain't got plastic enough back in that scoop to finish this here wall," Will shouted. Gathered along the side of the cross-tunnel—just as there had been in the last cross-tunnel—were submerged plastic curtains left by the miners. "Let's use these."

"Ain't we supposed to leave those for the investigation? I mean, don't this show they weren't using proper ventilation?" Sam asked.

Will smiled. "I reckon. But I seen 'em. And this mine didn't flood 'cause o' poor ventilation, Sam. Let's get 'em."

Everyone except Sergeant Freeman stooped to untangle the submerged plastic. The cop stood staring at Will.

"This is your brother's mine, isn't it?" the cop asked.

Will looked up, his arms filled with dirty, wet plastic. He smiled.

"Yeah."

The cop pursed his lips.

"You all do things a whole lot differently than we do."

"Yeah."

The cop shook his head. He did not join the others in retrieving the curtains.

"Why don't you go get that lumber?" Will asked. "We ain't gonna be able to bring the scoop any farther in this water."

Their two hours were up. They still had three breaks to go before the end of the mine. Will led the team beyond the next cross-tunnel without stopping to put up ventilation curtains. He'd decided to look for Rob.

Will had seen many dead bodies in his day, some of them horribly mangled. But he always approached coal-mine death investigations with a deep sense of dread. In everyday life, dead bodies are out of place. They lie in silent embarrassment on a bed, in a living room or by the side of the road. They shouldn't be there, and they are quickly removed to a morgue.

In coal mines, it was the living who seemed out of place. Looking for dead bodies in coal mines always felt like rooting around an antechamber to hell.

They passed another cross-tunnel. Will took out his hammer and started tapping the roof again. They were now groping for footing in water that had risen to their thighs. Almost half the space of the mine was filled with water. They sloshed forward and came to the last cross-tunnel.

"Jesus!" Sergeant Freeman screamed. He fished around in the water and pulled up a piece of wood. He closed his eyes and took a deep breath.

"Sorry. I thought . . . I thought it was the head," he said. The others edged forward again.

Will stopped, put away his hammer, and took out his air meter. He didn't shout out any numbers this time but stared at it silently. He turned around.

"Fellas, we're standing in about five percent methane. Sergeant, that's enough to blow us to Kingdom Come," Will shouted through his mask. "Leave your hammers in your belts. Keep your helmets from hitting the roof. Don't even snap your fingers."

Will glanced at Sergeant Freeman and realized that the cop was shaking uncontrollably—from fright or cold, Will didn't know which. Will was shaking a bit himself. The water felt like a malevolent force, seething and snatching.

They could now see the miner machine and scoop clearly but there was no sign of a body. Will held up his hand.

"That over there is where the roof bolts end," he said, pointing ahead. "Y'all stay back here. I'm gonna see if I can find Rob."

Will dropped to his hands and knees, submerging most of his body. He crawled forward.

"What the hell's he doing?" Sergeant Freeman asked Sam.

"That's unsupported roof. He wants to get below the miner machine so that if there's a cave-in the machine protects him," Sam said.

"Are we supposed to be doing this?" Sergeant Freeman asked.

Sam looked at him.

Will all but swam the remaining distance to the scoop. To the others, his helmet seemed to float forward. He went around to the right, didn't see anything but machine and rock, and circled back around to the left.

Rob was leaning back against the machine as if taking a nap. His face was swollen, his eyes were open, and his lips were drawn back in a grimace. His skin was chalky, bleached of much of its pigment. He could finally be mistaken for Will's brother.

Will came to Rob's side and put a hand on his shoulder, and the body slumped forward into the rock. Will pushed at the boulder. Nothing. He set his feet and strained against it. Not the slightest movement.

He reached up and closed Rob's eyes then lay beside him.

"Oh Rob," he said quietly. "How's that arm? I'm so sorry, buddy."

Will patted the dead man's back and closed his own eyes. When he opened them again, Will raised himself up and kissed Rob on the head. He stood with his hands on his knees for a moment, sighed, and dropped back down. He swam back to the team, and Sam helped him to his feet.

"Rob's right there, but there's a big block of coal on top of him," Will said to the gathered team. "Couldn't move it."

They said nothing.

"He's startin' to look kinda bad. We need to get him outta here pretty soon. Alvin, I want you to map this and call it in. They might as well know about it now as later," Will said. "And then let's get out of here."

"We just gonna leave him?" Sergeant Freeman asked.

"We ain't got the equipment to get him out, and we can't stay here," Will said. "Ready, Alvin?"

Alvin nodded.

"Retreat," Will yelled.

Back at the fresh-air base deep in the mine, Sergeant Freeman kept shaking his head. Will could see that the cop was having trouble breathing and guessed that he was starting to suffer claustrophobia. Will didn't want to embarrass the guy, but he was pretty sure that Sergeant Freeman should not be among those who headed back for more rescue work.

The sergeant was seated on one of the coolers, and Will went over to get a drink. The sergeant got up for a moment as Will fished out a bottle of water.

Will put a hand on the cop's shoulder.

"You all right?" Will asked.

The sergeant gave a shallow nod.

"Will, I'm sorry I asked to come down here. I don't know how much more of this I can take. I keep," and here the cop paused, "seeing things."

"It's the headlamps. They screw up your vision," Will said.

Twice on the way back to the fresh-air base, Will had glanced behind his team and seen someone standing in the tunnel. When he focused his lamp on the spot, the person had disappeared. His heart had leapt both times.

But he had experienced such things before and knew they were phantoms made from darkness, narrow lighting, fatigue, and fear.

"It happens to all of us, Sergeant," Will said. "It's just rough the first time."

There was a good chance the team wouldn't have to go back, that the other teams would finish building ventilation walls and get the equipment needed to get those men out. Another team was exploring the other working section and had already called back word that they'd found all six dead miners.

Will put off suggesting that Sergeant Freeman leave.

Quite suddenly, Will found that he was lying with his face pressed into the mud, his body covered by a great weight. Roof fall, Will thought, and now I'm gonna die.

# CHAPTER TWELVE

The buck had six points, and Amos had him perfectly sighted. He aimed for the animal's heart, breathed out slowly, and squeezed the trigger.

The buck sprang six feet into the air with the impact and bounded away. Amos thought he'd seen the rubber bullet hit precisely where he'd aimed.

Deer-hunting season had just ended, which wasn't a great concern to Amos. No one would trouble himself with a small buck shot out of season. More important, his freezer was full of venison, and Glenda was unlikely to want more.

For years, Amos had shot far more game than he could eat. Instead of killing needlessly, he now shot rubber bullets and BBs. Made the game jumpy, but Amos figured that wasn't such a bad thing. Tougher on the amateurs.

He watched the buck bound up the hill and then heard the cruiser.

Hazard City Police had recently painted all of their vehicles white with blue lettering. Made them seem less threatening than the old black and yellow. The cruiser parked beside his trailer.

A man wearing a white police shirt and blue jeans got out and stood with the door open, looking up at the hill. Most of his body was shielded. Amos looked through the telescope of his .22 and saw a barrel-chested officer wearing a police baseball cap. Amos could have easily shot him, but that seemed intemperate. Even a BB might cause real trouble.

Amos waited.

The man stood for several minutes, one arm on the top of his car door and the other on his roof. He seemed to decide something, closed the door, and walked slowly to the trailer.

He knocked. He knocked again. He opened the storm door and knocked vigorously. He spoke, then motioned. Glenda appeared. The officer took her by the arm. Glenda tried to pull away. The officer threw her on the porch, put her arms behind her back, and cuffed her.

All the while, Amos caressed the trigger of his .22. His breathing was less controlled than normal, but Amos had little doubt that he could kill the man.

The officer pulled Glenda up by her elbow. She sagged. He brought her down the porch steps to the cruiser. With a hand on her head, he bent her down and pushed her into the backseat of the vehicle. He closed the door.

He walked slowly to the front of the cruiser and sat facing the hill. He looked at his fingernails.

Amos could see only one of Glenda's knees through his scope. He put his crosshairs back on the officer, who was picking at something on his hands.

Amos put the weapon into a crook of the blind and walked down the hill. The officer looked up only when Amos was within a few yards, although he had to have heard Amos well before then. The officer nodded at Amos, pushed himself up, and went around to the backseat door.

He opened it, leaned in, and removed Glenda's cuffs. He pulled her out gently.

"Ma'am, you can go," the officer said. "I'm gonna have a talk with your husband."

Glenda's lips were trembling, her cheeks wet, her breathing labored. She seemed to be having an anxiety attack. Amos reached for her, but she pushed his hands away, strode to the trailer, and disappeared inside.

Amos was sure that she was headed straight to the bathroom. Probably wasn't a bad idea. Moments like these are what those drugs are prescribed for, Amos thought.

He turned to the officer, who held the back door of the cruiser open. Amos glanced at his nameplate. *Jones.*

Amos got into the backseat. Officer Jones shut the door and got in the front.

"Ain't you out of your jurisdiction?" Amos asked.

Jones stared out the windshield.

"Shame your wife had to be involved," he said, shaking his head. "I'd hate to have to do that again."

He paused.

"She got the nerves, don't she?" he said, still looking out the window. "We got a lot of them at the jail."

They sat in silence.

Dusk came. A great blue heron flew past the cruiser and flapped noisily onto a log about twenty yards away. It stepped gingerly onto the ground, pecked at something, rose and flew toward the cruiser. It disappeared over the vehicle and headed toward the creek.

The sky darkened. The trailer blackened. Glenda kept the lights off.

Amos stared at the back of Jones's head. Both men were immobile. An hour passed.

Finally Jones sighed, opened his door, and got out. He opened the back door and stood aside. Amos emerged.

"Your partner made some promises he couldn't keep," Jones said, still looking up the hill. "You won't make the same mistake."

Amos nodded. "The Lord is my shepherd."

Jones nodded. He looked directly at Amos, who was standing just outside the cruiser door.

"The fella you peppered's gonna tell you what to do," Jones said, his eyes and voice flat. "Don't make me come back here."

Jones closed the back door, opened the front again, got in, rolled down the window, and, as he was backing out, said, "You take care now."

Amos didn't move a muscle. The cruiser barely missed running over his foot. He watched it disappear and then walked back into the trailer.

. . .

"It was a mine bump," Will said.

"A what?" Sergeant Freeman asked.

Will smiled. He'd been sitting beside Sergeant Freeman for almost an hour. The doctor had said the cop might sleep for some time more. No telling. Will decided to sit with him for a bit in hopes that he'd wake up. Will thought he'd have some questions, and Will wanted to answer them. Sergeant Freeman had indeed roused himself a moment before, but Will wasn't sure if he was all there yet.

Will was actually sitting in the same seat that Sergeant Freeman had sat in just two nights before when they'd questioned the kid. Will imagined that the whole thing was rather confusing for the cop.

"We call them bumps," Will said with a forced smile. "One of the columns of coal holding up the roof collapsed. The water probably undermined the ribs around that area and that column just couldn't take the strain no more. It blew out—like a bomb going off."

"Jesus," Sergeant Freeman said. "I thought it was a cave-in. Thought I was dead for sure."

"Me, too."

Will held up a helmet that he'd been holding between his legs and swiveled it around to show a deep indentation on one side. "This is yours," Will said.

"What happened to that other guy's?"

"Sam took his helmet off. I don't know why," Will said, looking down. "He didn't make it."

"Oh. I'm sorry. You okay?"

"Just some bruises. They dug us out pretty quick. You were a little closer to the column than me, so you got it worse. Sam was on the other side a' you. He mighta saved our lives by shielding us a bit from the blast. But nobody really knows."

They sat in silence while Will fingered the damaged helmet. "Your captain's been here. Your sister's on her way from Louisville. Should be here pretty soon."

More silence. Sergeant Freeman sat up. "I feel okay," he said. "Just a headache."

Will nodded. "Doc says you probably have a mild concussion."

"Anybody else hurt?"

"Nope. Just you and Sam."

"What's going on with the rescue?"

"They pulled all the rescue teams out."

"They get those men?" Sergeant Freeman asked.

"No," Will said. "Too dangerous. Might try again tomorrow."

"Jeez."

"Yeah."

Will put the helmet on the table beside the bed. "This helmet's yours now. Saved your life," Will said and got up. "I'll see you soon. They say you'll probably be ready to go home tomorrow. Well, today. It's pretty late."

"I'm sorry about Sam, Inspector," Sergeant Freeman said.

"Yeah."

# CHAPTER THIRTEEN

H is heart leapt when his headlights washed over the gold Camry.
Tessy.

She'd been back before but never at night. He pulled his truck beside the car and resisted jumping out to run up to the house. He gathered his helmet and belt, stopped and took a deep breath before opening the pickup door.

The lights were out so he crept into the back door. He dropped his stuff in his bucket and took off his boots and coveralls. The dryer was going, and the thumping filled his heart.

She was doing the wash.

He walked through the kitchen. He deliberately didn't turn on the lights so he couldn't see what she'd done, but he could smell bleach. He was near tears as he approached the bedroom.

The door was open a crack and he was suddenly seized by a fear that she wasn't actually there. Were the smells of laundry, bleach, and pine—all bound up in a complex of feelings for her—just echoes mocking him? He didn't think he could bear the sight of an empty bed.

He stuck his head in the door. Her long, dark hair flowed over the pillows. She was wearing her favorite, let's-do-it-tonight gown. She must have brought that with her, which meant that she had been thinking for hours about making love to him. That thought blazed through him.

She was lying on the right side of their bed. Her side. Will stood in the door for a moment. He was more excited than he'd been in years. He worried that he wouldn't last more than a minute with her, but there was nothing he could do about that.

He opened the door and brought the rest of his body into the room. The floor creaked. She looked up at him sleepily, eyes half closed, an apologetic smile playing across her lips. She put her right hand to her brow and looped the left over her head. She was giving herself to him. Staring at her, he wordlessly took off the rest of his clothes. He was shaking as he crawled onto the bed.

"Oh, Will," was all she said, all she needed to say.


He wanted to get up and go to the bathroom, but he knew how much she loved to be held after making love so he put off the trip. They lay like spoons, facing away from the window and the world outside.

"I'm so sorry about Rob," she finally said. "And about Sam."

"Yeah."

He knew she wanted more from him, some show of emotion. But while he could easily put off a trip to the bathroom, this was beyond him. He wasn't going to mourn openly for either friend.

In a concession, he said, "It's really too bad."

She was quiet.

Will ached for his lost friendship with Rob, a rift that would now never be repaired. As for Sam, Will was mostly angry at the dumb shit for taking off his miner's cap. Sam knew as well as anybody the dangers underground—especially in a flooded mine. But they'd been slogging for hours, and maybe he'd wanted to brush back his hair.

Rob and Sam were the tenth and eleventh family members and friends Will had lost underground. It was the same number of kids on Will's high school basketball squad. It was enough for a football team, and it was numbing.

They all knew death was possible underground, and all had an abiding fatalism about it. And now death had struck again in a mine inundation and bump. Both would happen again. At least this time, it wasn't his fault. End of story. Move on.

It wasn't a speech he could make to Tessy. He wanted her to stay, and if he started talking like that, she might leave. He was always amazed at her reservoir of outrage for ordinary things.

The everyday corruption of eastern Kentucky that cost families their homes, that kept women from getting divorces and put crooks in office could get her eyes blazing and feet stamping almost any day—even though they'd both known such evils for as long as they could remember.

Tessy was probably the only person in his family who was happy that he'd become a federal mine inspector. And now she had come home in the midst of another coal tragedy.

Well, whatever it took, Will thought.

"I can't stay," she said. "We've got a game tomorrow."

"Hm."

"You gonna come?" she asked.

" 'Course."

"Don't sit too close. People will talk."

Will laughed.

"What? That we're going steady? Married even?" he asked.

"Yes," Tessy said simply.

Will sighed. His wife had filed for divorce because she wanted her daughter to join a better basketball team without penalty. And that meant they had to keep up appearances—bad appearances. They had to pretend not to like each other and to be a dysfunctional family. But they were doing it for the benefit of their daughter. It was all pretty confusing.

"I washed the sheets and towels. How you can wipe yourself off with the same old dirty towel week after week is beyond me. Fold them for me?" she asked, turning her head to kiss him.

"Sure."

She got out of bed. He watched her naked body as she retrieved her clothes. She was a bit too thin, and her breasts had flattened since her teens. But he could not take his eyes off her hips. Exactly what he wanted, they stirred something primal in him.

She pulled on her jeans. She wrapped her bra about her belly, snapped it together in front of her and then twisted it around before reaching her arms into the straps.

He'd always thought it was an eminently sensible way to dress—better than the two-handed backward reach that most women used to wiggle into their bras.

She buttoned up her blouse.

"You got enough food to last you through the week, and I left some mail on the front table," she said and bent down to kiss him on the cheek. "Take care of yourself."

He heard her retrieve her jacket in the living room. She went out the front door, like a guest.

Amos could see the TV trucks and sheriff's deputies still parked along the highway. A temporary light bathed the mine parking lot in a gray wash.

Amos slowed his truck. He had awaked at his usual hour and had decided to go through his usual morning routine. He needed to get out of the house and over to the mine. The news had reported yet another death, an inspector.

All that death had made the place unfamiliar, forbidding. He wanted to get the real image of the mine fixed again in his memory. And he wanted to pay tribute to the dead.

He slowed his truck. Dawn was about to break. The flashing lights on the deputy sheriff's cruiser still blazed brightly. It blocked the mine entrance, and no one was standing nearby.

Amos pulled to the other side of the highway just short of the mine and stopped. He leaned on the steering wheel and peered into the growing light.

The mine trailer was still there. The loader was parked well away from the mine. The conveyor belt was quiet. A few mine-rescue vehicles sat in the parking lot. Black water covered much of the mine area.

Amos leaned his forehead against the top of the steering wheel.

"God, take Rob and Crandall, the whole second crew, and this inspector fellow," he prayed. "Take care of their families."

Amos picked up his Bible from the passenger seat. He tilted it forward to read in the light.

"'Lord, Thou hast been our dwelling place in all generations,'" he recited. "'Before the mountains were brought forth, or ever Thou hadst formed the earth and the world, from everlasting to everlasting, thou art God.

"'Thou turnest man back to the dust and sayest, "Turn back, O children of men!" For a thousand years in thy sight are but as yesterday when it is past, or as a watch in the night.

"'Thou dost sweep men away; they are like a dream, like grass which is renewed in the morning: in the morning it flourishes and is renewed; in the evening it fades and withers.'"

He bowed his head again.

Looking up, he saw a car coming in the other direction. It slowed. The man inside looked toward the mine. As the car passed him, Amos thought the guy glanced in his direction. It sped away.

Amos shut his Bible and put the car back in gear. He took another look at the mine and made a U-turn to drive back home.

Will felt totally let down the next day. Rob and Sam were still dead. And Will still didn't understand his wife.

Everything had seemed so right the night before. They didn't argue—rarely had, in fact. The sex was great. And then she left in the middle of the night. Reminded him of being in high school.

He had briefly considered calling Tessy's bluff, saying that if she really wanted to go through with a pretend divorce that he'd give her a real one. But he couldn't. She had plenty of good reasons to leave him, and he didn't want to give her another.

He didn't think he could make it alone, and he was pretty sure Tessy knew that. Tessy had long been the glue to Will's life. She had always come up with their weekend plans, made all the decisions about families and holidays, and determined when and how they had sex.

When she left, she had all of their mail—hers and his—sent to Hazard so she could pay the bills and sort through the rest.

Several times, he had come home to find a fishing catalog or a letter from a family friend stuck on the inside of the screen door, put there by Tessy so he'd see them. It had been a shock to realize how little mail he actually received, once she filtered it.

She often brought over casseroles that would last nearly a week, and she left a few TV dinners in the freezer. But on at least two occasions, he had found himself with no food in the house and no idea whether to go shopping or wait to be rescued.

He had waited for Tessy, who showed up with food and a look that foster mothers must use with truant children. Will had only shrugged.

Being reminded that he was helpless was yet another reason he was angry at Tessy for leaving him.

He drove to the office to find out what arrangements were being made for Rob and Sam, and he decided to schedule a few interviews for the investigation, a formality that had to be observed.

The worst part of the day was having to endure condolences. When he came in, he could see that Myrtle, the office secretary, had been crying. He stood by her desk for a moment as she wailed anew. He nodded and murmured something stupid like, "There, now," and fled to his office.

Special investigators get their own offices. Will had always loved this separation, and today it meant he could close his door and not have to look hang-dog. He wrote up some notes of the rescue and returned a call from headquarters.

Thankfully, he only had to leave a message. He left early for the basketball game.

The gym parking lot was full by the time Will arrived. Will always got a thrill pulling into the school. When he'd played in high school, this gym was enemy territory. Now Helen had made it her home floor, but for Will it was still barely a demilitarized zone.

The Pikeville team bus was in the lot. Will had rarely beaten Pikeville in his playing days, but his daughter's team had a chance. Her mother's move to Hazard meant that Helen was part of something special. Hazard had a true center in a six-foot two-inch black girl and a pretty good forward. Helen was probably the region's best point guard. Together, they were favored to beat Pikeville—finally.

Will drove past the gym and parked on Lyttle Boulevard, a side street near the gym. He walked back down. The gym was shoehorned onto a narrow strip of land on a steeply pitched hill in the heart of old Hazard.

Ten years earlier, Hazard had built a new high school on the edge of town on fill from a nearby highway cut-through. They had a new gym, a couple of tennis courts, and even a football field. But the school decided to keep playing basketball in its shoe box of a gym in the center of town largely because fans' proximity to the court gave the team a huge home-field advantage.

Walking down to the gym, Will felt like he was walking in the footsteps of his father and grandfather. Both had made this same trek to the same building to watch their children play. Cheers rose from the gym, and Will broke into a jog.

Helen was bringing the ball up the court when Will stepped inside. He glanced over at the home team's bench and saw Tessy with Paul and his wife, Caroline, and Uncle Elliott sitting just above them. There didn't seem to be any room there, so he picked the nearest seat he could find on the home side.

The gym was packed.

Girls' basketball had been banned in the mountains in 1935 amid worries that the strain was bad for girls' delicate bodies. Thirty years later, the teams re-formed. Since then, the girls' teams in the mountains had become far more competitive statewide than the boys'.

Fan interest built with success. Tonight, he guessed, more than a thousand people jammed the gym—quite a crowd for an early-season game in a town with only eight thousand residents.

At the top of the key, Helen cut left and Will smiled. Over the summer, she'd walked everywhere bouncing a ball with her left hand to improve that side. She passed to one of the guards and cut around right.

Helen's team passed the ball again and again, probing Pikeville's defense. Helen got the ball back and cut toward the basket. The defense collapsed on her and Helen bounced a soft pass to the team's center, who put an easy lay-up in the basket.

Will's heart swelled.

Hazard led the entire game. Helen was one of the smallest girls on the court, but she was also the coolest. The Hazard coach, a middle-aged man named Gerry Morton, never substituted for her. She hustled on defense. She called almost every play on offense. Will wasn't counting, but he guessed that she racked up nearly ten assists—a lot for a girls' game. She even made a few rebounds.

Will could hardly stop smiling. He glanced down at Tessy and, although he couldn't see her face, knew by the way she was slumped over that she must be scowling. Will snorted.

Helen was doing a brilliant job, but Will was sure that Tessy would have several sheets of notes on things that she had done wrong. Whatever. Mother-daughter relationships were always complicated.

The score tightened four minutes before the end, when Pikeville came within three points. Cool as ever, Helen took the ball up the court and ran a perfect pick-and-roll with the team center to widen the lead to five points.

Pikeville never threatened again.

At the buzzer, Helen embraced everyone on her team before shaking hands with the Pikeville team. She was a leader—something Will had never managed.

Will waited as the crowd filed out. He noticed the driller Dee Singleton, who seemed to be trying to catch his eye. Singleton pointed at Helen and gave Will a thumb's-up. Will smiled.

Will joined a crowd of family members and well-wishers waiting for team members to emerge from a tight scrum around their coach. Tessy was one of only two adults standing with the team.

His brother, Paul, walked over.

"Where's Caroline?" Will asked.

"She went back to the house," Paul answered.

"Y'all drove separate?"

Paul shrugged.

"I haven't seen her in, I don't know, year or more," Will said.

"Yeah, she mostly stays in Lexington now, with the kids at UK. She came down for the reading o' the will tomorrow."

"She expecting some'm big?"

Paul smiled.

"My men are coming to see you tomorrow morning. Don't take too long with 'em 'cause you gotta be in my office at one o'clock for the will. Mom's coming and, by the way, she said you hadn't visited in forever."

"I saw her at the funeral," Will said defensively.

Paul shrugged. "Just lettin' you know."

"Okay," Will said to Paul.

He thought back to the last time he'd seen his mother. Driving up the hollow, he had slowed to get around Paul, who was driving away in a brand-new Jaguar. They'd passed brief pleasantries and Paul had said he had to go. Will drove on.

Several vehicles were parked outside the house. Two were the pick-ups of the guys who were renovating the kitchen—paid for by Paul. A third was the Chevy of a nurse caring for his mother—paid for by Paul.

Will walked up to his parents' bedroom, and as he mounted the stairs he heard his mother and the nurse.

"When are you gonna wear it, Kate?" the nurse asked.

"All the time," his mother answered with a laugh. "Look at the sparkles on the wall. Oh my Lord."

Will walked to the door and saw his mother cradling some sort of pendant. Her eyes were as fiery as the diamond at its center. She giggled like a schoolgirl as she rocked the diamond back and forth in the sunlight, throwing small rainbows around the room.

Following the light, she noticed Will, and her face fell. She slipped the pendant under her housedress and looked back at Will, her face rearranged into something approaching motherly—what was it?—patience? forebearance? dismay?

"Hello, Will," she said, the delight gone.

Will realized that his own expression had been rather sour, and he made a game attempt to rearrange it into something cheerful.

"Hey, Momma, how you feelin'?" Will asked.

She coughed once in answer, and this small cough led to more and more violent ones. The nurse started to flutter around with a towel and medicine. Soon, Will's mother said she just wasn't feeling well, and Will had left with a new hole in his gut.

Will was not looking forward to another visit like the last. "I'll try to get up there soon," Will said to Paul. Uncle Elliott walked over beaming.

"Helluva game, fellas. Helluva game," the old man said.

"She done good, Uncle El. She done good," Will said.

The team scrum broke up and Tessy joined the men.

"I thought you missed it," she said to Will. She didn't kiss him.

"Got here just as it started, but it was pretty crowded around you."

"Most important game of the season."

"She was great, Tessy," Paul said.

"She sure can shoot," Uncle Elliott added.

Tessy smiled proudly.

Helen ran up to Will and hugged him.

"Looked good," Will said.

"Thanks, Dad. Mom said something bad happened in that rescue. I'm glad you're okay."

"Yeah."

Will tried to smile. Helen did not make a similar attempt.

"So, it didn't look like you were favoring your right at all," Will said to break the silence.

"Yeah," Helen said. "I'm trying."

Will caught a look of annoyance on Tessy's face.

"Well, you were great. Listen, I got some frozen pizza if you and Mom want to come home for a celebration dinner," Will said.

There was a pause.

"I gotta go," Paul said. "Good game, Helen."

"Thanks, Uncle Paul." He and Helen embraced. He waved at Tessy and walked away.

Tessy put her hand on Helen's arm.

"Baby, we can't do that yet. Not till the season's over, anyway," Tessy said, and glanced around.

"Okay, sure," Will said. He wanted to add, "Why not?" but didn't want to argue in front of Helen. She couldn't actually believe anyone would care, could she?

Helen looked down.

"I gotta get my stuff," she said and jogged to the locker room.

Will and Tessy stood watching her. Tessy looked down and gathered her purse, clipboard, and another bag. Uncle Elliott kept smiling, oblivious to the rising tension.

"I'm gonna . . ." Tessy said, pointing toward the locker room.

"Sure," Will said, nodding. "Yeah."

"Helluva game," Uncle Elliott said again.


On the drive home, Will dove into his deepening reservoir of anger. It was a pool of vitriol born as much from confusion as hurt. Just last night, Tessy had made love to him with as much caring as ever. Her every touch had conveyed the message that she still loved him. She had seemed entirely at ease—even when she was naked.

And then today, she seemed to want to leave as soon as she possibly could. Granted, she was becoming increasingly anxious at Helen's games, but there seemed to be something more than that. And why did Paul's presence at yet another of his family dramas bother him? Tessy was living at Paul's. Will knew he should be glad that Tessy wasn't throwing away money on renting an apartment, but something about the whole living situation bothered him.

Will still remembered the day in June when the court server showed up at his office with divorce papers. Tessy had warned him that it would happen, but somehow the reality of it hadn't penetrated. The server asked him to sign something, and Will, unmoored, just looked at him.

"Divorce papers?" Will had asked in a voice whose volume he later regretted.

The guy was short, middle-aged, and had one of those rigid extended bellies that always struck Will as comical. For some reason, Will couldn't believe that this guy was serving him divorce papers. He realized that Tessy probably didn't even know the guy. Still. Why did he have to have such a potbelly?

Tessy had assured him that fake divorces among basketball parents were common, that it was the only way Helen could play on the team without losing a year of playing eligibility, and that a friendly judge would sit on their divorce petition for years with no action.

But Will had been suspicious that what she really wanted was a trial separation that would metastasize into a real divorce. Lord knew she had her reasons. But if that was it, he wished she'd just be honest about it.

Or maybe he didn't.

He hit the steering wheel and said, "Tessy didn't even like basketball." Or at least she didn't used to, he amended silently.

She had missed many of his games in high school and, later, had seemed to take no interest when Will signed up a seven-year-old Helen for a league. For years, Tessy attended the games without caring about the score. She had even chided Will if he suggested that winning mattered.

Then Helen started middle school, and in a switch that seemed to occur overnight, Tessy became intensely interested in the game. She slowly started boxing Will out of his coaching role until one summer night a couple of years ago he'd come home to find Tessy and Helen dancing around their home basket.

Will had quickly realized that Tessy was teaching Helen how to flop—or take dives in hopes of drawing a foul on the opposing player. Will couldn't help himself.

"What are you doing?" he'd asked Tessy.

"She's got to get to the free-throw line more, Will," Tessy had said, smiling.

Helen was clearly delighted.

"Honey, I don't want her to become a flopper," Will had said.

"Always a stickler for the rules, aren't you, Will?" Tessy had said and sighed.

"Well, yeah," he'd answered.

"If it gets us a few more points, we're gonna bend 'em, aren't we, Helen?"

Helen had nodded. Tessy then threw out her arms and fell back in an exaggerated flop. Helen squealed and fell down as well. Both laughed uproariously. Will had cocked his jaw and walked inside.

After that, Will gave in. At some point, he could tell that Tessy no longer even liked it when he gave Helen pointers. By then Helen was being taught by some of the best coaches in the region, and Tessy didn't want Will messing that up.

Will was both amused and somewhat hurt by this, but there was no doubt that Helen had grown enormously as a player. Tessy signed her up for AAU summer leagues. She got tickets for the whole family to go to Lexington to see the University of Kentucky play. She bought instructional videotapes. She started talking about things like "court sense" and "catch-and-release," phrases that led Will to smile when he first heard them come out of Tessy's mouth.

To Will, Tessy's change from disinterest to obsession about basketball was overnight. Her sudden decision to undertake a divorce had been just as abrupt. The previous day captured their marriage in a microcosm. Last night, everything was perfect. This evening, they lived on different planets.

"Damnit," Will said aloud.

He drove past Whitesburg and took the turn for Fleming-Neon. The car behind him made the turn as well, and Will flipped the rearview mirror to full strength to see whose car it was.

Seemed to be a Ford Taurus. Will didn't recognize it.

Will didn't think much of it until the car made the next turn. And the next. When the car headed up his own hollow, Will slowed and stared into his rearview. Somebody get a new car? Seemed unlikely that one of his neighbors had a visitor at this hour.

Will turned into his driveway, and the Taurus continued up the hollow. There were only three homes past Will's house, and Will wondered which of them might have such a guest.

He gave a mental shrug and got out of his truck. On his way up the front steps, the Taurus came back down the hollow. It slowed noticeably as it passed Will's house. Will couldn't make out the driver. He watched it disappear down the road.

"What the hell?"

# CHAPTER FOURTEEN

L et's just start with general conditions for a second. For instance, did the mine follow its ventilation plan?" Will asked.

The surviving members of the Red Fox mining crew had arrived at 9 a.m. sharp with Blue Gem's lawyer, Silas Wyatt. Will had said that he would interview each miner separately, as MSHA protocol demanded. A half dozen large men sat in plastic chairs in the waiting area.

Will commandeered the break room, and he sat across from the lawyer and the first miner, Carl Breathitt, the rescued scoop operator.

Will was mildly intimidated by the lawyer, who was a named partner in one of the most prestigious law firms in the state. The man exuded an oily confidence and his initial comment, "I'm sure we can clear this all up rather quickly," had bothered Will.

So Will started the questioning with something of a curveball.

"Ventilation?" Carl asked, surprise in his voice. "Sure. We done right by ventilation."

The answer was an obvious lie. Almost no mine followed its ventilation plan, and Will knew that Red Fox was no exception. If Carl had given a less definitive answer, if Silas Wyatt had been less of a prick, if eight guys—no, nine—hadn't died, if Tessy weren't in the midst of a sham/real divorce, Will probably would have let it go. After all, Blue Gem was owned by his brother.

But the whole thing was starting to piss him off.

"You put up your curtains to the face, built your brattices in step with your mining, and always mined from right to left?" Will asked with a look of mild annoyance.

"Yes, sir," Carl said.

"Uhm, when I was in the mine, the ventilation curtains looked like they were tied up seven or eight breaks away from the face. Any idea how they got there?"

Carl frowned and shook his head silently.

The lawyer intervened.

"Inspector, I thought you wanted to talk about the inundation," Wyatt said. "Mr. Breathitt has volunteered to cooperate in that investigation because he lost some good friends. But if you want to turn this into a witch hunt on ventilation issues, we may reconsider our cooperation. As you know, you can't compel any of this testimony."

Will raised his hands in surrender.

"No witch hunt here, Mr. Wyatt," Will said, trying to sound pleasant. "I was just curious."

Let it go, Will said to himself.

"But you're right, Mr. Wyatt, let's get on with it," Will said. "Why don't you tell me about that morning, Mr. Breathitt?"

"Well, sir, not much to tell," Carl said and glanced at the lawyer. "We done our preshift inspection, and everything was fine. We was following our mining plan. We tested everything. We checked the maps."

Carl again looked to Wyatt.

"That water just wasn't supposed to be there," the miner said.

Frowning, Wyatt gave a quick nod.

"Where were you when the water came in?" Will asked.

"Just coming back from the conveyor," he said.

"And then what happened?" Will asked.

"Well, then the water come in. Come in so fast, I couldn't get out of my buggy. I tried and tried. Finally, I got free but the water, h'it swept me back. I think I hit my head."

"Did you happen to see Rob Crane after the water started coming in?" Will asked.

"Who?"

Will blinked.

"Rob. Crane," Will said distinctly. "One of the other scoop operators. A black guy."

"Oh, the black guy," Carl said and then looked sickly. "No, sir, didn't see him."

"You didn't know Mr. Crane?" Will asked. "He was on your crew, wasn't he?"

"Yes, sir, but he'd only been there two, three weeks."

"Oh. Right," Will said. "But he'd been working for Blue Gem for years."

"Yeah, but he only just come from the Carcasone mine."

Will stared into space for a moment.

"Inspector?" Wyatt asked.

Will focused his eyes back on the miner. "So you woke up at the elevator?"

"No, sir. I come to about forty breaks short o' that."

"Long walk."

"Yes, it were," Carl said, nodding.

Will was quiet for a moment while Carl continued to nod.

"Why do you think you hit water?" Will asked.

"Got no idea. We done everything right. Studied on the map of the old works, drilled all the bore holes." Carl shook his head. "Dunno what could have gone wrong. That water just shouldn't have been there."

An hour later, Will was sitting in the same spot. Across from him was Darrell Penny, another scoop operator, who concluded his description of the inundation the exact same way as Carl and another miner before him.

"That water just shouldn't have been there," the scoop man said and glanced at the lawyer.

Will closed his eyes for a moment.

"Mr. Penny, has anyone told you what you should say here?" Will asked.

"No, sir. Just tell the truth, is all I heard," he said, nodding his head.

The lawyer frowned and nodded, too.

Will was back to being pissed off.

The law had very few real penalties for miners. During an investigation, miners could admit that they had ignored every rule in the book, and Will couldn't do a thing against them. Their only risk came if Will caught them lying or falsifying records—criminal offenses.

But here they were, lying to beat the band. Not that it really mattered. Will had little doubt that the whole thing was a tragic accident. Still, they were so blatant about it that the lies showed a lack of respect.

"Well, thank you for being so candid, Mr. Penny. I really appreciate it," Will said, getting up from his chair.

Darrell Penny and the lawyer rose as well. There was a pause. Will didn't reach out to shake hands, and the other two men didn't offer theirs. Brief glances approached an honest acknowledgment of the deeply dishonest nature of their encounter.

Penny and Wyatt shuffled toward the door.

"So we'll have Jeremy Porter and Amos Blevins tomorrow, Mr. Wyatt?" Will asked.

"Mr. Porter will be here at nine a.m., but I'm afraid that Mr. Blevins can't make it," the lawyer said, a concerned look on his face.

"When did you plan on bringing in Mr. Blevins?" Will asked in a bored tone.

"Actually, Mr. Blevins has declined to cooperate with the investigation, Mr. Murphy."

Will looked closely at Wyatt.

"Why?"

"Ah, he wouldn't say," the lawyer said, gesturing with his hands up. And for the first time, it sounded like the truth.

"Wow."

Will had never known of a miner refusing to cooperate in a mining investigation. Everybody knew Blevins's rescue efforts had been heroic. Will had been looking forward to meeting him and had been annoyed that he'd not spoken to him on the day of the disaster. Will laughed, although he wasn't quite sure why.

Will ushered Wyatt and Penny out the door.

"Well, let's see what Mr. Porter has to say, then," Will said. "I'll see you tomorrow, Mr. Wyatt."

As the lawyer and miner stepped out of the break room, Clete DeStephano, another MSHA inspector, leaned into the door.

"Ah, sorry, Clete. I'm done. You need the room?" Will asked.

Clete turned to watch the lawyer leave. He clearly had something to say but didn't want others to hear it. Will waited. Clete was short, nearly bald, and built like a fireplug. He'd been the sixth man on Hazard's basketball team, and he'd become infamous in the region for his dirty play—surreptitious elbows, quick shots to the groin, and edging underneath a leaping player so he'd come down hard.

For Will, there was something mildly reassuring about finally being on the same side as Clete. Still, Will usually gave him a wide berth.

The lawyer and his clients finally disappeared outside.

"Got a blitz on Friday, and I'm gonna need you there," Clete said.

"Look, Clete, I got this investigation."

"Like I care. This a blitz, Will. You know what that means."

"Yeah."

"We can't let 'em get away with this shit. Not no one. You're comin'."

Will sighed. "All right. I can switch things around."

"Seven o'clock. Wal-mart parking lot. We're gonna fuck 'em up." The little man grinned.


The lawyer's voice droned on. He'd written the will, and he seemed to cherish every boring word. He was old, tall, and gray. He sat bolt upright, his back as stiff as the wooden chair. The family was arrayed around him in a semicircle in what had been Paul Sr.'s office on the second floor of Blue Gem's two-story building.

Will's mother sat in one corner of the couch, an aluminum walker in front of her. Her hair was snow white and thinning. Will was again struck by how shrunken she looked. Tessy was on the other side of the couch and Caroline sat in a wing chair. The two women could not have presented a greater contrast.

Tessy was dressed in a black skirt that went just below her knees, a white blouse, and a black sweater. Her long, dark brown hair was pulled back from her face and gathered in a knot, and the only jewelry Will could see were two small pearl earrings.

Caroline wore maroon pants, a cream-colored camel-hair jacket, a silk scarf, and what looked like several ounces of gold around her neck, wrists, and ears. Her short blond hair was as stiff as a helmet. The skin on her face looked stretched.

Paul was sitting beside his father's giant oak desk. Muscular and richly hued, the desk dominated the room. It was entirely out of place in the modern office building. Its empty chair faced the room, its back turned to the mountains outside.

"To Katie, my wife," the lawyer said, and he looked at Will's mother with an undertaker's smile. "I leave the house and all its possessions not otherwise stipulated herein. I also leave my Merrill Lynch account and all of its securities.

"To Caroline." His smile broadened. Caroline puckered her lips and smoothed her pants as she heard that she had been left several antiques, to be given upon Katie's death. Paul Sr. had also given her $20,000 in cash "so you can go shopping without asking Paul," the lawyer read.

Everyone laughed. Caroline preened. She got several more odds and ends, some of which she was to give to her children. Paul Sr. had clearly been thinking about this for a long time.

"To Paul, I leave all my shares in Blue Gem."

Will glanced at his brother. Paul had that pressed-lip expression of a man trying not to look exultant. Will looked at Tessy, who was ashen. Will was pretty sure he'd just been screwed, and Tessy's face confirmed it. The shares in Blue Gem represented by far the bulk of his father's estate, and he'd gotten none of them.

"To Helen, I leave fifty thousand dollars in trust for her education, with Paul as the trustee. And that is the end of the family section. There is a five-thousand-dollar bequest to the First Christian Church and some odds and ends to friends, but—"

Will staggered up. "Bathroom," he said to his mother's questioning glance. There was a bathroom just outside the office that Will's father had commandeered for his sole use. Will went in, and he was hit with a familiar smell. The cleaning ladies at Blue Gem used something he'd never smelled anyplace else. For years, it had made him homesick. Now, it just made him sick.

He took the flask from his jacket pocket and poured the remaining

Jack down his throat. Will had put a dent in the flask before the meeting, although he was sure no one had noticed. The liquor burned a path down his throat, and when Will stopped swallowing, he felt he could breathe fire.

His father hadn't even trusted him to oversee his daughter's education money, which was barely more than Caroline was getting for her shopping trips.

Will had always hated Caroline. She had grown up in a fairly well-off family, and she made little pretense of her low regard for Will and Tessy. She'd spent the last bunch of years doing all she could to butter up the old man—laughing at his jokes, bringing him pies, and letting him slap her ass. Seemed like it all started after the explosion, when it was clear that Will and Tessy were no longer favorites.

Will's hand reached for the bathroom door and pushed it open. His body carried him back into the office. Everyone but his mother was now standing, and the lawyer was shaking hands all around. Tessy turned to look at Will. Her expression became worried.

Will drifted over to the group.

"Will, I hear you did your interviews today," Paul said.

"Yeah."

"Glad you're on this thing so quick. I'm gonna want that report of yours done by next week at the latest. Need to get the mine open again, and having that report'll help."

"May take a little longer'n that."

"Look, Will. If you need some help, I can send over one of the girls to type the thing up. But I'm gonna want that report right away."

"Nine people died, Paul. Nine." He said it somewhat loudly.

The lawyer puckered his lips. The women grew silent.

"Honey," Tessy said.

"All right, Will. Take a few more days." Paul spoke slowly, his mouth somewhere between a smile and a grimace. "But get that report done. This is pretty important for Blue Gem, and Dad woulda wanted it done right."

"This is . . . Dad woulda wanted?" Will nearly shouted.

"Will!" his mother said.

"For all Dad cared, I coulda died in that fuckin' explosion. Dad woulda wanted? Don't you mean that you want this report? And you want it your way, right?"

"Take it easy, little brother," Paul said. "You just need to do your job. You need to stop drinkin' and get it done. This is why you're there."

"Will! Paul!" their mother said.

"What does that mean, Paul? That I'm at MSHA to investigate disasters, or that I'm at MSHA to protect you? Which is it? 'Cause I ain't figured that one out yet."

Paul licked his lips.

"Will," Tessy said pleadingly.

But Will couldn't stop. "You're a piece o' work, Paul." He pushed his older brother, and Paul fell back, righted himself, and rushed Will, slamming him against the desk. The women screamed. Will got the wind knocked out of him and fell to his knees, his back howling.

"Stop this!" their mother said.

Tessy came over to Will and kneeled down.

"No," Will said. He got to his feet. Paul stared fiercely at him. Will put his hand on his father's desk and then seemed to see the desk for the first time. It was his father's pride, the embodiment of the company from which Will had finally and everlastingly been excluded. Will remembered the day that he and his brothers had taken it out of the house and brought it to Blue Dog's new office.

Now it was here, in Blue Gem's corporate temple, under Will's hand, in front of a huge pane of glass.

Will bent down and, with a roar, pushed the desk over and back. It broke through the glass wall and fell out of sight. They heard it crash onto the ground below.

# CHAPTER FIFTEEN

J esus," Paul said. "You fuckin' moron."

"Oh my Lord," Will heard Caroline say.

Will looked around the room, put a hand up to signal Paul to shut up, and walked toward the door. He knew he shouldn't, but he glanced at his mother on the way out.

Her mouth was open and her eyes were wide in horror, an expression that he'd seen only a few times in his life. The first had been when some drunk downtown pushed her to the ground. Just a boy, Will had been terrified. The man had haunted his dreams for years.

Now that man, that drunk, was Will himself.

Will squeezed back tears and left. He went down the stairs and burst out of the building. As he was fumbling for his keys, Tessy came out.

"Don't get in that truck, Will," she said. "You are not safe to drive."

"Oh, I'll be safe for another five more minutes. Ain't drunk yet."

She shook her head.

"It's a good thing I'm already gone," she said.

"Yeah," he said and opened the door.

"What're you gonna do?" she asked.

He paused.

"Investigate, I guess." He got into the truck.

"Helluva time to start."

Will rubbed his chin.

"Yeah." He closed the door and drove away.

Will made it back to work and fled to the privacy of his office. He crawled under his desk and pondered what he should do. Soon he fell asleep.

He awoke with a stiff neck, dry mouth, and full bladder. He rubbed his eyes and shuffled out to the office bathroom. When he came back, he paged through his notes, found the address he was looking for, picked up a blue and white plastic cooler thrown in the corner of his office, and left.

It was dusk when Will arrived at Amos's trailer.

There is an Appalachian protocol about making unannounced visits to someone's home that Will only became conscious of when, in one of his first investigations, he was briefly paired with a supervisor from Washington.

The official had gotten right out of the car and had walked straight up to the trailer door. Will had been too stunned to say anything. The guy inside hadn't even opened the door to talk to them, and Will was pretty sure why.

Will had talked the official out of trying another such visit.

In Appalachia, it's a good idea to let people inspect you and your vehicle before walking up to their door. Curtains may need to be drawn, clothes arranged. Bang on someone's door before they realize you're out there, and he may reach for a gun.

And since trailers are generally small and on occasion not too tidy, some people like to meet visitors outside.

Will sat in his truck and did nothing for a moment. He reached down into the well of the passenger seat and picked up the cooler. And then he waited again.

Finally, Will got out of the truck. He walked slowly past a car parked in the driveway and stopped before a ruined garden. The door to the trailer opened, and a large bearded man stepped out onto a small wood porch.

Will pointed his chin at the garden.

"Have any luck with the tomatoes this year?" Will asked.

Amos Blevins walked down the steps and stood beside Will, and both men stared at the garden's ruination. Frowning, Amos nodded. The two stood silently.

"That's one heck of a trellis," Will said, referring to an elaborate construction made of rebar.

"Yeah," the big bearded man answered and then lapsed back into silence again.

Both men nodded. Oh Lord, Will thought, another one. He charged ahead.

"I'm Will Murphy from MSHA, Mr. Blevins. Your lunch bucket ended up coming out of the mine during the investigation and, since we don't need it, I thought you might want to have it back," Will said, and handed the cooler over. "I also wanted to thank you for trying to save Rob Crane. He and I grew up together."

Amos looked silently at the mine inspector. He reached to take the cooler, which had "BLEVINS" stenciled on its side, but his eyes never left Will's. He nodded, put the cooler down on his porch, and went back to looking at the garden.

"He mentioned your name at the end," Amos said.

"Who?"

"Rob Crane, the scoop man. He mentioned you. Matter o' fact, they were his last words," Amos said, little inflection in his voice.

Will felt pierced.

"What'd he say?"

"Said to tell you it wasn't your fault,'" Amos said.

Will closed his eyes. Then he nodded.

"Before that, he said to tell Mary that the bank give him a life insurance policy, and to tell his kids that he was proud of 'em. And about the company's survivor's benefit."

Will nodded.

"I can tell 'em that," Will said.

"'Preciate it," Amos responded. "Mary's his wife?"

"Yeah."

"What wasn't your fault?" Amos asked. "You don't got to tell me. I just been wonderin' ever since."

Will looked away. "My drinkin'. Leastways, that's what I'm thinkin' he meant."

And they were quiet. Will wiped his eyes and his nose, fearing one of them would drip with sadness. The silence stretched. Will wasn't sure what to ask this big miner. He suddenly felt kind of stupid. What was he investigating?

So Will stared in silence at the garden, too.

At least three minutes went by, an achingly long time. Will marveled at the fullness of the silence, its beauty. Out of the corner of his eye, Will watched Amos. He seemed entirely unmoved, no hint of anxiety or uncertainty. He was a rock.

Will finally gave in. Another game of verbal chicken that Will had lost. He took a slow step toward his truck and said, "Well . . ."

"You a religious man?" Amos suddenly asked behind him.

Will turned back.

"No, not really. Used to go with my wife, but she stopped pushing about ten years ago so I stopped going."

Amos nodded, still looking at the garden.

"Pine Mountain Pentecostal is my church," Amos declared. "It's a God-fearing place."

And then, Amos turned to Will and stood squarely in front of him.

"Brother, you should come some day," Amos said, and with his right arm he gripped Will's left bicep.

Will had no idea what to do with his arms. He kept them at his sides, but they suddenly felt out of place.

"Come hear the good news," Amos said with a nod and released his grip. He turned back toward the trailer, walked up the steps, and disappeared inside.


Will drove with his left hand and used his right to knead his bicep. There had been nothing aggressive about Blevins's grip, but it had penetrated.

He had no idea what to make of the man. The visit had been a long shot, and it hadn't panned out. He hadn't learned anything about the disaster except that Amos was likely a nut.

Night had fallen, and Will flipped on his headlights.

Will had heard of Pine Mountain Pentecostal. The Pentecostal movement had grown strong in Appalachia, but it was hard to characterize, since churches often had very different practices.

Pine Mountain was known as a particularly fervent community, and Will had heard that its congregants spoke in tongues. There were rumors of snake handling, but Will didn't believe them. He'd heard the snake rumors about other Pentecostal congregations only to learn later that the stories were made up.

Folks loved to accuse Pentecostalists of snake handling. In truth, only a handful of churches in the area actually used snakes in their services, and those congregations tended to be made up of just two or three families practicing with a grim fatalism even darker than that embraced by miners. Not too many people were eager to test God's will on a regular basis. A fair number of those believers had lost their lives to rattler bites.

Will turned up his hollow and, just before his driveway, noticed a car sitting along the right side of the road. It was the same Ford Taurus Will had seen the night before.

He'd passed too quickly to tell, but Will had a sense that there was someone sitting in the car in the dark.

Will steered up his driveway, parked the truck, and walked inside his kitchen door. Flicking on the lights in the kitchen and living room, he walked back to his TV room and quietly opened a door that led to a small area directly behind his house. Will rarely used this door. A hill rose steeply up from the back door, so there was little point.

He walked up the hill a ways and then, staying on the incline, circled around his house and back down toward the road. His first few steps were tentative as his eyes adjusted. But a half-moon provided a fair amount of light, and Will soon was walking comfortably through the woods.

He took quiet steps as he approached the road. Twenty yards away, he squatted down to look at the car. There was someone inside. Will could hear a radio playing. The glow from the dashboard lit up the guy's face. Will couldn't make out his features, but it was definitely a man. And he was definitely looking up at Will's house.

Will felt a prickle run up his spine. He almost giggled.

Who the hell would be stupid enough to stake out his house? Will wondered. The guy had to know that Will would notice him. Was he dumb? Or was someone trying to send a message? Was this about the drugs? The murder of the foreman? And if so, why go after a mining investigator? Will had nothing to do with those things.

Will thought about confronting the son of a bitch. But there was no law against sitting by the side of the road. And Will didn't want whoever was behind this move to get the satisfaction of knowing that Will had been rattled. Will crept forward to see if he could make out the man's features. All Will could tell was that the guy seemed young.

Will turned around and, staying low, retreated back to his house, entered through the TV room, and walked into the kitchen. He stood at the kitchen table and considered calling the sheriff.

But what would he say?

Yeah, uh, there's a guy parked near my driveway?

Staring at the phone, Will realized that his message light was blinking. He pushed the button.

"Hi, Will. It's Charity Phillips. I was just calling because some guy in a Ford Taurus is looking at your house. Never seen him before. I'm gonna keep an eye on him for you."

Will picked up the phone and dialed.

"Hi, Charity," Will said. She was a retired nurse, and Will had always liked her.

"Heya, Will," she answered.

"Thanks for watching the house."

"Do you know him?" she asked.

"Can't say that I do."

"You gonna call the sheriff?" Charity asked.

"What for? He's just settin' there."

They were both quiet.

"Well, you know best," she said.

"I'll talk at you later," Will said, and hung up.

He finished his beer and shut off the lights in the front of his house. In the dark, he locked his doors and checked his windows. He briefly considered going out to his truck to get his gun but decided not to. He undressed, brushed his teeth, went to bed and, surprisingly, fell right to sleep.

# CHAPTER SIXTEEN

Carl's pickup showed up just after 7 a.m. Amos glanced out the trailer window and shook his head. Amos went out the front door and put on his boots. He waited on the porch. Carl did not emerge.

Amos walked down the steps and over to the driver's-side window. The sideview mirror was still shattered. Carl lowered his window and sighed theatrically.

"So you spoke to the inspector after all," Carl said.

A surge of adrenaline ran through Amos's body. Was the inspector dirty? And why'd Carl care about a mining inspector? Wasn't this just about drugs?

"I didn't say nothin'," Amos said.

Carl looked at Amos.

"Well, what did you say?"

So the inspector wasn't dirty.

"Nothing," Amos said. "I invited him to my church."

The man snorted.

"And I thought I's special when you invited me," Carl said.

"Got to share the good news." Amos answered automatically. "Why you care about me talking to an inspector?"

"Why don't you shut your fuckin' mouth?" Carl said and pointed with his right hand, which Amos noticed was bandaged. "You don't talk about nothin' to nobody. You do and you're gonna get more trouble than you know how to handle."

Amos was silent. It was not an idle threat.

"Here."

Carl held out an envelope without looking at Amos. Amos took it.

"You need to report to that there mine tomorrow," Carl said, looking straight ahead. "They need a scoop operator. It's outside of Middlesboro. Another one owned by Blue Gem."

He glanced up at Amos.

"We gonna need a new place to run things out of," Carl said. "This one here's low coal. Nobody's gonna find it."

Amos stared at him.

"How long you been in this?"

"Longer'n you," Carl said.

"And if I don't show?"

"You know the answer to that," Carl said, and glanced back at the trailer where Glenda still slept.

"I saved your life."

"You did. An' I 'preciate that. But I ain't gonna be alive for long if we fuck this up. You heard what happened to Mike?" His eyes narrowed. "Know anything about that?"

Amos shook his head.

"But why me? Why not you? I mean, I didn't even know you was involved. Seem like I'm the last guy in," Amos said.

Carl shrugged.

"Four months and your next crop'll be in, the investigation'll be over, everything'll go back to normal. You play along until then, you can do what you want. But I tell you this. I don't want to work with you no more."

"You don't . . ." Amos said. "Look here, you told me yourself I was the best miner operator you ever seen, right?"

Carl stared straight ahead.

"Never missed a day. Never broke a drum. Ran more coal than anybody, and I saved your life. Saved your life."

"Look, you wouldn't talk to the inspector. To tell 'em what the company wants you to say."

"Just 'cause I can't lie for 'em 'cause I been saved, you cast me out?"

"So wait. Sellin' drugs is okay but lyin' ain't?"

"Nothin' in the Bible 'bout marijuana."

Carl snorted.

"You don't get it, Amos. We can't run legal. You know that. I know that. Everybody knows it. So you got to say what Mr. Wyatt tells you to say in this thing, or Mr. Murphy's gonna get shut down. And then we all suffer. And not talking, you keep the investigation going, and then there's no tellin' what they'll find.

"So, yeah. You threaten my job and stop me from putting food on the table?" Carl said, nodding. "You ain't no hero to me nor nobody else. Take away my job and you might as well've left me and the kid to die. 'Cause I can't make it on this drug thing by itself."

Amos briefly wished that Carl would get out of the truck so Amos could demonstrate what an arm fortified by God's righteousness could do.

Instead, Amos said, "Yeah, it's working out real good for all a' us. I mean, how could Mr. Murphy not know about that old mine?"

Carl sighed and looked sideways at Amos. "That there, that's the question," Carl said and stared off into the distance. "I seen a map once," he mumbled, "but it didn't make no sense. Ain't talked to Mr. Murphy 'bout that, but I'm thinkin' I will."

Carl looked back at Amos. "But that don't concern you." He put his truck in gear and backed up, forcing Amos to step away.

"You best show up down there," Carl said and sped away.

When Will pulled into the Wal-mart parking lot, Clete had already parked his government-issued Jeep Cherokee well away from the store. Will pulled over to the adjoining spot, put his truck in park, and waved at Clete before gathering his gear.

Will got out and walked over to Clete. There were at least three butts on the ground at his feet.

"Been here long?" Will asked.

"Ten minutes."

Will shook his head.

"I almost feel sorry for the stupid sons of bitches."

"They got it comin', Will. They got it comin'."

"I'm sure they do."

Another Cherokee came into the parking lot and swung into a spot on the other side of Clete. The driver, MSHA inspector David Busby, rolled down his window. A fourth inspector was in his passenger seat.

"We ready to rumble?" David asked.

"Let's git," Clete responded. Will climbed into Clete's vehicle, and they pulled out.

They were both quiet for the first part of the drive. Jumpy as a horse in high grass, Clete was a miserable driver and Will didn't want to distract him any more than necessary. He chain-smoked and always seemed to be fiddling with something in the car—the radio, CB, a cup of coffee, stuff in the backseat.

Several times Clete caught himself failing to take a curve or to see a stopped car. There was nothing Will could do about it, so he tried to relax.

"Everything all right?" Clete finally asked.

"Yeah."

"Still getting divorced?"

"Ah. Yeah."

"You like the ham?"

"Still eatin' it."

Clete laughed.

Clete was the guy in the Hazard MSHA office who gathered and divvied up the gratuities from coal operators, and it seemed to take up every bit of his time. He kept detailed lists of who had given and what. He counted the cash down to the penny so that Will's monthly envelopes often had coins inside.

He made sure the Thanksgiving turkeys and Christmas hams that operators showered on the office were divided up by weight. Will had gotten a small bird at Thanksgiving, so Clete had given him a huge ham at Christmas. It was ideal for his newly single life. Will had been carving off pieces ever since.

"I ain't tole you about the mine we're visiting," Clete said.

"No."

"They stopped payin' into the kitty back in, like, September. David inspected 'em at the end of October, an' I went in there just after Thanksgiving. Still didn't get the message, probably, 'cause they ain't even paying their citations. So I been laying for 'em."

Clete cocked his jaw.

"Then a week ago Wednesday they had a roof fall. Big one. Seventy foot by twenty foot. Tha's all I need."

Clete shook his head for a while.

Will nodded.

Operators who stopped paying into the office kitty, or paid less than what Clete thought they should, drove Clete nuts. He would often take over the inspections of the mines and write a blizzard of citations. This was usually effective.

But on rare occasions, operators didn't get the message. When that happened, Clete organized a blitz—an inspection by four or five inspectors at once. Such inspections often resulted in temporary closure orders, which was MSHA's only true weapon against rogue operators.

The mine was closed until certain conditions were fixed. The orders, of couse, cited mining conditions, but everyone knew what condition most needed to change. The office always received a FedEx package stuffed with cash the day or, at most, two days after every blitz.

Will wasn't quite sure why Clete always asked him to go on these blitzes. The other guys on the team were far more enthusiastic about busting up the insides of offending mines. Could have been the basketball. People who played against Will often gave him a fair amount of deference. He'd been a star, and for them, he still was.

Could also be because of Paul, who was one of the biggest contributors to the kitty. Clete probably figured that Will would want to go after anyone who wasn't contributing because that was unfair to Paul.

Clete, Will, and the other guys used to meet at a gas station or coffee shop nearest the mine they were due to inspect, but they grew to suspect that the owners of the shops called the mines to warn the foremen. So they started meeting at the nearest Wal-mart.

There was no telling which mine they would visit from a Wal-mart.

Clete headed toward one of the old highways between Pikeville and Hazard that was full of underground mines. They listened to Reba on the radio and chatted about their families.

"I'm sorry about Sam dying," Clete said. "And somebody told me you grew up with one of the miners."

"Yeah. We weren't close no more," Will said.

Clete nodded. There didn't seem to be anything to say to that.

"You hear about Helen's game against Pikeville?" Will asked, smiling.

"No, but I'm thinking I'm about to," Clete said and gave that staccato laugh of his.

Will described how Helen shot and dribbled and how she controlled the tempo of the game. He didn't mention Tessy's coldness after the game or her passion the night before. He knew that Clete would just shake his head and compare Tessy to his wife and Will's divorce to his own.

Clete's marriage had dissolved in betrayal and bitterness. Will believed that his relationship with Tessy suffered none of those problems. So each time he and Clete had talked about Will's marriage in recent months, Will came away feeling morose. He hoped to avoid the subject this time.

After about fifteen minutes, Clete turned down the radio and turned up a CB radio installed below the dashboard. It squawked immediately, and the two men listened.

It was the usual talk of truckers: cops, road conditions, and loads.

And then, "The MSHA is headed up fifty-one near Crazy Creek. Pass the word."

Coal trucks drive every major road in Appalachia, and MSHA vehicles can get only a few miles on these arteries before one of the truckers reports their presence on CB.

Clete grinned. He picked up the radio handset and brought it to his mouth.

"You talkin' about that black Jeep Cherokee? I believe that's Missy Dungan," Clete said in the radio.

"What? Who was that, come back?"

Clete clicked the handset a few times then started in midsentence, "'Sides, that Jeep is turning off toward twenty-three."

Clete turned up his radio and held the handset to the speaker. He began to giggle. Will smiled.

Clete turned off the highway onto a well-worn, smaller road. The road dived and then rose steadily. He turned again, this time onto a wide gravel road, then slowed to allow a descending coal truck to pass.

He put the handset back in its place.

"Pete, you got company," they heard almost immediately. "MSHA headed your way. Better tell the crew."

Clete shrugged.

"So they get an extra couple of minutes," Clete said, his smile fading. "Ain't gonna be enough."

Around a sharp corner, the road suddenly opened into a wide parking area. There was a pile of coal to the right, fed by a conveyor belt that emerged from the mine like a snake's tongue. A tired wheel loader was working the pile and dumping black cascades into a coal truck. Another truck waited. Just as Clete parked, coal stopped falling from the conveyor belt.

"They're at it now," Clete said, nodding at the conveyor.

Will gathered his gear and, as soon as Clete swung the Jeep into a parking space, bounded out. Clete, David, and the other inspector were close on his heels, and the men walked briskly toward an office trailer.

Clete knocked. There was no answer. He knocked again.

"Just a second," they heard in response. "I'm on the john."

Clete rolled his eyes.

"Right," Clete said.

Clete opened the door. A man sat in a folding chair to the right of the door. He looked at them in surprise.

"You couldn't open the door?" Clete asked.

"He's on the john," the man said, pointing to the back of the trailer.

Clete pushed the man and he fell back in a heap.

"Hey," the man said.

David pushed his way past Will and went into the trailer. He kicked the man on the ground.

"Jesus!" the man shouted.

"Get on the radio and get us a ride into the mine," Clete said evenly.

Just then, a door in the back of the trailer opened.

"What the hell?" the man said.

"Get that guy outta here," Clete said, and David reached down and grabbed an ear of the man on the ground.

"Hey," he said as he got up. When he neared the door, David kicked him in the ass. The man crashed down the short flight of stairs to the outside and fell in a heap at Will's feet. Clete slammed the door.

"What's your name, son?" Will asked.

"Sneaky Caudill."

"We need a mantrip into the mine, Sneaky."

"We just sent a crew in. The mantrip probably won't be back for another hour," Sneaky said and struggled to his feet.

"And you don't got a buggy stored thirty feet into the fresh air?"

The man pursed his lips.

"Not that nobody's told me."

Will turned to the inspector behind him.

"Ray, sorry to do this to you, but do you mind crawling into that first entryway and seeing if there's a buggy there?"

"No problem," Ray said.

Ray reached into his helmet and pulled out two knee pads. He turned and walked toward the mine, putting his helmet on as he walked.

Will watched him go.

"What the hell's a special investigator doing here?" Sneaky asked.

"Just here to help, just here to help," Will answered.

They both watched Ray put on his miner's belt and knee pads and then bend down to enter the mine.

Will turned back to Sneaky.

"Now I'm guessing he's gonna find that buggy. If he does, I'll issue you a citation for impeding an inspection. If he doesn't, then you'll have thirty minutes from now to get us that mantrip. After that, I'll issue the same citation."

"People can't mine coal with you folks around."

"Is that right? I noticed the coal stopped coming off your conveyor as soon as we showed up. I don't suppose the miners down there are hanging curtains, are they?"

The man was silent, staring at the mine entrance.

Will shook his head.

A low scoop emerged from the mine, Ray at the wheel.

"Impeding an inspection. An S and S violation."

Will sighed and opened the trailer door.

"Hey, guys, we got a buggy. Let's . . ." Will stopped at the sight before him. David had the mine superintendent in a wrestler's hold. The man's face was bloody.

"Will, this guy wants me to fuck myself," Clete said, standing in front of the man. "Do I look like someone what wants to fuck himself?"

Clete hit the man, hard. The man grunted and sagged. David struggled to hold him up. Blood began to pour from a cut around the man's eye.

"Jesus," Will said.

# CHAPTER SEVENTEEN

C lete, David, let him go," Will said.

"You seen all the flowers he's got in this trailer, Will?"

Will looked around. He hadn't noticed before, but the trailer was surprisingly neat. And every window and shelf was stuffed with potted plants, many of them in flower. Will had never seen anything like it at a coal mine.

"Maybe his wife give 'em to him," Will said.

"Uh-huh," Clete said and poked the man. "Tell him."

"I just like flowers," the injured man said.

Clete grinned wildly at Will, who wondered why in the world the man would admit such a thing to a guy like Clete.

"All right, hit him one more time, but that's it," Will said.

Clete slapped the man in the face.

"Gonna call the state police," the man mumbled.

"Police?" Clete said and smiled. "He's gonna call the police, Will. Who do you think they're gonna believe? A dirtball like you that's lost two of his men—two deaths—in the past two years? That never pays his fines but dissolves his company and starts another? That had four major roof falls in the past six months, including one that killed his miner man?"

"Carroll's death's an accident," the man said through ruined lips.

"An accident?" Clete said and crowed. "Will, gimme that clipboard. That one right there."

Will reached into the trailer and picked up a clipboard that had been tossed on the ground. He gave it to Clete.

"Lemme see," Clete said and paged through sheets.

"October second, a roof fall twenty foot by seventy foot by ten foot dropped in the neutral entry. November seventeenth, a rock measuring fifteen foot by fifty foot by fifteen foot dropped in the fresh air, killing one Carroll Prater. January twenty-fifth, a fall measuring twenty foot by eighty foot by twelve foot dropped in the neutral."

"And there's more," Clete said, looking up. "You got rocks the size o' whales dropping all over your mine, Mr. Boger Man. And then you got the gall to stop contributing to the kitty? You, what needs more help from us than anybody? It's nothing more 'n a miracle that only two men been killed here. But your miracles are at an end, my friend."

Clete delivered another open-hand slap.

"Clete, that's enough. We got a buggy here. Let's take her in 'fore they clean everything up," Will said.

"David, you stay here with this dirtball. Make sure he don't do anything stupid."

David let go of the man, and he dropped to the ground. David giggled.

"Not like this, guys. Come on," Will said.

"Get some fuckin' balls, Will. We'd be doin' the world a favor if'n we killed the man."

Clete walked out of the trailer. Will stood for a moment and watched Clete walk toward the buggy. He turned back.

"David, don't fuckin' . . . ." He sighed. "Just leave him be." David looked at Will and shrugged.

"Come on," Clete shouted.

Ray and Clete were already in the buggy. Will jogged to the vehicle and got in one of the rear-facing seats. They plunged into the blackness of the mine.

. . .

"The whole fuckin' crew was hanging curtains to beat the band," Clete said, chuckling. "In the middle of nowhere."

Hours later, the two were sitting in the bar at Viper, a seedy hangout between Hazard and Whitesburg. Bikers, some miners, and a backwoods crowd made the bar dangerous. Fights were common, and there had been a few killings over the years. But it was the first real bar they'd come to on the way home, and Will had insisted on stopping.

"Twenty breaks," Clete said, shaking his head. "They hadn't built a brattice for twenty breaks, and they's hanging curtains at the face. Those guys are morons."

Will nodded blankly. He poured beer down his throat like a cook trying to put out a kitchen fire with water.

"I nearly lost it when you asked that foreman what he was doing with those curtains," Clete said, laughing. "'Help me out here, son,'" Clete said, stomping his feet. "'Your air is twenty breaks back, you said. What do you think this curtain is gonna do?'"

"Yuh," Will said. He put his hand up for another beer and one soon arrived. He took another long pull.

"And that kid done nothing but stare," Clete said, shaking his head.

Clete, who had been jabbering away ever since they got there, finally lapsed into silence.

"Thank God it ain't a gassy mine," Will said and looked at Clete. Will was having trouble focusing. "Otherwise, those guys'd be dead for sure."

Clete nodded.

"I don't think that guy's gonna put in a complaint, Will. He knows the score."

Will stared into space.

Clete continued, "When I give him the closure order at the end, he said, 'We'll get this worked out.' I'm a monkey's uncle if he don't got a contribution to the kitty in our office by tomorrow mornin'."

Will stroked the underside of his chin. His eyes wandered to Clete.

"Know my brother? Know that inundation there?" Will asked. He pulled the beer up to his mouth and drank deeply.

"Yeah?"

"'m investigatin' it."

"I know, Will. You'll get it done."

"No. I mean I'm 'onna investigate it. For real."

"What?"

"Lookin' into it. You know, asking questions."

"That's your job, Will. That's your job. But just remember—and I know you know this—but your brother's the best damn coal operator in the state. Always has his contribution. Gets those hams of his shipped all the way from western Kentucky."

"Still ain't found that guy's head. Roof bolter."

"That's a bitch, Will. I'm hopin' you're not the one that finds it, neither."

"Old Bethlehem map was wrong, but how's that possible? Bethlehem operations were damn careful. Always done things right."

"Will."

"Ever hear of a fellow from Virgie name of Amos Blevins? Miner man?"

"No. Listen, Will—"

"He didn't come in for his interview. Refused, they said." Will sipped his beer.

"So?"

"Just never happened to me before. Everybody comes in. Otherwise, it looks bad—for the company and them. People lie, but they always show up. There's just something funny about the whole thing."

"Will, it's your fuckin' brother."

"Yeah." Will kept nodding.

"You don't think you might be doing this for the wrong reason?"

"Been doing things for the wrong reason for a long time. Like today. Fuck. This may be the first thing I done for the right reason in years. Probably a waste of my time, but what better to waste it on? Nine people dead."

They were quiet.

"You ever been to a Pentecostal service, Clete?" Will asked.

"Don't tell me. Jesus, Will. You gettin' religion? Like, that kind o' religion?"

Will tried to laugh, but it made him dizzy so he stopped.

"No, this fellow Amos Blevins. He goes to the one up on Pine Mountain. Asked me to come."

Clete shrugged.

"BYOS, Will. Bring your own snake." And with that, Clete let out a peal of laughter.

Will woke up on his couch, a local newspaper on his chest. He had a vague memory of Clete helping him up the steps. He got up, and the newspaper fell to the floor. He reached down and needed a few tries to get it.

He went to the bathroom and sat on the pot. He looked briefly at the front page and then turned to the back and his favorite feature, "Speak Your Piece." It was a gossip column in which locals wrote anonymous stories—often complaints about neighbors.

"Keep your hands off my man," was the start to one item. "To the white trash from Deer Lick who's been flirting with my man. I'm going to tear that red dress off of you. He's never going to fall for you. He's mine. Why don't you take your trash someplace else!!!"

And another:

"To the poor man up Twin Forks who's working day and night to keep that wife of his happy. There's a blue Chevy pickup truck that's been visiting your house when you're gone. Watch IT."

Will loved trying to guess who the writers were. It was a kind of Appalachian crossword puzzle that he'd been piecing together since his teens. He would often talk about the items for days, even weeks. Tessy and then Helen started reading it themselves so they would understand what Will meant when he'd point someone out in a restaurant or on the street and say darkly, "The lady with the red dress."

An item quickly caught his attention.

"Why is a certain coal company still using a certain drilling company to look for water on Hell-for-Certain even though the drillers couldn't find water in a swimming pool? We got no hope of new water anytime soon. Why doesn't somebody else try looking that can get the job done?"

The "certain" coal company had to be Paul's Blue Gem, and the "certain drilling company" had to be Singleton Drilling.

That Paul was favoring Singleton wasn't that surprising. Everybody knew that Singleton did most of the drilling for Blue Gem. Too bad about the "no hope of new water" line, Will thought. Probably meant that Singleton was having no luck drilling new wells. It would mean the end of yet another community because of coal mining.

There was no need to investigate the item since proving it true didn't lead anywhere. At the moment, Will's investigation had simply confirmed what Paul had said from the start: every precaution seemed to have been taken. The old maps had been deceptive.

Didn't matter. Will was gonna take his time. Interview people. Maybe inspect some records. It was time Paul stopped taking him for granted.

He wiped his ass, got up, and went into the bedroom. He sat on the bed and picked up a book. He put the book back down, rose, and walked to Tessy's dresser. He opened the top drawer, kneeled, and put his face in the drawer.

He put his forehead on the top of the dresser and remained breathing in her fading smell. An image of Tessy dressing flashed through his head. He nudged the image toward nudity, but it remained firmly clothed.

It wasn't about sex. He just wanted to be near his wife.

Dawn was no more than a promise when Amos left for Middlesboro the next day. There were three ways to get there, none of them good. Amos chose the one that took him across Pine Mountain.

It was the most direct route, but it was also narrow and winding. The switchbacks up Pine Mountain had cost many lives.

Amos loved the old road. It was poorly built. It sloped in the wrong directions. Its curves were anything but gradual. It was a road that had barely tamed the old mountain, which Amos thought appropriate. If there was a Mount Sinai or Ararat in eastern Kentucky, Pine Mountain was it.

The road also went by Amos's church and passed near his best pot patches. Religious devotion had brought him on this journey of defiant truthfulness. It seemed right to give the church a nod on the way.

Just over the crest of Pine Mountain, the trees crowded and the road darkened. It was here that Amos had been tending his crop more than two years earlier when he stumbled onto the back of the church.

The noise had puzzled him at first. There was a babble of voices. Some of them sounded like foreign languages, others like bees in a hive. He listened for a moment, trying to pick out the rhythm of a hymn. There was none.

He crept closer and peered into a window. He realized that a church service was under way. He had never seen such rapture. Amos watched for more than a half hour, spellbound.

At some point, he became conscious of his gun digging into his right side. He slipped the gun from his armpit and held it in his hands. Feeling out of place, he crept away.

He headed to his other patch. Spreading Miracle-Gro, he kept thinking about the church. The memory of that service tickled his mind for weeks. Eventually, he decided to attend a service. He'd been going ever since. Tonight Amos's headlights washed over the dark and empty church for no more than a second. He arrived at the mine, Plover number 3, around six-thirty in the morning. By then, dawn had begun to lighten the sky. He pulled into the parking area. Three vehicles were already there.

Plover number 3, like many of the mines around Middlesboro, extracted coal from the Blue Jim seam, a narrow strip of unusually high-quality, low-sulfur bituminous coal that was nearly as hard as anthracite.

The coal was highly prized by some industrial buyers like steel makers because it burned hot and clean. But at its widest, the seam was no bigger than thirty inches and often narrowed to twenty-six. Miners here spent their working lives in a space no taller than a coffee table. The machinery was specialized, and its operators all lay prone. Miners had to bring straws with their lunches because there was rarely enough room to tilt a Coke can over their heads. Pissing required athletic agility and practice.

Despite having mined for nearly twenty years, Amos had never worked in such low coal. His size wasn't a problem, since standing was impossible for everyone.

He looked at the slits that served as the mine's entryways. A large hound would have resisted walking into them.

He got out of his truck, retrieved his cap, belt, emergency breathing box, and lunch bucket from the back of his pickup and walked to the mine's trailer.

Amos almost laughed as he opened the door. The trailer was almost identical to the one at Blue Gem's Red Fox mine. Same once-tan exterior, same dirty, tired interior, even the same musty, sweaty smell. It was oddly comforting.

"You Blevins?"

"Yes, sir," Amos said.

He was medium height, round, and had a graying beard. His eyebrows were bushy and wild, his hair thinning and white. He could make good money as a store Santa Claus.

"I'm Jim Craven, the foreman here. I'm sorry about all you've been through."

Craven offered a firm handshake.

"We need a scoop operator," Craven said. "You ever work the Blue Jim?"

"No, sir," Amos said. Amos realized that he had no idea who among the crew knew about the drugs. He decided to keep quiet until someone said something.

"It's different work, but I'm sure you'll get the hang of it," Craven said and smiled. "I'd give you the chance to work the miner, but we don't got one."

"Conventional?" Amos asked.

"You could say that," Craven said and smiled. "We shoot from the solid."

Amos blinked. He didn't think mines still shot from the solid, a hundred-year-old mining method that relied on explosives. Amos turned and saw another man sitting on a stool at the far end of the trailer. Amos and he nodded at each other.

Looking back at Craven, Amos motioned toward the open lockers along the wall.

"Take that'n," Craven said, pointing to one almost in front of Amos.

Amos pulled up a stool in front of the locker, which was nothing more than a small shelf over a few hooks.

He took off his coat and hung it on one hook. He wrapped his miner's belt around his midsection and got up and retrieved a battery and lamp from a charger. He assembled his cap.

Three more men entered the trailer and quietly prepared. They all nodded at Amos, who returned the greeting.

"Let's go," Craven said, and the men shuffled toward the door.

Two scoops were parked in front of one of the mine's entryways.

"Blevins, I'll drive it in, then it's yourn," Craven said over his shoulder.

The two men in front of Amos walked to the first scoop and lay slightly sideways across the shovel. Amos did the same in the next scoop, and the man behind Amos lay down beside him.

Craven climbed into the middle of the first machine, away from its shovel, and lay down on a narrow bed in front of the motor. The bed was angled slightly upward, so the operator's head was supported, and it jutted out from the side of the scoop so he could see forward and back. Another driver did the same in the machine in which Amos was riding.

The scoops surged forward. For a second, Amos was sure that the entryway was too small for either vehicle. But the mine swallowed them both, and Amos lay staring at the scarred roof flashing by just inches from his face.

Amos found his breathing somewhat shallow. Tombs had better head room.

Twenty-five minutes later, they arrived at the face. Amos rolled out of the vehicle's shovel and crawled on his elbows toward the scoop in front of him. Craven crawled back.

"We still got some coal to pick up along the return air," Craven said, pointing his thumb to the left side of the mine face.

"Yes, sir," Amos said, and crawled back to the scoop.

The scoop's controls were slightly different from the ones Amos had driven for decades, but he got the hang of it. And the task put to him was so basic that Amos was pleased.

He had been a miner man for years, riding a bucking, deafening machine that ground away tons of coal in minutes. The entire operation had relied on Amos, something he had always liked.

Now he was sweeping up a few thousand pounds with a relatively small shovel. He could have stopped and no one would have noticed. It was nice. And the mine was blessedly quiet. The only sound came from two drillers boring holes into the face.

Amos finished his sweep of the left side of the mine and drove back to the power center. Craven was there.

"We's just fixin' to blow it," Craven said. "You might want to drive the scoop back another break. You can wait back 'ere."

Amos nodded, nearly opened his mouth and thought better of it. He drove the scoop away from the face.

Two other miners were lying on the ground when he drove nearby. Amos parked the scoop, lay quietly, and then decided to crawl over to the others.

The two men nodded at him without obvious pleasure.

A warning siren rang. The other men put plugs in their ears. Amos did the same. The explosion that followed made his head ring. He crawled back to his scoop, and the other men went to theirs.

He drove up to Craven, who was lying near the power center. Both men took out their earplugs.

"Clean out the right tunnels first and go left," Craven said. "That way Charlie and John can come in behind you with the roof bolter and the driller."

Amos nodded.

It meant he would be under unsupported roof much of his workday.

# CHAPTER EIGHTEEN

W ill burst out of the church, furious. He was not sure that he would attend the burial. He could say something happened to his truck. But then people would accuse him of being a baby, and he didn't want that.

Nothing about his life was going well. He looked up at the sky and wanted to shout or stomp his feet. He felt like something was squeezing his nuts.

The first part of the funeral had been fine. It had taken the mining company another two days to retrieve Rob's body after Will found it. By then, the body was in bad shape, so the casket was closed.

Rob's oldest daughter had read, and she had stopped before the end of the passage, unable to continue.

The Reverend James Profit spoke. As pastor of one of two black churches in the region, he spoke at pretty much every black funeral. And he was good, saying just the right things about Rob.

Then the friends of the dead spoke. One of Rob's cousins spoke first. And then Tickle Jenkins spoke.

Tickle Jenkins.

He was the kid from Nigger Hollow whom Will and Rob had toler-
ated, first because their parents had told them to and later because the
two of them couldn't bring themselves not to. Rob had actually be-
stowed Tickle's name upon him when the boy, then known as Peter,
showed up at Will's house with his hand in his pants.

Rob had asked Peter what he was doing.

"Ticklin' my britches," the boy said, an answer that had led to peals
of laughter from Will and Rob—much to the boy's delight.

From then on, Will and Rob had called the boy "Tickle Britches," a
name later shortened simply to "Tickle." Now an insurance salesman,
Tickle had never grown out of being the shy kid still yearning for affection from more popular peers.

Tickle had started his eulogy by saying that he'd known Rob Crane
all of his life, and that he'd considered him his best friend. Both of which
were true, Will had to concede, but Rob had hardly felt the same. And
then he told a story about the two of them running naked through the
high school gym after the janitor had mistakenly locked the door between the showers and lockers.

Again, the story was true. But Tickle had failed to point out that he
had turned around almost immediately after entering the gym, and
that it had been Will and Rob who had streaked through the girl's vol-
leyball practice to reach the lockers on the other side, later opening
the door for Tickle and the other boys.

Tickle hadn't even been there when Rob, safely in the locker room,
had poked his head back into the gym and announced to the giggling
throng, "And no, we ain't all this good-lookin'."

Tickle had stolen Will's story and even his place as Rob's best
friend. It had been years since Will and Rob's falling-out, but Will
realized that he still had a proprietary feeling about their friendship.

Will beat his thigh. He might not have been so furious if his own
home life were better. Tessy had insisted on coming separately to the
funeral, and she and Helen had sat several pews behind him. She had
not been invited to the burial—everyone knew of their divorce, appar-
ently.

He pressed fingers into the space between his eyebrows and

imagined his head splitting. The service was still going on. Will could hear a hymn, which swelled in volume as someone else opened the doors.

Will fled to his truck, where he sat and listened to the radio for a while. Finally, he started the engine and steered toward Nigger Hollow.

Will drove past his childhood home, past Rob's home and then parked behind a line of other vehicles near the hollow's end. He got out and walked to the cemetery at the top of the hill. This small plot had twelve graves—all kin of Rob's. Will had known each headstone intimately.

It was a glorious, cold day. The sun was setting behind a sky filled with reddening popcorn clouds. The fading light put the sheer rock wall of the highway cut-through—visible to the west—in stark relief. The cemetery, trimmed and raked, looked beautiful.

Will nodded at several old friends and saw his brother, looking solemn, standing near the grave, his mother and Tickle by his side. Will had spoken to neither Paul nor his mother since he'd tossed his father's desk, and he was hoping to avoid them now. He shuffled to the back of the crowd of about two dozen mourners.

Prayers were said, dirt was thrown, and the casket was lowered. Will caught only snatches of the brief ceremony. Everyone began shuffling away, and Will followed them back to the cars.

Then Mary Crane, Rob's widow, appeared by his side.

"Will," she said and put her arm through his.

"Hey, Mary."

He had always liked her. She and Rob met in high school. She was one year older than he but two years ahead in school, and she was white. She got pregnant when Rob was still a senior, and they moved in together as soon as he graduated and went full-time into the mines.

They were never married but lived together for so long that the common law treated them as husband and wife. They had three children, the youngest of whom was still in high school.

Rob had been wild. Rob had been morose. And Rob had been hurt. Through it all, Mary was rock solid, accepting Rob however he presented himself. Will was always a little jealous.

"Heard you nearly got killed in that damn mine," Mary said. "Lord, I'm glad you made it out. If that mine had taken you, too, I don't know what I woulda done."

They walked a few steps in silence.

"Listen, I been meaning to come by," Will said. "The miner man at Red Fox, he said Rob said to say good-bye to you. Said he'd gotten a life insurance policy with the bank and had a survivor's policy with Blue Gem. And said to tell the kids he was proud of 'em. They were his last words."

She stopped, her mouth open. Tears sprang from her eyes. She wiped her eyes and nose, patted Will's arm, and began walking again.

"He talked a lot about you in the last month," she said and gave him a sad smile. "I mean, for the first time in years."

Will found that his throat had closed. He cleared it.

"Really?"

She nodded.

"He was happy. Maybe the happiest I'd ever seen him. Laughin' all the time," she said. "And he wanted to see you."

Will looked at her curiously.

"Why?"

"He loved you. Maybe even more'n he loved me."

"That was a long time ago, Mary. I said, I did, some things a man can't forgive."

"He never blamed you for the explosion, Will, he said—"

"Wasn't just the explosion."

"I know. I know."

"I called him every name in the book. Nigger. Spook. Gorilla. He didn't care. Wouldn't let me go."

Will thought back to his last weekend with Rob. Rob had come over at Tessy's urging and thrown out every liquor and beer bottle in the house, smashing them into the trash. Already drunk, Will could hardly resist.

And then Rob drove Will to a cabin in the Virginia woods to dry out.

"I begged him, cursed him, spit on him. He was a rock. He finally fell asleep, and I . . . Oh, I can hardly even think about it."

Will shook his head and looked off into the mountains. He breathed deeply.

"You didn't hurt him too bad, Will. I guess he was just surprised."

"I coulda killed him. I woulda. I was in a bad way." Will pursed his lips. "I never did know how he got back after I took his truck."

"Hiked out. Finally flagged down a logging truck. Took him most of the day to make it home."

"See. The thing is, I don't know if I coulda been friends with him again, after all I did. Just couldn't face him."

"I think there was a part of him that knew that. Still, I guess he was hoping you'd call, you know, after you got his letter."

"What letter?"


"Blevins, I need you to finish laying out the explosives on this charge. Charlie's gotta go."

Amos blinked again. He had not handled explosives in more than fifteen years. He vaguely knew that things had changed since then, that packing an explosives charge involved more steps and more safety issues.

He hesitated.

"I'll learn ya," Craven said. "We'll do the first few together."

They both crawled toward a scoop whose shovel was filled with equipment. Craven took out some explosives, crawled toward the face, and stuffed them in the hole, with a lead hanging out. He stuffed wadding into the hole and crawled on to the next one.

"Some people tie up the leads at the end, but I like to do it as I go," Craven said. "Simpler."

Amos nodded. After watching Craven fill two holes, Amos tried one himself with Craven watching. Craven soon nodded and left Amos to his job.

Filling his third hole, Amos's stomach suddenly felt sick. He'd felt fine just a moment ago but now he worried that he'd throw up. His first thought was that he was getting the flu. And then he knew that it was something else. He looked around. No one was near. Even the sound of the scoops had receded. He disconnected the lead on the hole he was working on.

He paused for a moment, shook his head, and went on working. But he didn't connect the leads on the next two holes, either. Even so, the sudden explosion tossed him into the air and, as he flew, Amos wished he'd stopped connecting the leads one hole earlier.

# CHAPTER NINETEEN

M ary stopped walking.
    "You never got his letter?"

Will shook his head. She closed her eyes.

"Oh, that's so sad," she said. "He thought you'd just decided not to see him. Oh."

Will felt the dams on his emotions beginning to burst.

"All my mail is being forwarded to Tessy in Hazard. She drops it off only now and then," he said. "I think I got a couple of letters on my bureau right now. I just haven't checked 'em."

She shook her head and started walking again.

"Can you walk back to the house with me? Leave your truck?"

Will nodded.

"What did he write?"

"I don't know. He wouldn't show it to me. I think he just said he wanted to get together. Some'm happened last month that changed things for him."

Will groped for a response amid the grief pouring through his heart.

"Last month? What was goin' on last month?"

"Don't know that neither," she said. "He come back from Frank's—that's the hair guy for black folks around here—with a lot less hair and a ton less worries."

She stopped again.

"He come in the door, pinched my bottom and kissed me like, oh, like he ain't kissed me since high school."

She hugged herself, and tears pooled in her eyes.

"This last month been the best of my life," she said. "No drinkin', no shoutin', always there. And laughin' like, well, like he ain't never laughed."

She started walking again.

"I'm sorry you didn't see it," she said with a far-off look.

They walked the remaining distance to the house in silence. After Rob's mother died, he and Mary had moved into the family home-place with their kids. Will reached for the doorknob, one he had touched thousands of times in his life, but the door opened on its own. Paul came out and nearly ran into Will.

"Oh, sorry," he said, and stopped in front of them.

"Paul," Will said.

"Mary, I'm so sorry for your loss," Paul said stiffly.

Mary suddenly seemed stricken. Paul ducked his head and slipped between Will and Mary.

"Paul," Will said. Paul turned back. "Sorry about the desk."

"Don't come to the office again, Will. 'Least not for a while."

A silence stretched.

"Like I said, I'm sorry."

"You've said that a lot."

"All right." Will squinted. "I'll try to cut down. Leastways with you."

"Somebody said you're actually investigating this inundation."

"That's what I'm paid to do, Paul."

"Oh? Since when?"

Will frowned.

"Mary," Paul said and nodded. He turned and left.

Will glanced back at Mary, who gave a wan smile.

"Will, I know he's your brother, but I have never liked that man. Never," Mary said. "Even Rob's been pissed off at him lately. Or was."

"Why?"

"Don't know. I think they had an argument a few weeks back."

"About what?"

Mary shrugged, a gesture of both ignorance and resignation. She walked into the house, where she was immediately caught up in being the hostess and chief mourner.

Will followed her in, spotted Tessy and Helen, and walked over to them.

"You okay?" he asked.

"Yeah," Tessy answered.

"Okay. I gotta go home. Rob Crane wrote me a letter. I gotta find it," he said.

"Oh my Lord," she said. "There was a letter. It came about two weeks ago. I left it for you t'other night."

"Probably it. Shit." He shook his head. "I'll see ya."

He touched Helen's arm and headed for the door. He was nearly out when Uncle Elliott appeared in front of him.

"How ya doin', son?" the old man asked.

"Fine," Will said, and gave the old man's shoulders a squeeze.

"Son, I heard about the will and the desk and you and Paul," Uncle Elliott said, undeterred. "And I'm tellin' ya, I know just what you're goin' through."

"Okay. Well, that's good. I gotta go."

"You take care," the old man said.

"Yes, sir. You, too," Will said and made it out the door. Outside, he broke into a jog.

Amos came to and found himself in a world without light, sound, or space. He discovered that he could move, and he pushed piles of rocks from in front of him. He reached up to his helmet light. The glass was broken.

As the dust settled, wash from distant lights gradually illuminated the area around him. He started to crawl. He couldn't move one of his feet. He pulled himself along by his elbows.

He crawled into the return air tunnel, where few miners ever venture. He pressed himself against a rib.

He saw a growing light and heard a scoop. With the shovel down, Craven plowed his way through the rubble and stopped just short of the return air. Amos saw Craven's helmet lamp sweep over the mine face, and then he saw Craven crawl out of the scoop.

The mine was deathly still.

Amos heard the approach of a second scoop. It stopped next to Craven's.

"He dead?" the man in the second scoop asked.

"Think so. Body's gotta be in here somewhere," Craven answered.

"He had it comin'," the man in the second scoop said.

"Yes, sir," Craven said. "They said he's a snitch."

The two were silent.

"You want me to help look for him?" the second man asked.

"No, I'll find him," Craven answered. "You better get to the mine phone and tell 'em we had that accident they wanted."

The second scoop disappeared.

Craven swept the face of the mine several more times with his helmet lamp.

His foot now functional, Amos rose up on his hands and feet and skittered, crabwise, straight at Craven. Just as Craven turned back to the scoop, Amos hit him in the face. Amos caught a glimpse of shock on the Santa-like face before it disappeared in a flash of headlamp and motion.

The blow knocked Craven onto his back. The old man didn't move. Amos, pretty sure that he wouldn't for some time, crawled back to Craven's scoop, got in, and headed back toward the fresh-air tunnel. He passed two miners, who looked at him in surprise as he drove to the surface.

*Dear Will,*
*It has been a long time, old buddy. I was wondering if you wanted to grab a beer sometime. Or maybe we should get a Coke! I am trying to cut down on the beers, too. Ha ha! Give me a call sometime.*

*—Rob*

*P.S. I have been thinking a lot about that deal with Paul and the condom!! Ha ha. Remember how you were not sure if you had done it?*

The writing was in clear block letters, painstakingly cast and deeply familiar. Sitting on the edge of his bed, Will chuckled at the postscript. Paul and the condom. What a story.

Rob and Will were juniors in high school, already heroes on the basketball court and dating the girls who would eventually become their wives. That following summer, Mary would become pregnant, which sobered them all.

But Will remembered that junior year as the best of his life, as Tessy and he explored each other everywhere they could—cars, fields, bathrooms, creekbeds, and, of course, the cemetery.

Their parents knew the two were seeing a lot of each other but chose to ignore any suggestion of sex. At one point, Will's mother said at breakfast—pretty much out of the blue—"Now, Will, I know you and Tessy wouldn't do anything so stupid as to have intercourse, right?"

Jeff, Will's younger brother who would leave school for the mines within weeks, hooted.

"Momma, did you just say 'intercourse'?" Jeff asked.

But she kept her eyes on Will.

"No, ma'am," Will lied.

"Good boy."

No more than two weeks later, Will's mother and father took one of their many weekend trips to Lexington, taking Jeff with them. Will, Rob, and Paul worked at the mine in the morning. Will met up with Tessy just after lunch and spent the rest of the day with her. It was early spring, the weather was beautiful, and they had sex—glorious lovemaking—three times that afternoon.

He arrived home with the fading light around 7 p.m. His mother was sitting at the kitchen table. As soon as Will entered, Jeff got up from the table and headed for his room, his raised eyebrows a warning that Will was in for it.

"Sit down, Will," she said firmly. "Paul!"

"What? What is it?" Will asked, his heart suddenly racing.

She flexed her jaw muscles and said nothing until Will's father came down the stairs and pulled out a chair beside her. Then she turned over one hand and, fingers extended, placed a yellow and orange condom in the center of the kitchen table.

"I found this on my nightstand," she said. His father stared into the distance.

"Momma, it's not mine," Will said in a rush. "I got nothing to do with that."

"Are you and Tessy having sex?" she asked quietly.

"Ah," Will stammered as images from the afternoon flooded into his brain. "No, ma'am."

Both parents frowned, and Will knew he was lost. He could not now admit to having sex but deny doing so in their bed—a repellent thought.

"William," his father intoned. "Our bed is sacred to us, and you have violated that."

"Dad, I didn't—"

"William," his father repeated, and his tone quieted Will instantly. "When you are not at school or practice, you will be at home or in the mine. No Friday night dates. No Saturday night dates. You are grounded for the rest of this school year. We will not discuss this ever again, but I cannot remember ever being more disappointed in any of my sons."

"But Dad—"

"This ends this discussion."

His father rose and went back upstairs. His mother remained, glaring at him.

"Mom," Will said in a stage whisper. "I didn't leave this condom by your bed. Tessy and me didn't do nothin' in there."

"Oh, and who left it there?" she whispered back.

"I don't know. Paul?"

"Paul? He's got his own apartment. Why would he bring a girl here?"

"I don't know. Maybe somebody else did it. All I can say is that I swear it wasn't me. I swear!"

And as he said it, Will suddenly wasn't sure himself whether he'd left the condom there. A small part of him glimpsed what his parents saw: he was the only possible suspect.

But his condoms were blue on the outside, he insisted to himself.

And truth be told, he and Tessy often skipped protection altogether, preferring the "pull-out" method. He took a closer look at the package. It said, "Ribbed, Lubricated." He'd never bought anything like it.

But his own doubts must have been apparent to his mother. She sighed heavily and got up.

"I am just so disappointed," she said, words that filled Will with dread. She went upstairs. Will remained at the table, his head in his hands.

It would be weeks before he and Tessy managed to sneak away long enough to have sex. Months passed before the pall lifted with his mother. His relationship with his father never recovered. Jeff snickered and Paul was condescendingly dismissive of the whole affair.

And then, just as the school year ended, Will popped into Paul's Mustang looking for a stick of gum in his glove compartment and found a trove of yellow and orange condoms. Will stared at the plastic squares until a honk from Rob's battered Delta 88 roused him. Will got out of Paul's car, slammed the door and briefly thought about defacing it.

Rob honked again, and Will sprinted to the passenger seat. They had left the mine early to attend an evening team meeting, but, as usual, they were late.

"What the fuck you doing?" Rob asked and gunned the motor.

"I can't fuckin' believe it. I can't fuckin' believe it," Will said and punched the dashboard.

"What?"

"In Paul's car! There's a whole shitload of condoms just like the one Momma and Daddy said I left by their bed. I mean, the same kind."

"Holy shit."

"Yeah, the bastard. All this time. Fuck! I took the rap and he didn't say a fuckin' word."

Rob shook his head and then started to chuckle.

"Well, you gotta get him back. I mean, big-time-revenge stuff."

"By doing what? Momma and Daddy are never gonna believe me, even if I show 'em the condoms. They'll say I put 'em there."

"I ain't talkin' 'bout your Mom and Dad. I'm talkin' 'bout revenge, son."

Will looked quizzically at Rob and then shared his smile.

"What you got in mind?" Will asked.

"We got to think long and hard 'bout this, my friend. Can't rush into it. It's got to be right. We got to get him back, but he can't know we're getting him back. Leastways, he can't be sure."

It took them two days to come up with a plan, and it only fell into place after Rob told a hilarious story about a sexual mishap he'd had with Mary. Rob had been grinding up his mother's dried hot peppers to make a spice she sold to friends, and some of the dust from the blender drifted onto his lips.

Some time later, he and Mary became entwined, and Mary soon complained of a burning sensation in a delicate place. Rob realized that it must have been the pepper. Mary wasn't amused, but Will roared when he heard the story.

"Hey," Will had said. "What if we put that pepper in some of Paul's condoms?"

And the idea was born. Rob got a hypodermic needle from his mother's medical kit, and Will threw out most of the condoms in Paul's glove compartment. The rest they injected with a paste of dried jalapeños.

Two days later, Rob appeared as usual in Will's kitchen to pick him up for work, but he was having a terrible time suppressing his laughter.

"What's so funny?" Will's mother had asked Rob.

"Nothing, Mrs. Murphy. Sorry." At which point, he broke into another fit of laughter.

"What?" Will said, joining in the laughter.

"Nothing. Listen, Will, we gotta go," he said, and then gave up the effort and doubled over.

"Bye," Rob managed to say before bolting out the door. Will ran after him.

Rob was sitting in the passenger seat of his own car.

"You drive. I can't drive," he said and fell into another fit.

Shaking his head, Will walked around to the driver's side, got behind the wheel and put the car in gear. Will couldn't get another word out of Rob until they were almost at the mine.

"Momma said that Paul showed up at the emergency room last night with Mrs. LiBassi," Rob managed to say.

Another fit delayed any more information.

"Yeah?" Will asked, feeling bad that he was laughing about such a thing.

Mrs. Anne LiBassi was the wife of the chairman of the school board and one of Fleming-Neon's leading ladies. She was also at least twenty-five years older than Paul, and she lived about a half mile from Nigger Hollow.

"Both of 'em had a severe allergic reaction to a condom," Rob said.

And Will nearly drove off the road.

Sitting on his bed, Will laughed at the memory, a happy sadness filling him.

But why had Rob mentioned the story? And why had he mentioned the part about Will briefly thinking he might have actually left the condom himself? Will couldn't remember telling Rob about that.

Mary said Rob had learned something at the barbershop. But what?

Will had a weird feeling that it was all somehow connected to the Red Fox flood, but he had no idea how. Something about Paul's reaction to his apology earlier that night felt all wrong. Paul was way too pissed off, and he was something else. Scared? And what had Paul and Rob argued about? Was that why Paul had transferred Rob to the flooded mine? Was the flood somehow connected with that argument? Did Paul do something to flood the mine to get back at Rob? Didn't seem likely. Nothing made sense.

Will decided that he needed to take a trip to Frankfort.

# CHAPTER TWENTY

H ey, Tessy," Will said.

"Will," she answered on the phone, surprise in her voice. He'd called her at work.

"Listen, I know this probably is nothing you're interested in, but I'm headed to Frankfort tomorrow, and I was wondering whether you wanted to call in sick and come along. I could drop you at the mall in Lexington on the way out, and on the way home we could have dinner at Fleet's."

Fleet's, a Lexington institution, was her favorite restaurant.

There was silence.

"Oh, Will," she finally said.

Like most folks in eastern Kentucky, Tessy adored trips to Lexington. For years, Will had teased Tessy about her Lexington hang-up. He pointed out that Lexington was no metropolis; that its cultural offerings were minimal, and that its citizens were famous for spurning the affections of their Appalachian neighbors.

Without some connection to Thoroughbreds or the University of Kentucky, you were nobody in Lexington, Will said, "and we got neither."

Didn't matter. Tessy loved the place. She devoured the restaurant reviews in the *Lexington Herald-Leader*. She often checked the meager theater offerings in town. And every few months, she planned a big weekend trip to Lexington.

Those weekends, which usually included Helen, became the highlight of their marriage. Truces were called and wounds were healed. Their union was at its healthiest in Lexington. The glow from one of those trips lasted for days.

Asking Tessy to go on a trip to Lexington was a transparent attempt at reconciliation. He wasn't saying that he accepted her decision to move to Hazard and file for divorce, but the invitation certainly suggested that he could live with it.

"Oh, Will," she said in a whisper. "We'd probably run into someone from home."

Will gripped the phone harder.

"And then word might get out that we actually loved each other?" Will asked sarcastically.

He heard Tessy sigh. Will couldn't get his tongue unstuck.

"You know, we can go someplace else, maybe someplace out of state, but we should probably wait till the season's over," Tessy said, still whispering.

"Why are you whispering?" Will asked, his anger rising.

"You know why," she answered in a normal voice.

"This is insane."

They hadn't been this secretive in high school when they were dodging their parents.

"Oh, Will," Tessy said.

"I'll talk to you soon," he said and hung up, miserable.


The waiting room was mobbed, so Amos stood. Glenda cleared away a few old magazines and sat on a side table. They both settled in.

Amos recognized a few of the patients. None belonged to the chamber of commerce. Most wore sad, tired expressions. A few fidgeted nervously.

Since Glenda was surrounded by seated patients, Amos was forced to stand almost ten feet from his wife. She fitted into a depressing tableau, and Amos realized that she differed little from the rest of those waiting. Glenda didn't fidget, but she looked anxious and defeated.

A group portrait of The Nerves.

The door opened and a beautiful young blonde in a skirt suit walked into the waiting room with a grocery sack in one arm and dragging a black roller bag with the other. She approached the desk, which was glassed in.

"Hi, Patsy!" the new arrival said, waving to the woman behind the desk.

"Hi, Cheryl!" Patsy answered and rolled the window all the way open.

The two women beamed at each other.

"How's everything? How's John?" Cheryl asked.

Patsy nodded.

"Fine, fine. He joined the track team t'other day," Patsy answered.

"Oh, that's great! That'll help his training for basketball." The blonde smiled. "He'll be on the varsity yet."

The two nodded.

"Here," the blonde said. She reached into the grocery bag and took out a smaller paper bag, then handed the larger bag to Patsy.

"Lunch for you and the girls," the blonde said, and then held up the smaller bag. "I wanted to give Dr. Shrisrapan his lunch myself. Is he available?"

"Oh, I'm sure he can spare you a minute," Patsy said with a laugh that the blonde joined. "Just go right into his office."

"Okay, let me check that you've got enough samples first," the blonde said.

A buzzer sounded, and the blonde opened the door into the inner part of the doctor's office. Because he was standing, Amos had a view going well into the office. He watched as the blonde opened a set of double doors and transferred handfuls of red and white medicine boxes from her roller bag into the closet.

Finished, she closed the double doors and headed down the corridor. She opened another door and stepped in. A moment later, Glenda's doctor entered the hallway, walked toward Amos, and then opened the same door the blonde had entered. He smiled as he went in.

"Well, I was wondering if you'd come today," Dr. Shrisrapan said as he closed the door.

The two were in the office for about fifteen minutes. The crowd in the waiting room grew. Dr. Shrisrapan emerged brushing his hair back with his hand, went back down the hall and entered an exam room. The blonde followed him out a moment later and returned to the front of the office.

"Okay now," the blonde said.

Patsy, who had been sitting glumly at her desk, brightened.

"Take care, Cheryl," Patsy said.

"I'll be back next week," the blonde said. "You still want the chicken salad?"

"Oh, yes," Patsy answered. She patted the grocery bag on the desk.

"Okay then," the blonde said as she exited the inner office and rolled out of the waiting room.

Another hour passed before Patsy announced Glenda's name. Glenda was back in five minutes carrying a red and white medicine box.

"All set," Glenda said.

Amos nodded and held the door for his wife.

As they walked to the truck, he decided to ask.

"What's that?"

"What do you mean?" Glenda asked without looking.

"The box."

"Doctor said it was the best thing for me. It's new," Glenda said, obviously pleased.

"You got everything you need in the box?"

"No. This is just a sample. I gotta fill the prescription," Glenda said, unclenching her hand long enough to show a slip of white paper.

"I thought you liked the other stuff," Amos said, knowing that he should let it go.

"I did, but this is new, Amos," Glenda said, surprised that he failed to see the obvious.

To Amos, the blonde's influence on his wife's prescription was obvious. What remained a mystery was whether she would be hurt by the new drug any more than she had been by the old.

Like much about Glenda, he saw no way of untangling that mystery.

. . .

Will loved driving out of Hazard toward Lexington because he felt decades pass along with the miles. Around Whitesburg, abandoned coal tipples—hulking steel squares where rock and coal were separated—sat rotting in tangles of kudzu. Train tracks were braided with the main roads. Classic Appalachian shacks—small buildings with large front porches—were easily visible. Hanging footbridges still swung gracefully over many creeks.

Leaving Perry County, he saw an old gas station that still had a sign which warned, "Last Chance for 100 Miles," a reminder that most of the counties between Lexington and Hazard allowed no alcohol sales.

West of Jackson, the mountains began to falter. Fields appeared. The sky began to open up. White clapboard farmhouses dotted the landscape. At Stanton, the road geared up from two lanes to four. Dark clouds were visible at least an hour before rain arrived.

At Winchester, a mountain parkway gave way to Interstate 64. Appalachia faded away, and rich, loamy bluegrass took hold. Barns sported cupolas. Horses grazed instead of cattle and sheep.

Lexington's constantly changing haphazard sprawl thrilled Will because it was so different from the ever-familiar mountains around Whitesburg and Hazard. Will liked leaving Appalachia almost as much as he savored each return.

Frankfort, though, was just a bit too far. By the time he turned off the interstate, his back was bothering him and he'd heard a few songs on the radio several times.

He drove through town, parked, got out of his truck and glanced at the state capitol. It was a glorious building. Behind it was a campus of state office buildings. Will entered the first and stared at a legend posted just inside. He finally walked to the elevators and rode to the fourth floor.

When he got out, he looked left and right, shrugged, and went right. He opened a large wooden door and walked into a room crowded with beige metal cabinets and cursed with mottled brown carpeting. Fluorescent lighting gave the room a bluish glare.

There were two desks to the right of the entry door, and a thin middle-aged man wearing khakis and a Western-style button-up shirt sat at one.

"This the mine map room?"

"Can I help you?"

"Yes," Will said. He walked over and stood in front of the man's desk, where the day's newspaper had been spread.

"I'm looking for the maps for a mine from Letcher County. Bethlehem Number eleven. Pretty old. Like nineteen-twenties old," Will said.

The man nodded.

"All right."

The man turned to his computer terminal and then looked down at the keyboard and used his index finger to hit "enter." He pecked away uncertainly for more than a minute.

"Bethlehem number what?" the man said.

"Eleven."

"Drawer fifteen forty-one."

"Where's that?"

"That side," the man said, pointing to the southern end of the room as he again looked down at his newspaper.

Will nodded. Saying thanks seemed a bit much. Not too many visitors, Will guessed.

There were numbers on the drawers and legends on the tops of cabinet islands. Will found 1250 through 1300 and figured he was headed in the right direction. He soon found the cabinet "1500–1550" and scanned down its side. Each drawer was about five inches high and nearly four feet wide. Near the bottom, he found 1541 and opened the drawer.

It was empty.

Will stood there for a moment, pursed his lips, and walked back to the clerk.

"It's empty," Will said.

"What?"

"The drawer, fifteen forty-one. It's empty. Come see."

"No, I believe you," the clerk said.

"Well, where's the map?"

"Got no idea."

"Well, why would you have it indexed and put aside a drawer for it if it's not gonna be there?"

The clerk shrugged and went back to his newspaper. Will stood over the man for a moment.

"Can you punch in the number of another mine?"

The man sighed theatrically.

"Like what?"

"Like Bethlehem number ten."

The man looked at Will and then glanced back at the screen. He pecked out more digits.

"Drawer fifteen forty-two," the clerk said, now exasperated.

Will marched back to the cabinet and opened drawer 1542, just below the one he'd opened before. It was filled with large mine maps, maybe two inches deep.

Will looked at the left-hand corner of the top map. Bethlehem No. 10.

Will closed the drawer and opened the next one, which was still empty. He shut it and opened the next. Dust billowed up. He looked at the corner of the top map. Bethlehem No. 12.

He closed that drawer and again opened the empty one, this time pulling the drawer all the way out.

The drawer was clean except for the very back, where a faint line of dust seemed to outline a gap between the end of the drawer and something that might once have been inside the drawer.

He ran his index finger along the line and brought the finger up to smell it. He sneezed.

"Dust," he pronounced quietly to himself. "What a sleuth."

# CHAPTER TWENTY-ONE

Amos stood in front of the bathroom medicine cabinet, paralyzed. He had managed to pry the red and white box out of Glenda's hands, but she was expecting him to appear with a pill.

He'd watched out of the corner of his eye as she'd opened the box and found a blister pack of pills.

"Oh hell," she'd said.

She reached for a kitchen knife and Amos, uncertain about what he actually intended to do, found himself talking.

"Honey, don't use a kitchen knife on that thing."

"Why?" she asked.

"It ain't sterile."

They paused, both a bit surprised that he'd come up with such a word.

"Give it here. I'll get the scissors from the first-aid kit."

"All right."

And here he was.

He wanted to do something, but he wasn't sure what. He was quite certain that the pills in the pack would do Glenda no good and might do her real harm. He figured that her doctor had that blonde's interests and his own more at heart than Glenda's.

He chucked the blister packet out the window and retrieved a bottle of generic ibuprofen. Glenda never seemed to use these pills. They were red and had a white *w* inscribed on one side.

He shook five onto his palm, returned the bottle to the cabinet, and walked out of the bathroom, cradling the pills like communion wafers.

Glenda was still standing in the kitchen, one hand on her hip. Amos walked up and offered his palm. She took one of the pills, and he dropped the rest into a glass.

"We'll leave these here," he said. He retrieved a small dish and covered the glass. "I'll get the rest of the prescription later."

Glenda gave him a grateful smile.

"Thank you, Amos. Thank you for understanding," she said and put her hand on his arm.

"I'm just sorry that what I done made it so much worser," Amos said.

She frowned, sighed, and got a glass of water. She took the pill. She closed her eyes and exhaled. She opened her eyes slowly and smiled.

"That's better," she said.

Amos smiled back.

She reached for his hand, kissed it, and looked at him with hooded lids. She backed into the bedroom, pulling Amos along with her.

Thank the Lord for ibuprofen, Amos thought.


"There's some'm wrong," Will said. "I just can't figure out what."

Will was sitting on the same uncomfortable stool beside Uncle Elliott in the Hazard dialysis clinic. And Uncle Elliott, who could sense his nephew's need, was trying to give Will all the attention that a man could while having his blood drained.

"Son, I'm sorry. I still don't understand what happened at the map room."

"The drawer was empty," Will said.

Uncle Elliott smiled that soft, crinkled smile of his and closed his eyes briefly. Will wasn't sure whether any of this was getting through to him, but it sort of didn't matter. Uncle Elliott had always been the one person in Will's family with whom he could discuss difficult subjects.

The old man rarely gave Will answers, but Will often arrived at one anyway.

The old man opened his eyes.

"Look, Will, I'm sorry if this sounds insulting, but I never got the sense you gave a rat's ass about coal mine investigations. That fair?"

Will squinted. "I guess."

"And then they assigned you to investigate your own family's mine?"

"Yeah."

"Strike you as odd?"

"I guess."

"Again, I don't mean to put you down, but I'm thinking they thought you were gonna whitewash this whole thing. Right? Now you're actually investigating?"

Will nodded.

"Why?"

"I don't know. Pissed off, mostly, I guess. You know, it wasn't my idea to become a MSHA inspector. But now that I'm doing it, I guess I'm gettin' tired of pretending. Plus, this whole thing at Red Fox is starting to bother me. I mean, nine people died."

"There's been worse, but I'm proud o' you, son. Feel like you're waking up, or fighting back, something like that. And your brother, well, it's been a long time since he treated you right. Just like your father," Uncle Elliott said and nodded to himself.

"They got their reasons," Will said and looked down.

Uncle Elliott patted him and pursed his lips.

"Look, if your brother wanted to get some maps out of there, he wouldn't have any trouble. The Kentucky Department of Mines and Minerals is open for business with coal operators. You got money and a coal mine, you just gotta ask with them people."

Will waited on the old man, knowing more was coming.

"You just gotta figure out why he'd go to the trouble," Uncle Elliott said. "I mean, what'd happen if you did find an old map? What'd it matter?"

"That'd depend on whether it was different from the one he filed with his mining plan and give us," Will said. He tried to sit back, remembered he was on a stool and stopped himself before he fell back.

"And if it is different?" Uncle Elliott asked.

"Well, if it's real different, then Paul could be charged with falsifying records, Uncle El. And that's a felony."

Uncle Elliott whistled and nodded his head for some time. "Reason enough," the old man finally said.

"Yup," Will agreed.

Will looked around the room. There were at least twenty other people getting dialysis. Most were watching a few shared TVs, dozing, or doing some combination of both. It was warm, and there was a languid air about the place. Even the staff seemed to move slowly. Although every patient in the clinic had their toes curled over the end of their lives, they paradoxically had loads of time to kill.

"So what's happening with you and Tessy?" Uncle Elliott asked.

Will spread his hands, smiled, and said, "Women."

Uncle Eliott nodded and closed his eyes.

Will sighed. "I can't figure out anything. This investigation. My wife. Nothing makes sense."

Uncle Elliott made a slight movement with his head that showed he'd heard.

"If only God would whisper me the answers," Will said.

"He's never said nothing to me," the old man said. His eyes still closed, Uncle Elliott pointed toward the floor. "Maybe you should try the other guy. I hear he gets things done."

"That is one fine idea, Uncle Elliott," Will said in a jocular tone. He made a show of addressing the floor: "Devil, you got any ideas about where else I can look for this map?"

"To the mine or your marriage?" Uncle Elliott said, opened his eyes, and smiled at Will.

Will laughed.

"The mine. I don't think even *he* could set Tessy straight," Will said, his smile fading.

Uncle Elliott closed his eyes again and licked his lips.

"You tried Bethlehem yet?" the old man said, and opened his eyes briefly to look at Will, who shrugged. "I doubt they kept all this stuff after their bankruptcy, but you never know. And what about that mining museum in Kingdom Come? They got a lot of old maps."

"Wow. Those are pretty good ideas, Uncle El."

The old man looked at Will through narrow eyes. "I get 'em every now and again."

"Yes, you do," Will said, admitting to himself that Uncle Elliott's good ideas still surprised him.

"Worth a try, anyway," Uncle Elliott said.

"I just can't shake the feeling that Rob, my old friend, wanted to tell me something," Will said.

"The, uh, black guy?"

"Yeah."

"Wasn't he in the Blue Dog explosion with you?"

"Yeah."

"Maybe when he wrote about that condom story, he was really talking about the explosion, not what was going on at Red Fox."

Will froze. He hadn't even considered that.

"You mean, like, that somehow I wasn't to blame for that? But I lit the cigarette. I remember that."

Uncle Elliott shrugged. "Just thinking out loud."

"No. I think it's got something to do with this Red Fox thing. His wife said he and Paul got in an argument recently."

"She's white, though, right?"

Will didn't answer. He'd always known that his uncle was racist and disapproved of interracial marriage, but Will chose to ignore this failing.

"Listen, I'd be careful if I were you, tellin' this theory to anyone at MSHA. They might start to worry about you."

Will nodded. They were quiet for a few moments. Uncle Elliott seemed to nod off for a moment.

"Well, thanks," Will said. He patted Uncle Elliott's shoulder and got off his stool.

"Where you off to now?" the old man asked without opening his eyes.

"Home, then I'm going to a Pentecostal service," Will said with a smile.

"What?" His eyes were open now.

"Yeah. I know it's a waste o' time, but this miner that got stuck in

Red Fox, he invited me, and I'm hoping to gain his trust. Maybe he can tell me something. I got nothing else to do anyways," Will said, a sheepish look on his face.

"Which church?"

"Pine Mountain."

"You're kidding," Uncle Elliott said.

"No, sir."

"Be sure to grab the snake by the head," Uncle Elliott said, laughing.

"The first snake I see, I'm outta there," Will said and laughed, too.

"Pretty sure there're no snakes," Uncle Elliott said, still smiling. "I grew up with the preacher, Rusty Seymour. Good kid but jumpier'n a jackrabbit. A snake'd scare the shit out of him."

The both laughed again and then sat quietly for a moment. Uncle Elliott's gaze drifted into the distance. His eyelids drooped.

"Take care, Uncle El," Will said.

Uncle Elliott nodded slightly and fell asleep. Will stood over him, looking sadly at the shrunken body. He patted the air above Uncle Elliott's head and left.

# CHAPTER TWENTY-TWO

Until the preacher mentioned the inundation at Red Fox, Amos had felt the service was going to be one of Rusty Seymour's best. He had mentioned the evil in Russia, the confusion in Washington, and even the sins of the flesh in Lexington—all familiar themes.

But Preacher Seymour always found a local event to use as an illustration. This time, he picked Amos's mine.

"The Lord does not make it easy on us, oh brothers," Preacher Seymour said. "He tests us. He challenges us. For Brother Amos, that challenge came this week, when the waters poured in upon him. Dark waters!"

Amos had not spoken to his preacher since the disaster. Hearing it cast as a battle between good and evil pulled Amos out of his growing reverie. He opened his eyes and looked around.

The church, which had once served as a country store and then as a bingo hall, was filled with more than one hundred worshipers, about average for a Saturday night. Most were women. Almost everyone was standing in front of black metal folding chairs. Maroon indoor/outdoor carpeting ran between the walls. There was nothing—not even a cross—on the whitewashed walls. Many of the male congregants wore coats and ties. The women wore dresses and skirts.

All had started to sway. The first couple came forward to witness for their sins. He wore a brown polyester three-piece suit with white pinstripes, a purple shirt with a high collar, and tan loafers. She wore a black dress with a scoop neck, wide red plastic belt, and two-inch black heels.

The couple had their arms intertwined. Preacher Seymour held his hands above their heads.

"Oh God, our heavenly Father," he intoned. "Let these two be saved. Bring them into Thy household and keep them from the wickedness that threatens to devour them on both sides."

He pressed both lightly on their foreheads, and they staggered back.

"To the Lord, all things are possible," Preacher Seymour shouted.

The male witness fell to one knee. Shouts of "hallelujah" and "amen" rose from the congregation.

Amos looked around. Near the back, he saw the inspector. Their eyes met. Amos nodded and smiled. Will nodded back.

Maybe some good could come out of this inundation, Amos thought.

With that, he began to sense the Spirit in himself.

He began to sway. It had been months since Amos had witnessed. He had a feeling that would change tonight.


Will had been curious about Pentecostal services for years. The number of Pentecostal churches in the area had grown from just a couple to a dozen or more over the past twenty years. He'd always assumed that those who went were lost, desperate, or just stupid.

Then came the invitation from Amos. He wasn't sure why, but Will felt he needed to go. If he gained the big miner's trust, maybe he'd learn about the inundation.

He entered after the service had already started and crept along the back wall. He saw the big miner near the front on the left side. Amos already seemed to be in a trance. With growing discomfort, Will watched the service get more heated and louder.

He was just beginning to think he should leave when Amos appeared at his side.

"First time ain't easy," the big miner said.

"Yeah," Will said.

"Come witness with me," Amos said, and he reached for Will's hand.

"Uh," was all Will managed. He was so surprised that he allowed himself to be led to the aisle.

Amos raised their clasped hands and shouted snatches from an old revival hymn: "What will wash my sins away . . . nothing but the blood, nothing but the blood of Jesus."

They began a slow, rhythmic march forward, possessed by Amos's spiritual ecstasy. Will felt his face flush and adrenaline surge through his body. His palms grew wet. He couldn't remember ever feeling more embarrassed. He looked down at the maroon carpeting and tried to breathe more easily. Women and men reached out from the pews and, their fingers splayed, pressed their palms onto his right shoulder.

Will looked right and saw a bald, elderly man with few teeth wearing a zip-up gray shirt that was open halfway down his chest. The man's white chest hair spilled out of his shirt, and Will found himself staring at the shrunken chest like he would at a woman displaying generous cleavage.

He looked away, closed his eyes for a second, and then looked up. The preacher was holding his hands up, waiting for them. He thought briefly of Rob and how he would laugh his ass off at the whole situation.

"Jesus," Will whispered to himself. Rob would have done better than that, he thought. "Jesus!" he shouted.

Amos chimed in with "Nothing but the blood! Nothing but the blood of Jesus!" and the two fell into a call-and-response between "Jesus!" and "the blood!" The volume roared up into the gabled roof of the little church.

Just as the two reached the altar, the preacher stepped onto one of the metal chairs.

"Take them, Lord," he shouted. "Receive them!"

The preacher put his palm on Amos's forehead, and the big man fell back. Two men behind Amos caught his body and lowered him gently to the floor. Amos looked like an epileptic having a seizure.

Will looked back toward the preacher, who stooped toward him. Will thought the preacher was about to kiss him on the forehead, but he stopped just short and simply blew.

Hands grabbed his shoulders and cradled his head, and Will let himself be lowered backward to the ground. Bodies lay limp around the altar. Some rose speaking in tongues. Others rose quietly and walked back to the chairs.

Amos had stopped shouting. The big miner was still shaking, but now he was babbling unintelligibly, his eyes closed and arms raised. Will looked up at the people standing around him. A woman was kneeling near the wall, sobbing. The preacher dropped to one knee quite near Will's head.

In the midst of this strange chorus, Will heard the preacher say, quite distinctly, "Hear me, Inspector. Hear me."

Will turned his head to look directly at the elderly man.

The preacher's eyes were closed. He put one hand on Will's forhead and whispered fiercely, "The map you seek is at Joe and Gaynell's store. Go there," he said.

It seemed to come out of nowhere. Will swiveled his eyes around toward a few of the worshipers near them, but none seemed to have taken note.

"What map?" Will asked in a conversational tone that he hoped would not be overheard by the others.

But the preacher had thrust his arms to the ceiling and was shouting, "Salvation! Jesus! Salvation!" He rose to his feet again. Will stared at him. Next to Will, Amos finally seemed to run out of gas and fell silent. The big miner opened his eyes and rolled to his feet. Will got up, too.

Two women had started their trek down the aisle, their arms linked. Will realized that his turn at the altar was over. He looked at Amos, who seemed drunk or dazed. Will grabbed the big miner's arm and led him to the side of the church.

Amos leaned against the wall. Will turned to watch the service mostly to give the big man a moment to compose himself.

When he turned back, Amos seemed to have recovered.

Will patted him on the back.

"That was somethin'," Will said.

Amos looked at Will but didn't say anything.

"Did you hear the preacher?" Will asked.

Amos just stared at him.

"I mean, what he said about the map?" Will amended.

Amos blinked.

One of the women who had walked down the aisle started shouting "Jesus" again, let out a scream, and fainted. Will and Amos looked toward the noise. Amos pushed himself away from the wall and hustled over to help carry the limp woman out of the church.

Will followed.

Amos stood while others fanned the woman and slapped her hand. She revived and made an exhausted smile of gratitude for those around her just as Preacher Seymour appeared. "You all right, child?" he asked. The woman nodded.

Will couldn't help himself. "Preacher, sir, you mentioned something about a map," he said.

"Pardon me?" Preacher Seymour said, a concerned look on his face.

"In there. When we were, ah, testifying. You mentioned a map and a store, Joe and Gaynell's. What—"

"Sir, I know of no map or such a store. I'm afraid I say quite a few things when I am in the throes of the Spirit. And if you'll pardon me, I must return."

The man gave a small, strangely formal bow and headed back inside. "But . . ." Will said and looked at Amos, whose impassive face showed no acknowledgment of just how bizarre the situation was. Amos nodded at Will and went back into the church, too. Will almost said something to Amos, but the big miner was gone too quickly.

Will looked back at the reviving woman, who was now laughing. He walked quietly around the small group surrounding her and out into the parking area. He reached his truck and, with a surge of near-panic, gunned his engine and fled.


Amos woke in the middle of the night. He watched the moonlight pour in through the bedroom window and reveal the outlines of his sleeping wife. Glenda was still beautiful. Her hips traced a full outline that sloped down to a narrow waist. Her long hair was still a rich, dark brown.

He loved her and always would, but he had no idea how to protect her.

He guessed that they wouldn't leave it alone, especially after trying to kill him. Something was bound to happen and pretty soon.

But he was out of ideas. Glenda wasn't about to leave, and he couldn't leave without her. He was stuck. He decided to give himself up to the situation and see what happened.

It was an attitude he had perfected over decades of mining. If the mountain wanted to take you, there was little you could do about it. Best thing was to pray to God and run like hell when the roof started to fall.

Glenda stirred.

She opened her eyes, focused on him, and smiled. He laughed quietly, smiled back, and stroked her hair.

"Howdy," Amos said.

She closed her eyes and put a hand on his chest.

Glenda had had a baby on her hip and two older children with her when he first met her at a gas station. She had seemed young to have so many children, but young mothers were not rare in eastern Kentucky.

She was at the counter. The two older boys had their hands curled around the counter's edge, and they were staring at candy bars Glenda had placed beside the cash register.

"Y'all sure, now? Ben, you want this'n? And you, too, Eli?"

She waited for both boys to give unambiguous nods. Amos was behind her, but she showed no sign that she knew or cared. Her whole focus was on the boys.

"All right then." She laid a dollar bill onto the counter.

The baby stared at Amos.

A clerk took the dollar and gave Glenda back a dime. Amos raised one eyebrow at the baby, who promptly screwed up its face and cried.

"Oh sweetie," Glenda said. When the baby hid its face in Glenda's breast—clearly hiding from Amos—she turned on the stranger.

"Sorry," Amos mumbled. "I, ah . . ."

"It's okay, it's okay, Abby," Glenda said. She put her lips to the baby's head and bounced her.

"I can see you got a way with women," Glenda said, a laugh in her eyes.

Amos smiled.

"Aunt Glenda, can we get another?"

It was one of the older boys.

Glenda turned on the boy.

"Eli, you know you only get one. Now let's get out the store."

Glenda turned back to Amos and saw that he had a six-pack in his hand.

"Don't hurt yourself, cowboy," she said, and held the door for the two preschoolers.

Amos was smitten. Glenda would later admit that she knew exactly who he was, but at that moment he was lost. He ended up buying a can of Skoal chewing tobacco just to keep the clerk busy while he figured out how to ask Glenda's last name.

While digging a bill out of his wallet, Amos blurted out, "That, ah, Glenda, where?"

"Beg pardon?" the clerk said.

A middle-aged woman was now behind Amos in line. Amos chewed his lip. Everyone paused.

Amos cleared his throat.

"She live around here?" Amos asked.

"Who?" the clerk said.

"That's Glenda Petrie," the woman behind Amos offered. "Lives up Lick Creek. Those are her sister's children."

"Oh yeah," Amos said.

The woman smiled.

"She's a good girl."

Amos flushed.

"Thank you," he said and floated out of the store.

A week later, Amos drove up Lick Creek, wondering if he'd see her. It was a glorious summer day. Someone had planted sunflowers along the road, and they were ablaze in yellow. Amos slowed as he passed the Petrie place. It was an older house but had two stories and a nice front yard. He turned around about a half mile later.

Just after passing the Petrie place for the second time, Amos slowed. Ahead, Glenda was walking in the middle of the road. She glanced behind her when he crept up, but she made no move to get out of the way.

He watched her walk. She was knockout pretty, and she walked like she knew it. In fact, Amos thought, her walk was sassy enough to convey that she knew that Amos knew that she knew that she was pretty, but she didn't care.

He smiled at all the "knews" on his mind.

She finally wandered to the side of the road and looked at him full-on, a smile on her face. He stopped beside her.

"I heard you asked who I was," Glenda said.

Amos swallowed.

"You gonna ask me out?" she said, mischief on her face.

"You wanna go out sometime?" Amos almost whispered.

"Sure. Why don't we go get us some ice cream right now?"

And she walked around to the passenger door, Amos chucked his bag in the back. She slid in, closed the door, and stuck her elbow out the window like it was her car.

Amos stared at her.

"Well, let's go, cowboy," she said.

Amos let his foot off the brake and never again spent a day without her.

"Whatcha thinkin' about, cowboy?" Glenda asked back in the present. She gave him a sleepy smile.

"You," Amos said.

She lightly drew her fingernails across his chest. She closed her eyes again.

"Hm. Can't sleep?"

"No, ma'am."

"You got a job?"

"Not no more."

"Watcha gonna do?"

"Dunno."

She closed her eyes and nodded. She lifted her head and put it on his chest. She traced with her fingernails a delicate path to his underwear.

She picked up her head and let her breasts fall on his chest. She kissed him.

"You want me to go to my sister's, don'tcha?" she said, her lips less than an inch from his.

"Yes, ma'am," he said.

"You can't get rid of me that easy, cowboy," she said, and she kissed her way down his chest.

Some time later, Glenda rolled over and went back to sleep. Amos watched her for a while but his head was too full to sleep. The flood, a bad cop, an explosion, his wife's pills. There was no telling what plague might be visited upon him next.

And then tonight, God had spoken to him. Amos, though, couldn't figure out the message. He needed to think, which meant he needed to hunt. He got up, dressed, and tramped into the blackness.

Hours passed. Dawn arrived, and still Tessy slept.

*BAM!*

The door to the trailer slammed open and several men with automatic weapons poured in. Glenda had enough time to roll onto her side before the bedroom door flew open and a man stuck a rifle in her face.

"Stay down," the man shouted. "Where's your husband?"

Glenda was speechless.

"Where is he!"

"Don't know," she croaked.

The man turned to the others.

"Find him."

# CHAPTER TWENTY-THREE

S he ain't takin' her medicine again," Myrtle said when Will entered. Will paused as he hung up his coat. Just the other day, Myrtle, the office secretary, had been sobbing over Sam's death. Now she was back to talking about her mother's health. Poor Sam seemed forgotten.

Will nodded absently.

"I keep tellin' her she'll wind up back in the hospital," Myrtle said with an exasperated air. "She won't listen!"

Will had learned some years before not to make inquiries or even sympathetic noises when Myrtle made these pronouncements. Any encouragement and Myrtle would launch into a soliloquy without end.

Will kept nodding and started back to his office. He stopped.

"Oh, uh, Myrtle?" Will asked.

"Yeah?" she said eagerly.

"Ever hear of Joe and Gaynell's, some kind of store?" Will said.

"Whose it?"

"Joe and Gaynell's."

Myrtle eyed him suspiciously.

"Whatcha need?"

"Oh, it's, uh, you know. Lookin' for an old mining thing. A tool folks used to use," Will said, reddening.

"Nope. Never heard of 'em. You tell me whatcha looking for, and I might likely be able to find it."

"Oh, that's all right. Thanks." Will retreated to his office.

He unlocked the door and flipped on the fluorescent lights. The room was small—about 250 square feet. There was a desk and three chairs on the right and a bookcase on the left.

Newspapers, catalogs, and sticky notes covered his desk.

Will sighed and dropped into his chair.

He looked at the bookcase, got up, and retrieved an agency phone directory and brought it back to the desk. He paged through it, squinting. He picked up the phone.

"Mine Safety and Health Administration," someone answered.

"Charlie Tillinghast, please," Will said.

"Hold, please."

A few seconds later, Will heard several rings.

"This is Charlie."

"Hey, Charlie, it's Will Murphy from the Hazard office."

"Will Murphy. Long time. What can I do for you?"

"You got anyone I might be able to call over at Bethlehem to ask if they got some old mine maps?"

"How old?"

"I dunno. Twenties? Thirties?"

There was a snort.

"You gotta be kidding. From Bethlehem? You can call their operations guy, Sanford Teeley, but I can tell you right now they are not going to have your map. Not a chance."

"You got a number for this guy?" Will asked.

"Yeah, just a second." Will heard the sound of a drawer opening.

"This have anything to do with that inundation down there?"

"Maybe."

"Here it is." Tillinghast gave him the number.

"Thanks."

"Listen, Will. I think they were thinking this investigation wouldn't be much of a deal, you know, that it would be pretty straightforward."

"Yeah, it seems to be. Just, you know, checkin' a few things."

"Sure, whatever you need to do."

"All right," Will said. "Take care."

"Yeah, you, too."

Will hung up.

He sat in his chair for a moment staring at the phone. There was a knock. Will looked up to see Lucius Haverman, the district director, standing in his door.

"Morning," Haverman said.

"Morning," Will answered.

"Just checking on that Blue Gem investigation."

"Still working on it."

Haverman nodded. Nominally, Haverman had no power over Will.

"You're done with the mine, though, right?" Haverman said.

"Think so."

"All right, I'm gonna release the site back to the company today. It'll probably take 'em a couple weeks to get it back on line. And we'll inspect again before they start production."

"Makes sense. They ever find that head?"

Haverman shook his head.

Will whistled.

"You need any help?"

This was the second attempt in less than two minutes by someone at MSHA to get Will to wrap up his investigation. Will wondered what Paul was telling people about him. Paul didn't need to stretch the truth to get people concerned. Will had not been doing a bang-up job. Never had.

"Don't think so," Will said, still pleasantly.

Haverman nodded again and pursed his lips.

"Think you'll have it done in the next couple of weeks?"

"Hope to." All smiles.

"All right, partner." Haverman tapped the door again and ambled away, his message delivered.

"Hey," Will called, and Haverman appeared again.

"Yeah?"

"Ever hear of Joe and Gaynell's store?" Will asked. Haverman seemed to know everyone in the mining industry, sometimes a bit too well. He was the perfect person to ask.

Haverman shook his head.

"All right. Sorry," Will said,

Haverman looked at Will curiously as he turned to go.

Will stroked his chin. He sighed. He picked up the phone. He quickly reached Sanford Teeley, who, as predicted, laughed at the very thought that he might have an eastern Kentucky Bethlehem mine map from the 1920s.

"You realize how many times we have reorganized this company since then?" Teeley asked.

"Y'all don't have a library or some records room?"

"Sure we did. We got rid of it ten, fifteen years ago."

"All right, thank you for your time."

"Sure. Call anytime," Teeley said with a chuckle.

Will hung up. He sat for a moment again. He picked up the phone and dialed.

"What listing?"

"In Hazard, Kentucky?"

"Yes, what's your listing?"

"I'd like the number for Joe and Gaynell's store?"

"What's the last name?"

"I dunno. Could be just Joe, *J-O-E*, and Gaynell's. I don't know how to spell that, but probably starts with *G-A-Y* or *I*."

Will heard some clacking.

"Nothing listed under Joe and Gay anything, sir."

"Okay," Will said and hung up.

Will stared at the ceiling. He sucked his teeth. He retrieved a large file sitting on the corner of his desk, the transcripts from his interviews with the miners. He took a yellow highlighter from a desk drawer and started reading.

At first, the cops scoured the hilltop around the trailer. When Glenda told them that Amos was probably out hunting, they came back and lay in wait for at least another hour.

The whole time, Glenda sat on the floor of her bedroom, her hands cuffed behind her back.

Finally, they gave up and systematically destroyed his and Glenda's home. Glenda watched as a man took each drawer of her bedroom dresser and dumped its contents on the floor. He threw the empty drawers in a pile, and since they were made of pressboard, several broke.

They pulled off her bedding—tearing the fitted sheet—and took apart her bed.

There were several crashes that sounded like the contents of the kitchen cabinets were being chucked to the ground.

"I got a whole shitload of drugs in the bathroom here," a voice shouted. "Scripts."

"I tole ya," another shouted. One of them came back into the bedroom. Glenda recognized him. "Jones" was stenciled across the front of his black jacket.

"Mrs. Blevins, we're arresting you on suspicion of trafficking in controlled substances. But we need your husband."

Glenda just shook her head.

"When does he usually get home?" Jones asked.

"Shoulda been here by now."

"It'd be better for the both of you if you told us where he is."

Glenda shrugged.

"All right, let's get her out of here," said a man who peered in from the living room. "I believe you boys can pick her up."

Jones came over and grabbed her left arm. Another man reached down and grabbed her right.

They carried her out between them, the cuffs digging painfully into her wrists and her feet dragging along the floor. As they went down the steps outside, Glenda tried to raise her feet slightly so they wouldn't bang painfully, but she succeeded only in levering her knees further down. They threw her onto the backseat of a police cruiser, the second time in less than a week that she'd been deposited like that.

As before, she lay there for some time. Finally, someone pulled her left arm and brought her to a sitting position. It was Jones again.

"Well, Mrs. Blevins, I told you I was worried about your nerve condition, didn't I?" he said with a smile.

Glenda looked around. They were twenty yards from the trailer, which was swarming with men. She could see through the trailer's front window someone peering into her kitchen cabinets. Two more men were visible through the open door. Another was outside the trailer, looking up into the hills. Jones seemed to be alone with her.

"Now, we have reason to believe that your husband has been trafficking marijuana," Jones said.

He was standing outside the cruiser, his black helmet pushed back from his blond hair and his left arm resting on top of the cruiser's open door. He reached inside his black jacket and fished out a pack of cigarettes.

With one hand, he shook the pack and mouthed a cigarette. He put the pack back in his shirt, took out a lighter and lit the cigarette. His left hand remained motionless throughout the operation.

He was handsome, Glenda had to admit. But he seemed supremely aware of this fact. Glenda had the feeling someone was taking pictures, the way he was acting.

"Amos?" Glenda said.

"Thas right," Jones said.

"Selling drugs?"

"Thas what I said."

"It's a lie," Glenda said.

The cop smiled. "Mrs. Blevins, you should probably be more worried about yourself. You have a pharmacy worth of pills in that trailer, many of them controlled substances."

"They's all prescriptions my doctor tole me I needed."

"But you got four different doctors, Mrs. Blevins. One of 'em is Dr. Shrisrapan, and I'm sure he'll tell us that he didn't know about t' other doctors. He's mighty helpful that way," Jones said, nodding. "Thas medical fraud, yes, ma'am, it is."

Glenda scowled.

"What's this really about? That accident?" Glenda said, peering suspiciously at the officer. "What's Amos done? Didn't he save one of them fellers?"

Jones took a long drag on his cigarette and looked up toward the hills. He smoothed his jacket and straightened his gun belt.

The Inter-Agency Mountain Drug Task Force was a prestigious posting for two dozen officers from departments across eastern Kentucky. Squad members got top-notch training and the best equipment. More important, the squad brought in money. Police departments are allowed to seize any property suspected of being used in drug crimes. Even when suspects are acquitted, the unit gets to keep the money taken in property seizures.

Jones surveyed the Blevins's property. The trailer and land might net $20,000, and the truck would bring in another $2,000. That alone would justify the raid to his supervisors even without a conviction of Amos Blevins, against whom Jones had no intention of making a case.

"Mrs. Blevins, you can blame your husband for this," Jones said, not looking at her. "I told him that it would be a shame to involve you."

"What you want with him?"

"Want? Now?" Jones said, and looked back down at Glenda. He smiled. "Nice friendly talk. Just to talk, yes, sir."

He nodded his head several times and took another long drag on his cigarette. The cigarette was near its end, and Jones considered it for a moment and then flicked it over the front of the cruiser. He watched it tumble.

When he turned back, Amos was standing in front of him.

"Whatcha wanna talk about, Officer?" Amos asked.

Jones reached for his gun.

Glenda had never seen a man get his nose crushed. She would remember the sound for years—like a boot being pulled out of deep mud. Amos threw Jones into the well of the backseat, donned his black helmet, and assumed the officer's casual pose at the door of the cruiser.

Amos wasn't wearing a bulletproof vest or a black jacket, but his pose seemed to fit. The other officers were far enough away that no one heard the commotion or noticed anything amiss. Jones did not stir.

"Glenda, honey, I'm real sorry about this," Amos said.

"Oh baby, I know," Glenda said. She leaned out the door and put her forehead on his stomach.

"Come on," Amos said. "Let's go."

"No, sir," Glenda said, rolling her forehead across his belly. "They's gonna come after you now, and I cain't run like you do."

"Baby, they gonna lock you up. Maybe for a while."

"I need to lose some weight anyways, honey," Glenda said and looked up at him. "If I come with ya, they'd just catch us both."

Amos nodded.

"Hold on just a second," Amos said.

In no obvious hurry, he ambled to the back of the cruiser. When he returned, he held a dead possum dripping blood. He tossed it on top of Jones.

"Shame to mess up that purdy uniform," Glenda said.

"You'll tell him how to dress it?"

"Parsnips or potatoes?" Glenda responded brightly.

Amos put his hands on Glenda's shoulders and closed his eyes. His lips moved in prayer. He kissed her forehead, doffed the helmet, and was gone.


"You got a visitor," Myrtle said when Will returned from lunch. In the midst of hanging his coat, Will looked around. All four visitors' chairs—a sad plastic parade beside Myrtle's desk—were empty.

"She's outside in her truck, black Ford," Myrtle said. "Didn't seem happy."

"I got that effect on a lot of women."

Myrtle gave a brittle laugh.

Will hesitated, then decided not to put his coat back on. He opened the door, went outside and saw the pickup. The woman in the truck looked at Will. He nodded to her. She gathered her things.

Remaining outside, Will closed the door, keeping his hand on the doorknob. She got out of her truck and approached. He opened the door again.

"Come on in. We can go on back to my office."

Will was sure that he'd never seen the woman before. She remained silent. Will motioned for her to precede him. He unlocked his office and held the door for her. He edged past her to get behind his desk. They both sat.

"How can I help?" Will asked.

She had black shoulder-length hair and brown eyes. She wore an aqua blue blouse and shiny dark blue slacks of indeterminate material. Her mouth was set, more angry than sad.

"My name's Missy Hogg, Mr. Murphy."

They were both silent. Will raised his eyebrows.

"Yes, ma'am?"

She looked perplexed.

"It were my husband, Virgil, who shot hisself up on that mine bench."

"Of course. I'm so sorry. Terrible."

The image of the jagged edge of Virgil Hogg's forehead leapt before Will. He closed his eyes to banish it.

"He was a stubborn one, Virgil," she said.

They were quiet.

"But he loved Hell-for-Certain," she started again. "Said he'd never leave. Said they'd have to drag him out. They done that."

Quiet again.

"Mrs. Hogg, I'm sorry for your loss. Is there something I can do for you?"

"We's out of water up 'ere. Everybody is. The company's bringing us bottles, but you can't wash with that. Can't hardly flush. They're saying they don't got to do nothing else. Dee Singleton's tried drilling new wells, but it ain't working."

Quiet.

"Again, I'm very sorry. I'm still investigating the circumstances surrounding the inundation, of course, but I don't know what I can do for you," Will said, splaying his fingers.

"I heard you're brothers with the feller what owns Blue Gem."

"That's true."

"Somebody got to make Blue Gem do something. We can't live without water."

"Mrs. Hogg, me and my brother are not on the best of terms."

"Well, make 'em do it. You got the power, don'tcha?"

"Not over things like that. You want to talk with the Federal Office of Surface Mining or the Kentucky Division of Mine Reclamation and Enforcement. They deal with surface problems from mining. Not us."

"Uh-huh. They told me to see you. That you could do something," the woman said. Her mouth seemed to set even more firmly.

Will opened his mouth. Nothing came out.

"Mr. Murphy, my Virgil was right. We can't live like this. But he's gone, and I'm stuck with the mess. We got three kids, so's I can't shoot myself. We got to move, but I can't leave with nothin'."

Will nodded.

"Look, I know somebody at OSM. You want that I call him?" Will asked.

"I sure would appreciate it," Mrs. Hogg said.

"Give me your number, and I'll get back at you and tell you what he says," Will said, lifting a pen from his desk.

"We lost our phone."

"Oh. Well, I can come up and see you. I gotta be around there anyway."

The woman nodded. Will rose. She looked at him appraisingly and then rose as well.

"Promise I'll look into it," Will said.

The woman turned to leave the office. Will trudged along behind her. He stopped at the end of the hallway.

"Bye-bye now," Will said. "Promise I'll call ya—I mean, come see ya."

She gave Will a withering look and left. Will blew out his cheeks. He walked back to his office and flipped his Rolodex. He retrieved a card and picked up the phone.

"Hey, it's Will Murphy at MSHA."

"Will Murphy at MSHA," the voice said, drawing out the "aaaww" in the agency's name. "I used to know a Will Murphy from MSHA. Heard he got arrested for showin' his willy to little girls."

"Yeah, sorry, I owed you a call. Listen, I need to talk to you about something. Buy you lunch at France's tomorrow?"

"Lemme check my schedule," the man joked. "The governor just cancelled so it appears that I'm free."

"See you at noon."


Amos sat for hours wedged between two trees, clear lines of sight in almost every direction. A soft rain was falling, and he was soon soaked to the skin. He couldn't move.

The tasks before him were overwhelming.

He would have to hide for weeks, maybe months, maybe years to keep away from the cops and the criminals. He had to find a way to free Glenda from jail. And, more than anything, he had to return to that glorious state that had allowed him for the first time to hear God.

"Save my mountains" could not have been clearer. The words and the voice had filled him with a sense of belonging and awe that he had never felt before. The glory of that secret moment while witnessing with the inspector had left him happier than he had ever been.

But slowly, the meaning of the words had begun to worry Amos. What did it mean? Which mountains? Save them from what?

It was an impossible task, one of several now facing Amos. He could not move.

It was the mist that finally delivered him. It crept up the hill, hiding the ground a few dozen yards away. Winter mist is a fragile and wonderful thing. The temperature and humidity must be just right. The mist rarely rises more than a few feet off the ground. And it can disappear in seconds with the fall of just a few degrees in temperature.

Such a mist always made Amos remember working as a boy in the tobacco barns of western Kentucky. A farmer had once told Amos that winter mist is the breath of Jesus. Farmers watched for it, knowing that it brings the tobacco leaves in their barns "in order," or ready for stripping.

Quite suddenly, Amos had somewhere to go.

# CHAPTER TWENTY-FOUR

It took him all night and several rides to hitchhike to Todd County, Kentucky—about six hours and another world from Hazard. A fat mailman told him of a farm about two miles outside of town that would likely be stripping that day. He walked past the town cemetery, past a Mennonite school, and past acres soon to be planted with corn and soybeans.

The mist was gone. It cleared early on the Pennyroyal, the western third of Kentucky. But the ground was wet, and Amos thought the tobacco was likely ready.

The mailman had described a farm with a two-story white farmhouse off to the right, two more barns nearby, and a tobacco barn in the midst of a soybean field to the left.

The tobacco barn was nearest the road. Amos needed no sign to find it. Tobacco barns are remarkably uniform. Few are less than one hundred years old. Nearly all are rectangular with gable roofs, boards so weathered that they look like driftwood, and long, vertical openings for ventilation.

Several pickups were parked in front. Light seeped from the barn's cracks. Dawn was still an hour away when Amos pushed open the door and walked in.

The barn was full of drying tobacco plants. Spiked onto ancient, hand-split oak sticks, the plants made the barn look like an upside-down aquarium. In its midst were three bare tables with legs made from saw-horses and tops from sheets of plywood.

Two small Hispanic men crouched to the left. A white man wearing a green John Deere cap, blue jeans, and a blue, short coat looked around at Amos. Deep crow's-feet creased the skin around his eyes, which fastened onto Amos.

"Someone said you was looking for strippers," Amos said.

"Yuh," the man said and stared some more at Amos.

Amos unshouldered his backpack and looked down.

"Who are you?" the farmer said.

"Andy Hughes," Amos said. "And I could use a job."

"Yuh," the farmer said and laughed. "Boy, how long has it been since you done this?"

"Been a few years."

"You from the mountains, ain't ya?"

"Yes, sir."

"I ain't had one a' you fellas in ten years. Been nothin' but Mexicans since."

Amos was quiet.

"Even Mexicans are getting hard to come by," the farmer said. "You can start with the reds."

Amos nodded and set his backpack against a barn wall. He walked to where the Mexicans squatted, and he stood next to them. They seemed to take no notice of him. The barn smelled like a barbecue.

"All right, Pablo, *vamanos arriba*," the farmer said.

The younger of the two Hispanics rose and climbed to the first tier of tobacco plants. Amos, the other Hispanic, and the farmer walked beneath them to the edge of the barn.

The man in the rafters put his feet on the lowest tier of wood supports. The distance between the rafters was about three and a half feet, and it was a stretch for the small man. He bent at the waist and lifted one of the sticks laden with six plants. He handed it down to Amos, who handed it to the other Hispanic.

That man and the farmer pulled the six-foot plants off the end of the stick and laid them carefully on the first of the three tables. More laden sticks followed, and the operation continued.

When the pile of plants on the table reached several feet high, the farmer said, "okay, okay." The man in the rafters came down. He had cleared about a quarter of one row. There were six more rows on that tier and two more full tiers in the barn.

"All right, let's get started," the farmer said.

One of the Hispanics picked up a tobacco plant and started stripping the bottom leaves with his left hand. The leaves were a light, bright brown. He flipped the stalk to the next table and then twisted the leaves into a bundle or "hand" that he tied together with what seemed to be the largest of the plant's bottom leaves. He put the hand into a wide, flat basket behind him. He started again on a new plant.

The farmer and the other Hispanic man took the partly stripped stalk and simultaneously stripped off more leaves. They each made hands, put the bundles in baskets, and went back to stripping. The farmer tossed the plant to Amos.

The leaves left on the stalk were near the top and were smaller and reddish. Amos copied the others, only his was a far smaller and redder hand. He laid each bundle in a basket behind him in a stack—away from those made by the others.

Like riding a bike, Amos thought, your hands and feet don't forget.

Amos threw up about midmorning. He managed to make it outside just in time, and he didn't think anybody else knew. But the farmer had a slight smile when Amos came back in.

"Don't lick your fingers or wipe your eyes," the farmer said. "The nicotine'll get ya."

His stomach had steadied by noon when the farmer's wife brought in food from the farmhouse. He had not eaten in more than a day.

He went to his pack as a diversion, not sure what to do if the farmer failed to offer dinner to the hands. It had been a tradition when he had worked the fields as a boy, but maybe that was no longer true. He busied himself checking and rechecking some of his things.

"Ain't you hungry?" the farmer asked with a smile.

They had swept off the first table, and the farmer's wife had set several plates.

Amos nodded and came over.

Stripping was not nearly as hard as cutting tobacco, summer work that remained the hardest job Amos had ever done. Still, he was tired and hungry, eager for the break and for the food.

"This here's Eda," the farmer said to Amos. "This is Andy."

"My husband said you're from the mountains."

Amos nodded.

"Ain't too talkative, are ya?" She laughed.

Amos shook his head agreeably.

Husband and wife seemed always ready to laugh. Being so close to selling their tobacco crop, which represented most of their yearly cash income, likely added to their cheer. But Amos thought their good humor didn't depend on money.

"Where you stayin'?" Eda asked.

"Down the road."

"Where?" she said and laughed again. "Andy, we got nothin' but Mennonite farms around us nowadays. And they won't take too kindly to a stranger camping on their land."

Amos had no response.

"We got some old nigger cabins on the north part of the farm here. They's overgrown and the roofs've mostly fallen in, but one of 'em's got a roof and hearth. You could stay there."

Amos wasn't sure whether to acknowledge his earlier lie. But then again, he needed someplace to stay.

" 'Preciate it."


"The good people of Hell-for-Certain are fucked," the man from the federal Office of Surface Mining said as he bit down on a fried chicken breast.

With his mouth full, he added, "It's hell for them, I'm certain of that. But there's nothing I can do." His laugh died when he noticed that Will did not seem to find it funny.

His name was Ephrom Mainard. He was medium height with a full, red beard. He wore the environmentalist's uniform: Nike hiking boots, a plaid shirt, and blue jeans. A Gore-tex jacket was hung over the chair. His brown hair was gathered in a thin ponytail.

Mainard had started at the Mine Safety and Health Administration about the same time as Will but had transferred to OSM after a roof fall during an inspection nearly killed him. He said he couldn't face going underground again. Will suspected he'd moved because inspectors at OSM did even less than those at MSHA.

"Nothing? You can't even pipe in some water from someplace, or send out a drilling team?"

It was Tuesday, so they had both ordered fried chicken. If it had been Wednesday, it would have been meat loaf; Thursday, the turkey special; Friday, chicken-fried steak.

On the outside, France's looked like a down-at-the-mouth diner. It looked that way on the inside, too, but the food made up for it. Will had already finished his chicken and was waiting for Ephrom to finish his so they could order pie, a dessert for which France's was famous.

"I could put in a request, but I can tell you now that it wouldn't even get past my supervisor."

"Why?"

"They just don't qualify," Ephrom said, and he pushed his plate away.

Will looked around for the waitress, although he still hadn't decided whether to get the banana cream or apple pie à la mode.

"I'm gonna have to tell this lady some'm, and 'don't qualify' is not gonna cut it. She's a tough old bird. Can you tell me more?"

"All those folks were getting their water from an old mine, not from an underground aquifer. They shouldn't have been sipping out of a deep mine in the first place."

"But Eph," Will said, shaking his head. "They were sipping out of that deep mine because their wells got screwed up way back in the twenties by mining, and you guys are supposed to help folks that's water is lost 'cause of mining, aren't you?"

Will managed to catch the waitress's eye, no small feat. Like all of France's staff, she was well over sixty and moved slower than cold chocolate syrup.

"I'll have the banana cream pie and some coffee," Will said before she even arrived.

"Make that two," Mainard said.

The waitress—her uniform said "Belle"—began clearing plates. Will watched her with some unease, feeling he should help.

"The thing is," Mainard continued, "a lot of those houses were built in the forties. Their first and only wells were sunk into that old mine. There hasn't been any good water left to find up there for seventy years."

Will nodded.

"So fix the ones that were built first. Or just run a water line up there and save 'em all."

"Yeah," Mainard snorted.

Will just looked at him.

"Do you realize how expensive that is? It'd cost us four million dollars upfront, and another, I don't know, seven hundred and fifty thousand dollars every year after that. There's only twenty-five, thirty homes up there. We'd spend more on each house in the first year than any one of 'em was worth."

Will sighed.

"So you're telling me they're fucked," Will said.

"Been trying to tell you that all day."

Will looked out the window for a moment. The pies and coffee arrived.

Mainard took a forkful of pie, put it in his mouth, and then pointed the fork at Will.

"You know, you could try to get a story in the *Courier-Journal*," Mainard said. "It's amazing how much that can change things. The problem is the paper just closed its Hazard bureau, and I don't see them sending a reporter all the way out from Louisville to write about water problems on Hell-for-Certain Creek. Still, you could try."

Will nodded.

"Or—and I can't believe I'm telling you this—you could call KFTP and have them picket us," Mainard said, laughing. "Drives my supervisors nuts. Might get us to spend that money, although I doubt it."

"KFTP?"

"Do-good outfit opposed to every mine we permit." Mainard shov-eled in another heaping pile of whipped cream and banana pudding.

"They lose just about every time, but once in a while they get some-thing done," Mainard said. "I think Tessy knows one of their coordi-nators, Lauren something."

"Oh, that's right." Will perked up.

Mainard gave Will a quizzical look.

"Somebody told me you two were getting divorced."

Will nodded.

"And that's how we got Helen as our starting point guard?" Main-ard added.

Will looked out the window.

"If only one of my kids was such a good ballplayer," Mainard said, smiling. "I could use a break from the wife."

"What?" Will said.

"Nothing, Will. Sorry. Probably shouldn't joke about it."

Mainard quickly finished the last of his pie.

"Thanks for the lunch, Will. Hope it helped."

"Oh yeah. No, I appreciate it." They both rose. Will got out his wallet. Mainard stood a few steps away as Will counted out the bills.

"I never asked you why you cared about this," Mainard said as Will laid the money on the table. They started out of the restaurant.

"I got assigned the investigation."

Mainard held the door for him.

"What's there to investigate?"

"Nine men died."

"That's true, but they've lost that mine for months. And they can't be so stupid not to drill bore holes in front of a mine that deep," Mai-nard said, still standing in front of the restaurant.

"Probably right."

"'Sides, your brother runs that company, doesn't he?"

"Yup."

"You pissed at him or some'm?"

Will shrugged. "Listen, have you ever heard of a Joe and Gaynell's store around here?"

"What?"

"Joe and Gaynell's? Some kind of store?"

"No," Mainard said simply.

"Well, I'll see ya'," Will said and waved as he walked to his truck.

On his second day, Amos didn't throw up. His hands, sore despite years of coal mining, stopped bothering him. The farmer no longer checked the hands of tobacco Amos had stripped, and Amos began to lose himself in the work.

Even better, one of the Hispanic men failed to show, so Amos was more vital to the operation. If he could prove himself—and he felt he was well on his way—he could probably get another two months of work on the neighboring farms.

Amos's heart skipped a beat when the farmer asked him to get up into the barn's rafters. He had yet to go higher than the second tier—the little Hispanic guy took the third—but he still balked a bit at the height. There was nothing like it in coal mining.

The farmer's wife had even given him some bread and cheese, so Amos had managed to have supper and breakfast.

At the end of the day, the farmer asked Amos to finish up while he drove the Mexican back to his bungalow at another farm. Another good sign, Amos thought. Amos finished making hands out of the last few tobacco sticks. He was ordering the stacks of baskets when he noticed the flashing lights.

He crept to one of the barn's ventilation slats and peered up at the farmhouse. There were two state police cruisers in the driveway, their emergency lights piercing the gathering gloom.

One of the troopers was talking to the farmer, who had returned. The other was staring directly at the tobacco barn, a shotgun in his hand. If Amos left by either the front or the back door of the barn, the trooper would see him.

He was trapped.

# CHAPTER TWENTY-FIVE

Will drove out Highway 15 back toward Fleming-Neon. He turned off the highway well short of town, crossed the railroad tracks, and slowed to a crawl. He knew vaguely where Frank Royals lived, but he'd never actually been there.

He passed a brown house with pressboard siding and a large parking area with two cars in it. He stopped, backed up, and drove into the parking area. There was a door just in front of the cars, but Will saw a worn trail going toward the back of the house, and he followed it.

The back of the house was framed in grooved plywood. The gravel path ended in a somewhat sad entryway that looked like the end of a mudroom. Will knocked, and someone shouted, "Come in."

He walked into a cramped but typical-looking barbershop. There was a large mirror on one wall, two barber's chairs to the left, and three visitors' chairs along the right wall. The floor was black-and-white-checked linoleum.

The framing was less than square, and the drop ceiling was graying. But all in all, the bright, clean room was such a contrast to the tired, unfinished exterior that Will almost laughed.

A man in one of the chairs was just getting out as Will entered, and the barber—who had to be Frank since this was Frank's Place—gave him change out of his pocket. Everyone seemed to pause when Will entered. There were four people in the room, and Will was the only one who was white.

Frank completed his transaction, and the customer headed toward the door. Will stepped aside to let the man out.

"I'm Will—"

"I know who you are," Frank said. "You, Rob Crane, and Lefty Smitz made up probably the best back court Fleming-Neon ever had. If y'all had had a real center, you woulda gone a long way."

"Uhm-hm," said the man sitting in one of the visitors' chairs. Will couldn't place him but he was familiar.

"Thanks," Will said.

"Too bad about Rob Crane," Frank said.

"Yeah."

"You here for a cut?"

"No, actually, I'm here about Rob. His wife, Mary, said he come in here about a month before he died."

"I suppose that's so," Frank said. "But then again, Rob come in here just about every month. Fact, I was expecting him about the time he died."

"Yeah, well, you did somethin' for him that last cut that Mary said changed him. Said he came home a different guy. Fewer worries. Can you tell me why?"

He wore a short white coat over a T-shirt and black jeans. He had on white, newish running shoes. His hair was close-cropped, his face clean-shaven. The room had the tangy smell of men's cologne and shaving cream. Frank looked at his visitor then turned away to his mirror and started brushing one of his clippers.

"No, can't say as I can," Frank said with his back to Will. He glanced again at his visitor.

Will looked closely at the visitor and realized that he had been the other guy in Dee Singleton's drilling rig. The guy who'd thrown up after Virgil Hogg shot himself.

"You work for Dee Singleton, don'tcha? You were there when that guy killed himself."

"Yup," the man said.

"Did you tell Rob somethin' that made him different?"

"You an inspector for the MSHA, ain't ya?"

"Yes. But that's not . . . I mean, I just want to know about Rob."

"You got burned in that explosion, right? You were the one what lived, along with Rob."

"In the Blue Dog blast? Yeah." Will blinked several times. "Is that what you told him about? Something about the explosion?"

The man was silent. Frank still had his back turned to Will but had stopped brushing his clippers and made no pretense of his interest in the conversation.

"He deserves to know, too," Frank said, looking sideways at the visitor.

The man shook his head.

"He's an inspector," the man said.

"Look, that was years ago. I mean, the statute of limitations on anything you tell me is long gone," Will said.

The man continued to shake his head.

"Dee drilled the bore holes for Blue Dog, too, didn't he?" Will said. "I remember him being around back then."

The man just stared at Will.

"Oh, come on. He was my best friend," Will said.

"Was," the man answered.

Frank turned back around. Will looked at him in appeal. Frank shook his head. Will slumped.

"Shit," Will said.

They all stood in silence.

"You know where to find me," Will finally said, and he walked slowly out.

He sat in his truck for several moments wondering what he should do next. The sun was setting, so he had no thought of returning to the office. He put his forehead on the top of the steering wheel and closed his eyes. Finally, he sighed, started his truck, and headed home.

. . .

Amos had climbed into the rafters with his backpack and stepped over laden sticks to get to the side of the barn opposite the house. He figured he could squeeze out one of the air vents, but he worried that he might break a leg from the fall.

He edged back across the rafters to the other side of the barn to watch the officers. If they started walking toward the tobacco barn, he would return to the other side, chuck his pack out, and then risk the fall himself. He was having a hard time balancing with the pack on, but there was nothing for it.

The officer who had been speaking to the farmer turned away and started walking toward Amos. Amos took a step back toward his escape route when he saw the officer stop at his cruiser and get in. The guy with the shotgun got in the other cruiser. They headed back toward the road, their flashing lights disappearing over the hill.

Amos stood for a moment, almost unwilling to believe his good fortune. Then he climbed down.

The farmer came into the barn just as Amos made it to the ground.

"I don't think they're comin' back, Andy," he said and smiled. "I'm 'onna pay you now."

He took out a wad of bills.

"Twenty hours. We ain't talked about a rate, but I figure twenty dollars an hour'd be fair. You all right with that?"

Amos nodded. The rate was more than fair, but that's not what Amos wanted to know about.

"Here. Four hundred."

Amos pocketed the bills.

"You know, when I was a kid, there was a big old man from the mountains. Somewhere around Hazard. Had a beard like you. Quiet like you, too.

"'Cept he was missing most of a thumb," the farmer said and grabbed his own thumb. Amos blinked. "Said he'd spiked it onto a tobacco stick one time. Said they sewed it up in the field and he was back to spikin' 'fore they finished the row."

The farmer looked out the barn door into the growing darkness.

"First season I ever cut tobacco, he was my spiker. Matter of fact, he was my spiker till I got into my teens. We made a pretty good team.

"One of my first days in the fields, I got to feelin' pretty sick, and when we took a break, I went over to the Blue Hole over there. It's the biggest spring in the county. It's pretty deep and real cold," the farmer said, pointing with his thumb.

"I guess I passed out and fell in. That old guy must have been watching. He fished me out and brought me to. Saved my life."

The farmer began to laugh.

"Best part, though, is that he never told nobody. I'd rather'd died than have my old man know that I'd passed out cuttin' tobacco. And he never did know."

The farmer was quiet.

"One year that old guy just didn't show. Got no idea what happened to him."

The farmer looked up at Amos.

"Those state troopers said they was looking for a big man from the mountains. Beard. Said his name was Amos Blevins. Said he was wanted for selling drugs and beatin' up a Hazard police officer."

They were both quiet. Amos looked at his backpack.

"That's why Pablo—hell, I think that's his name"—the farmer laughed—"that's why he didn't come today. Already knew this mornin' they was lookin' for ya. Scared he's gonna get deported.

"He called you a Jonah. 'Yonah, Yonah,' he kept saying. Crazy bastard. What's that mean?" The farmer laughed again and looked at Amos, who shook his head.

"I barely got his buddy to come."

Again they were quiet.

"There's some railroad tracks about a half mile down the road. A freight goes by about one of the mornin'," the farmer said. "If you take a right along the tracks, there's a turn there where the train slows down. Always blows its whistle. Love that sound."

A horse on the nearest Mennonite farm whinnied.

"Here." The farmer handed Amos a plastic bag. "The wife fixed you some sandwiches."

Amos nodded and shouldered his backpack.

"Good luck to you."

The farmer held out his hand. Amos shook it.

"Thank you kindly," Amos said.

The farmer didn't release Amos's hand.

"That old man from Hazard? His name was Blevins."

The farmer turned away and walked out of the barn.

# CHAPTER TWENTY-SIX

Jumping trains sounds easy. It is not. Even a slow-moving train travels between five and fifteen miles per hour—somewhere between an easy jog and a breathless sprint.

A train taking a curve complains loudly, and the screeching can be disorienting. Figuring out which cars might prove companionable is difficult—particularly in the pitch black conditions required for successful hobo travel.

Ponder the question too long, and the train can quickly get out of sight. Jump too soon and the engineer is likely to spot you.

The train that passed through Todd County had only a handful of boxcars scattered among a parade of flat and tanker cars. After letting two boxcars pass, Amos set out after a green one that seemed to have a simple door mechanism.

As he ran alongside, Amos worked on the lock. His backpack was jumping, making both the jog and handwork mighty awkward. He finally got the door open and found he had almost no energy left for the jump. He made it, though, and slammed his head against a metal container inside.

After a moment's rest, Amos turned back to the door and pulled it most of the way closed, making it less likely that someone might check on him.

The train lurched violently, and the door that Amos had carefully left propped open slammed shut. Amos felt for several minutes around the door and its edges, but he could find no way to open it from the inside.

The car was cold and smelled of fish. It was filled with two metal semicircular containers and what appeared to be broken packing crates. There was a narrow place for Amos to stand between the containers, but it wasn't long enough to lie down.

Amos leaned back on one of the containers and fell asleep—again and again. By dawn, he was bone-cold and dispirited. The train seemed to be headed east, but it was moving no faster than ten miles per hour. He was down to his last sandwich. He had little water left. Light seeped into the car from dozens of holes, but he could tell little about the landscape outside.

He knew he could reassemble his rifle and find some way to shoot off the door, but that would attract attention. Even if it didn't, what would he do when he got off the train?

Amos needed a plan and not just for the next few days. He had run from eastern Kentucky, the police, and maybe even God. No, he realized that he had the order wrong. First God and then Glenda. If he figured out those two, he decided, the rest almost didn't matter.

He opened his Bible and turned to Revelations, the book Amos saw as the Bible's most mysterious, darkest, and most powerful. There was just enough light to read, and he did. For hours.

He came back again and again to the passages describing the end of time and the sounding of the seventh trumpet.

"The nations raged, but thy wrath came, and the time for the dead to be judged, for rewarding thy servants, the prophets and saints, and those who fear thy name, both small and great, and for destroying the destroyers of the earth."

"The destroyers of the earth" rolled around in his head. To Amos, it shouted "strip miners."

At some point, Amos fell asleep or fell into a trance. He wasn't sure which. He came to. He had not reached that place of clarity. Maybe he never would again. But his charge nonetheless seemed clearer to him. He would do something to slow the destroyers.

About when this thought distilled in his head, the train lurched again and the boxcar door—for no apparent reason—slid open.

Another sign, Amos decided. He jumped out.

The next morning, Will got back in his truck and instead of heading north to Hazard, he steered south on Highway 119 toward Kingdom Come. It was a beautiful drive through one of the only true valleys in eastern Kentucky, the birthplace of the Cumberland River.

He drove through several old company towns similar to the one in which he'd grown up. He finally stopped in Benham, whose tightly packed clapboard houses were surprisingly well preserved. Even its old downtown survived, and the company's old commissary had been turned into a mining museum that Will had always loved.

The museum mostly presented a sanitized version of mining, the better to attract industry funding. Its mock mine on the first floor suggested plenty of head room, and the equipment was first-day clean.

Will parked his truck in the museum parking lot and went in. He lingered in front of a picture of underground miners using mules. Such photos always made him smile. Having animals in the industrialized cacophony of a mechanized mine was unimaginable for any modern miner. It'd be like riding a horse on a superhighway.

When looking at such photos, Will often wondered how many of the men pictured had left mining alive. Thousands died annually in underground mines in the 1920s. Cave-ins, fires, and explosions were routine. Some explosions were so powerful that they were felt for miles and shot pieces of mining equipment hundreds of feet from mine entrances.

Will's own, now-rare experience—surviving a devastating explosion—was once common.

Will asked the cashier where he could find the curator. She pointed to a door marked "Employees Only." Will went in.

The door opened into what appeared to be a reception area. There was a desk with boxes on it and no chair behind it. There was another door. Will knocked lightly and opened that. It led to a corridor. The drop ceiling, present in the outer room, was gone. The only light in the corridor came from what looked like several office entries along the left-hand side.

"Hello?" Will called.

A man with salt-and-pepper hair popped his head out of an entryway halfway down the hall.

"Yes?"

"I'm looking for the curator," Will said.

"That would be me," the man said, smiling. "What can I do for you?"

"My name's Will Murphy. I'm an MSHA special investigator and . . . " Will started to explain.

"Oh," the man said and stepped all the way out into the hallway. "Please come in."

"Thanks," Will said and walked down the hallway.

He shook the man's hand. "Will Murphy," he said.

"Peter Goodnough. I'm the museum director."

"Nice to meet you, Mr. Goodnough," Will said.

"It's, uh, Doctor, actually," Goodnough said, bobbing his head. "I'm also a professor at Southeastern Community College, which, as you may know, owns the museum."

"Oh. Sorry."

They stood for a moment.

Goodnough looked a bit like Norm from the TV show *Cheers*. If he lost thirty pounds, he'd be called barrel-chested. His belly hung over a low-slung belt and pushed out his trousers so much that Will could see the white lining of his khakis. He wore a rumpled blue shirt and a blue jacket and didn't seem quite as relaxed as Norm.

"Let's go into my office," Goodnough said.

Boxes lined the walls. A bookcase was stuffed with small mining memorabilia—hooks, headlamps, and buckets.

Will sat in what appeared to be the visitor's chair, and Goodnough edged around his desk.

"What can I do for you?" Goodnough asked, as his chair creaked under his weight.

"I'm looking for a mine map, Bethlehem Number eleven. From the

Viper, Red Fox, Hell-for-Certain area. Be from the nineteen-twenties or so," Will said.

Goodnough gave Will a penetrating look.

"That's odd," he said.

"What?"

Goodnough kept staring. Will suddenly worried that the man might have a speech impediment.

"Well, I can show you what we have," Goodnough finally said, without explaining his delay. He rose from his chair. "I'm afraid it's not too well organized."

"That's all right," Will said eagerly.

Will followed Goodnough out of the office. They turned left and went to the end of the corridor and through another door. Goodnough flipped a switch and several fluorescent lights bathed a room packed with rusting junk.

There were piles of picks and shovels, a large weighing scale, dozens of four-foot-long corkscrews, and piles of silvery boxes.

Goodnough headed to a corner of the room where several large metal shelves stood. He pointed to piles of long, flat boxes.

"They're in there, and I'm afraid you're going to have to look for yourself," he said.

Will approached the shelving and pulled one of the boxes toward him. It was heavy. He pulled a flap and saw what looked like hundreds of mine maps inside.

"You have any idea where Bethlehem Number eleven might be?" Will asked.

"Nope," Goodnough said with a shrug. "We hope to organize this someday, but we just don't have the money. It might be in there. I just don't know."

"How many maps you figure you got?" Will asked.

"No idea," the director said. "Five, ten thousand."

Will's shoulders sagged. He wanted to be thorough and do his job right—if only this once. But weeks of searching through stacks of old maps would be too much.

"It'd take forever to get through 'em all," Will said.

"Yeah, some guy came about a year ago and spent almost two weeks here, and I'm pretty sure he didn't make it through 'em all," Good-nough said.

"Some guy?" Will asked.

"In fact, that's what I was thinking of," Goodnough said, wagging his finger. "I think he was looking for a Bethlehem map, too."

"Who was he?" Will asked.

"From some coal company," Goodnough said, rubbing his chin. "Carl something."

"You can't remember which coal company?"

"'Fraid not."

"Was it Blue Gem?" Will asked, trying to sound casual.

"Could be."

"Carl? Carl Breathitt?"

Goodnough again gave Will a silent stare.

"That sounds familiar," Goodnough said.

"What he look like?"

"Little guy, about this tall," Goodnough said, putting his right hand in the mid-five-foot range. "And skinny. I mean everybody's skinnier 'n me," he said, and he bobbed his head. "But skinnier even than you."

"How old?"

"Forties, fifties maybe."

Sounded a lot like the Red Fox miner.

"Did he find what he was looking for?" Will asked.

"Said he didn't."

"Did anyone watch him?"

Goodnough shook his head. "Don't have the staff."

Will was quiet again.

"What district did you say you were in?" Goodnough asked.

Will got out his badge.

"Hazard? You investigating that inundation there?" Goodnough asked.

Will nodded and went back to looking at the boxes.

"Well, I'm gonna . . ." Goodnough pointed a thumb back toward his office. "If you need anything, don't hesitate to holler."

"No, I'll come with you," Will said. "No sense in staying."

Will followed Goodnough out of the storage room. Goodnough

stopped at his office and Will kept walking. Will waved absently at the director and walked back to his truck.

If Carl Breathitt had come down here to get that old mine map, he'd either failed to find it after two weeks of work or he'd found it and taken it away. Either way, it didn't make sense to spend time following in his tracks.

Time for another visit with Mr. Breathitt. Will would have to call Blue Gem's lawyer and tell him that he wanted to talk to the miner again. Will couldn't wait for the interview.

There was no way that Carl Breathitt was down here looking for the map to satisfy his own curiosity. A guy like that wouldn't spend more than an hour in a museum—never mind two weeks—unless it was part of his job.

Did Paul know or was Carl ordered to come down by the now-murdered foreman, who might have been a drug dealer?

There had to be something hokey about that old mine map, but Will had no idea what. If it showed earlier mining to be more extensive than the map Will had seen, that would mean Blue Gem deliberately cut into the old works.

But why would any sane person want to do that? The inundation had been a disaster not only for Blue Gem's crew but for the company itself. Millions of dollars in equipment had been lost, and Will doubted that any insurance fully protected the company against the lost profits caused by the flood.

And while he could believe that Paul and Rob had argued, and that Paul might have transferred Rob to Red Fox because of it, he simply couldn't believe that any disagreement between the two would have led Paul to destroy an entire mining operation on the off chance that an inundation would kill Rob.

There were more certain and far cheaper ways to kill a person.

And what did drugs have to do with any of it?

Will badly wanted to see the old map. What could it possibly show? Even if Carl had found the map, it seemed unlikely that he would admit it or dig it up for Will.

"Pretty please?" Will mumbled to himself and chuckled. He got into the truck and thought about what he'd tell the lawyer, who was going to want to know precisely why his client was being re-called.

Will suspected that the best way to get a truly honest answer was to surprise Carl with the question, but Will was almost certain that the lawyer wouldn't let his client answer such a surprise inquiry.

Will decided to tell them his questions about the map ahead of time. What the hell? There's no way they'd deny that the miner had been looking for it or had found it, if either had actually occurred. There were too many chances that someone—the curator or someone else—would contradict Carl.

And at this point, they didn't dare risk calling the curator to see what he'd told Will for fear this would be interpreted as witness tampering. They'd have to assume that the curator's memory was more solid than it actually was.

They had to come up with a reasonable explanation, which was hard for Will to imagine. The company would have been required to get a copy of the old map years earlier when it filed its mining plan. Why look for more copies? Did they have some doubts about the reliability of their earlier copies? If so, why?

If the search had been an effort to round up stray copies of the old map—as Will suspected—what possible explanation would they give for that?

Will felt like he was still looking for a stick of gum in Paul's car but was about to stumble on the cache of condoms in the glove compartment. He was pretty sure that his brother was up to something. He just couldn't figure out what.

Will decided to call the lawyer as soon as he got back to the office. When Paul found out how far and wide Will's investigation was going, he was going to flip.

Will put his truck in reverse and backed out of the museum parking lot.

# CHAPTER TWENTY-SEVEN

The lawyer had betrayed no hint of anxiety when Will called, which had been a bit of a letdown. Will was so eager for an answer that he had even agreed to meet Carl and the lawyer at the mine site the next afternoon. Why the hell not? Will would have driven to Lexington to hear their answer.

He was so jumpy after the call that he could not force himself to work his way through the depositions that he needed to read to finish his report. He left for Helen's basketball game an hour early.

As always, Tessy was sitting just behind the home bench trying to look relaxed, a clipboard in her hands. She clapped as the Hazard girls broke from their huddle. Tessy was watching Helen and the others so intently that she didn't notice Will until he was beside her.

"Hey," Will said.

"Oh, Will," she said and glanced around the gym's bleachers.

Will sat and lapsed into silence.

"The girls get new uniforms?" Will asked.

Each team member had identical yellow warm-ups. The pants seemed to have side seams just like the pros', and there was a Nike swoosh on the front of each top.

"Just got 'em yesterday," Tessy said with a nod.

"That's great," Will said. "Can't see Letcher County coughing up the money for those. Hazard's something."

It was an attempt to say something nice about a move that still rankled Will. Tessy didn't seem appreciative.

"The school didn't pay for those, Will," she said.

"Oh, well. I'm glad to have contributed to the cause," Will said, still trying to be nice.

Tessy was silent for a moment. She seemed to make a decision.

"You didn't contribute," Tessy said, looking straight at the girls. "Paul bought those."

Will swiveled his head away from the girls to Tessy.

"Paul's dressing my daughter now?"

Tessy didn't look at him.

"Where do I send a check to pay for Helen's uniform?" Will said, his voice flat.

"School board," Tessy said, still not looking at him.

"Hazard Independent?"

"Sure."

"How much?"

"For which part?" Tessy said, and she finally looked at Will. "The warm-ups cost about one hundred and fifty dollars each. The uniforms are another two hundred dollars each. The video equipment cost about five thousand dollars, I think. And the repairs to the gym, I just don't know, Will. Maybe seven hundred thousand dollars.

"Paul paid for all of it. It's one of the reasons Hazard has such a good team," Tessy said, her voice even. "You want to start kicking in some money, that's fine. But I don't want you spending thousands of our dollars in some pissing match with Paul. A pissing match you can't win."

She left her eyes on Will. He was silent. She went back to watching the warm-ups.

"Thataway, Jeannie!" Tessy shouted. "Drive straight at it."

"Did you know this before?" Will asked quietly.

"Before what?" Tessy asked. "Attaway, Cindy!"

"Before you moved in with Paul so Helen could get on this team?"

Tessy looked back at her husband.

"Yeah, I did."

"Why? Why do this?"

"Because I want Helen to make some'm of herself," she said defiantly. "I want her to have the chances I didn't get."

"And basketball gets her that? Workin' for Paul gets her that?"

"You know a basketball scholarship is the only way she's gonna be able to go to a good school. And I don't mean UK or U of L."

Will glanced over at the court. Helen had stopped warming up and was staring at her parents, concern written on her face. Will tried to smile.

Tessy looked at the court and clapped.

"Come on, baby," Tessy said, in something less than a shout. "Keep going."

Helen got back in the layup line.

"Let's not talk about this, Will. I knew you wouldn't understand. I knew you'd have a problem with it. But it's what Helen needs," Tessy said, her lips barely moving. "And if you can't see that—"

"Are you sleeping with him?"

Tessy rolled her eyes and turned back to the court.

"Go, Hazard!" she shouted as the girls gathered for another huddle.

Will was quiet. He had an overwhelming sense of déjà vu. Paul had won the affection or loyalty of every important person in his life—his father, mother, best friend, and now his wife.

Will closed his eyes and opened them to see a woman—a sex that could be bought with jewels and yellow warm-ups. He looked over to the court and saw Helen, a future member of this sorority. Or, now that he thought about it, already a pledge. Helen must have known about Paul's involvement with the team.

Helen was in the middle of a scrum of players, her hair pulled back in a ponytail. The scrum broke and several of the players—one nearly a foot taller than Helen—high-fived her. The coach called Helen over and walked with her to the court's edge, talking earnestly into her left ear with his arm around her shoulders.

Helen was clearly thrilled with the new arrangement.

"You're probably right," Will said. "Paul's more important to my daughter right now than me."

Tessy sighed heavily but didn't look at her husband.

"Ladies and gentlemen," the public announcer said over a surprisingly clear address system. "Before tonight's game, the Hazard Independent School System would like to express its heartfelt appreciation to Paul Murphy, whose generous contributions have helped these girls through thick and thin. Let's give him a round of applause."

Paul came out of the players' entrance, smiled and made a brief wave. He had on black slacks and a shiny black, button-up shirt. After a moment, he retreated back into the entryway. Will had a wild urge to trot down to the entryway and have it out with his older brother.

Will looked over at Tessy, who, with a determined look, joined in the general applause.

"Now please welcome . . ." the public address announcer continued.

Just then, Uncle Elliott appeared wearing a broad smile.

"This gonna be good," the old man said.

Wanting to shout, Will got up and left his seat.


Will watched the first half from the walkway at the top of the gym. Helen was not playing her best, but against Leslie County, she didn't need to. Hazard was up 28–19, a comfortable margin.

He decided to stop pouting and move down near Tessy just before the second half began. When he sat down, Tessy gave him a soft look. He nodded to her.

He decided to break the ice. The girls were still in the locker room, so he had only a moment.

"Tessy, you know that inundation a couple weeks ago?"

"Yeah?"

"Well, all the homes up Hell-for-Certain lost their water, and they aren't getting help from Blue Gem, the feds, or the state," Will said in a rush. "I was thinkin' you might talk to your friend Lauren about organizing somethin' for 'em."

Tessy raised her eyebrows.

"I thought you didn't like Lauren," Tessy said, a playful smile on her face.

"I never said that," Will said and smiled back. "I don't consider her my best friend or nothin'."

"I'll talk to her," Tessy said, nodding.

She looked intently at Will.

"Helen's sleeping over at Cindy's tonight," she said. "What do you think if I came over, spent the night at home?"

Will blinked several times.

"That'd be great," he stammered.

"All right. I can't stay—"

The girls came out of the locker room in a rush, the crowd roared, and Will lost the rest of what Tessy said.


At the end of the game, Will walked down to the floor and waited for Helen, stepping from foot to foot. He wanted to kiss her, congratulate her, and bolt for home to clean up for Tessy.

Uncle Elliott walked up, with the same smile he had after the last game.

"Helluva game," he said.

"Yeah," Will answered.

Paul appeared.

"You're making me pay my lawyer to come up here again?" Paul asked, shaking his head and paying no attention to Uncle Elliott. "You know how much that costs?"

"You don't have to send your lawyer if you don't want. I just want to talk to one of your miners."

"You already did that."

"Need to ask him a couple of other questions."

"About a map?"

"Yeah. You know why he'd spend two weeks of work time huntin' for it?"

"Ya know, if Dad were alive, and you were doing this? He would tar your ass."

"You two need to stop this," Uncle Elliott said. "Not gonna help either one of you."

Will looked at the locker room entrance, hoping Helen would appear. Another player came out. She was wearing yellow warm-ups.

"Thanks for the warm-ups," Will said.

"Sure. Somebody's gotta buy 'em for these girls."

Will bit his tongue.

"By the way, if you show up drunk to Momma's eightieth birthday party tomorrow, I'm gonna throw your ass out," Paul said. "You can count on that, son."

"Paul, damnit," Uncle Elliott said.

"Paul, you can go—" Will started at the same time.

Helen appeared. All three men smiled.

"Great job, honey. You were terrific," Will said.

"Best point guard in the state," Paul echoed. "You were fantastic."

"Helluva game," Uncle Elliott said.

"Thanks Dad, Uncle Paul, Uncle Elliott." The girl kissed each man in turn.

"All right, I gotta go, honey. Congrats again," Will said. He nodded at Paul and his uncle and jogged out of the gym.

The road from Hazard to Whitesburg had two lanes and a lot of curves. Speeding required blind passes that only idiots, drunks, and teenagers were willing to make. Will sped.

Since Letcher County was dry, Will didn't have to decide whether to stop by a liquor store or get a bottle of wine. Wasn't possible. He thought they might have one in the basement, but if not, he'd put out a bottle of Jack. Come to think on it, Tessy'd probably prefer he didn't drink at all.

Most important, he reminded himself, was that he find any and all stray socks and put them away. Maybe in a bag outside the back door. Tessy hated Will's dirty socks. He tended to forget them when taking off his shoes, so they were often scattered about the house as if it were a gym locker room.

Even when he'd make an effort to pick up, Tessy would often find one that he'd missed and walk to the washing machine holding it like a dead rat. Dirty socks would cast a pall over her for some time.

Not tonight.

He skidded to a stop in front of their house and got out as soon as the wheels stopped. He was giddy about the prospect of his wife of eighteen years coming home. It was stupid. Sort of.

He found five socks in what he thought was a very thorough search. The odd number bothered him, but there was nothing he could do about it. He put them in a trash bag and put the bag in the garbage can. He'd retrieve the bag before putting out the trash.

No wine. He decided that if she asked, he'd get out the Jack. Otherwise, it'd stay hidden. He checked to make sure the whiskey was in the cabinet and—what the hell?—took a quick swig.

He jumped in the shower, thinking Tessy would be at least a half hour behind him. He was done in less than two minutes and was dressed before five had passed.

He got out candles, opened a can of soup and put it in a pot to simmer. He sat on the couch and popped up seconds later to get the day's *Lexington Herald-Leader* from his car. He ran up the steps, feeling like a kid in a game of tag.

He jumped on the couch and opened the newspaper. Five minutes passed before he understood a word he was reading.

Two hours later, he blew out the candles and finished the last of the Jack. He was angry at himself for being so disappointed. She must have gotten cold feet. Or Helen's sleepover had evaporated.

He was on his way to the bedroom when the phone rang.

"Will, I'm sorry."

"Sure," he said.

"There's somebody watchin' the house, and I just got scared."

"What?"

"A black Ford Taurus. It was sitting down the hollow—between us and the Udall place," Tessy said. "Scared me."

"Shit," Will said, and looked out the window.

"You've seen him before?" Tessy said, her voice rising.

Will wondered what the right answer was.

"Uh, yeah. He's been out there a few times."

"Jesus."

"Baby, it's probably just, I don't know, somebody trying to make a point. Coal company or something."

"What? A coal company? You think Paul is behind this?"

"I don't know, probably not. But they're not doing anything, far as I can tell, so you can't let it rattle you."

"Are you kidding? Will, everything's going so well for Helen now. I don't want anything to happen."

"How does you and me having a night together have anything to do with Helen?" Will said, his voice rising.

"Will, I can't talk to you when you get like that. I'm sorry about tonight."

She didn't hang up, but she didn't say more. The silence stretched.

"Well, I'll try to figure out who that guy is," Will said, trying to sound conciliatory. "I'm sorry you came all the way down and then had to turn around."

"Yeah."

More silence.

"Well, I'll see you," she said.

"Have a good night," Will said and hung up.

He went out on the porch, but there was no sign of the Taurus. He padded back inside and, just as he was headed toward the bedroom, stopped and headed back out to the trash. He retrieved the bag, came inside, flipped it upside down, and walked back to the bedroom, socks dropping to the floor as he went.

# CHAPTER TWENTY-EIGHT

It was a group of thirty or forty people. About a third wore white cotton robes. As Amos watched from the trees, two of those in robes waded into the river and turned back toward the others. One gestured and spoke. A woman—small and plump in her robe—walked down the slope into the water, her head looking down and her arms raised toward heaven.

She had white-blond hair down to her shoulders and wore a thin cotton frock. She stumbled slightly then righted herself. One of the men in the river, the quiet one, sloshed out of the water to take her hand so as to lead her through the immersion of baptism.

It was about 10 a.m. The temperature was in the mid-thirties. The breath of the woman wading into the river came out in short gasps—each briefly visible. Someone in the crowd along the shore strummed a guitar and started singing. He was young, his voice barely audible to Amos.

Halfway through the first verse of "Amazing Grace," the rest of those on shore had joined the sweet sound "that saved a wretch like me . . ." The woman in the water didn't seem to notice. She spoke with one of those in the river, who waved his hand over her.

The quiet man put his arms close to his chest, one hand holding his nose. The woman mimicked him, and then the two men each grabbed an elbow, cradled her head and lowered her backward into the river. A half second later, they raised her up, water streaming from her hair, her thin cotton dress plastered to her graceful young body. She wiped her face and beamed at the singers onshore. Some shouted and clapped, briefly interrupting the rhythm of the song. She quickly walked out, and someone wrapped her in a towel.

Another young woman waded into the river.

Amos walked down the slope toward the crowd. When he got to the group, he took off his backpack. He was wearing camouflage pants and jacket, and he had on construction boots. Since most in the crowd were women, he stood out like a thumb.

He stood next to the boy with the guitar, who was now singing "Jesus Loves Me." Amos didn't sing. The boy didn't seem to mind. Amos stepped away to stand behind several folks in white robes who seemed to have formed a line. He watched each enter the water.

Most had chosen a friend who waited with a towel, although two middle-aged women had to rush to get their own towels.

A balding man wearing a white cassock over a tan jacket who had been in front of Amos waded into the water. Amos took off his camouflage coat, a brown button-up cotton shirt, and his boots and socks. He stepped gingerly up the hill to lay the pile of clothes on his backpack when a fiftyish woman with jet black hair, prominent cheekbones, and coal dark eyes put out her hands. Amos paused. She reached out and took his clothes.

"Need a towel, honey?" she asked.

"Yes, ma'am, that'd be nice," Amos answered.

She nodded, and turned away.

Amos walked back to the river's edge just as the balding man came up from his dunking. Amos looked down and gingerly stepped into the water, feeling with his toes for rocks. He closed his eyes. When the water passed his knees, he opened his eyes. The balding man was almost beside him and headed out of the river. They smiled at each other as they passed.

The pressure on Amos's feet lightened, and he looked at the two men waiting for him in the water. A black wetsuit showed under the cassock of the preacher, who smiled curiously at Amos. The other man held out his hand for Amos to hold. The hand was cold. Amos didn't see a wetsuit under his cassock.

The boy with the guitar began playing "Hotel California." No one sang.

"Son? Where do you come to us from?" the preacher asked.

"I been wandering in the wilderness," Amos answered.

"You have now come into the sight of the Lord," the preacher said, nodding.

"Reverend, I'm fixin' to go on sabbatical. And the Lord said, 'Six years you shall sow your field and six years you shall prune your vineyard and gather its fruits but in the seventh year there shall be a Sabbath of solemn rest for the land, a Sabbath to the Lord,'" Amos said.

"You know your scripture," the preacher said, nodding approval.

"Been studyin'," Amos answered.

"You sure you shouldn't be the one baptizing me?" the preacher said and laughed. The man next to him didn't seem to get the joke.

"That wouldn't be right," Amos said. "It is right that you do this. Yes, sir."

"Well, praise the Lord and turn around," the preacher said.

"Lord, let this man be baptized in your sight, and let him follow in your ways."

Amos held his nose and fell slowly backward full length into the chill water.


Will was uneasy the second he parked. There were no vehicles in front of the trailer and the front door was open behind the storm door. It was a cold morning, the heart of winter. He sat in his truck for a long minute.

"Well," he said and got out of his truck.

The ground in front of the trailer was torn up with tire tracks, like somebody had been joyriding. Will walked up to the front door and, standing a step down, leaned in and knocked.

No answer.

He opened the storm door.

"Hello? Mr. Blevins?"

He stepped inside. The couch cushions were strewn about the living room. He poked his head a little deeper into the trailer. The kitchen cabinets were open and their contents spilled onto the linoleum.

Will pulled his head back out and let the storm door close. He sucked on his teeth.

A car approached from the head of the hollow. It stopped in front of the brief driveway, and a woman rolled down the driver's window.

"Lookin' for the Blevinses?" she asked.

"Amos," Will answered.

"You a cop?" the woman asked, her face blank.

"Not really," Will said.

The woman's face remained blank.

"I'm a mining investigator. Amos was involved in an accident."

This seemed to meet with her approval.

"The narco squad came, arrested Glenda. Amos got away," the woman said. "They say he knocked out one of the officers. Say when they find him, he's gonna go away for a long time."

Will let his surprise show.

"Guess that means he won't be helping in my investigation."

"They ain't gonna find him," the woman said. "Not Amos."

She let the brake out. The car disappeared.

"That's that," Will said to himself.

Will had wanted to make one last effort to ask Amos about the mine. Will wasn't sure what he would learn, but he had an odd feeling that Amos could be the key to his investigation. And he'd wanted to press Amos on that church service. Had he told the preacher that Will was a mine inspector? That he was looking for a map? How would even Amos know that? It was all just too bizarre. The answers were now lost. Amos could not serve as a witness in the investigation. His credibility was shot.

"Oh well," Will said to no one in particular.

Will would have to see the miner and Paul's lawyer empty-handed. He got back in his truck.

The largest strip mine in eastern Kentucky is the Sunfire mine, a behemoth that straddles three counties and thousands of acres between Hazard and Hindman. On satellite maps, Sunfire looks like a cluster of shingles blisters running along the middle of Kentucky's eastern flank.

It was where Amos decided to begin.

It took him more than an hour of walking to find the active part of the mine. The mine workers were almost finished with their preparations for blasting.

The bore holes were in a grid pattern. Wires snaked out of each hole and joined feeder wires like roads in a subdivision.

In each hole was a cylindrical plastic bag filled with ammonium nitrate, explosive fertilizer. Amos used a long knife to cut three central wires and then, just to be sure, he started cutting the smaller wires.

Walking through a grid of primed explosives was generally frowned upon by safety advocates. Amos knew that he had a good chance of dying. He knew that, even if he succeeded in delaying the explosion, his efforts could be reversed quickly.

But he figured he had to start somewhere, and he was in a mood to test God as well as man.

With all the wires cut, Amos took off his backpack and set about assembling his .22 rifle. He didn't know what was going to happen next, but he was pretty sure somebody would get hot under the collar, so he wanted the gun handy.

He sat down, crossed his legs, and put the assembled rifle on his lap. He prayed, "Not my will but Thine be done."

Twenty minutes later, a pickup drove up from below. Amos was sitting atop a bench nearly sixty feet above the rest of the mine. The pickup stopped well short of the bench on a dirt ramp. Two men got out, stood for a minute, and then walked toward Amos.

Both men wore black mining caps with a red blaze on the front. One wore a white button-up shirt under a black down jacket. He wore pressed jeans and construction boots. The other man wore brown overalls.

They stopped fifty feet from Amos.

"Sir, this is an active mine site," the man in the black down jacket said.

Amos didn't answer.

"Sir, it is extremely dangerous for you to be here. We nearly blew you to kingdom come," the man said.

Amos sat, his eyes closed.

They seemed to notice Amos's gun for the first time.

"We will call the authorities, sir. You will be arrested," the man said.

Amos opened his eyes and calmly looked at the two.

He reached for the gun. The men quickly turned back toward their pickup. Amos put the gun on the ground and stood. They stopped. Amos walked toward them, leaving his backpack and gun behind. The men waited. Amos halted about twenty feet from them.

Amos was an imposing sight. His hair and beard had grown somewhat wild in recent weeks. He had thinned to sinew and muscle, a lean, genial menace. His eyes burned but his tone was that of a teacher.

"You fellas are destroying the earth. God wants you to stop. These mountains are His, not yourn," Amos said.

The man in brown overalls pursed his lips and looked sideways at the man beside him.

"Are you with some kind of group?" the man in the pressed jeans asked.

"Pardon?"

"Some environmental group? You an activist?"

"No, sir. No group," Amos answered and smiled.

"So what do you want?" the man said.

"For you to stop."

"Sir, this is a three-hundred-million-dollar mine. It's the biggest mine east of the Mississippi."

"Yes, sir."

They all stood for a moment.

"Give me your radio," the man in the pressed jeans said to his companion. The man in the brown overalls complied.

"Gil," the man said into the walkie-talkie.

"Yes, sir," squawked the response.

"Call the state police. The guy says he's a freelancer. Tell 'em he's got a rifle."

"Roger that."

They stood still.

"I don't think I'm supposed to hurt you," Amos said and half smiled. "But I'm pretty sure I don't wanna be arrested."

The men whispered to each other and turned back to the truck. They climbed into the vehicle and backed down the dirt ramp. Amos walked back to his backpack and gun and sat.

An hour later, a dark blue state police cruiser appeared some way off, laboring in the dirt.

Amos stood, shouldered his pack, picked up his rifle, and walked into the woods.

It took Will a second to realize that the police cars and coroner's van in the Red Fox mine parking lot and the TV truck parked just outside signaled something alarming. They'd all been there during the inundation and rescue, but that had been nearly two weeks earlier. Their return meant trouble.

He eased up to the sheriff's car blocking the entrance.

Will flipped open his identification and showed it to the deputy. Will didn't offer an explanation and, thankfully, the deputy didn't ask for one before waving him in. Will almost asked the kid what had happened but decided to wait.

He parked his truck and got out, his puzzlement written on his face.

He saw Sergeant Detective Gene Freeman of the Kentucky State Police standing in a huddle of other officers near the mine trailer, so he headed toward the group.

As he got closer, Will saw what looked like a body lying a few yards away from the officers. The officers eyed Will curiously as he approached.

"Detective," Will said.

"Mr. Murphy," Sergeant Freeman said.

"Didn't think I'd see you back here."

"Didn't think I'd need to come back."

"What happened?"

"Murder."

# CHAPTER TWENTY-NINE

Who?" Will asked.

"Fellow named Carl Breathitt," Sergeant Freeman said.

Will sighed. "I was supposed to interview him again today."

"I know."

Will noticed that his heart was pumping. "So, Detective, I came here to ask Carl about a missing map. Might be important."

"Hm," Sergeant Freeman said. One of the cops standing next to the sergeant suppressed a smile.

"Can I see him?" Will asked.

The sergeant cocked his head. "Sure. We're pretty much done here."

Will stepped around the men and walked to the side of the body. Dead, Carl looked even smaller. He was wearing jeans and a blue denim jacket. He lay on his back as if placed there. His right eye was pulp and his ear filled with brown blood.

A bit of it had pooled on the ground next to the body, but Will was surprised there wasn't more.

"Probably a twenty-two," said Sergeant Freeman, who walked up to stand beside Will. "Went in the eye and never came out."

Will noticed that Carl still had his car keys in his right hand.

"Those small-caliber bullets can actually do a lot more damage than the bigger ones because they like to bounce around inside," Sergeant Freeman continued.

"So what happened?" Will said.

"The company lawyer said he was driving in just as the victim was walking across the lot. Said he saw the victim fall. Said the victim was alone."

Will looked up at the mountains surrounding the mine.

"No way to tell where it came from, with that bullet still in his brain," Sergeant Freeman said. "But we figure the shooter was laying for him up in the hills. Probably the same guy that shot Mike Barnes, the foreman. I'm betting the bullets are gonna match."

"Holy shit."

"Yeah."

"You figure all this is about drugs?"

"Probably."

"What the lawyer do when he saw it?" Will asked.

"Said he ran over to see what was wrong. Said the victim was already dead when he got there."

"You believe him?"

The cop's expression remained neutral. "Think so."

"So why didn't the lawyer get killed, too?"

The cop shrugged.

"Kind of a coincidence that I was gonna talk to Carl today about that map," Will said.

Sergeant Freeman blinked. "The lawyer said they were gonna tell you that there was nothing in the map thing. Routine safety check, he said. He said you were, ah, being very thorough."

The two were silent.

"Thorough's good, 'course. But now it's a murder investigation," the cop said.

Will nodded.

"We're pretty sure the shooter was Amos Blevins anyway. He's supposed to be a crack shot, he's been a fugitive on drug and assault charges for several days, and he may have stuck up the Sunfire mine early this morning," the cop said.

"The Sunfire mine?" Will asked. "Then how'd he get over here?"

"It's actually not that far. About a four-mile walk through the mountains. He coulda done it in two hours, plenty enough time to get here and set up a shot."

"And why would Amos Blevins want to kill this guy?" Will asked, pointing to the body.

"The lawyer said that Blevins kicked the shit out of some other foreman down near Middlesboro, and Carl Breathitt is the guy that sent him down there. We figure they must have all been part of some drug ring."

"Huh?" Will said skeptically.

"Look, I don't really have a clue. Maybe he got cheated out of his share of the money from selling drugs. Maybe he was pissed about the inundation. Maybe he didn't like Breathitt or Barnes or even your brother. Doesn't really matter."

"Doesn't matter?"

The detective looked at Will and then turned to the other cops.

"Why don't you fellas head back? I'll be there soon," Sergeant Freeman said. The three moved away. "Will, you were nice enough to introduce me to your world. Now I'm gonna tell you a little secret about mine: I really don't give a shit about motive."

Will let out an involuntary chuckle and then realized the cop was serious.

"TV cops are always talking about motive, but the truth is it just doesn't matter to us. In most of my cases, I got no idea why somebody shoots somebody else, and it doesn't really matter. I look for the guy with the gun. Or the dangerous criminal that happens to live next door. Or the husband. Or the wife. Pretty much in that order. Never fails."

The sergeant gave a wry smile. "But maps and motives?" he said, shaking his head.

Will's cheeks colored.

"By the way, you guys ever find that head?" Sergeant Freeman asked.

"No."

"Jesus."

Will looked out at the mountains. He bit his lower lip.

"I gotta tell ya, sergeant. I'm kinda lost in my investigation. There's just some'm not right about a lot o' this. Like there's this problem with an old map. And Rob Crane, the guy on the scoop, remember? He and Paul argued just a few weeks before the flood. Least that's what his wife said. And he sent me a letter just before he died that, well, I don't really know what it said. But it was kinda angling that Paul did some'm bad.

"But I don't know what it was," Will said with a shrug. "And it's hard to figure it would mean somethin' anyway. I mean, I can't get past the fact that nobody in their right mind would want their own mine to flood. And all these murders? I gotta figure it's got nothing to do with mining, but who knows?"

Sergeant Freeman nodded.

"We're pretty sure the murders are about drugs," the sergeant said. "And I don't figure your brother had anything to do with it. Still, I'm impressed you're worried about it. I've heard MSHA inspections aren't always, well, thorough. And what with you being brothers . . ."

"Yeah. Paul's a little surprised, that's for sure. Maybe even a few people at MSHA are, too. Likely a waste. And now that Carl can't answer for himself, I'm not sure what to do."

"Didn't you tell me in the hospital that first day that this had to be an accident?"

"Yeah."

"So has something changed that?"

"Not really. But just because there were drugs down there doesn't mean there wasn't some'm funny about the mining."

The sergeant shrugged.

Will rolled his eyes. "Yeah. I shoulda never agreed to do this investigation. At first, I was gonna give Paul a break 'cause he was my brother. Then I wanted to bust his balls 'cause he was my brother. And now, well, I should probably just write it up."

"Let it sit for a day or two. You never know what'll come in. That's what I do when I'm stuck."

"Not sure I can hold out for too long, but that's a pretty good idea."

A young cop, maybe a trainee, approached.

"Can they take the body, Sarg?"

"Sure," Sergeant Freeman answered. "All right, I gotta go, Will. Good luck."

"Thanks."

And Will left.

Dusk was approaching. Will had no interest in returning to the office, and his mother's birthday party wouldn't start for a couple of hours. He decided to go see Missy Hogg on Hell-for-Certain and go over her options. He'd promised her he would, and this wasn't a bad time to do it. One more loose end to tie up.

Driving up the creek, Will saw plenty of signs of the neighborhood's sudden decay. A U-Haul truck was parked in front of one small house. At another, junk spilled out of an open garage door. Several houses looked empty.

Then he came upon a tidy blue house with white shutters, and Will was glad to see several cars parked in front.

He parked, got out of his truck, and walked to the front door. His knock was answered almost immediately by what looked like a thirteen-year-old girl. She was wearing jeans, a Gap T-shirt, and a playful smirk.

"Is your mother—?" Will began.

"Come on in, Mr. Murphy," Will heard from within.

The girl stood silent, betraying no sign that she'd heard her mother.

"Howdy," Will said to her quietly and walked in.

Stairs headed straight up from the door but there was a living room to the right. Will walked in and hesitated after the first step. The room was dazzlingly modern, with white carpeting and furniture, a glass-topped coffee table, halogen lighting, a large-screen TV, and colorful abstract prints. Will suddenly worried that he hadn't wiped his feet.

Missy Hogg sat on the couch. Beside her sat Lauren Carroll, the activist—another surprise.

"Lauren," Will said.

"Hello, Will."

Small, thin, and muscular, Lauren Carroll had short salt-and-pepper hair, a firm grip, and a tar pit where her heart should have been. Will had not seen Lauren in years and didn't feel the least bit deprived.

"Mrs. Hogg, I came to tell you that you need to introduce yourself to an activist named Lauren Carroll," said Will, smiling. "Late again."

"A truer word was never spoken," Lauren said.

Will's smile immediately became as false as Lauren's.

"Come on in and set down," Mrs. Hogg said. "We was just talkin' 'bout the protest."

"Protest?" Will said, still standing.

"Tomorrow in front of OSM," Lauren said. "We'll have the Letcher, Perry, and Knott county committees all there. Thirty people at least. And if we can get some of your neighbors," at this Lauren gave a hard look at Mrs. Hogg, who nodded, "we'll put on quite a show."

"Tomorrow?" Will said and gave a laugh.

"You got a better day for it, Will?" Lauren said.

"No, it just seems mighty quick," Will said.

"To an MSHA man, I can see how it might," Lauren said. There was that hard smile again, Will thought.

"Mrs. Carroll was explaining that the sooner the protests start, the better," Mrs. Hogg said, sounding conciliatory.

Will smiled encouragement at Mrs. Hogg, not because he believed a quick protest was the right strategy—he had no opinion on that—but because she'd called Lauren "Mrs. Carroll." An unmarried feminist, Lauren insisted on being called "Ms."

Will thought he'd seen Lauren blink when Mrs. Hogg had spoken.

"I'm sure Mrs. Carroll is right about that," Will said. Lauren's jaw tightened.

"Well, there is nothing wrong with starting with a smaller action and having it build," Lauren said in a Brooklyn rush.

The more annoyed she became, the more Lauren sounded like the New Yorker she was.

"Somebody also told me that putting a story in the *Courier-Journal* might help," Will said, delighted to be suggesting work for Lauren.

"You can't just 'put' a story in the *Courier-Journal*, Mrs. Hogg," Lauren said, using two fingers on each hand to signal the quotation marks around "put." "And they've got corporate owners now that try to keep our stories out. But I've got some contacts there. We might be able to slip something past their overseers."

Mrs. Hogg, her mouth slightly open, nodded at Lauren.

"If only we'd taken that offer a few years ago," Mrs. Hogg said. "All this trouble . . ."

"You can't think about that now," Lauren said, and forcefully patted Mrs. Hogg's knee.

"What?" Will said. "What offer?"

"A man came by and offered to buy our house. Said he'd pay fair value," Mrs. Hogg said, nodding. "Virgil run him off."

"Who?" Will asked. Lauren scowled at him.

"Dunno," Mrs. Hogg said. "Said he'd pay cash, too."

"Why? I mean, it's a beautiful house, Mrs. Hogg. It truly is," Will said, trying to recover. "But out of the blue? Up here?"

"Said he liked the area," Mrs. Hogg said, frowning.

Will didn't know what to say to that.

Lauren rose.

"I have to go now, Mrs. Hogg. But I'll expect to see you with at least ten of your neighbors at eight a.m. sharp tomorrow in front of the OSM office," she said.

Mrs. Hogg rose with her. Will, who had not sat down, moved toward the door as well.

"Sounds like you've got things in motion, Mrs. Hogg. I'll leave you to it," Will said.

" 'Preciate you stopping by, Mr. Murphy," Mrs. Hogg said.

"Good to see you, Mrs. Hogg," Will said, completing a call-and-response couplet as common to Appalachian visiting as "swing-your-partner" is to square dancing.

Will sensed that Lauren was uncomfortable leaving at the same time as he, as if worried that their common departure might suggest a shared purpose. He decided to walk close to her for several paces just to heighten her tension.

"Good to see you, Lauren," he said.

"Hm," she answered. She stopped and looked down at the creek.

"What?" Will said.

"They got a straight pipe," she said.

"A what?"

She eyed Will coldly.

"You lived here all your life and never heard of a straight pipe?"

Will looked down at the creek. He now noticed a pipe that ended several feet above the trickle of water in the creekbed. He realized that he was looking at the Hoggs' sewer output.

"Yeah, I guess I have," Will said.

"The thing is, if we win this fight, that's only going to get worse," Lauren said, shaking her head.

"Why?"

"Because if OSM pipes in water up here, that's just more water to flush down those straight pipes. All these houses have wells, and those wells are not the best. Some only bring in enough water for two showers in the morning and laundry at night. It's so little water that some of these homes put their sewage into a hole. There isn't enough flat land for a proper septic system, but a hole is better than nothing. But they get water piped up here, and everybody will be flushing into the creek."

She shook her head and began walking again.

"Well, why fight for it?" Will said, still standing there.

Lauren turned back to him.

"Sewer systems are four times as expensive as water systems. OSM has yet to build one of them."

"Like I said, why fight for a water system then?"

Lauren's eyes blazed.

"I fight for people, Will, not creeks. The environment's somebody else's job."

She'd almost made it to her car.

"You ever heard of Joe and Gaynell's store?"

It had come out almost of its own. Will had all but given up on the lead, but why not try Lauren?

Lauren stopped and looked at him quizzically.

"Are you serious?" she asked.

"Uhm, yeah."

"You've never heard of Joe and Gaynell Begley or the C. B. Caudill store?"

"No," Will said, almost regretting that he'd asked.

"Who'd you ask before me?"

"I don't know. A few folks."

"At MSHA?"

"Yeah."

"And they didn't know? Incredible," she said and turned to get into her car.

Will threw up his hands.

"So you gonna tell me?"

Lauren put her hand on the car's roof.

"Joe Begley was one of the most famous anti-strip-mining advocates ever to come out of Appalachia. He used to lay down in front of bulldozers. He was on *60 Minutes*. He went to the goddamn White House when they signed the law in 1977. And nobody at MSHA has ever heard of him? It's just incredible."

Will shrugged.

"So where's the store?"

"It's in Blackey. You know where that is, don't you?"

"Ah, yeah," Will said, although he wasn't honestly sure.

"Get a map," she said and got in her car.


It was almost full dark when the red Chevy pickup pulled up to the tidy house on one of Hazard's nicer streets. Joe Fercal got out of the cab, glanced around, and retrieved a bag from the back.

He walked into the house, dropped the bag near the front door, took off his coat and put it on a hook, retrieved a remote from the coffee table and turned on the TV.

Fercal fell into a chair and took off his boots, still watching. He got up, unhitched his belt, dropped his trousers—a pair of stone-washed jeans—and stepped out of them. He reached under a pair of boxer shorts with purple hearts, scratched his ass, and then sat back down.

At a break, Fercal got up and went through a swinging door into the kitchen.

"Jesus!" he shouted.

"Evening, Joe," said Amos, sitting at the kitchen table.

# CHAPTER THIRTY

"Oh my God. Amos, what the hell you doing here?" Fercal said, breathing deeply.

"Thought you was dead, didn'tcha, Joe? Never felt sorry for ya till jus' now. Must be hard always worrying if some old friend is gonna show up and kill ya."

Years before, Joe Fercal had avoided prison by agreeing to testify against his drug-dealing partners, who also happened to be his brother and childhood best friend. Amos had known both, which meant he knew that Fercal had reason enough to fear for his life.

Fercal generally kept his doors and windows locked, and he often checked the surroundings before venturing into anyplace dark—like the parking lots of bars or restaurants. Fercal had to know that if his old partners really wanted to kill him, there was little he could do about it. Since both were still serving time, he probably thought the risks were not immediate.

"Goddamnit, Amos. I ain't seen you in fifteen years. What the fuck you doin' bustin' into my house?"

"Want to talk to a client a yourn."

"Client? What are you talkin' about?"

"Chrissy Icovelli. She just got out a' jail, right? I need to talk to her."

Fercal was silent, his mouth agape.

"She ain't no client."

"Your wife know you swap the Vicodin she gives you to Chrissy for sex, Joe?"

Fercal scowled. He went to the refrigerator and got out a Budweiser. He didn't offer one to Amos. Along with his underwear, Fercal was wearing a red and black long-sleeved Chicago Bulls T-shirt. His slight paunch made his legs look even scrawnier.

Amos always thought Fercal looked exactly like the Maytag repairman guy—fleshy face and sad eyes.

"Why'd you bust in here? Whyn't you go see Chrissy yourself?" Fercal asked after his first gulp.

"She lives downtown. Too many people."

"I heard you had some troubles," Fercal said and laughed. "Amos Blevins hit a cop."

"Yeah. They mixed us up with you, Joe. Said Glenda was selling scripts. And here you're doin' it near every day just up the street from the Hazard Police Department."

Fercal shook his head.

"Not no more. Through with that."

"Yeah. Let's wait for Chrissy."

They were quiet.

"How'd you get in here?" Fercal asked.

"You taught me how to do that, Joe. Remember? Breakin' into the Fister place when we were kids?"

Fercal smiled.

"You shoulda been a teacher, Joe. I always thought so."

Fercal sucked his teeth.

"What you doing now? Still surveying?" Amos asked.

Fercal nodded.

"Saw you up Hell-for-Certain last year," Amos said.

Fercal glanced quickly at Amos and then looked out the kitchen window.

"Chrissy ain't comin' for 'nother hour, Amos. Whyn't you watch some TV while I fix me some supper. Can even make some'm up for you."

"You sold out your own brother, Joe. You'd have no trouble selling me out. How about we just sit here and talk and you cook."

A cloud passed across Fercal's face. He turned to the refrigerator and got out some salad fixings—lettuce, tomatoes, cucumbers, and cold lentils. He cut the cucumber and tomatoes and washed the lettuce, put the vegetables into a glass bowl and spooned in the lentils. He sprinkled the salad with some olive oil and a little rice vinegar.

He sat at the kitchen table.

"I got high cholesterol," he said almost apologetically.

After several mouthfuls, Fercal glanced up at Amos.

"What you want with Chrissy?" Fercal asked, chewing.

"That's between me and Chrissy. Where's your wife?"

"Boston. Workin' at a hospital there till June."

"She own this house, don't she, Joe? Nice."

"Yeah."

They were both quiet for some time.

There was a knock.

"Stay here," Fercal said. "Lemme talk to her."

Amos followed Fercal out of the kitchen. Fercal turned to look at him, swallowed what he was about to say, and opened the door.

Outside was a small, pretty woman in her late twenties with short blond hair, a thin waist, and wide hips—a cheerleader going to seed. She smiled when Fercal opened the door, but the smile wavered when she saw Amos.

"Joe, I don't—" she started to say.

"Chrissy, this here's Amos Blevins," Fercal interrupted. "He was just fixin' to leave."

"Oh," she said, and her eyebrows shot up in a clownish look of surprise.

"Heard about me, Chrissy?" Amos asked in a low rumble from inside the room.

"Yeah. They're lookin' for you."

"Come inside," Fercal said brusquely.

She glanced at both men, pulled her hair back behind one ear, and stepped into the house.

"You got out yesterday," Amos said.

She nodded.

"You see my wife?"

Another nod.

"She all right?"

She looked at Fercal.

"Don't look at me," Fercal said.

"She cain't get bailed out," Chrissy said.

"Yeah," Amos said. "She usin'? Fightin'? Eatin'?"

Chrissy seemed at a loss.

"She didn't get in no trouble, if that's what you's askin'," Chrissy said. "Leastways, no worse than she was already in. They said they's just holdin' her to get at you. Or maybe she said that."

Amos nodded.

"Oh, she give hell to Penny, once," Chrissy said. "Lost her exercise privileges. But that's about it."

"Thank you, Chrissy. If you get yourself back there anytime soon," Amos glanced at Fercal, "tell her I'm gonna find a way."

"All right," she said.

Amos walked toward the door.

"Joe, I'm figuring you gonna be too busy to call the cops for the next hour or so," Amos said. "After that, I don't care. I don't plan on another visit."

"That'll be fine by me," Fercal said.

"You take care," Amos said.

"I will," Fercal said.

Amos smiled and left.


Each MSHA district office has a large wall map with pins showing active mines in the region. Will had often stared at it in part because Appalachia's mountains distorted distances. Towns that seemed far apart by car were sometimes geographically side by side. The map was also a handy way to look for obscure towns in the region.

Will parked the truck, walked quickly into the office, did no more than wave at Myrtle, and went straight up to the map without taking his coat off.

"Blackey, Blackey, Blackey," he mumbled.

He eventually found it on Route 7 between Jeremiah and Cornettsville at the intersection with 588. Will had inspected at least two mines near the town, but he couldn't picture it. Couldn't be much, he thought. He headed toward the door and stopped. Clete, Will's fellow inspector, was standing in the way.

" 'Scuse me, Clete."

"Guess who I just heard from, Will," Clete said, not moving.

"Ah. I don't know."

"Blue Gem. Your brother's company."

"Yeah?"

"Know what they said?"

Clete's eyes were on the ground.

"No."

"They said that they're not gonna contribute to the kitty this spring. You know why?" He looked at Will, his eyes blazing.

Will let out a long breath.

"You know why, Will?" Clete persisted.

"No," Will said, his voice flat. "I don't."

" 'Cause of you. They said you were being a hardass. Said you turned a simple inundation into a major case. Said they had to spend so much in legal fees that they can't afford to contribute to the kitty."

"Nine people died, Clete. Nine. Sam was one of 'em."

Clete nodded his head.

"We all liked Sam, Will," Clete said. "His death was a tragedy. But Sam died in a mine bump, Will. And that's nobody's fault."

"And the miners?"

"They died in a inundation, Will. A inundation. Now, did this mine drill bore holes?"

"Yeah."

"So what the fuck are you investigating?"

"Well, that's complicated."

"Complicated? There's nothin' complicated about this, Will. You need to fuckin' write up this report, maybe fine 'em for one or two things, and move on. And maybe they'll play ball again this summer. Did I mention that Blue Gem was our biggest contributor?"

"You know, Clete, maybe this whole kitty thing is not the best idea."
Clete frowned.

"Will, I know you've had some troubles at home, so I'm gonna forget you just said that. 'Cause I wouldn't want the other guys in the office finding out that you might turn rat. 'Cause the last time somebody said somethin' like that around here, his truck ended up in the river, his garage ended up gettin' torched, and his wife left him. You remember all the shit that came down on Eddie?"

Will set his jaw. The two men were now involved in a serious stare-down.

"Move out of my way, Clete," Will said. "Now."

Clete scowled and backed out of the doorway. Will waited until he was well clear and then left the office.

Like most of the old roads in eastern Kentucky, Route 7 is a winding deathtrap braided with a creek and an old railroad track. At times, the road almost falls into the creek.

By the time he arrived at the intersection between routes 7 and 588, it was full dark. Will slowed his truck after passing Route 588 but didn't see anything that looked like a store. The creek was on his left. The store had to be on the right. After a couple of miles, he turned around.

This time, after passing the intersection again, he saw a white building to his left. He stopped and pulled in.

A cornice over the building's front porch had large letters that read, "C. B. CAUDILL." The building was dark. Will walked up the steps to the porch and tried the door. Locked. He knocked. There was no answer.

A curled and faded door sign that purported to list the store's hours said that it was open until 6 p.m., which was five minutes away. Will frowned. The sign also said that the store opened at 8 a.m.

He peered through the window. In the dark, he could see a few spare shelves of convenience goods. The wood floors were bowed. On the porch sat several rocking chairs. Will had not seen a store like it in decades.

The night was getting cold. Two cars passed along Highway 7, and Will suddenly had an urge to run back to his truck and flee. He forced himself to look calmly around the porch, although he now saw little in the twilight.

The whole thing seemed so bizarre. He had heard of the place during a shriek-filled Pentecostal service with a guy who ate dead animals whole and was now a drug fugitive, and from a preacher who said moments later that he didn't remember what he'd said. The place itself seemed from another time.

Will felt as if he were standing beside himself, a feeling he was sure was more common in Appalachia than almost anyplace else. The past seems somehow present in the mountains. People have family picnics at graveyards. Buildings are allowed to decay in place. In most of the rest of the country, the new replaces the old. Here, present and past live side by side.

Will smiled.

He seemed to have abandoned the reasonable and taken refuge in the supernatural.

"Nothin' else's worked," Will said out loud.

He climbed back into his truck. He would return the next day, although he decided not to test the 8 a.m. opening. His report would have to wait.

He put the truck in gear and steered toward his family homeplace. His mother's eightieth birthday party was about to start.


Paul Murphy lived on one of the few mountaintops left in Hazard. At one end of the ridge sat a hotel, The La Citadelle (which translated roughly into "The The Fort"), that had once been the swankiest spot in town.

The hotel had hosted the launch party for the TV show *Dukes of Hazzard*. In the booming days of the OPEC oil embargo, its bar had been swimming with drunk coal operators and fading moonshiners who brawled over who had the best-looking cowboy boots and the toughest woman.

But a Quality Inn sprang up on Highway 80 just outside town, and business at The La Citadelle—where rooms were small and the plumbing uncertain—dried up. The hotel closed and, although there had long been talk about opening it up again or redeveloping the site, it sat empty.

On the other end of the mountain sat Paul's aerie and those of his fellow coal operators. It was Hazard's equivalent of Belair. The driveways were steep, winding, and among the first roads to be salted and plowed by the county when the forecast even hinted snow.

Local wags joshed that the operators were hoping for an unobstructed view of the University of Kentucky—one hundred miles away. Surface-mining coal companies were flattening nearly every mountain in between.

The house was modern, with huge picture windows and a cantilevered terrace that stretched out over the mountaintop. And standing outside it for several hours, Amos had noticed almost no security. Not that he expected any. Burglarizing Paul's home would be as unthinkable to most eastern Kentuckians as knocking over a Mafia castle would be to Sicilians. It just wasn't done.

But Amos's visit to Sunfire had made him realize that only violence or sabotage would slow down those huge strip-mining machines. In either case, workers' lives would be endangered. Amos decided that unless he heard otherwise from God, he could not walk that path.

This led him to Paul. He seemed the key to so many of the things swirling through Amos's life. Somehow, Paul Murphy needed to understand the needs of the natural world.

Amos decided to assemble his 30.06 rifle.

The shell for a 30.06 looks like a small missile. The report from the gun sounds like a cannon. Held incorrectly, the kick can cause a separated shoulder. It was designed to take down sizable game—elk, moose, bear. Nothing but hamburger is left if the gun is used on smaller animals.

It is a big gun.

Amos walked to a nearby mountain and set up a blind and waited. Deer are plentiful in eastern Kentucky, and Amos had little doubt that he would see one or two as the night wore on.

He was hoping for something small. Anything sizable would be mighty hard to carry back across the mountain.

Just as night fell, he spotted a pair that would do nicely. They seemed to be a young doe and her mother. Amos took aim at the smaller of the two, breathed out, and gently squeezed the trigger.

The rubber bullet struck the doe just over her left eye. She collapsed. Her mother bolted. Amos waited until the echoes of the shot died out. He couldn't be too careful, though, or he'd lose his window of time.

He walked over to the doe and laid his hand on her neck. She was still alive. He looked at her head. She was bleeding from the blow of his rubber bullet, but the wound didn't appear to be serious.

He tied her feet together and hoisted her over his head.

By the time he got to Paul's house, Amos was drenched in sweat. Even at less than a yearling, the doe weighed close to eighty pounds. She had twitched several times. Amos figured he had only a few moments until she woke up.

He stood beneath Paul's house and listened. There was no sign of any occupant. After a few tries, he found a window that pushed open. Amos cut the ropes from the doe's legs and placed her inside the house. He closed the window, crouched, and waited.

The doe suddenly flailed its legs. It shook its head and sprang to its feet. It froze and then seemed to see Amos. It ran in the other direction. Amos heard a crash. He smiled and walked away.

Nature was paying a visit on her destroyer.

# CHAPTER THIRTY-ONE

Maybe two dozen people were already crowded into the modest living room. Almost all were standing. In their midst was Will's mother, sitting on the couch. Like everyone else, Will had to make obeisance. When he bent to kiss her, she caught his wrist in a cold grip.

"Now, Will, I want you to listen to Paul," she said loudly.

Will was certain that everyone in that room—family, friends, neighbors, and a couple of secretaries from Blue Gem—knew that Will had rolled his father's desk out a second-story window in a fight with Paul. He would have preferred this little rebuke to have been privately delivered. But his mother was firmly in her dotage, and she seemed oblivious to Will's embarrassment.

Or maybe she wasn't, Will thought.

"Stop this foolishness," she said. "This is a family."

"Yes, ma'am," Will croaked.

"Now that your father's passed, I told Paul to take you back into the company. He said he would. As a foreman."

"Foreman," Will said and gave a tight smile. When hell freezes over, Will thought.

"And then you can go back to being respectable. No more drinking. No more inspecting. No more nonsense."

Will dropped even the pretense of smiling.

"Paul? You hear?"

"Yes, ma'am," Paul spoke up, standing just a few feet from Will.

His eyes down, Will walked back to stand in the doorway between the living room and the TV room. The crowd parted, giving him a wide berth. Will hoped that, being out of his mother's sight, he would eventually drop from her mind. He was not immediately successful.

"Investigation and interviews and lawyers. Can't have that. Got to stop, Will. Got to. Poor Paul. I mean, after all."

Will kept his eyes on the ground.

"Katie? The new kitchen looks wonderful."

"What? Oh," Will's mother said, and Will's humiliation was done.

Uncle Elliott was his rescuer—again. The old man glanced over at Will with a twinkle in his eye, and Will mouthed a silent "thank you."

Will walked straight to the table with the liquor and poured himself a tall glass of Johnnie Walker. He felt better after the third swallow.

Tessy came and brought Helen. Will wandered the house, talking little, nursing his drink. It was his childhood home, and he rarely saw it anymore. His parents long ago could have afforded a better, bigger place, but they'd remained in the same house for more than fifty years, and Will was glad of it.

He walked down the back steps, stopped on the landing, and looked out the window. He could see the Cranes' house beyond the driveway. The lights were on, and Will vaguely wondered how Mary, Rob's wife, was coping that night. Nighttime had to be the worst. It was for Will, and Tessy was only thirty-five miles away. He couldn't imagine what it would be like to be permanently separated from your partner.

Will's mind wandered to Rob's letter and the story of the condom. What could Rob have meant by it? His eyes drifted down, and Will saw Paul's car pulled up near the back door. Will got a wild notion. Why, he couldn't say.

He walked down the rest of the stairs into the kitchen and went out the back door. Paul's Jaguar presented itself. Will acknowledged to himself that what he was about to do was stupid, that it could only lead to trouble, but that he was powerless to stop himself. He walked around to the passenger door and tried the handle. It wasn't locked. He opened the door, sat in the passenger seat, opened the glove box and saw . . . an owner's manual, an insurance card, and a brochure for a Florida resort. That was all. No condoms, no drugs, and no answers to the mystery of the Red Fox inundation.

Paul didn't even have a handgun.

Will looked back up at the house. He'd been an idiot to do this, but it didn't look like anyone had noticed. If he snuck away now, no one would be the wiser. Problem was, he couldn't stop himself. He pushed the button for the trunk, which thunked open.

He got out and walked to the back. He leaned over and peered into the trunk. There was a golf bag. Still no condoms or drugs in sight. Then it caught his eye, a long black object in some sort of case. Golf club? Or, Lord, maybe a rifle? Will leaned in and reached for the object. Quite suddenly, the trunk lid crashed down on his head, and Will fell to the ground.

Paul came around the back of the car and kicked Will in the side.

"What the fuck you doing, Will? You searching my car?"

Will grabbed Paul's legs and tried to pull him down. Paul managed to get one foot out of his grasp and then he kicked Will across the head. Will let go of Paul's other leg and curled up into a ball.

Paul kicked his brother again.

"You fuckin' piece o' shit moron. I wouldn't take you back at Blue Gem even as a miner. You're fuckin' stuck at MSHA."

Will took his arms off his head and looked up at his brother. Blood poured from a gash just above his hairline and dripped out of his nose. Will coughed.

"Sorry," Will said. He spit blood. "It was Rob's . . ." Then he stopped himself. He didn't want to tell his brother about Rob's letter. And he wouldn't be able to explain it anyway. As far as Will knew, Paul still didn't know that he and Rob had put hot peppers in those condoms.

"Rob's what? You blamin' me for Rob's death? That why you're do-ing this?"

Will sat up. Blood poured down his face. He put his hand to the gash, and blood ran down his arm.

"That a rifle in your trunk, Paul?"

Paul snorted. The trunk was still slightly open. Paul closed it and did the same to the passenger door and then locked the car.

"Stay out of my fuckin' car, and stay out of my fuckin' life, Will. And get your shit together and stop fuckin' drinkin'."

They both breathed heavily.

"Christ, come on inside. Clean yourself up," Paul said.

"No. Not looking like this," Will said, and rolled to his feet. Will got out his keys and gingerly entered his truck, with Paul watching silently the whole time.

"You shouldn't drive," Paul said in a flat voice.

"I'll be all right," Will said.

"It's not you I'm worried about."

Will closed his door and rolled down the window. He backed up the truck, and Paul stepped aside. Will drove away.

The next morning, Will had a large lump on his head, his scalp was caked with blood, his nose was cherry red, and a dark bruise had appeared on his rib cage. He got up anyway. He had never before been midwife to a protest rally, so he was bent on watching it unfold.

He bought an Egg McMuffin breakfast and drove around to the OSM office near the old hospital. He parked in the hospital parking lot and maneuvered so the government office was in front of him. With the truck's engine running and the heat on, Will dug into his McDonald's bag and folded the *Lexington Herald-Leader* over the steering wheel.

It was seven fifteen, almost an hour before the protest was due to start. Will figured he'd be reading recipes by the time anything interesting happened, but that was fine. He didn't want to miss a thing.

It was a brilliant early March day. The temperature rose into the forties, the sun was shining, and the smell of burning coal seasoned the air. Will rolled his window down halfway but kept the heat going in the truck.

At seven thirty, he saw Lauren pull up in a gray Subaru wagon. She parked in the OSM parking area, popped her hatch, and unloaded several bundles. Two other women pulled up in a battered green Datsun pickup and came over to greet Lauren. Both had fold-up chairs.

Missy Hogg arrived in her pickup, followed by two other cars. A gaggle of six women led by Mrs. Hogg approached Lauren and the others. The two groups shook hands like players on opposing softball teams. Lauren handed out several dog-eared picket signs that read "UNFAIR!" which the Hell-for-Certain women accepted with embarrassed laughs.

Then Lauren unfurled a banner strung between two poles that read, "OSM MUST ACT!" The two other activists, both young women with shoulder-length hair, took hold of the poles.

Everyone seemed to stand uncertainly for a few minutes. Several cars turned into the OSM parking area, paused in front of the protesters, and then drove gingerly around the thicket of signs and people to parking spaces beyond.

When the occupants of the cars walked past and into the OSM building, the protesters ignored them entirely.

Lauren stepped in front of the protesters and turned her back to the road. She had a bullhorn.

"We are here because it's unfair!" Lauren shouted.

"Yeah!" the two young activists shouted.

"It's unfair OSM has done nothing to help the people of Hell-for-Certain," Lauren said.

"Yeah," the two young activists yelled.

"OSM has got to do something!" Lauren said.

"Yeah," the activists said, but this time several of the residents— clued into the timing—chimed in.

Will smiled despite himself.

Lauren switched hands on the bullhorn and there was a brief electronic screech.

"Unfair!" she shouted, and raised her right fist.

The activists and then residents echoed her. "Unfair!" rang through the north end of Hazard. Just as the volume was beginning to fade, Lauren said "All right!" into the bullhorn, and the two young activists clapped and shouted "All right!" back to her.

Lauren walked back into the group of protesters, and everyone smiled. After a few minutes, the smiles faded. The young activists got out beach chairs, which they set up for themselves. They invited two residents to sit as well. Others sat down on the curb, still holding their signs. After about fifteen minutes, most put down their signs.

"Well," Will said to himself.

He put his truck in gear and backed out of his parking spot. He drove slowly past the protest, deciding to take the long way back to his office. Then he found that he had turned into the OSM office. He knew he shouldn't, but he wanted to find out what was next.

He pulled up to the group and rolled down his window. Lauren turned and saw him. Seated in her own beach chair, she did not walk over.

"Got everything organized, I see," Will said, trying to sound friendly.

"We're telling truth to power, Will. You should try it sometime," Lauren shouted back so all could hear.

There was a prickle across the scars on Will's back.

"What's next?" Will asked, still smiling.

"We keep telling truth to power," Lauren shouted. "All day long. Every hour we'll rally. Want a flier?"

"Sure," Will said.

Lauren got up and handed him one. It showed an accurate map of Hell-for-Certain Creek Road dotted with cartoonish house figures in what appeared to be the correct locations. "Save Our Homes" was emblazoned across the top.

"Pretty good," Will said. He folded it and put it in his pocket.

He saw Mrs. Hogg and smiled. A scolding look had returned to her face.

"Good luck," he said. He put the truck in reverse.

Will swung back past the OSM entrance and was about to complete his three-point turn to reenter Main Street when he saw his uncle Elliott emerge from his white Cadillac, which as usual he'd parked illegally on Main Street. Will waved, but the old man didn't see him.

Uncle Elliott walked up to the group of protesters. Lauren rose from her beach chair. He stopped a couple of yards away from the group and seemed to say something to all of them. Will wasn't close enough to hear Uncle Elliott's brief speech, but the cheers that followed were clear.

Will shifted the truck into park, turned off the ignition and got out. Uncle Elliott had just finished saying one more thing, which had been mostly lost in the cheers. He turned to walk back to his car, and Will caught up to him.

"Uncle Elliott, what are you doing here?" Will asked.

"The right thing," the old man said, his face creased into a sad smile. "Told 'em I'd pay fair value for their homes."

"Really?"

"Yup," Uncle Elliott said. "Someone in the family had to."

"But why you? Why not Paul, for chrissake?"

The old man pursed his lips and shook his head.

Ephrom Mainard stuck his head out the door of the OSM office, saw Will, and came over almost on tiptoes.

"What happened?" Mainard whispered.

"Uncle Elliott said he'd buy their homes," said Will, his pride and amazement showing.

"No shit?"

"No shit."

The old man just stood there with a half-smile. Will clapped him on the shoulder and gave him a hug.

"All right, that's enough. I got work to do. Need to get a real estate appraiser up that hollow and start writing checks," Uncle Elliott said, and he ambled off to his car.

Will watched him go, affection shining in his eyes. He shook his head and hit Mainard in the arm.

"Ow," Mainard said and rubbed his arm. "I can't believe this," he pointed his thumb at the protesters, "actually worked."

Will looked at the protesters, who seemed to have sobered a bit.

"What happened to your nose?" Mainard asked. Will waved him off.

"I'll see ya," Will said and walked toward the gathering.

Lauren was speaking without a bullhorn to the protesters. She didn't need amplification.

"And if he doesn't pay what's right, we'll be back," she said.

There was no applause.

Will walked over to Mrs. Hogg.

"Congratulations," he said.

Mrs. Hogg seemed to take a moment to recognize him.

"My family's lived up that creek for more than one hundred years. Virgil and I grew up there," she said. Then she smiled.

"Can't wait to get out. Lexington, here we come." She gave a little shimmy.

Will laughed.

"Have a good trip," he said and backed into Lauren, who turned to hug Will and then, recognizing him, stopped.

"You won," Will said to help her recover.

"When you fight, you win," Lauren said.

Will raised his eyebrows. Not in his experience, but he let it pass.

"Congratulations," he said and walked away.

"Will," he heard Lauren say. He turned back.

"You asked about Joe and Gaynell Begley?" She turned and motioned to a frail woman sitting in a straight-back wooden chair on the walkway beside the OSM building. Will had not noticed her before.

"This is Gaynell Begley."

Her hair was white and pulled into a bun. Her eyes were pale blue. She wore khakis, a blue button-up blouse, and no jewelry. She had a soft smile and a calm but focused expression. Will liked her immediately.

"Mrs. Begley," he said, suddenly lost. "I'm Will Murphy. I'm a special investigator with MSHA."

She nodded, and her smile seemed to deepen.

"Nice to meet you, Mr. Murphy," she said with a soft lilt.

Lauren turned and hugged someone else. Mrs. Begley and Will briefly watched her, and then Mrs. Begley turned her eyes back to Will. The silence that followed did not seem to bother her at all.

"Someone suggested that I should visit your store," Will finally stammered.

"Someone?" she said simply.

"He was, ah, he was part of an investigation," Will said, flushing.

"I no longer drive, Mr. Murphy. Sheila," she nodded in the direction of one of the young activists, "drove me here. If you would drive me back, we can visit the store together."

"I would be delighted," Will said.

"I'll just tell Sheila," she said.

"I'll get my truck," Will said and strode the fifteen yards back to his vehicle.

He pulled up to the curb and sat for a second. When he realized that Mrs. Begley was not moving, he bolted out his door and came around to her.

"If you could be so kind," she said, motioning to her chair.

"Yes, ma'am," Will said and lifted the chair into the back of his truck.

Will turned to her and she walked gingerly toward his door. Will edged in front of her and opened it. He held out a hand, and she grabbed it. Her hand was cold but firm. She pushed herself up into the seat. Will closed the door and jogged back to the driver's side.

They were mostly silent on the drive. Mrs. Begley seemed only partly there. Will wasn't sure if it was a sense of inner peace, a lack of energy, or diminishing faculties that kept her quiet. But he was pleased to be able to do her a favor and would have driven her to Lexington if she wished.

When he pulled up outside the store, he ran around to open her door. She was halfway out by the time he got there, but he again proffered a hand. She did not take it. She walked slowly up the steps of the store, got out a lone key from her pocket—no chain—and opened the door.

She flipped a sign that read "CLOSED" to "OPEN." She held the door for Will. He walked in feeling as if he were entering a museum or a time warp.

She turned on a light but it wasn't enough. The large space was still dark around the edges. Two rows of shelving just in front of Will were filled with convenience items like Alka-Seltzer pills, candy bars, laundry soap, and breakfast cereal. But the shelves only reached about five feet high.

There were more shelves, but they seemed filled with flea market items, junk and maybe a few antiques. Will guessed that few of the convenience items were within their expire dates.

Mrs. Begley turned left and sat in a chair beside the counter, which was against the wall. Will suddenly wondered whether the sales counter—between the sales staff and the customer—was a modern invention. He was a bit surprised to see a computer register beside

Mrs. Begley instead of one of those old manuals that looked like an organ and played like a bell choir.

Then he saw it.

Above Mrs. Begley was a mining map. It looked just like the map he'd seen at the rescue, except for what seemed like an entire continent of mining along its left side.

Will walked over and stared. The map was framed, and the bottom of the frame hung at least a foot above his head. The lights in the store were also hanging, so the top of the map was dark. But he could make out its title: "BETHLEHEM NUMBER 11."

Mrs. Begley was looking placidly at him.

"This map," Will said. "Uhm, why do you have it?"

"I don't know. It's been there for as long as I can remember. I think my father put it up there," she said.

"Might I borrow it?" Will asked.

She considered.

"Surely," she said.

# CHAPTER THIRTY-TWO

After a nearly disastrous attempt to take the map down, Will accepted an offer by Mrs. Begley to get help. A teenager who lived nearby—a Goth with long black hair, black army fatigues, and a black T-shirt—came right over and happily pitched in.

The boy mounted a ladder, and Will stood on the counter. Together, they managed to get the map down and gently place it into Will's truck. It weighed nearly one hundred pounds, with thick glass in its frame. Will waved good-bye, feeling like one of those art experts who finds a Renoir at a yard sale, suckers the owner into selling for pennies, and then can't drive away fast enough.

If the Begley map was as different from the other Bethlehem map as he suspected, Carl Breathitt's murder might have been about something mighty different from drug trafficking.

Will wondered whether Paul was capable of murder. He remembered the time Paul got a shotgun for his birthday. He and Will had gone to a little pond near their house as evening fell. They had taken turns shooting any frog that popped its head out of the water.

Will still remembered how the frogs sprang into the air when they were shot, all four legs stretched out. Must have been some kind of involuntary reflex. Will stopped asking for a turn while Paul blasted away until the box of shells was empty.

What did it mean? Will had no idea. Was that really a rifle in his trunk? It seemed unlikely that Paul would actually shoot someone, but Will didn't rule out the idea—sorry, Mom—that Paul would get someone to commit murder for him.

If Carl was about to reveal that he had doctored the map on Paul's order, his murder made total sense. And the few felonies that MSHA could pursue were those involving fraudulent records.

Will had never heard of anyone altering an old mining map, but he was pretty sure that the charge would fall under the felony statutes. That would mean arrest and maybe even jail time for whoever did it. Will could imagine Paul doing just about anything to avoid that.

Still, before Will took any of these suspicions to the state police, he had to figure it out himself. Why in the world would Paul want to change the old map in the first place? To get an extra one hundred feet of coal? Maybe, but he'd have to go to an awful lot of trouble just for what would amount to $10,000 or $20,000 more in his pocket.

Old works were every miner's bogeyman. Stories abounded about horrible deaths—asphyxiations, poisonings, drownings—that no miner would willingly face. It was almost impossible to believe that Carl and the murdered foreman, Mike Barnes, would continue to work underground if they knew the possible danger.

And it had been a costly mistake. Paul had lost an operating mine and all of its equipment. The rescue effort alone probably cost him $500,000. And what for? A few thousand extra tons of coal? Even at $35 a ton, it just didn't seem likely.

Maybe it was all about drugs, but Will just couldn't believe that Paul would get mixed up in something like that. So who did it?

Will slapped his thigh. He had no answers, but he no longer wanted to surrender. At least not yet.

He pulled into the district parking lot and bounded out.

"Myrtle, who's around?" Will asked.

"What?" she said.

"Who's in the office?" he asked, trying to contain his impatience.

"Lucius," she said.

Will bolted back to Lucius's office, down at the end of the hallway. On the way, he glanced out the window at his truck to make sure the map was still there. Will knocked and opened the door at the same time. Lucius was on the phone. Will looked down.

"It's in the cabinet under the phone," Lucius said, and raised his index finger to Will. "Found it? All right. No problem. Honey, I got to go. All right. I love you, too. Bye-bye.

"Yeah?" he said.

"I need some help bringing something in. You mind?" Will asked.

Lucius sighed.

"Will, I got a call a few minutes ago from Stan Maylor, head of the state coal association?"

"Yeah?" Will said, feeling less certain that he wanted to hear what was next.

"He told me that you searched your brother's car. Without a warrant or a police officer present or anything. Said you and Paul got into a fight."

Will shrugged.

"Will, do you realize how much heat I have taken from having you on this investigation? Hell, any investigation? I've defended you for years, and you do this?"

"Look, are you gonna help me carry this thing in or not?"

Lucius nodded his head.

"Doesn't look like you won the fight," Lucius said with a slight smile and then raised his great frame from his overburdened chair.

He followed Will out. "You gotta know that Maylor's not gonna quit complaining on this thing. Somebody in Washington's gonna hear about it."

Will nodded and held the door for him.

"What is it?" Lucius said as they approached the truck.

"Some'm I picked up. Old mine map. Probably nothin'."

"Old mine map," Lucius said evenly.

The map was still covered by the old blanket Will had thrown over it. Lucius reached over the truck wall and pulled the blanket down. He looked at the map for at least fifteen seconds before speaking.

"This here's a map of the old works up at Red Fox and Hell-for-Certain, ain't it?"

"Think so," Will said quietly.

"Looks like it's a bit different from the one we were lookin' at," Lucius said, still staring intently at the map.

"Looks like."

Lucius sucked on his teeth.

"I reckon this means you ain't done with that report."

"I reckon so."

"Come on," Lucius said, and started pulling on the huge frame.

Will jumped in the truck and picked up the other end. When they got into the office's back hallway, Lucius stopped.

"Leave it here?" Lucius said.

"No, let's see if it'll make it into my office."

It did, but barely. They leaned it up against a pile of boxes.

Lucius stood looking at the map, but Will could tell that his eyes were elsewhere.

"You're on real thin ice here, Will. I wouldn't take too long noodlin' around with an old map."

"I know."

Lucius gave Will a rogue's smile, patted him on the shoulder, and left.

As soon as the big man left, Will swept a pile of documents off his desk to get at the map of the old works that had been given to him by Paul. He taped it to the framed version, got down on his haunches, and compared the two. Paul's version was missing an entire section.

Will got out a pen and twice counted the tiny lines signifying breaks on the ghost section of the older map. Forty-five. Will wasn't quite sure of the spacing in older mines, but he thought he remembered that they were about forty feet between centers—two-thirds the size of modern mines. He got out the calculator from his desk. About 1,800 feet—a third of a mile.

Will stood up and stared at the doctored map.

What the hell did it mean?

He turned back to the floor behind him and fished out the map of Blue Gem's Red Fox mine. He pulled the doctored map off the framed one and tried to line up the end of the modern mine with the true picture of the older one. He tried to imagine the spot up on the mine bench where they had drilled that well as something near the meeting point between the two mines. Didn't work.

So he laid the framed map on the floor and then put the map of the modern mine to the side of it.

No words of wisdom presented themselves to his brain.

He walked out of his office.

"Hey, Myrtle," he said.

"Yeah, sugar," she answered sassily. Her mother must be back on her medications.

"Where do we keep our topo maps?" Will asked.

"Break room."

"Right," Will said and walked past Myrtle to the lunchroom.

Maps dripped out a large cabinet that stood in one corner.

Will pawed through several drawers and eventually found one he thought might work. He strode back into his office.

The framed map had several survey points and Will found similar coordinates on the topographic map and lined them up. The two maps were of wildly different scales.

Still, Will felt he could see some kind of pattern here.

Then he remembered the flier handed out at the protest. He took it out. It showed a map of Hell-for-Certain Creek Road and the location of the houses. He lined the bend in the creek up with the one on the topographic map. And then it hit him.

Every house along the creek sat on top of the ghost section of the old mine.

Made total sense, Will thought. All those houses had been built where wells drew their water from the old works, so they had to be sitting on top of the old mine.

It still didn't answer why Paul or anyone at Blue Gem would knowingly cut into that aquifer. Not only would it endanger the mine and its miners, but it would destroy an entire community.

"What the fuck?" Will muttered to himself.

"It is not an accident, my friends, that the Middle East is in crisis," Preacher Rusty Seymour nearly shouted, his arms raised. "It is the work of the devil. He is here on earth. Amongst us. Even here, here in eastern Kentucky, in our beloved mountains, you can see his hand at work."

As the congregation started shouting, "Praise Jesus!" the passion spread. "Save us!" "Glory!" and a plain "aiee" built into a crescendo.

The church was nearly full, and the service soon was in full swing. Preacher Seymour's shirt was soaked through with sweat. His forehead glistened. Two teenage boys were strumming guitars near the front of the church and singing "Onward Christian Soldiers." Other worshipers chimed in.

Preacher Seymour had a microphone and a small amplifier. Its sound was tinny but effective. Everybody could hear him over the music.

"That's right, we are soldiers of God! Soldiers in His cause! And we must defeat Satan! We must defeat him by accepting Jesus into our hearts. Jesus!" he shouted.

The shout had a physical effect on the crowd, which swayed and echoed back, *"Jesus!"* A woman near the front collapsed to the floor. Preacher Seymour looked down at the woman and only then noticed Amos near the right wall of the church.

"There is one among us who has been through the valley of the shadow of death. One who has seen the devil face-to-face," Preacher Seymour said, looking directly at Amos.

"Who?" echoed around the church.

"Brother Blevins, you have wandered in the wilderness. Come and testify and cleanse yourself!"

Amos remained standing, frozen.

"Come! Help him, brothers. Help him to come before us."

Hands reached and pulled Amos toward the front of the church. Amos resisted and then let himself be led by two strong young women.

"Testify," the preacher shouted when Amos reached him. He pulled Amos around to face the crowd and then moved off.

Shouts of "Hallelujah!" and "Praise Jesus!" erupted through the pews.

"The Lord has spoken to me," Amos said, "right here in this church."

Amos didn't shout. He didn't use the microphone. His deep voice filled the church like incense.

"He told me to take a sabbatical from my worldly concerns, and I done heard Him. For the Lord said, 'Six years you shall sow your field and six years you shall prune your vineyard and gather in its fruits; but in the seventh year there shall be a sabbath of solemn rest for the land, a sabbath to the Lord.'

"And we must rest, friends. Rest ourselves and rest the land here," Amos said. "We got to stop tearing it up."

This was greeted with "Praise Jesus!" and "Hallelujah," but the enthusiasm seemed diminished. Several parishioners opened their eyes.

"God done told me to save His mountains," Amos said, his voice dropping. "We gotta stop what we been doing."

No more shouts. The singers began "Nearer My God to Thee." Most of the congregation took up the hymn. "Though like the wanderer, the sun gone down, darkness be over me . . ."

Amos closed his eyes.

"We are destroying God's work," he said. "We—"

"YES!" boomed Preacher Seymour's voice, and it crackled with feedback. He was at the back of the congregation, and he held his hands up high in supplication.

"We must repent, sinners!" he shouted into the microphone. "We must not destroy what God has given us, for God has given us His love."

Amos opened his eyes. Several congregants had turned their backs on him to look toward Preacher Seymour.

Preacher Seymour was done with him and was back to his sermonizing. Amos wanted to keep talking, keep trying. He had come to the service with a vague idea that he needed somehow to preach about man's stewardship of God's land. He knew that Preacher Seymour would ask him to testify. And he had failed in his mission.

Amos quietly returned to the side of the church, kicking himself for citing Leviticus. Nobody liked Leviticus. He should have used another passage—maybe Revelations.

The service carried on for some time without Amos paying much attention. And then Preacher Seymour's tone changed, and it snapped Amos out of his reverie.

"For Jesus did offer Himself up to the Pharisees. His followers offered to fight with the sword. And they did strike. But Jesus said no more of this. And He did heal the ear of the wounded slave. So we shall offer ourselves," Preacher Seymour said.

Something about the story struck Amos wrong. It didn't feel like the time to surrender.

Amos edged closer to the wall and looked out the window. It was pitch black outside, and he could see nothing but the skeletons of bare trees. He edged around to look back toward the parking lot. Still nothing. Then bright headlights. He heard two car doors slam.

Amos tried to open the window. It was painted shut. He lifted his chair and threw it through the glass. The guitarists stopped playing. The congregants stopped singing. Preacher Seymour, though, reached a fever pitch.

"And Pilate sought to free Jesus. Three times, he sought to free Him," Preacher Seymour said. "But the people were urgent, and Pilate gave way."

"Pontius Pilate is burning in hell, people!" Amos yelled. "And the Lord told me that we will too lessin' we stop tearin' up His mountains."

And with that, Amos threw himself out the window.

# CHAPTER THIRTY-THREE

He rolled in the undergrowth and came up with a sharp pain in his right arm. He must have jammed it against a piece of broken glass. Then he heard a shot. He felt more than heard the bullet whiz by his head. Amos broke into a run.

His backpack—with his weapons—was in the church.

Amos headed downslope, stumbled, pitched forward, and rolled down the hill. He sprang out of the roll still running and realized that his left shoulder was numb. He wondered if he'd been hit.

Amos had heard no challenge. No one had demanded that he stop. He didn't stop.

His eyes had yet to adjust to the light. He ran headlong into a tree and fell. Stunned, he got up and ran again. He sensed that the woods looked a bit thicker to the right. Amos ran toward the thicker screen.

He ran around bushes and down a few steep pitches. He no longer heard any pursuit. He ran around a large oak and stopped on the other side. His lungs burned.

He looked around the oak. Nothing. He strained to see more. He saw some flashes by the church. Maybe flashlights.

He knew that he had to start moving soon, but he needed another minute to rest. Still gasping, he looked at his right upper arm and probed the wound with his fingers. Just a cut.

He felt along his left shoulder. There was a bullet hole. He pushed a finger inside. Amazingly, he could feel the jagged top of the bullet. It seemed to have flattened itself along his shoulder blade. Something to worry about but it wouldn't kill him. At least not right away.

He heard a dog. And then another. He pushed away from the tree and headed sideways along the ridge. He figured he'd have to stay away from roads, where his pursuers could get help. This ridge would eventually take him eastward into Virginia, if he could get that far.

But if they had a couple of good dogs, sticking to the woods wouldn't help him. He needed a different answer. He had no idea what. He walked fast.

He had probably walked the whole length of Pine Mountain over the course of his life. There were several dangerous drop-offs, so he had to stay alert. Certainly the dogs would not be fool enough to walk over them.

Amos thought about sliding down some of those near-cliffs. Taking a risk on a steep slope might buy him some time. The dogs could make it down, but their handlers would want to be more careful. Depending on the slope and the risk, he might earn five or ten more minutes doing that—not enough to change the odds of escape.

He couldn't climb any trees, and the only lake on the mountain was behind him. Nothing.

There were a few homes. If Amos could stumble on a house with a car or something, he'd do what? Hold the occupants hostage? No. Steal their car? Maybe, but he would likely need a key. And the only way to get a key from somebody would be to threaten him, and he couldn't do that.

He certainly wasn't going to be able to flag down a car with his arm and shoulder dripping blood without getting reported immediately. And there wasn't another road that crossed Pine Mountain for at least five miles.

People were not the answer, Amos decided. The mountain, this sacred mountain, somehow had to take him.

The mountain!

Amos looked up. He'd already passed the path to his easternmost pot patch, but he thought he was about level with it. That would mean the Hazard number 5 coal seam would be above him. He went back to walking but edged a bit higher along the ridge.

He could hear the dogs in full bay now. They were at least a half mile behind him.

Amos saw a plateau above him and headed for it. The last few feet he had to use his hands to pull himself up.

The bench of the old strip mine was no more than seven feet wide—an early and crude toehold on the mountain. Amos kicked the wall in front of him. A hint of black rock showed. Encouraged, he pushed onward in his eastward march.

Finally, he came upon what he'd been hunting for—a hole in the mountain. It was no more than four feet high, but it was clearly an old mine. Amos ducked down and headed in. He was blind. He felt along the walls for several yards. He couldn't raise his left hand above waist level, but he could still feel the wall. The dirt gradually gave way to rock. He felt the contours of the work.

The coal was rough. He kept moving. He reached over with his right hand and stroked the wall. Too rough. Amos turned around and walked back out.

He needed something more than an old dog hole—a tiny effort by a few men to scrape a bit of coal out of the mountain. He needed a true mine, and the only way to tell from the entrance was to feel the quality of the work along the wall.

He emerged back into the night. The dogs were nearer. Amos continued along the bench. He passed another hole, but it was little more than a cave. He had to remind himself not to panic. He was walking fast—about the pace of a good dog handler. He figured that as long as he was moving, it was unlikely that they were gaining on him.

But he knew that he only had time for one, maybe two more failed attempts. Any more than that, and the dogs and handlers would come in sight. Then he could be shot, or the dogs would be let off the leash. Either would do him in.

He kept pushing himself.

The bench widened slightly, which was encouraging. The cliff to his right grew higher. A fair amount of labor had gone into carving the bench from the mountain. Amos strained to see any signs of early mining.

And then there it was. A portion of a concrete skirt that had surrounded the entrance was still visible. There was a wrought-iron fence that had rusted almost entirely through and then the remnants of a chain-link fence in front of that. Amos yanked the fencing away. There was no concrete cap.

It was perfect. The concrete and wrought iron were just the kind of touches that major mining companies had used on their biggest mines in the 1920s.

He jogged a bit farther along the bench and came to another entry, this one better preserved. Again he wrenched the fencing away. He decided to risk going even farther along the bench, and he stumbled into a third entrance.

Amos guessed that there were likely to be three or four more entrances along the bench and maybe even a possible exit out of a bore hole. It was exactly what he needed. Again he wrenched the fencing away from the entrance.

He stood for a moment thinking. The dogs raised the pitch of their barking. They knew he was near.

He crouched down and felt around the floor of the bench. He moved toward the ridge and carefully stepped over the side and down a few steps. After discarding several possibilities, Amos eventually settled on a clublike stick, which he put into his waistband at the small of his back.

He kept hunting around.

He took a few more steps down the slope and came up with a long, strong stick that could serve as both probe and spear.

Satisfied, he clawed his way back to the bench, walked to the entrance, and ducked into the mine.

He held the long stick in front of him, sweeping along the floor of the mine. The stick struck something solid, and Amos's heart went into his throat. A rock fall. But it seemed to block only a portion of the entrance. Amos went to the right of the fall, probing farther along. By facing straight into the mine instead of bending slightly to the side, he squeezed past the first part of the fall. He had no idea how long this tiny tunnel would last, but he kept going.

If he failed to reach the first crosscut, he was dead. The men outside would simply camp in front of this one entrance and wait for him to crawl out for a drink of water.

His tappings on either side suddenly widened to the point where the stick hit nothing.

He had reached an intersection. He might make it.

He turned and his stick hit something that didn't sound like stone or coal. Amos reached out a hand and edged forward. It was a column of wooden roof supports.

Modern mines use long screws to tie together the layers of rock above a mine and prevent roof falls. Older mines used columns of wooden wedges laid out in rising squares. The pillars were far less effective and made maneuvering around in the mine mighty difficult.

Amos felt gingerly down the pillar. Several wedges crumbled at his touch. He doubted that the column provided any support. He prayed for a moment and went back to tapping.

The sound of barking grew intense. The dogs were at the entrance.

His heart racing, Amos stumbled into another roof support. It fell entirely away. The roof above Amos rumbled. Amos ducked, expecting a fall. Nothing happened. He got to his knees, felt for his probe, then got to his feet. He lurched forward.

The dogs yapped excitedly. Amos guessed they'd been let off their leash. One dog suddenly yelped. It had probably run blind into that first roof fall.

Amos backtracked and felt around for the remains of the disturbed roof support. He separated the wood into two piles several feet apart and then rested his long stick upon them. The stick nearly touched the ribs on either side of the crosscut.

Amos stepped a few feet away. He got the club from his waistband.

The dogs—there seemed to be only two—covered the distance rapidly, whining their excitement.

They paused only briefly at the intersection. Amos could hear their breathing and snuffling. They came his way.

Amos could see nothing—no movement, no glowing canine eyes. The dogs were likely blind as well. Amos was counting on it.

The dogs approached. The stick clattered. Amos lunged. His left hand went directly into the dog's mouth. Amos swung with his right. The club caught the dog on its left shoulder—well away from its head.

The dog thrashed and kicked away. Amos grabbed a leg with his left hand and, from his knees, swung the club again. The heavy club crushed the side of the dog's head. It yelped and scrambled madly away.

The second dog sank its teeth into Amos's right calf. Amos flinched and released his grip on the first dog's leg. Before it could scramble away, he swung one more time at its head. He hit a glancing blow. The dog's yelp was lower in tone.

The second dog was now ripping at Amos's leg. Amos put his entire strength into clubbing its head. Stupidly, the club struck the roof, so Amos's first blow just made the dog loosen its grip. It quickly bit him again and continued thrashing. The second blow stopped its movement. The third and fourth fell with sickening thuds. Still, the dog's jaws remained sunk into Amos's leg. Blind with pain, he felt along the rib for the other dog. It was several feet in front of him, crawling away.

He grabbed a handful of its fur with his left hand and dragged it back. The dog snapped at Amos, who clubbed it again on the head, and again made only a glancing blow. The dog whined pitifully.

Amos found its neck and, with his left hand, held it down, finally making an easy target for his right. He clubbed it to death in seconds.

He let the club drop and put both hands on either side of the jaws gripping his right calf and tried to pry them open. He couldn't. He pressed his leg to the ground, digging the teeth further into his flesh, and tried again. The jaws were locked.

He felt around for the club, found it, and chopped at the side of the dog's head. He switched hands and chopped at the other side. He soon beat the dog into pulp.

He set the club down and pushed again at the jaws. One side of the lower jaw levered away. Amos picked up the club and chopped again at the other side.

Finally, he was able to pry the jaws off his leg.

He sat for a moment, breathing. He heard a whistle from behind him—the handlers calling their dogs.

Amos started to crawl toward one of the entrances he knew would lead him out of the mine.

# CHAPTER THIRTY-FOUR

After two hours of wracking his brains, the only thing Will had decided was that his brother Paul was up to something pretty nasty, but Will just couldn't quite figure out what it was or why.

With that, Will decided that his brains had had enough. He headed for a bar.

A local builder had bought an old bank downtown and turned it into a fancy bar called The Bank. It had a tin roof, stained-glass windows, a restored vault, and lots of brass and dark wood. It felt out of place in Hazard, and Will guessed it was a money loser. He wanted to get as much enjoyment out of it as he could before it closed.

Like most alcoholics, Will justified each trip to the bar as a release needed because of his peculiar set of burdens. He was investigating his brother. It was tough. He needed to get through this.

The drinking had started after the explosion, after his brother died, after his best friend got disabled, after Will nearly died, and after everyone realized—Will particularly—that these many disasters were his fault.

His wife and his best friend had both tried to get him to stop drinking. The only result had been that his wife had left him and his best friend had stopped talking to him.

He slid into a chair at the bar and ordered a Bud. A Duke-Virginia basketball game had just started on the TV behind the bar. For a true-blue Kentuckian, there are few pleasures greater than rooting against Duke. Will settled in.

An elderly couple sat eating at one table. He wore brown slacks and a brown jacket that didn't quite match. She wore a handsome black dress with white lace at the collar.

Three ladies who appeared to be in their late fifties or early sixties sat together at another table. They were drinking whiskey sours and occasionally burst into loud peals of laughter. They each wore blue jeans, tennis shoes, colorful sweatshirts, and large gold earrings. One had on a baseball hat with an outline of a dog.

The only patrons who appeared to be under thirty were a group of five at the pool table, three guys and two girls. The girls wore the sorority uniform: V-neck white T-shirts, blue jeans, black half-boots, and blond ponytails pulled through the back of blue UK baseball hats. Each wore stud earrings and slender necklaces. When lining up their shots, they leaned over just enough to offer glimpses of white, lacy bras.

The boys wore khakis, blue shirts, black belts, and hungry looks. They laughed loudly and at least one of them would wake up the next day to find that he was fifty years old with a soul-crushing job, a balloon mortgage payment due, and a wife who was thinking of leaving him for a tennis pro.

Will watched them with a mixture of pity and envy.

The blaze of youth grew too bright, and Will looked away. He saw a black Taurus pull up to the curb just outside. Will watched a young guy, tall and rail thin, get out of the car. He walked toward the entrance of the bar, hunched over as if barely making headway against a howling wind. He had short, light brown hair and was wearing a long, somewhat formal winter coat, dark pants, and basketball sneakers. He came into the bar, looked up, and locked eyes with Will. He turned right around and left.

Will got off his stool and took several steps toward the door. He saw the guy almost run to his car and quickly drive away. Will noted the license plate number, but he had no idea what to do next. He could call the police, but what would he say? "Sheriff, some guy has been sitting at the end of my driveway, scaring my wife away from coming back to have sex with me? And now he just ran away from me?"

Will went back to his stool and tried to watch the game. But with five minutes left in the second half, Duke stretched its lead to fifteen points. Will decided he couldn't stand to watch until the final whistle.

He paid his tab and left. When he got to his truck, Will quickly did the math. Six beers in two hours. He was probably okay.

He got in, started the truck, and pulled out. Within a block, a Hazard police cruiser turned on its emergency lights. Will pulled over, his heart pounding. The officer walked up and Will rolled down his window.

"Some'm wrong, Officer?" Will asked.

"Get out of the car." He was blond and his name badge said "Jones."


Amos opened his eyes to see three squatting children staring intently at him. Each had dark eyes and dark hair. The two boys, who appeared to be about four and seven, wore matching gray pants, blue shirts, and old-fashioned straw hats. The girl, between them in position and age, wore a dark green dress and what appeared to be a bonnet.

Amos tried to rise up on his elbow, but a jab of pain in his back made him settle back on the floor.

He looked past the steady gazes of the children. He was in a house, but it seemed to be under construction. There were curtains where doors should be. The interior walls had lathing but no plaster. The floor was wood, its planking wide and its finish satin.

There was a large sink pulled slightly away from the wall. There were kitchen cabinets, but none hung on the walls as they would in a finished kitchen. There was no refrigerator yet, no dishwasher, and no modern stove, although what appeared to be a large wood-burning stove hissed happily to one side.

Behind him, a fireplace kept his left side warm. He was covered in what appeared to be a handmade quilt of blues and greens. He realized that he was wearing a blue shirt identical to the one worn by the boys.

He reached down to his waist. He wore what looked like pajama bottoms with a drawstring. His own clothes were gone.

A small, fat woman walked in from outside wearing the same green dress as the girl, only she also wore a white apron. She set what appeared to be a heavy pot on the wood-burning stove and turned toward Amos. A smile broadened her face.

"You're awake," she said.

The accent was foreign.

Amos briefly worried that he had died and that this was some sort of antechamber to hell or heaven. There was something distinctly odd about the family and house before him.

Then he remembered the dogs and struggled to his feet. The two youngest children bolted to their mother's skirts. The seven-year-old remained, his head tilted back to continue to stare at Amos.

"It's all right," the woman said. "You are safe here."

She spoke in a foreign language to the seven-year-old, who rose up from his haunches and, still staring at Amos, backed toward the door.

Amos heard a clock tick, a horse whinny, and a man shout. The light from the windows suggested dawn or dusk, and then Amos realized that it must be dusk and that he had been out for almost a full day. The woman looked at Amos with a kindly smile. She turned away from him and set to chopping vegetables that were piled on one of the cabinets. The children continued to stare at Amos wordlessly.

"You should sit," the woman said with her back turned to him. "You lost blood, and bandages should not be moved."

The accent wasn't Hispanic.

There were four chairs around the fireplace, all wood and handmade. Amos gathered the quilt and sat in one of the chairs. His right calf and upper back screamed as he sat. He reached down to feel his leg. Strips of cloth had been wound around it. He could feel some sort of cream underneath.

He reached around to his shoulder blade. There seemed to be tape over cotton. Amos pushed and was rewarded with a pain so intense that he couldn't breathe for a moment.

He looked up to see the woman laughing and shaking her head.

"I will get Jacob before you pull your wound apart," she said.

She wiped her hands on her apron and stepped outside. The children, who had been clutching at her skirts, stayed behind and silently stared.

Amos looked into the fire.

A moment later, a man came in dressed like the boys. At a chair near the door, he took off his boots. He stood again, although with some difficulty, and walked over to Amos. Amos rose, and the man put out his hand.

They shook.

"Welcome," the man said. "Before introductions, you had a bullet in your back. Do you wish to call the police?"

The man held Amos's hand and looked into his face. Amos stared back.

"No? I thought so," he said and smiled. "If you had, I would have had to apologize for digging it out instead of calling an ambulance. I am Jacob Fellinghausen, but do not tell me your name. Let me get you some water."

Fellinghausen went over to a bucket on one of the counters, dipped in a mug, and brought it back to Amos.

"Sit," said Fellinghausen, and he lowered himself with a sigh into a chair. Amos drank the mug dry in a couple of gulps and then sat beside his host.

"You have done me a great favor," Fellinghausen said. "I have long wished to perform the gesture of the good Samaritan by helping a traveler in need. All the better that you may be a dangerous traveler."

Fellinghausen laughed and slapped Amos on the knee. Amos grimaced.

"Oh, I am sorry," Fellinghausen said, and laughed again, almost giddy. "I will squander this chance yet by injuring you anew. I cleaned the scrapes on your knees and wiped them with honey but bandages I did not put."

Amos nodded and felt the bandage on his left shoulder again.

"You sure done a good job," he said.

"I thought you would sound that way," Fellinghausen said, nodding.

"Bram!" Fellinghausen said, and the seven-year-old pushed himself away from the door. Fellinghausen turned to the boy and spoke in a foreign language.

The boy came forward and haltingly gestured at Amos's mug. Amos gave it to the boy, who took it back to the bucket, got more water, and returned it to Amos, who drank it all again and handed it back to the boy, and the process repeated.

When Amos sipped his third mug, Fellinghausen spoke to the boy again, who retreated back to the door.

"We feared that you would be pursued here, and so my two oldest swept your tracks for some distance away from the house," he said.

Amos glanced back at the seven-year-old.

"Not Bram," Fellinghausen said, and laughed again. "I have a fourteen-year-old and a thirteen-year-old. They can be trusted to do good work."

"'Preciate that," Amos said.

"Hm," Fellinghausen said and cocked his head.

"You have been shot, cut and mauled by an animal," Fellinghausen said. "Your hands and knees show that you have been forced to crawl a long distance. You have not bathed in some time. And you had this in your pocket."

Fellinghausen turned over his left hand to reveal Amos's New Testament. Leatherbound and with gold on its pages, the book was not much bigger than an address book. Fellinghausen had been holding it the whole time, but Amos had not noticed.

"It was this that made my path clear," he said and patted it. "If you bring evil to this house, I would say that it is God's will. But I think this was in your pocket to remind me of my duty.

"Here."

He gave the book to Amos, who began rubbing his thumbs across its cover as someone might worry a rosary.

Fellinghausen, who had a neatly trimmed brown beard and glasses, watched Amos cradle the book.

"Now tell me why I am here to save you, and don't spare the details," Fellinghausen said, and he edged his chair closer to Amos. "I may get the chance to be God's instrument only once in my life."

# CHAPTER THIRTY-FIVE

It would be hard to compete with the ten worst moments in Will Murphy's life. Learning Jeff had died in the explosion; hearing Tessy say he couldn't drive Helen anymore; listening to his father banish him from Blue Dog.

There were lots to choose from, but sitting in a Hazard jail cell charged with drunken driving and realizing that he couldn't think of anyone to call had to sit somewhere on the list.

There was no way to reach Tessy without calling Paul, and he couldn't do that. His mother was in no shape to pick him up. With Rob dead, he couldn't ask Mary to put up the money. And he didn't want anyone from work to show because he hoped no one there would find out.

The only one left was Uncle Elliott, and when Will was led out of the holding area and saw the kindly old man, his heart was filled with gratitude. Will gripped Uncle Elliott's arm and nearly cried.

"Thanks. Thanks so much, Uncle El."

"Come on, son. I'll drive you home."

They walked outside into the cold, black Hazard night. The front door of the jail looked like the back door to a pizza shop, and it opened out into a small street parallel to Main. Uncle Elliott's white Cadillac was parked illegally in an area reserved for police officers, but nobody had bothered it.

Will climbed into the passenger seat, although he was feeling chastened enough that he, like some busted teenager, almost climbed in the back.

Uncle Elliott was blessedly quiet for the first few minutes of the drive.

"Mind if I smoke?" Will asked.

"Go ahead."

Will rolled down the window, and the frigid air came pouring in. Uncle Elliott shrugged his shoulders, an involuntary reflex to the cold. Will thought he should probably stub out the cigarette and close the window. He didn't.

"Your father ever tell you about what happened between us?" Uncle Elliott finally asked.

"Between you and Dad? No."

Uncle Elliott put his lower lip over his upper one and nodded.

"Well, we was just like you and Paul. I mean, same damn stuff. I look at you, Will, and it's just amazin' how much you remind me of myself."

"I heard you were some kinda hell-raiser, Uncle El."

"You could say that again." The old man chuckled. "Sold moonshine. Drank a fair bit of it, too. Shot up the neighbors. Made a general idiot of myself. Just like you."

"Get arrested?" Will asked.

"Oh yeah."

"Get beat up by Dad?".

"Yeah. He hit me so hard one time messed up my eye. Got no peripheral vision in this'n here," he said, and pointed to his left eye.

Will's face fell.

"Blow up the family's mine and kill your younger brother?"

Uncle Elliott sighed. "No. Never done that."

They were quiet for a moment.

"Your granddad, he didn't take too kindly to my antics. He got sore and kicked me out of the house. We never really made up. Then he died, and I lost the chance to. He mostly cut me out of his will, just like your dad did to you."

Will's brow furrowed.

"But Uncle El, I thought you said you owned a lot of the land around Hell-for-Certain and all the coal rights underneath."

"I do. But it ain't like it's beachfront property. You seen the people what lives up Hell-for-Certain, right? Most of 'em ain't got two nickels to rub together. There's some coal there, that's for sure. And I think your granddad's idea was to give most of the coal company to your father, and give me most o' the rights to the land. That way we would have to get along.

"Least, that was the idea. Your dad didn't go along. He just decided to buy the rights to other people's land. And all the other companies figured that if your dad didn't want it, there must be some'm wrong with it. Couldn't sell it for nothin'. And I didn't have enough shares in the company to do nothin' about it."

"Wow. I had no idea."

"Yeah. It was rough."

They were quiet again.

"But isn't the Red Fox mine on that land?"

"Oh yeah. I mean, once Paul Junior took over the company, he saw right away that a mine there made sense. And he got it done. I leased the whole thing to Blue Gem. Paul struck a tough deal, I'll tell you that. So for years, I got nothin' outta that land. Worse than nothin', 'cause I had to pay the taxes. Made it hard."

"I'm sorry, Uncle El."

The old man shrugged.

"And now it's you, doing the same thing, facing the same problems. You gotta do it different."

"Uncle El, I didn't even get any land."

"Probably just as well. Having that land and not being able to do nothin' with it tore me up inside. Tore me up. And now? Now I'm spending every dime I made from leasin' it to your brother just to help those people move outta there. Wasn't no blessing, son. No blessing."

"I just didn't know."

"I know, son. I know. But I'm tellin' you now 'cause you need to figure out a way out of this. Don't make my mistakes."

Will looked out the window.

"Uncle El, you just picked me up from the jail. I think it's a little late to be givin' me the turn-around-your-life-'fore-it's-too-late talk. And if you're tellin' me that I gotta make up with Paul, well, that ship done sailed."

"Makin' up with Paul is one way. And you could try that. I tried it with your father, and it didn't work for me. But it might could work for you. There is another way, though," Uncle Elliott said and pursed his lips.

"Sir?" Will said.

"I been watchin' Paul beat on you your whole life. I always took your side. Always. Just like you were my child. And now that you got Helen, I feel it even more. Like she's my grandbaby."

"I 'preciate that, Uncle El. You've always been good to me, but—"

"It's time you beat Paul, and beat him bad. And I don't mean with fists," Uncle Elliott said.

Will's eyebrows shot up in surprise. "What'd you have in mind?"

"How's that investigation going?" Uncle Elliott said and smiled.

Will laughed. "Why, Uncle Elliott, and here I thought you was just a nice old man."

"Nice don't always get you very far, Will. Sometimes you gotta get mean."

"I found that map," Will said, his eyes agleam.

"You did? What's it say?" Uncle Elliott asked eagerly.

"Says that Paul lied to us, big-time. Says that he should be facing felony charges for falsifying records, at the very least. I just been trying to tie up some loose ends, and when I do, I'm gonna recommend charges," Will said.

"You know, if'n you charge Paul with a felony, he won't be eligible to head up Blue Gem no more," Uncle Elliott said and chuckled. "Your dad put something in the bylaws saying anyone charged with a felony is disqualified. He did it 'cause we both thought I was fixin' to be charged with reckless endangerment for firing my gun in the air over the parade. I never got charged, but the rules stayed changed."

"So who'd run things?" Will asked.

"I guess it'd be me," Uncle Elliott said. "I don't have near the shares that your brother does, but I got some."

"Really?" Will said and laughed. "Wouldn't that be a shock."

"Yeah," Uncle Elliott said, smiling.

Will took a long pull on his cigarette and flicked the butt out the window. As he rolled up the window, he looked around the car. He'd always admired Uncle Elliott's choice in vehicles. No one who spent any time at a coal mine would buy a white Cadillac or a white car of any kind. Will had long thought that his uncle had simply rejected the family business. He didn't know that it was the other way around.

"Maybe I should buy me a white Caddy, Uncle El."

The old man laughed loudly.

"Maybe you should, son. Maybe you should."

# CHAPTER THIRTY-SIX

The barn was large, well-built, and clean. The timbers were mortise and tendon—not a nail in the structure. Amos knew good work when he saw it, and he was impressed.

The lighting could have been better, but there was an obvious fire risk with having lanterns in barns and the Fellinghausens didn't have electricity.

Feeling useless and in the wrong place—only the girls and two youngest boys seemed to enter the house during the day—Amos had insisted the following day upon joining Fellinghausen and his older boys after the midday meal. In a long conversation the night before, Fellinghausen had told Amos that his family's principle business was manufactured homes. They cut their own wood with a gas-powered sawmill.

Amos was soon helping, albeit poorly because of his wounds, to frame out a wall.

Besides Fellinghausen, three of his boys built the structures. The youngest to swing a mallet was eleven. The boys' English was rudimentary, and they mostly gestured when they wanted Amos to do something.

Fellinghausen came over at one point and asked Amos to follow him. They went to a corner of the barn. Fellinghausen picked up a roll of fiberglass insulation, and Amos got another. They brought it over to a nearly completed wall and began stapling it between studs. It was far easier than swinging a hammer and didn't seem to aggravate any of his injuries.

"You cannot stop the mining machines. That is clear," Fellinghausen said, picking up the threads of the previous night's conversation as if no time had passed. "And you are unlikely to persuade families that depend on mining to agree to stop it. These cannot be the actions that God expects of you."

Amos nodded, stapling all the while.

"How much have you made from your pot patches?" Fellinghausen asked, pronouncing each word distinctly.

"I don't know. Nine thousand dollars, maybe?"

Fellinghausen smiled.

"And for this, you think someone has murdered your foreman, your colleague, and sought to murder you?"

Amos shrugged.

"Amos, the Lord has spoken to you. It is the most important thing in your life, in anyone's life. You must assume that everything that has happened to you is related to that."

Amos went back to stapling. When he had finished the row, he gave his shoulder a rest and stood staring out the open barn doors.

The Fellinghausen farm could serve as the model for a child's book. There were three barns—one stone, one wood, and one made of corrugated metal. Each was well maintained. The stone barn had cows, several draft horses, sheep, pigs, and ducks.

One of Fellinghausen's children—he had nine, all born at home—led a draft horse past the barn door. The horse dwarfed the boy, but the boy showed no fear. A moment later, a girl carrying a bucket walked in the other direction. Behind her waddled at least thirty ducks. She headed off toward the stone barn.

"When did y'all move here?" Amos asked.

"Two years ago. We came from Louisiana," Fellinghausen said.

"Why?"

"There was a schism, and our leaders decided that the land prices and timber made this the right place to settle," he said. "There are six families with us."

"What'd y'all split over?" Amos asked, not sure that it was an appropriate question but too curious to resist.

"Kitchen cabinets," Fellinghausen said with no trace of humor.

"Sir?" Amos said.

"They wanted kitchen cabinets hung from the walls," Fellinghausen said, looking up from his work. "We thought such things were the devil's work."

Fellinghausen sighed and went back to his stapling. Amos realized that his mouth was open and closed it.

"I seen some Amish out in western Kentucky recently. They weren't wearing no shoes, but you got 'em," Amos said.

"We do," Fellinghausen said, and he continued to staple.

Amos felt he'd pushed just one step too far, and he worked quietly beside Fellinghausen for the rest of the afternoon.

Just before dark, Fellinghausen stood up and spoke to the boys in what Amos had decided was probably German. He smiled at Amos and added, "Time to eat."

They put away their tools and cleaned the barn thoroughly. It was almost black by the time they closed the barn doors. A faint wash of light from the house guided them.

The house was a hive of activity. With Amos, there were twelve people crammed into the kitchen and living room. The boys all took off their hats and handed them to one of the older boys, who stowed them on a shelf in a closet set off by curtains.

The children lined up at the sinks to wash their hands. Mrs. Fellinghausen seemed to delight in teasing the children, who laughed and pinched their mother in return. Mr. Fellinghausen joined in the conversation at places, and his remarks were often followed by general roars of laughter. Amos couldn't understand a word, but he never forgot the warmth he felt that evening in that kitchen. He had previously assumed that all Amish were dour.

The family eventually settled down to a light supper—chicken soup, cornbread, and greens. The older girls did much of the serving, with the mother directing traffic. Amos sat next to Fellinghausen, who said grace and then turned to Amos.

"So the passage from Leviticus did not persuade?" he asked with a gleam in his eye.

"No, sir," Amos said and chuckled.

"Try Psalms next time," Fellinghausen said. "It is a passage that I have memorized in English even."

Fellinghausen looked up, and the children nearest him fell silent.

"'The earth is the Lord's and the fullness thereof, the world and those who dwell therein; for He has founded it upon the seas, and established it upon the rivers,'" he said.

Felllinghausen smiled apologetically and shoveled another spoonful of soup.

"Where is that?" Amos asked, moved.

"Psalm Twenty-four. A good one. I have put a list of such passages on the first page of the Bible we placed into your backpack," Fellinghausen said.

"Backpack?" Amos said.

Fellinghausen spoke to one of the oldest girls, who rose from the table and returned with a bag. She handed it shyly to Amos.

"Rachel has sewn you a new one," Fellinghausen said. "And we have given you an extra shirt and another pair of pants, all fit for you. And there are dried fruits and nuts and some beef jerky."

Fellinghausen handed the bag to Amos, and he pointed to a pocket in the front.

"Here is your Bible," he said. "And there is room here for your own New Testament."

"I will forever be obligated to you, sir," Amos said.

"Just the opposite," Fellinghausen said. "You must preach again. But maybe at a different church."

A smile rippled across his face.

"You can become like your namesake," Fellinghausen said and fished the Bible out of the backpack and turned its pages.

"'Then Amos answered Amaziah,'" Fellinghausen read, "'"I am no prophet, nor a prophet's son; but I am a herdsman, and a dresser of sycamore trees, and the Lord took me from following the flock, and the Lord said to me, 'Go, prophesy to my people Israel.'"'"

He closed the book, a triumphant look on his face.

"That prophet is you."

Amos smiled.

"Not had much luck at that," Amos said.

"No," Fellinghausen said gravely. "Let us sit before the fire and talk of what you must do. And then you must sleep for a few hours. You have a hard journey ahead of you."

Fellinghausen rose, grimacing. One of the boys appeared at his side, and Fellinghausen put a hand on the boy's shoulder.

"Rheumatoid arthritis," he said to Amos. "It only hurts when I stop moving."

"Arthritis?" Amos said. "How do you run a sawmill?"

"I try not to stop moving."

# CHAPTER THIRTY-SEVEN

Will finally put the vehicle in gear and headed back toward the center of town.

He hadn't been to a practice since Helen had started at Hazard. He needed cheering up, and watching Helen practice was a sure-shot way to do that. Helen always worked hard, which was gratifying to see. She often seemed to learn something. And in practice, there was none of the tension present in games.

When Will got to the gym, the girls were sitting on balls near the bench. The coach was talking to them, and Tessy was seated on the bench along with two other mothers. Tessy was staring straight ahead. The coach was talking without animation. The players were looking at the floor. Bad news was clearly being delivered.

Will walked through the stands to a point just above the home bench and sat down quietly. Neither Helen nor Tessy seemed to notice him.

"We got nothin' to worry 'bout," the coach said. "We ain't done nothin' wrong. It's all just harassment. We been tearing up this conference, and that's made some folks jealous. So don't y'all worry."

The coach gestured to the women on the bench.

"I'll be talkin' to each of your moms, and we'll just make sure the paperwork for each one a'y'all—but especially for the new girls—is squared away," the coach said.

He clapped his hands.

"All right, let's get started. Layups, two lines," he said. "Let's go!"

The girls rose slowly to their feet and picked up their balls.

"Come on!" the coach said. "I will not let you girls slide because of this."

Will reached down and touched Tessy on the shoulder. She jumped, turned, and seemed deeply annoyed to see him.

"Jesus, Will," she said. She sighed, got up, looked around and stepped back to him.

"What are you doin' here?" she whispered.

"Just come to watch practice."

"Why?"

"What d'ya mean, why?" Will said, raising his hands in mock surrender. "Just want to see Helen practice."

"You ain't done that all year," Tessy said. "And what happened to your face?"

Will opened his mouth to spit back at Tessy and then furrowed his brow.

"What's the matter? What'd the coach just say?" he asked.

Tessy spun around to watch the girls do lay-ups. She clapped grimly. Will waited. She turned back.

"Someone," she paused for effect, "someone has complained to the KHSAA about recruiting violations," Tessy said.

"What's the KHSAA?"

"Oh, come on, Will," Tessy answered. She half turned back to watch the practice.

"I'm sorry, Tessy, I don't know."

"The Kentucky High School Athletics Association," Tessy said. "They put on the state high school basketball tournament every year. I guess you never knew about 'em because you never won the tournament."

Ouch, Will said to himself. She is steamed.

"Who they supposed to have recruited?" Will said.

"Not them. We," Tessy said. "And Helen's a suspect, along with Kaitlyn and Jemicka."

"Why Helen?" Will said. "Oh, right."

So sham divorces were frowned upon by state officials? Will thought. And that's a bad thing? For obvious reasons, he decided not to voice these thoughts.

Still, he doubted the investigation would go anywhere. Who could prove that he and Tessy weren't really getting divorced? Will sometimes wasn't sure himself. He shrugged it off. Powerhouse high schools always engendered regionwide jealousy, and that inevitably led to more scrutiny. Just part of basketball.

He watched the practice.

Girls' basketball is an entirely different game from boys'. With less foot speed and jumping ability, the girls must rely on strategy. There is more passing. The game remains on the ground. Plays are often executed more consistently. Being the point guard, Helen was even more important than a boy would have been in a similar position.

The lay-up drills were over, and the coach was having the team run through plays. The coach whispered to Helen at half-court. Helen nodded and she dribbled the ball toward the rest of the squad like a quarterback approaching the line.

She held up her left hand to signal the play and shouted, "Two two!" The team swirled around the basket, and Helen handed off the ball to another player, ran across the key to the other side of the basket, ran back and got the ball, handed it off to a third girl, and eventually retrieved the ball and took a shot. Swish.

Will smiled. Because they lacked upper-body strength, many girls shot the basketball from their chests—making them more vulnerable to being blocked. Not Helen. She shot from above her head in a motion similar to Will's own. She didn't look like him at all, but she shot the rock like him—and it pleased Will to no end.

Will glanced over at Tessy, who was watching the practice anxiously. Tessy likely knew the team's playbook better than Helen and was far more aware than Will of any subtle mistakes their daughter made.

He realized that he hadn't seen his wife take any obvious joy in

Helen's basketball all year. She had taken over responsibility for this part of Helen's life, and it was killing her. Will's smile widened. He leaned back and made a show of enjoying himself.

By the time practice was over, Helen was drenched in sweat and Tessy looked a wreck.

"That was terrific, honey," Will said cheerfully when Helen walked over.

In for a dime, in for a dollar, Will thought.

Tessy shot Will a cutting look.

"Honey, you gotta listen to Coach," Tessy amended. "And your cuts have got to get sharper. But it was a good practice. We'll keep working."

Helen nodded at her mother and drank the water her mother gave her. Tessy held a jacket and Helen shouldered her way into it.

"Can I take you guys to dinner?" Will asked, still playing the jovial one.

"Not tonight, Will," Tessy answered immediately. "Helen's got homework and, well, it's just not the right time. And you need to put some ice on your face anyways."

Will sighed.

"All right, but this weekend, Helen, can you come stay at, uhm, at home?" Will asked, his smile forced.

"Will, not now," Tessy said.

Helen looked sideways at her mother.

"What do you mean, not now? Tessy, she's only stayed with me twice since the summer," Will said, trying to keep his voice even.

"Will, let's not fight about this now," Tessy said.

"Who's fighting? I'm just asking for a visit from my daughter," Will said.

"Helen, let's go," Tessy said and pulled Helen by the arm.

"Mom," Helen said.

"Helen, what was Coach talking about before practice?" Tessy said.

Helen looked at her mother and then started walking with her.

"Tessy," Will said, shaking his head. "You can't . . ."

He watched them walk out.

. . .

She got out of the car and walked slowly into the gas station. Standing in the trees above the station, Amos smiled.

Glenda could still write poetry with her hips, with stanzas about the impossibility of possessing another person and the indescribable need to do so anyway. She was that rare woman who could feed the animal in a man without blush or bribe while still knowing more than his hunger.

She wore a knee-length blue skirt with no pleats or ruffles, black heels, and what appeared to be one of Amos's white button-up shirts. She was both over- and under-dressed for the hour—about eight of the morning.

She was a good woman who seemed to be losing her battles with drugs and real life more and more often. But Amos loved her head over heels and knew he would never be shed of her.

Somehow, they had both settled on the gas station at Lick Creek, where they had first met. Neither had been back to this place in years, nor had they discussed meeting there. But she had to know that neighbors were watching her, and that he would never be able to see her where she was staying.

Amos remained hidden for a moment more, waiting to see if another car or any sign of a tail appeared.

He crashed out of the brush and down into the station.

He found her looking at Cheerios.

"I still ain't had breakfast," she said when he approached. "Lucinda, bless her, is now making greens for breakfast. I can't stomach 'em."

She turned around and languidly wrapped her arms around his neck and kissed him.

"Miss me, cowboy?" she asked in a whisper.

His throat closed down tight, and Amos could only nod.

They kissed again.

"Glenda, honey, I'm so sorry," Amos said. "I heard they kept ya' in prison for more 'n a week."

She gave him a half-smile.

"I tol' 'em I wasn't leavin' till I got back down to one hundred and ten pounds," she said. "I only just made it 'fore they kicked me out."

"You look fine," Amos said.

"Fine? I look dern good," Glenda said. "Wanna see?"

She raised an eyebrow and looked past Amos to the restrooms. She swung around him and sauntered back. Amos loitered around the breakfast cereals for half a moment and followed.

He opened the door to the women's bathroom slowly, feeling stupid, and found Glenda staring at herself in the mirror, her hands on either side of the sink and her bare legs shoulder-width apart. Her skirt hung on the door. She wore a black thong and heels and had hiked the tail of her shirt up to the middle of her back.

Amos's knees nearly melted. He put a hand on her hip and wrapped the other around her belly. She turned her head and they kissed again. He slipped his hands inside her shirt, which she had unbuttoned to her belly. Her breasts had always struck him as the perfect size. As he cupped them in his hands, he was reminded again.

She broke the kiss, edged her feet a bit farther back, and seemed to brace herself against the sink. His mouth slack, Amos hooked his thumbs onto either side of her panties and pulled them down to her ankles.

He lasted only a few minutes. Amos felt he should apologize again.

Glenda turned around and, still bare-assed, leaned into him. She put her hand under his shirt and only then noticed the bandages on his shoulder.

"Oh baby," she said. She opened his shirt and found the more serious wound on his back. Her fingers probed it, and Amos flinched. She looked at him reproachfully, closed her eyes and folded into him again.

"They trying to kill you, ain't they?" she said.

Amos was silent.

She sighed and reached down to pull up her panties. Amos pulled up his pants and buttoned them. She retrieved her skirt and stepped into it. While she was fastening it, a smile suddenly played across her lips.

"Amos, what are you wearing, honey? A disguise?" she asked.

She reached out and pulled at the collar of his button-up black quilted jacket. She pulled it aside and took in his shirt and pants.

"A friend gave 'em to me," Amos said. "Got another set in my pack up the hill. Pretty comfortable."

"Hm," she said. "They look hand-sewn. You get too many more o' those shirts, and I'm gonna find that girl and scratch her eyes out."

"You got nothing to worry about," Amos said, smiling.

She put a hand on Amos's face, and Amos reached out to kiss it.

"Go on. I'm gonna fix my face. I'll meet you in Lucinda's car," she said.

Amos nodded and left. He went back to the cereal aisle and gathered a cornucopia of quick eats—some Cheerios, Chips Ahoy, several candy bars, and some Gatorade. He carried them up to the counter and awkwardly dumped them before the clerk, who eyed him strangely.

Amos did not meet the man's eyes. He pulled out a pocketful of bills, paid, walked quickly out to the car and hustled into the passenger's seat.

It was a black Chevy Camaro with silver racing stripes. It smelled of cigarettes and one of those tree-shaped air fresheners, which hung from the rearview mirror. There was no smell of Glenda.

Amos turned to see her flirting with the clerk. She came out holding a Snickers bar and ran through the light snow to the car. She jumped in, jammed the keys into the ignition and started it.

"Ohhh," she said. "Lord, it's cold. Where we going?" she asked.

"I'm getting out," Amos said. "I'm thinkin' you should go on back to Lucinda's. They got somebody watching you?"

Glenda nodded.

"They'll get nervous if you're gone too long, and next time we might not be able to have that romancin' in the restroom," he said.

Glenda laughed.

"Should I have resisted, baby?" she said, a coquettish look on her face.

"Sure," Amos said. "But this time worked out just fine."

Glenda tore open the wrapper on her candy bar and took a bite.

"Starved," she said and laughed again. "I may not look this good the next time I see ya. I'm eatin' like a horse."

Amos laughed and ripped open another Snickers and started eating. He reached out to hold her right hand. She put the candy bar on the dashboard and reached over to him with her left hand as well.

"Next week, same time?" he said.

Glenda nodded.

"Amos, how're you gonna fix this?" Glenda asked.

"I don't know. I gotta find out why I'm such a threat to 'em," he said. "When's your court date?"

"March twenty-third," she said.

Amos nodded.

"Baby, I dunno how to tell you this." He patted her hands. "I switched all your pills to headache medicine," he said.

"What?" she said.

"Yeah. They ain't a one of 'em that were what you thought."

They stared at each other.

"So get your lawyer—you got a good lawyer?" he asked. She nodded. "Well, get him to have them pills tested," he said. "Should be the end of this mess for ya."

She wetted her lips.

"I guess I thought I was getting resistance to 'em," Glenda said, looking inward. "I knew I wasn't gettin' the kick I used to. I thought I was an addict."

She looked at Amos with pleading eyes.

Amos kissed her on the forehead.

"I'm sorry, baby," he said.

Her head snapped around as if she'd been struck.

"Well, this means they cain't go after you, neither," Glenda said. "You can go on in there and give yourself up."

Amos shook his head.

"Baby, I go in that jail, I ain't comin' out alive," Amos said softly. "Now that you been there, you know that. This was never about scrips."

She hit his knee with her hand. Still sore from crawling, he flinched.

"What is it about, then?" she said. "You not talking in that investigation?"

Amos wagged his head.

"Might be. Seems kinda stupid, though," he said. "That Amish fella said he thought it must be some'm else. Some'm I know but don't know I know."

"Well, think," she said.

They locked eyes and both laughed.

"Don't worry if I ain't here next week," Amos said. "I got some things to do. This could be the last meal we eat together for a while."

"Heckuva meal to end with," she said and took another bite of her candy bar. Her smile suddenly dissolved into a sob. She put her head on to his shoulder for a moment then pulled back and wiped her eyes.

"Sorry," she said.

Amos patted her, took her Snickers bar, and cradled it.

"This here Snickers bar is a part of me," he said. "When you eat it, remember me."

He held it out, and she solemnly took a bite. He smiled and put the candy bar on the dashboard. Then he took the Gatorade bottle out of the plastic bag at his feet, opened it, and held it for her.

"And when you drink Gatorade, I want you to think of me, too," he said.

She sipped and dribbled slightly when he tilted the bottle too far.

"Sorry," he said with a chuckle.

She laughed, shook her head, and wiped her chin all at once.

"Ya know, I got a box a' wine in the backseat," she said.

"I'm not gonna be drinkin' wine till this thing is over," he said sadly. "Gotta keep my head."

She nodded and sighed.

"Got to go," he said.

He kissed her on the forehead, picked up the plastic bag of junk food, and got out. He walked up toward the start of the hill, waved, and plunged into the brush.

She watched him until he disappeared and continued to hunt for him in the brush for several minutes more. When she was sure that he was gone, she laid her forehead on the steering wheel and sobbed.

# CHAPTER THIRTY-EIGHT

Wat did you expect?" Ephrom Mainard asked. "That they'd give you a medal for searching a coal operator's car and getting arrested for drunk driving?"

Will had called Mainard, the man from OSM, in hopes of getting a drinking buddy who would be understanding, maybe even consoling. Will had been mistaken.

They were sitting at The Bank bar, which Will had come to know far too well. It was barely five o'clock. Will had already been there for an hour and was on his fourth beer. Mainard was sipping his first and laughing grimly. Will realized that he wanted to hit Mainard.

"These people aren't here to protect anyone but themselves, Will," Mainard said. "How many times do they have to prove that to you 'fore you realize it?" Mainard let out a manufactured chuckle and a theatrical sigh. He pulled at his red beard. He flattened his mustache. He was having a high old time. "The whole damn thing is just a joke. A joke!" Mainard said and thumped his hand on the bar.

"But tell me again anyway," Mainard said, suddenly calmer. "When you showed up this morning, Lucius and that guy from Washington, uh, Foster?"

"Forrester," Will said.

"Yeah, Forrester, that prick. They were there waiting?" Mainard asked.

Will motioned to the bartender. "Another."

"They called me yesterday afternoon, but I didn't pay no attention," Will said. "I suppose I shoulda known that wouldn'ta won their hearts."

"No," Mainard said with a laugh. "So Forrester had to stay overnight in Hazard? Not a good move."

"I don't expect he's used to a Quality Inn."

"How'd they break it to you?"

"Forrester's sitting in the waiting room, and the first thing he says when I come in is, 'Murphy, we're taking you off the Red Fox case.'"

Mainard sipped his beer.

"Yeah, I remember that about Forrester. Never would get to the point," Mainard said.

"I walked straight back to see Lucius. Forrester followed me."

"And what'd good ole Lucius have to say?" Mainard said, still appearing to enjoy himself.

"Nothing," Will said. "Said it wasn't his call. So I turned to Forrester and I told him. I told him, 'I don't understand. You're taking me off this case because I'm actually investigating this thing?'"

"And he said, 'No, I'm taking you off this case because you conducted an illegal search, and you just got busted for drunken driving.' And then I couldn't think of anything else to say."

Will shook his head and kept shaking it for some time.

"So what're you gonna do?" Mainard asked.

"I almost quit," Will said. "Got any jobs at OSM?"

"Not for a drunk that breaks into people's cars," Mainard snorted.

Will looked at him sideways.

"I honestly don't know what I'm gonna do," Will said. "I truly don't."

"Yes, you do," Mainard said, and his eyes wandered to the TV. "You're gonna go back to work tomorrow, and you're gonna punch the clock like you and the rest of us been doing for a long time. And maybe some days you'll go out to some coal mines and visit with the foreman in his office. And maybe just 'cause it's Tuesday, you'll write him up on a few citations. And every quarter you'll get money from the kitty, and you'll go buy yourself somethin' nice."

Will was staring at Mainard, his brow furrowed.

"Yeah."

Mainard looked back at Will.

"I mean, what the hell do you care, anyways? It's not like your brother is celebrating. He's gotta close that mine. And your uncle is taking care of all those people. That's not bad. There wasn't nothin' to investigate anyways and now you don't gotta write up the report. They did you a favor."

Will stared at his bottle.

"You know, I kinda got some'm," Will said and pursed his lips.

Mainard raised his eyebrows.

"Well what?" Mainard finally said.

Will shrugged.

"A map," Will said.

Mainard eyed him.

"A map? I guess they got it now," Mainard said.

"No, I took it home last night. Dragged it out of there."

More silence.

"Why?" Mainard asked. "You can't do nothing with it now."

"Maybe," Will said.

Mainard, who had been about to finish his beer and leave, ordered another.

They both sat in silence.

"Forrester told me to give what I got to the special investigator up in Pikeville, who'll finish the thing," Will said. "And I will. I just want to copy that map first."

Mainard shook his head.

"You never did know when you were beat," Mainard said.

"Damn right."

"Ya know, one of these days you're gonna realize that you're just window dressing," Mainard said. "The politicians don't want anyone to really investigate coal mining. If they did, they would have given you a gun. They would have given you criminal penalties. They would have done something about collecting fines."

It was almost full dark outside. Snowflakes swirled past the window, blazing like stars in the wash of the bar's lights. A figure trudged by covered in a blue hooded sweatshirt and then the street—Hazard's busiest thoroughfare—was empty.

Will finished his beer and stood.

"Well, you take'er easy," Will said.

"Yeah," Mainard answered.

And Will left.


The perfect camping spot. It was sheltered enough that Amos wouldn't have to worry about snow or rain. It had a commanding view of the landscape around so he'd see any pursuers well before they were close enough to threaten him. And it looked like no one had been there for years.

The only problem was that it was right under Paul Murphy's cantilevered terrace. If Amos coughed or sneezed, Paul or someone else in the house might hear him.

As he scouted the house, the idea of camping right under Paul's nose had sort of grown on Amos. It was reckless to the point of lunacy, but if Amos truly hoped to figure out if it was Paul who wanted him dead, this might be the best way to check that out.

The terrace was on the northwest side of the house, looking up toward Lexington. The drive and entrance to the house were on the southeast side. From under the terrace, Amos could hike up to the ridgeline beside the house and watch the home's driveway and entrance. The only risk was a window from what appeared to be the house's basement. Someone standing at that window could see Amos moving between his camp and his perch at the side of the house, but Amos had yet to notice any movement behind that window.

Amos thought he might even be able to have a fire. Any smoke would seem to outsiders to be coming from a fireplace in the house, so it wouldn't draw attention. And as long as he lit the fire only late at night, nobody in the house would likely notice.

Amos keenly missed his guns. He had just enough food to last a few days. He either had to put out some traps or walk to a store well away from Hazard. Either brought risks; both were laborious. A gun would also make his camping spot feel a bit less vulnerable.

Almost apologetic for not having guns, Fellinghausen had provided a thin rope and some netting. But Amos hadn't trapped in years, and he wasn't sure he still could.

He got out one of the zip-lock plastic bags filled with trail mix in his pack. He took the bag to the ridgeline and settled in to watch any comings and goings. From his perch above his campsite, Amos was beside and about level with the terrace. He could see inside the house and down both sides of the hill.

He wondered idly why such bags passed muster with the Amish if wall-mounted kitchen cabinets didn't. A blue Chevy Lumina drove up. A plump lady got out and retrieved what looked like dry cleaning from the trunk. She walked up to the house, disappeared inside, and came back in less than a minute. She drove away.

Amos popped a few more nuts into his mouth.

Some time later, a gold Camry pulled up. A middle-aged woman and a teenage girl got out, walked to the door, and disappeared inside.

A few minutes later, Murphy's blue Jaguar screeched into the driveway and disappeared into a garage. It happened so fast that Amos didn't get a glimpse of the driver.

Night fell.

It started to snow.

A Ford pickup came slowly up the drive. A man, rail thin and wearing a navy peacoat, got out of the truck and sauntered up to the door. He seemed to knock—Amos couldn't see for sure—and then stood back. He disappeared inside.

The snow stopped. Amos ate more nuts.

Quite suddenly, there was a noise a few feet from Amos's head. His heart leapt. He froze.

It was the terrace door.

"Quite a smell," a voice said.

"Fuckin' deer got in here and pissed and shit all over the place," a deeper voice responded. "They tried to clean it up, but they can't get rid o' the smell."

"Lordy," the first voice said.

Amos was no more than three yards from Paul, who was holding the door and seemed to be looking down directly at Amos. The other man exited the living room. Paul closed the door.

No longer wearing his peacoat, the man crossed his arms at his chest. "Quite a view, Mr. Murphy."

"It's nice," Paul agreed. "Listen, Dee, you and me, we go way back."

"Yes, sir, sure do."

"Just wanna make sure we're on the same page on this thing."

The other man nodded.

"You drilled all the bore holes. They all came up dry, right?"

"Yes, sir."

"All right. My brother Will is investigating this thing, and, you know, I don't want no surprises."

"Won't be no surprises."

Paul got out a pack of cigarettes and shook one out. He put it to his lips and lit up. He took a long drag.

"What're you figure he's gonna do?" the man asked.

"Will? Hell, I don't know. Don't think *he* knows," Paul said.

The other man nodded.

"So there's nothing else I need to know, right? You ain't been talking to no one else?" Paul asked.

The other man frowned and shook his head.

"All right, thanks for coming by. I'll show you out. Gotta watch the broken glass."

Paul took a last drag of his cigarette and flicked it over the railing. It flew over Amos's shoulder and dropped out of sight. The two disappeared inside.

Amos let his breath out slowly, still trying to be quiet. The inspector who had come to visit and had showed up at the service was named Will Murphy, Amos remembered. Must be Paul Murphy's brother, Amos thought. And it didn't sound like the family was too close. Amos heard the front door. He pivoted and saw the skinny guy head for his truck and drive away.

The house was quiet. Amos felt tired, like it was the end of a shift. He had gathered some dead grass to serve as a bed, and, like a cat kneading a couch cushion, nudged some of it into place. He sat on the bed and positioned his backpack as a pillow.

When he heard another vehicle arrive, he got up to look. It was a red pickup. And although Amos couldn't see the face of the guy who got out, he would always know the slightly bow-legged gait of the man who walked toward Paul's door: Joe Fercal, the old drug dealer Amos had just visited.

Amos could not begin to guess what Fercal was doing at Paul's house this late at night. He would be surprised to see Fercal there even during the middle of the day. Paul Murphy was high society. Joe Fercal, on the other hand, was a lowlife.

Drugs? Girls?

Fercal rang the bell and stood for a moment in silence. When the door opened, the light from inside briefly washed over Fercal's face. He looked serious.

He nodded and then passed inside and out of Amos's sight. Amos waited for the two to come out on the porch, but they didn't. Twenty or thirty minutes passed before Fercal emerged again. He walked straight to his truck without looking back and drove away.

The lights in the living room went out.

Amos crept back to his grass bed and leaned his head on his backpack. He lay awake for some time.

# CHAPTER THIRTY-NINE

The phone was ringing when Will unlocked the door. He almost let the machine get it. He picked it up on the third ring.

"Hello."

"Will?"

"Yeah. Hey."

It was Tessy. "Something wrong with Helen?"

"No, she's in bed."

"Oh," he said.

"Will?"

"Yeah?"

"Let's go to Abingdon, Virginia, this weekend. Just you and me. Helen can stay with Kaitlyn on Saturday night, and we can just get away."

Will would not have been more surprised if she had said she was moving to Bangladesh.

"This weekend?" Will said.

"Yeah," she said brightly. "I saw an ad. We could stay at the Abingdon Inn. Only ninety-nine dollars. And we haven't been there in, gosh, ten years," she said.

But we're getting divorced, Will almost said. And you were so cold at Helen's basketball practice. Will briefly wondered whether she had developed some personality disorder. And why Abingdon? Nobody they knew ever went there—and then he realized that was probably the point.

"Tessy, I would love to do this with you. Really. But I can't. Not now."

"Oh. Okay."

She was quiet again. Will sighed.

"Red dress was back in the *Mountain Eagle* today. You still think it's that same woman?" she asked.

"I haven't had a chance to read it. Still in my truck."

"Oh. Well, there was something else I thought you'd know about. Something in there about an explosion."

"What?"

"Yeah. Right in the middle. Had a funny name. The Crawl and Vomit."

"Crawl and Puke?"

"That was it. You mean it was real?"

"Tessy, I gotta go."

"Oh, okay. Well, I'll talk to you soon. Love you."

"Yeah. Okay. Bye." Will hung up the phone without waiting for her response and ran out to his truck to fish the *Mountain Eagle* out from under a McDonald's bag that he'd also picked up on the way back. He ran up the porch steps and stopped at the top, turning to the gossip column called "Speak Your Piece" by the porch light. It was cold enough that his breath steamed around him.

He scanned down the items and found it.

"The Crawl and Puke explosion wasn't caused by a faulty fan, folks. Or even a cigarette. No, the cause was a gas well right there in the mine. The Phantom knows!"

Will and Rob had jokingly referred to the original Blue Dog mine as the Crawl and Puke because it was low enough that they often had to crawl, and it sometimes smelled so badly that miners would occasionally get sick. The Phantom was Will's mining nickname for Rob, since his black skin made him hard to see underground.

It was a message from Rob, weeks after he had died. Will looked up into the blackness beyond his house.

A gas well? In a coal mine? Was it possible? Was this what Rob had learned at Frank's? Was this why his last words were that it wasn't Will's fault?

Will bolted down the stairs, got back into his truck, and spit gravel backing out. He tore down the hollow and out onto Highway 15. He turned into a parking lot near Whitesburg and headed to the back, where the *Mountain Eagle* offices were located. It was late, but the lights were still on.

Will parked in the fire lane, jumped out, and banged on the glass door in front.

The reception area was empty, and he couldn't quite see into the newsroom beyond. He banged again, and Will saw a shadow move. Someone appeared in the reception area and looked suspiciously at Will.

"Please, open up. It's important."

The guy nodded and came to the door, turned a bolt, and opened it.

"What can I do for you?"

"Hi. I'm Will Murphy, a special investigator for the Mine Safety and Health Administration. And you had an item in this week's issue about the Crawl and Puke explosion? Is there any way that I can see the letter that came from?"

"The Crawl and Puke? But that wasn't real. That's the only reason I let it go."

"No, but I think it was referring to a real explosion. One that I was in. And it could be important to my investigation of the Red Fox inundation."

"Red Fox?"

Will had the man's attention.

The man sighed. "Look, we don't give out those letters. I mean, the whole point is that it's anonymous."

"Makes sense. I understand that. But I think the guy who wrote that letter died at Red Fox," Will said.

"Wow."

"Yeah."

They were quiet.

"Do you actually remember the letter?" Will asked.

"Oh yeah. I almost didn't put it in."

"Was it handwritten?"

"Yeah."

"Neat little block letters?"

The man just looked at Will.

"If the author was Rob Crane, he died. You wouldn't be protecting nobody. Come on. You gotta show it to me."

The man stared at Will for a long moment, nodded, and silently let him in.

They walked into the newsroom. Six desks were spread across a surprisingly large area. One of the desks was piled with papers.

"We have to edit the entries, sometimes a lot," the man said when he got to one of the neater desks. "Can't be any real names or real people. Can't libel anybody or anything."

He bent under his desk and pulled out a small blue cardboard box, opened the top, and started paging through its contents.

"I keep every entry for about a month, just in case," he said with his back to Will. "Here it is."

He stood up and handed Will an eight-and-a-half-by-eleven-inch sheet of paper with Rob's neat block lettering on it. Will scanned down to the bottom of the page and saw Rob's name and address.

"People have to send in their name and address with the entries, so at least we know who they are. We started that about ten years ago. Cuts down on the crazier ones," the man said.

Will nodded, suddenly finding it difficult to talk. He started at the top of the letter and read.

TO THE WHITESBURG MOUNTAIN EAGLE. SPEAK YOUR PIECE. ABOUT 10 YEARS AGO, A MINE BLEW UP. LET'S CALL HER THE CRAWL AND PUKE. FOLKS THOUGHT IT WAS CAUSED BY A CIGARETTE. NO, THE CAUSE WAS A GAS WELL IN THE MINED-OUT AREA. IT WAS DRILLED BY SINGLETON DRILLING. IT'S TIME PEOPLE KNOWED. THE PHANTOM KNOWS.

Will stared at the page, suddenly aware of the lack of feeling in his back. In the weeks leading up to the Blue Dog accident, Will now remembered that Paul had spent very little time underground. He was working on some kind of "project," he'd said. And Dee Singleton had been around quite a bit.

And then his mind, like a horse to the barn, wandered back to the events of The Day. He'd been replacing a roller on the conveyor belt, and the thing was giving him fits.

He saw the short film clip of himself banging on that roller in frustration—one he'd seen over and over mostly because it was his last clear memory of his life before it all went to shit. As the years passed, the memory became richer. The belt had no guard despite a clear requirement, and its feet were buried in coal dust—an obvious, even outrageous explosion risk.

Surrounded by dangerous conditions that needed his immediate attention, Will was instead trying to fix a few stuck rollers that did nothing more than slow the exit of coal from the mine. It was like worrying about the plumbing on the *Hindenburg*. He'd been kicking himself ever since for being such an idiot.

Then he'd stopped, shook out a cigarette, took a lighter from his pocket and flicked it. He seemed to remember getting blown back and hearing a huge roar. But Will suspected that that memory wasn't real, that his mind—after repeated attempts at recalling the actual events—had simply reconstructed them.

And then he remembered the hospital, the sorrowful awareness of his terrible injuries and that day when his mind awoke to the blistering pain in his flanks. A nurse was picking at his scabs, and Will remembered that her efforts on the middle of his back—where the worst of the burns were—had caused him little discomfort. But then she worked her way around to his flanks.

The pain was blinding. Lying on his stomach, his face over a hole, Will began to scream.

"I'm sorry, honey," she said and kept right on picking.

Will screamed and screamed, his vocal cords fraying like worn rope.

He closed his eyes to banish the memory and opened them to an entirely new world in which the death of his brother, the wounding of his best friend, and the destruction of the family's coal mine were no longer his fault. At least not entirely.

"Why'd you cut out Singleton Drilling?"

"It's a real company," the man said. "I was gonna cut out 'Crawl and Puke' and just put in 'C and P.' But, I don't know, decided not to. What's it mean?"

"Means I need to go see Dee Singleton. And my brother. I only wish my father was alive."

Will took a step away.

"Come on now," the man said. "You gotta do better'n that."

Will looked back at him. "All right, but no story till this is through, or at least till I decide whether to file charges."

The man nodded.

"Look, deep-coal miners are always worrying about methane. The deeper the mine, the worse the problem. We set up fans, complicated ventilation plans, and curtains to get rid of the methane, which we just throw away even though it's almost as valuable as the coal. When a mine is really gassy, operators sometimes drill a methane well just as soon as the coal mine closes.

"Some operators don't want to wait that long, since by the time the coal is played out you've lost a good deal of your methane already. And I've heard some say that a methane well, drilled into a closed section of a mine, could limit the amount of methane going into the working part of the coal mine by directing the gas someplace else. If that ever proved true, it would be the best of all worlds—you'd make the mine safer *and* make money on the methane.

"Probably nine times out of ten, everything would work out. Problem is, there's that tenth time when the methane doesn't do what you think it's gonna do, when the pressure suddenly spikes and it's got nowhere to go but into the old mine. Or when a cave-in in the coal mine blocks the well and directs the methane into the coal mine. Neither of which is much of a problem as long as no one's down there or ever gonna go down there. But if there's an active mine nearby . . . I mean, we always seal off closed-out sections, but the seals are never all that good. So a pressure differential between one part of a mine and another will always even out."

The man nodded. Will looked up at the sky.

"I mean, it's almost the same thing that happened at the Red Fox mine. At Red Fox, you had an old mine filled with water next to an active one. The active one got too close, and all that water pressure evened out between them, flooding the active mine and draining the old one. At Blue Dog, we had an older part of the mine that—because someone drilled a methane well 'fore he shoulda—pushed that methane right into the active section. Least that's what Rob said in this letter."

The man blinked. "So the Crawl and Puke was Blue Dog? The mine that blew up, what, ten years ago?" he asked.

"Blew up with me, my little brother, and my best friend in it," Will said and closed his eyes.

"Who drilled the well?" the man asked.

"Singleton drilled it, but I'm sure it was my older brother, Paul, that got him to do it. And he kept quiet about it all this time," Will said, anger now flashing in his eyes. "But that's fixin' to catch up with him. I gotta go."

And he walked to his truck.

# CHAPTER FORTY

The house was black, the nurse asleep. Will picked his way through the front hall and up the stairs like a burglar. He hesitated at the door of his parents' bedroom then turned the knob.

"Momma?" he said.

He walked in. The room was truly black, and there was no way he could advance without risk of stumbling. He flicked on the light.

"Oh!"

"Sorry, Momma. It's me, Will."

"Will?"

"Yes, ma'am."

She was lying on her bed, clutching the blankets to her chest. Her hair, wispy and white, was unkempt. Her mouth was open, her eyes scared. The bedroom was smaller than Will remembered it. His father's bureau, tall and dark, took up much of one wall. His mother's, lower and longer, ranged along the back wall near the closet door.

He walked up to her bedside and kneeled.

"I was asleep."

"I'm sorry, I had to talk to you."

"What is it? Something happen? Someone hurt?"

"No. Well, yes. Sort of."

"What?"

She pushed herself up to a near-sitting position. Will took a deep breath.

"I don't know how to tell you this, but I got to. I just learned tonight that Paul put a gas well in the mined-out section of the Blue Dog mine."

"What?"

"Yeah. It was in a letter Rob Crane left for me. I haven't talked to Paul about it, but for a bunch of reasons, I'm pretty sure it's true."

"A gas well?"

"Yes, ma'am. That's why the mine blew up. I mean, me lighting a cigarette didn't help. But I woulda never done that if I'd known there was a gas well down there. And Paul never told me. Probably 'cause it's illegal. Paul probably thought it'd be okay in the mined-out area, which we walled off from the rest of the mine. But those walls never get a true seal. Anyways, what I'm trying to tell you is that the explosion wasn't really my fault. I mean, not entirely, not mostly. Jeff dying. Everything."

The surprise, even fear, had not left her face.

"How could Paul put a gas well down there?"

"He got Dee Singleton to drill it."

"Without your father knowing?"

Will's mouth dropped open. He hadn't thought of that. "I don't know. That's a good question. I guess I'll have to find out."

"Don't."

"What?"

"Leave it be."

"Momma, I been living with the guilt of Jeff's death for ten years now. It's just about done me in. I got to find this out."

"Will, I lost two of my three children in that explosion, Jeff and you. You keep looking into this, I might could lose my third."

"But Momma, it wasn't my fault."

"I never blamed you for it in the first place."

"But Dad did. And everybody else did."

"No, it was mostly you that did. And now you're too far gone. You think this letter from Rob can bring you back? Stop all the drinking and the nonsense?"

"Maybe."

She frowned and shook her head.

"Not worth it," she said.

Will closed his eyes and put his head on the bed. The smell, so familiar and welcome but now tinged with old age and camphor, filled his consciousness.

"I gotta find out."

"You do this, Will, you go after Paul like this, about somethin' so old, and I will never speak to you again."

Will rose from his knees, looked down at his mother, and said, "All right."

He walked out of the bedroom, leaving the light on behind him. In the hallway, he turned on another light and walked down the steps and out of the house. He got into his truck and pulled out of his parents' driveway for what he felt was probably the last time.

He drove in a daze, barely able to see through the tears welling in his eyes. He stopped in front of a modest house near Whitesburg. He stumbled out of his truck and knocked on the door, gently at first and then more urgently.

"Jesus, what in the hell . . ." Uncle Elliott said as he opened the door. "Will?"

Will closed his eyes and leaned into his uncle, who caught him awkwardly. Will bent his head down to the old man's shoulder and began to sob.

"It's okay," the old man said. "It's okay, son."

Amos spread the netting around the edge of the containment pond well before dawn. Several geese were sleeping nearby, but they didn't seem to wake. He tied two ends of the netting around trees and staked a third. The last end he let run down the incline toward the creek below.

The geese were so docile that Amos wasn't sure that he would need to hide, but he decided to play it safe.

His trap ready, Amos circled around the bottom of the pond and came up on the other side of the group of a dozen or so sleeping geese. He walked toward them and yelled, "Hey, hey, hey."

The geese groggily walked away from Amos and toward the netting. He stopped when several stepped onto the netting. He then walked the other way and circled back around. When he got to his string, he pulled the net over several geese.

They honked and flapped but none got out.

Amos ran to the nearest one and stepped on its neck. He took out his knife and sliced off its head. Blood spurted out of the animal, and the body continued to struggle for several seconds more.

One of the other trapped geese managed to free itself, but the third continued to struggle. Amos reached down and picked up the netting, freeing the trapped bird. He needed only one, and not much of that. It wouldn't take too much goose meat to catch a cat.

He took it back to his campsite. To his surprise, the lights in the living room were back on. Someone was up mighty early. Amos butchered the goose, got as much meat as he needed, and crept down the Hazard side of the hill.

# CHAPTER FORTY-ONE

His head was pounding. His tongue didn't fit his mouth. His arm was dead.

Will brought his arm down and felt the blood flow back into it. The pounding started again.

Will realized that the noise originated outside of his body. He rolled out of bed and got to his feet. He still had his socks on. Will hated sleeping in socks. After telling Uncle Elliott of his discoveries, Will had driven home and drunk himself into such oblivion that he hadn't even pulled off his socks.

He walked out of his bedroom and rounded the corner to the living room.

The light was so blinding that it was like God Almighty had come down from heaven in all His glory.

Will held up his hands to block the morning sun. When the door came into view between his squinting eyelids, he advanced. The fella on the other side started pounding again.

Will wrenched the door open.

"What the fuck?" Will asked.

"You Will Murphy?"

He was fat. He had a mustache. Will vaguely recognized him, and he knew that he didn't like the guy but couldn't remember why.

"Yeah?"

Will flinched when the man stuck something in Will's gut.

"This is official service," the man said. "Sorry, buddy, but you should get a lawyer."

The fat guy turned and walked quickly down the steps. Will watched him reach his car. The man glanced back as he got in.

Will looked down and found that he was holding an unsealed envelope. He heard the car back up. The sound of the car moving over gravel felt like sandpaper on his brain. Will shut the door and headed back to the bedroom. He sat on the bed and took a sip from the water glass on his bedside table. He sighed and looked back at the envelope in his left hand.

It was far smaller this time. He pressed it between his thumb and forefinger. Probably only two pages.

He flipped the envelope open, reached in, and got a paper cut on the pad of his index finger. He reached more cautiously into the envelope and took out the letter. He carefully unfolded the pages, his finger still smarting, and read them through.

There were only three paragraphs on the first page. The crucial one seemed to be the second, which announced that they now had a tentative court date of April 22.

Will turned to the second page. Only signatures.

He dropped the letter.

She'd said *just last night* that she loved him. Bile swelled into his throat. He picked up the phone and dialed Paul's number. No one answered. He phoned the school where Tessy worked. She hadn't arrived, a woman said.

"Fuck!" Will yelled. Last night, his mother all but disowned him. This morning, his wife had set a court date for divorce. And then there was the bit about being arrested for drunken driving, maybe losing his job, and having a brother who just might be a mass murderer.

He sat cradling the phone, his anger seeping out of him. He sighed and stood to go to the bathroom. Taking an aspirin in the morning was pretty routine for him now. He shook out three small pills, popped them into his mouth and chewed. His mouth full of chalk, he bent down and drank deeply from the sink.

He felt instantly better.

Will took off his socks and rubbed his feet. He turned on the shower and took off the rest of his clothes. When steam billowed out of the shower, he stepped in. He let the hot water beat on his head. He opened his mouth and let it soothe his tongue and flow up into his sinuses. He turned around and felt that bizarre but now familiar numbness as the water played over his scars.

Being reminded of his scars generally cleared Will's head by reminding him that things had once been far worse. He stood like that for several minutes.

"Time to see Dee," he said to himself and got out of the shower.


The cat's meows were not the usual brief spits and growls from a confrontation with another cat. They were far more persistent, even plaintive. It was still morning, though, and Joe Fercal had no interest in coming to the stupid animal's rescue. It was his wife's cat, and Fercal had never made peace with it.

Fercal didn't like cats—or dogs, for that matter. He would occasionally reach out to pet Market, but the cat never seemed to appreciate the gesture. Most often, it would move away. On occasion, it would bite him, and Joe would respond by chucking one of his wife's embroidered pillows at the animal.

With his wife gone, Fercal was forced to take care of the animal, which he did in a minimal way. Fercal put the cat out at night and allowed the animal inside only briefly in the morning to eat before he put it out for the rest of the day. If not for raccoons, he would have left Market's food outside and never let the cat in.

Even when the cat was inside, their truce was tentative. Fercal would empty a can of cat food into a bowl, and Market would approach only after Fercal had moved away. Fercal would then go about his morning business, but he kept the door to the second bathroom closed so that Market couldn't use the litter box. As soon as Market slowed down in her eating, Fercal would use a foot to shoo her out the back door.

And now she had roused Fercal out of a deep sleep.

"Shut up!" Fercal yelled.

The yowls continued.

Fercal climbed out of bed and padded toward the back door. He peered out the window into the cold gloom but couldn't see the cat. It continued to yowl.

Fercal put on some slippers, opened the back door, and went out. After a few steps, he caught sight of the cat. It seemed to have its back leg caught in something.

Fercal took another step toward the animal, and it quite suddenly leapt away. Less than a second later, Fercal found himself on the ground from a blow to his right ear.

He grunted slightly, but he was too stunned to scream or cry.

Someone immediately picked him up, put him into a chokehold, and carried him into his house.

Joe Fercal thought he was about to die from the attack he had long feared from his brother and former best friend. He struggled to breathe, pulled at the forearm around his neck, and kicked.

"Fercal," the voice said. "Quit your thrashin'."

Fercal stopped struggling. The voice was familiar enough, but it wasn't one of his old partners. Nor did he fear it.

"It's Amos," the voice said. "I'm gonna loosen up on ya, but if you make a loud noise, I may have to hit ya again. This time hard."

In an aside that made Fercal's blood run cold, Amos added, "God forgive me."

Fercal lay still, his head jammed against Amos's hip. Amos loosened his grip on Fercal's throat and Fercal remained still. Amos lowered Fercal's head to the floor, rose, and stepped back.

"What the fuck?" Fercal croaked.

Amos pulled out a kitchen chair and sat. Fercal reached up to massage his throat.

"What ya do to my fuckin' cat?"

Amos was quiet for a moment.

"Seem like you was always teachin' me the rules when we was kids. Now I got a few rules," Amos said with a sad smile. "First, don't move. If'n you do, I'll hit ya and tie ya up. Second, don't shout. If'n ya do, I'll hit ya and tie ya up. Third, answer my questions. If'n you don't, I'll hit and tie ya up. And then I'll pray on what's next."

Fercal blinked several times. He didn't otherwise move.

"The Lord works in mysterious ways, that's for sure. And no man can know the Almighty's plan. But I don't figure He's gonna worry too much about what happens to you."

They both went quiet.

"You said you weren't comin' back," Fercal said, almost a squeak.

Amos nodded. "Didn't figure to."

Fercal was paralyzed. His eyes, prominent anyway, bugged out of his head. His hands pressed against the floor. His body was awkwardly twisted, but he made no move to get more comfortable.

"I . . . I . . ." Fercal stuttered. "I didn't know Chrissy'd flunk her probation."

Amos raised his eyebrows.

"Chrissy's back in jail?" Amos asked. Fercal glanced wildly back and forth. "Joe, you take the cake. You surely do. But that ain't why I'm here."

Fercal raised a hand.

"Then what?"

"Why was you at Paul Murphy's last night?" Amos asked calmly.

Fercal's mouth opened but no sound came out. His eyes seemed to spin around the room. Amos could almost see the tumblers turning in his brain.

"Last night?" Fercal finally decided on saying.

"Yeah," Amos responded blandly.

Again the mouth opened. Again no sound came out.

"Look, Joe. I don't think the Lord wants me to kill you. But short o' that, I think I got a fair bit a' latitude."

Fercal tried to swallow. It didn't seem to go well.

Amos's shoulders sagged a bit. He got off his chair, leaned toward Fercal, slapped his face and then sat back again.

Blood dripped from Fercal's chin. His tongue explored his lip. Otherwise, he didn't move. The blood continued to drip.

They were silent for a moment more.

Amos started to get out of his chair again.

"I just went to talk about a survey I done," Fercal said in a rush.

"What survey?" Amos asked.

"Some, you know, property survey," Fercal said and tried to shrug.

"What property?"

"Around Little Fork."

"Little Fork?"

"Yuh."

"You mean in Knott County?"

"Uh-huh," Fercal said and nodded hard.

"This property include Red Fox or Hell-for-Certain?"

"No, I don't . . . no," Fercal said, shaking his head.

Amos tilted his head, shrugged, leaned forward and slapped Fercal again.

"Jesus," Fercal said.

"You know, I seen you. A year ago. No, more. You was up Hell-for-Certain surveying," Amos said, his eyes unfocused. "You was with another guy."

More nothing came out of Fercal's mouth.

"I said some'm to Mike about it 'fore the accident," Amos said, nodding. "Mike got all weird."

"That why you shot Mike?" Fercal asked, now clearly terrified.

"I ain't shot nobody. Not yet, anyways."

Amos frowned.

"The thing is, I'm 'onna need to know this, Joe," Amos said. "Got to."

"I can't . . . I don't . . . I ain't," Fercal said.

Amos stood up, stepped just outside the back door, and picked something off the ground. Fercal saw that it was a coil of rope. Amos took a hand towel from a rack by the stove and then stepped over Fercal.

Amos leaned down, his face within inches of Fercal's.

"You ready to talk?"

Fercal just looked at him.

Amos nodded and wrapped the towel around the lower part of Fercal's face, covering his mouth. He took the coil of rope and forced the rope and hand towel into Fercal's mouth.

*"Aaa aaaa."*

Amos took the rope and hand towel off.

"All right," Fercal said. "Paul Murphy asked me about some survey of the land around Hell-for-Certain I did more'n a year ago."

"For Murphy?"

"No, it was for some guy at the strip-mine agency."

"Who?"

"Guy named Mainard. Ephrom Mainard. Kind of a hippie."

"Why'd Murphy want to talk about it?"

"Said he wanted to check to see if it was all okay. I guess it's fixin' to get filed."

"You got that permit here?"

Fercal frowned.

"Naw," Fercal said. "Don't keep that stuff at home."

"It ain't like you got an office, Joe. Where's it at?"

When Fercal didn't answer, Amos got off the chair and tied the towel back on Fercal's face. Fercal didn't protest this time. Amos wrapped the rope around Fercal's legs and arms and left him on his side on the kitchen floor. Then Amos walked into the living room through a swinging door, which he left open.

There was a desk almost immediately in front of the kitchen door under a pair of windows looking out on the street. Amos glanced back at Fercal and then stepped in front of the desk. It had two wide drawers. Amos opened the left-hand one and took out a folded paper. He unfolded it and brought it back to the kitchen.

Amos put it on the floor in front of the prone Fercal. He squatted down next to Fercal.

"Looks like a survey map to me, Joe," he said. "This line's the mine, right?"

Fercal simply looked.

"Well, there're the houses. They's inside the mine, Joe," Amos said. Amos scratched his head.

"Maybe that's what's so secret. Murphy's been planning to push those families out of Hell-for-Certain for years. He needed to cut into the old works so's he could take away their water and get those folks outta the way for his strip mine. That right, Joe?"

Amos stood and looked down at Fercal.

Fercal spoke. Amos couldn't understand a word so he pulled the rope and towel off Fercal's face. Fercal grimaced and sucked air deep into his lungs.

"You are one dumb fuckin' hillbilly," Fercal finally spat out. "I told 'em you didn't know shit, that you was so stupid that they didn't have to worry. Goddamn. You're just figuring this shit out now? Shit. You saw me doing that survey more 'n a year ago. Me and that guy from OSM."

"Is this why they been after me?" Amos asked.

Fercal looked at Amos sideways.

"They said you didn't show up for some interview. Said they thought it was because you knew about the strip mine and how they been planning this flood for a long time."

Amos looked at Fercal sadly. Then he reached down and replaced the towel and rope over Fercal's face.

He picked up the map and carefully folded it. He stepped over Fercal and went into the living room, where he found the phone. He pulled it out of the wall, breaking the cable. He walked into the bedroom and did the same to the phone there then walked back into the kitchen.

"Joe, I'm gonna mostly untie your hands, all right?" Amos said. "With a little work, you'll be able to get 'em out. Then you'll have to untie your head and your feet. I'm thinkin' it'll take ya a while."

Amos was quiet for a moment.

"Then you can go outside and get your neighbor's phone and call the cops. Or you can call Murphy instead."

Amos pursed his lips.

"Or maybe not. Who else knew about this map? There's that guy from the federal strip agency. And Mike and Carl, right?"

"Look what happened to Mike and Carl," Amos said and shook his head. "You got nowhere to go."

Amos squatted down behind Fercal and loosened the knots. He stepped over him and left the house.

Fercal sat still for several moments. His hands began to work the knots. He got them loose and then wrenched his arms free. He sat up and began to work on the rope tied around his face.

Someone stepped into the kitchen. Fercal looked up to see a man in black holding a rifle. Fercal pulled furiously at the rope on his face.

"He was just here," Fercal said with a gasp. "Amos Blevins. He was here."

The man made no move to leave.

"But you can still catch him," Fercal said, still sitting on the kitchen floor.

The man pulled a pair of gloves out of his pocket and put them on. He closed the door. Still staring at the man, Fercal reached down to the rope around his legs and began pulling at it.

"I didn't say nothin'. He don't know shit."

The man cocked the bolt on his rifle. Fercal began crawling toward the living room.

"Help!" Fercal shouted.

The first shot hit Fercal in the back and he collapsed on the floor. A dog barked. The second shot came out Fercal's nose. The man bent down and picked up his shells. He opened the door and left.

Amos heard the muffled shots and looked back. He had a clear view of the back of Fercal's house and saw the man emerge dressed in black fatigues and a black jersey with a police patch.

Amos felt a surge of anger burst into his chest, and he stepped back toward Fercal's house. Then he saw the man look his way and raise his rifle. Amos dove behind a stone wall and, crouching, began running.

Amos didn't hear a shot. Yet.

# CHAPTER FORTY-TWO

Will drove up to Dee Singleton's house and headquarters at the head of Dead Indian Creek. He had only been to Singleton Drilling a couple of times, but each time the house had been flanked by so many drilling trucks that it was hard to get through.

Will saw only one truck, and it was nearly rusted through.

He had no trouble finding a parking space right in front of Singleton's house. The yard—a muddy expanse of rusted pipes, cables, and other drilling detritus—was unusually barren.

Will got out of his truck and listened to the silence. The last time he'd visited—was it two years or three?—the place had been a hive of activity. The sound of cutting and repair work had at times been deafening.

This was a puzzle.

Will knocked on the door. No answer. Out of the corner of his eye, he saw someone walking across the yard. Will turned to see the man from the barbershop walking from some outbuilding and carrying a bag.

"Hey!" Will shouted.

The man turned his head but kept walking.

"Hey!" Will shouted again and started jogging toward the man, who stopped.

"So there was a gas well in the mined-out section of Blue Dog? That was the reason for all the methane? That's why it blew? And that's what you told Rob Crane?" Will asked somewhat breathlessly.

The man just stared at Will.

"I came to ask Dee about it," Will said.

"He gone. Be back in about four or five hours," he said.

"What's your name again?" Will asked.

The man shook his head.

"Don't got no name no more. Ain't never been off, but I gotta live there now." "Off" was the word oldtime Central Appalachians used to describe everywhere but Appalachia.

"Buddy, Blue Dog was ten years ago. I am not gonna file no charges against you or Dee."

"Not you I'm worried about," the man said. "That brother of yourn can read, too. And he ain't gonna worry 'bout filing no charges."

Will had no answer to that. He'd long known that his brother was a son of a bitch, but Paul's capacity to bully, threaten, and maybe even murder was new to him. The man resumed walking, stopped at a maroon sedan, threw his bag in the back, and after nodding at Will, drove off.

Will blew his cheeks out. He still wanted to talk to Dee, but he had hours to kill. He'd brought the maps with him, at least the ones that would fit in his truck. Will decided he'd drive to Hell-for-Certain and see if, finally, he could put the whole thing about the Red Fox inundation together.

He drove the length of the community, stopped at the head of the hollow and drove back. At the bottom, he unfurled the topographic map, stared at it for a few minutes, and then turned the truck around and drove back.

A mongrel with brown stripes chased him on his way up the hollow and did the same on his way back. On his third pass, the dog ran only a few yards. On his fourth, the dog just barked.

He sat at the bottom of the hollow for nearly an hour, listened to the radio, and watched a few cars drive by. The entrance to the Red Fox mine was about a mile away, but Will knew that the mine ran under his feet.

Will had a dry tongue, a slight headache, and a keen sense that the answer to the case was right on the tip of his mind.

A yellow Ryder truck passed by, heading up the hollow. On a whim, Will decided to follow. The truck stopped in front of a tidy white clapboard house just beyond a cement bridge over the creek. The house had a screened-in porch crammed with toys. There was a small yard, a garden, and a swing set.

A man in jeans, a brown barn jacket, and tan boots got out and headed inside.

Will drove across the bridge and parked behind the Ryder truck. He sat in his truck for several minutes. The man came out carrying a small table, which he put on the grass beside the truck. He looked at Will.

Will got out of his truck.

"Howdy," Will said.

The man nodded.

"I'm Will Murphy. I'm an MSHA investigator looking into the disaster over the Red Fox mine," Will said.

"How ya doin'," the man said. He continued to look at Will in apparent confusion.

"Help ya out?" Will said.

"Buddy, you'd be here all day. I got the whole house to do."

"I'm a little stuck anyways. How about if I help ya with some of the big stuff?"

"All right. Thanks," the man said. "My name's Jimmy Stanley."

"Will." They shook.

"I'd love some help with the couch."

Will nodded and they headed inside.

It took some maneuvering and several attempts—straight-on, sideways, and end over end. Both smiled when they finally succeeded in getting it out the door. Then came a dining table and more maneuvering, a bookshelf, and some large boxes.

"You want a Coke?" Jimmy asked after nearly an hour of work.

"Sure," Will said.

"What kind?"

"Regular Coke'd be fine," Will said.

Jimmy nodded and disappeared back inside. Will sat on the front steps.

The weather was in the forties, but the sun was shining. There were a few clouds, and the light sparkled through the bare trees. The house sat in a flat spot of the hollow. There were four or five houses within a few hundred yards. It was almost a neighborhood.

Will looked up the hollow and realized that, if you ignored the trash in the creek, Hell-for-Certain was beautiful.

Jimmy came back with a Coke and sat beside him.

"It's beautiful here," Will said.

"Yeah," Jimmy answered sadly.

"Lose your water?" Will asked.

Jimmy nodded.

"Selling out?"

He nodded again and took a swig of his Coke.

"I'm just as glad it finally happened," Jimmy said.

Will furrowed his brow and looked at him.

"Why?" he asked.

"We knew it was comin'," Jimmy said. "Houses down the hollow kept losing their water. It'd happen to somebody and then a few weeks later, somebody else. About two dozen homes lost their water that way over the last three years. Matter a' time 'fore it happened to us. The last year, the wife was fixin' to go off the deep end. She couldn't stand not knowing from one day to the next whether we'd lose our water and have to leave."

"I can only imagine having to live with that," Will said.

"Yeah, it was rough. Couldn't sell. Who'd want it? So we couldn't leave. I'm sorta glad it hit all a' us"—Jimmy pointed to the surrounding houses—"at once. About eighteen, twenty of us all lost it at once when the disaster hit."

Jimmy glanced at Will.

"I'm sorry those men got killed. Real tragedy," he added.

"Yeah," Will said. "One of 'em was my best friend."

"Real sorry."

"Elliott Murphy's my uncle. The guy that's buying all these houses."

"Really? Helluva man to make the offer. We'd be in a heap o' trouble without him."

"He's truly a nice guy," Will said with a smile. "My brother, on the other hand . . ."

Jimmy smiled. "Family," he said.

They both laughed.

Will finished his Coke.

"I think I saw a couplea beds up there," Will said.

"If you're game," Jimmy said.

"Let's get it," Will said.

They wrestled three box springs out of the house and then dragged down the mattresses. When they'd gotten the last of them into the truck, Will sighed.

"I think that'll do it for me," Will said. "Sorry to leave you with so much left to do."

"Lord, I appreciate the help," Jimmy said with a smile.

"I left my jacket inside," Will said and went in to get it.

Jimmy was waiting for him on the steps when he came out.

"Where y'all movin'?" Will asked when he came out with his jacket on.

"Hazard," Jimmy said. "The wife doesn't want to live in a hollow no more. She figures nobody'll undermine a town that size."

"Don't be too sure," Will said and laughed.

Jimmy didn't laugh with him.

"Sorry, I just seen this all my working life," Will said.

Jimmy nodded.

"Did no one get their water back after they'd lost it?" Will asked.

"No, there was a family just down the hollow that got water again," Jimmy said. "I think they had to run a line a ways."

"What happened to 'em?" Will asked.

"They lost it again along with us, you know, when that disaster happened," Jimmy said.

"They did?" Will said. "Where can I find them?"

"Dunno. They might already be gone. It's the blue house, white shutters. This side of the creek. Just down about a quarter mile."

"All right. Thanks," Will said, now eager to leave. "See ya."

Jimmy waved.

Blue house, white shutters. That was Virgil and Missy Hogg's house. The guy who'd shot himself on the mine bench; the widow who'd helped to organize the protest. Will jogged to his truck.


Amos knew that the worst thing he could do was panic. He was being hunted, and panic would get him killed.

At the end of the stone wall, he straightened up and jogged at an easy pace. He had no idea whether his pursuer was alone or would call for backup.

The guy had to be at least fifty yards behind him. Amos didn't think the rifle he carried had a scope. So the man would have to be an outstanding shot or would have to get a lot closer to hit Amos while he was moving.

Amos kept moving.

Amos tried to remember the man's name by picturing his uniform splattered with blood.

Jones.

The cop was obviously dirty. He'd made that plain at his first visit. But Amos was surprised that the guy would shoot Fercal. Then he realized that Jones had probably been the one who shot Mike and Carl as well.

Amos's pulse quickened. He was in trouble.

Amos turned a corner and began running up a steep incline toward the top of a hill.

He heard a siren start down on Main Street. Another picked up the chorus.

Amos reached the top of the hill and turned up a narrow driveway that came off the street at an angle. Amos glanced back down the hill and saw Jones turn a corner and run up the street that Amos had just ascended. Jones held his rifle in both hands military-style and seemed to be running easily.

Jones looked up.

Amos turned away and ran. He heard a shot and the *fwip* sound of a bullet passing nearby. Amos automatically ducked a little but tried to continue running at his same, even pace.

There was another shot. Amos didn't hear the bullet this time. He ran up a small, steeper incline and then, with relief, ducked into the trees. Amos knew that it would now be harder to follow him at speed, and that it would be almost impossible for Jones to get off a good shot.

Still, the trees were bare, and Jones was close enough that he might be able to continue chasing him.

Amos headed up the slope but soon came to a rock wall roughly eight feet high. He ran along the wall for some time, but he could see that it was heading back toward a road that would bring him to Hazard and trap him. He had to get up the wall.

Amos stopped, took a breath, and began to climb.

The rock was sedimentary and soft. Its edge was ragged and gave way several times when Amos tried to get a foothold. He almost fell back at one point. But he pulled himself up. Just as he got to the top, Amos heard the crunching sound of footsteps.

There was another shot, and this time Amos felt the bullet whiz by his arm. He plunged on.

There was no deep-mine entrance that would save him this time. Amos could probably lose himself on the old mine bench, from which he could head in three different directions. He had trapped geese on that hillside earlier in the morning and had left his backpack there.

His only hope was to get back there.

# CHAPTER FORTY-THREE

Will remembered that Virgil Hogg had said something just before killing himself about not wanting to live without water again. And he had said that Dee Singleton knew about that. In addition to his work ten years ago for Blue Dog, Singleton had drilled the bore holes for Blue Gem to make sure there were no old works in front of it.

Will had just taken Singleton's word that he'd drilled the holes correctly.

Will drove about a quarter of a mile down the hollow and pulled in front of the Hogg house. There were no other vehicles. He knocked on the door. No answer. He knocked again. He turned to go. The door opened. He turned back.

It was the girl with the playful smirk. Instead of a T-shirt, she was wearing a white button-up blouse and a skirt. The blouse revealed budding cleavage that Will couldn't help but glance at.

She was probably about Helen's age. He tore his eyes away from her breasts. Her smirk grew.

"Howdy, I was here a week or so ago, remember?" Will said lamely.

"I remember."

"Is your mom here?"

"Nope. She gone into town," she said.

"Oh. Uhm," Will said, suddenly at a loss about what to do. "When are y'all gonna move?"

"Next week."

"Ah."

The girl began to rock the door back and forth.

"Listen," Will said and sighed. "Do you remember when y'all didn't have water? Before this time?"

The girl nodded.

"When was that?" Will asked.

"Last spring," she said.

"Oh," Will said. "But you got another well?"

The girl nodded. Instead of rocking back and forth with the door, she started to throw it between her hands. Will could see her face only in snatches. It was unnerving.

"Remember who drilled it?" Will asked. He was on pins and needles for the answer.

"Dee Singleton," the girl said.

"Right," Will said. "You mind if I go in back and see the new well?"

She stopped throwing the door and pressed her cheek against it with an expression of evident boredom.

"It ain't in back. It's on up the hollow," she said, pointing up the road. "They had to run a line, and Daddy said they had to get permission from some coal company to put it in."

"Who had to get permission?" Will asked.

"Dunno. Mr. Singleton, I guess," the girl said and sighed.

Will was speechless. A coal company? The only one with rights around here was Paul's company. The Hoggs' new well had been drilled into the old works. Singleton had to know that.

But if Singleton was drilling straws into the old works to get water for residents in advance of the mining, he had to know its real boundary and that the Red Fox mine was at risk. If Paul was approving these wells, he had to know exactly where.

"My mom'll be back in about an hour," the girl said and she looked away.

"Okay," Will said, nodding. "You don't mind if I walk along in back and try to trace that line?"

The girl shrugged.

"All right," Will said. "I'll try to stay out of your hair. Tell your mom I stopped by, and I'll try to come by and see her again."

She nodded. Will stepped back and waved. She closed the door.

Will walked around the house on the uphill side. The gravel driveway ran to a grass yard that was about twenty feet wide. It extended behind the house until it fell away into the creek. Next to the house were some holly bushes. Will didn't see any pipes. He walked to the edge of the grass and looked up a gentle slope overgrown with tall grasses and narrow trees. He noticed that the grass seemed thinner at one point, and Will walked toward that spot.

A hose sprouted out of the ground about five feet from the end of the lawn and continued up the slope. Will stepped into the brush and followed it.

He walked about two hundred yards, mostly uphill, and finally emerged into an area covered by kudzu that, it being winter, was the color of weak tea. In the middle of the field, the hose reentered the ground. Will pulled a few vines away to uncover a small cement cap that seemed to have been recently installed.

He looked around to try to get his bearings but failed. He hiked over to the road, found a long stick, and put it beside the road pointing toward the well. He walked back down the road to retrieve his truck, drove back, and parked next to the stick.

He glanced back and forth between the topographical map on his passenger seat and the view outside the truck.

"I'll be damned," he said.

He could see a collection of houses in front of him. All had obviously been situated directly over the ghost section of the Bethlehem number 11 mine, the section that had been present only on the map Will had found at Joe and Gaynell's store. The section seemed to end just beneath where Will was sitting, which was the start of a flat area on the creek. The Hoggs' well seemed to have been drilled at the very end of the ghost section. Its placement suggested that Singleton knew the precise contours of the old works.

Will looked to his left and dropped his head down to look up the hill on that side. He thought he could see the bench where he and Singleton had drilled that bore hole to drain the mine. It seemed to be about almost exactly on the boundary of the old works.

The Hoggs' well showed that Singleton knew exactly where the old works were. And the hole he drilled for the rescue showed that he had also translated the position of the new mine onto the land exactly.

Will fished out the Red Fox mine's official map and looked at the small X's that indicated where Singleton had supposedly drilled bore holes to ensure safe mining. One of them was almost directly over the spot he'd picked for the Hoggs' well.

The bore holes were obviously bogus. They'd never been drilled. And if Blue Gem had approved the Hoggs' well, the company would have had to have known about all this.

There was no way the inundation had been an accident.


Amos was soaked in sweat and starting to tire. He stumbled over some rocks, fell to his knees, and suffered a gash on his leg. He rose and, limping slightly, continued to run. He tried to concentrate on keeping his feet, raising his knees, and staying calm.

He resisted the urge to look back. Like any sprinter, he had nothing to gain by checking on the competition. He simply had to move as fast as his legs could carry him.

He guessed he was about halfway to the containment pond. His spirits began to flag. He wasn't sure that he could sustain this pace the entire way, although he was increasingly sure that he'd die if he didn't.

Jones obviously had no interest in capturing Amos alive. The shots that he'd heard from Fercal's house made that clear.

He wondered idly how Jones planned to blame Fercal's murder on him. Amos's fingerprints were all over Fercal's house, of course. And there would be obvious signs that Amos had bound Fercal.

But the shots would have come from Jones's weapon. How would he explain that?

Likely by disposing of the gun, Amos guessed. It all seemed rather easy.

Poor Joe Fercal, he thought.

Amos looked up and saw the end of the hill above him, and a sense of relief flooded his body.

He dropped down onto an old dirt mining road that headed up to the mine bench. Amos knew that he had to cover ground quickly now. The road was helpful to his speed, but it would also make him an easier target. And once he got up to the mine bench, he would have to run across a clearing of one hundred yards—twice the distance between him and his pursuer.

Amos would again have to count on Jones being less than a perfect shot. It was a good bet. They both had run a considerable ways, and even without the exercise, few shooters could hit a moving target with a rifle even at twenty yards.

Just before he reached the top of the hill, Amos took a second look behind him. Sure enough, Jones was right at the bottom of the hill, still running with his rifle. There was no sign, however, of other pursuers. Jones looked up. Amos turned back to running and fell. He scrambled to his feet. No sound of a shot this time.

The road crested, and Amos began running across the clearing. The pond was in front of him. A flock of geese milled in the water. Amos counted seconds. When he reached twenty, he started weaving a bit in his running.

A second later, Amos heard the first shot. And then another. And then another. With the fourth shot, Amos fell.

"Oh yeah," Jones said aloud. Keeping his finger on the trigger and the gun before him, the cop jogged toward the pond.

"I'm gonna gut you," Jones said aloud.

When Jones caught a glimpse of Amos's body at the back edge of the pond, he slowed to a walk.

"You done run your last," Jones said to the prone miner. "I'm hopin' you ain't dead yet, 'cause I want to take a few minutes to work on you. I owe you that."

Amos was lying on his right side, his right arm extended. His eyes were open and his expression suggested that he knew that death was before him. Jones smiled.

"I'm gonna have to dig that bullet out of you," Jones said. "Can't have you gettin' killed by the same gun that killed the surveyor. Then you wouldn't get the blame. This is gonna hurt a bit."

Now only a few feet away, Jones took his finger off the trigger of his rifle and shifted the long gun to his left hand. He reached his right hand toward his handgun.

Just then Amos stood up, and netting sprang up in front of Jones. As he fell back, Jones tried to pull his handgun from his holster. He couldn't. Amos ran to Jones's left, holding one end of the netting. Jones dropped the rifle to leave his left hand free to break his fall.

On the ground, Jones finally managed to pull his handgun. By then, Amos had reached him. He kicked the officer in the head and then stepped on his right hand. Jones groped with his left hand for the rifle. Amos stomped on Jones's head again, and the officer's left hand stopped moving.

Amos reached down, picked up the handgun, and tossed it into the pond. He freed the rifle from the netting and used its butt to strike the officer again in the head. Jones didn't move.

Amos sagged. He bent over and breathed deeply for a moment.

The sound of a siren came closer.

Amos looked up and turned away. He pulled his backpack out of a bramble, put it on, and began walking back around the containment pond. He carried the rifle with him.

Insurance. It was the only possible answer, Will thought. Paul must have suckered someone into giving him an unusually generous policy on the Red Fox mine. This was almost unheard of in mining, since everyone knew that mining was dangerous.

Who would be stupid enough to offer such a thing?

Still, Will could think of no other explanation for the evidence that the Red Fox inundation was deliberate. Will thought of Sergeant Freeman and his admission that he rarely paid attention to motive during a murder investigation. Will, too, was stuck on motive, but in the end maybe it wouldn't matter.

At the very least, Will knew that he had a terrific case of criminal negligence. Maybe more. Even the state police had to acknowledge that, with this new evidence, the foreman's murder could have been an effort by Paul to shut the guy up.

Or, Will suddenly thought, maybe the inundation was Paul's way of trying to kill Rob. Maybe Rob had told Paul that he knew about the gas well at Blue Dog.

Sitting in his truck, Will shook his head and clucked. Now that he'd figured it out—part of it, anyway—Will wondered what he should do. He was officially off the case. His bosses were not going to like hearing that he had continued to investigate a matter they had ordered him to stop looking into. If he could solve the case and tie it up with a bow, they probably wouldn't complain. But while Sergeant Freeman might not care about motive, he knew his bosses would. More work needed to be done.

What to do?

Conceivably Paul might be able to blame the whole thing on Dee Singleton and say that Singleton had never told him that the Hoggs' well had been placed into the old works. Or that Singleton had assured him that the bore holes revealed no problems. And now that the foreman was dead, Paul could also claim to know nothing about the old map.

Singleton was the key. He was also trapped. Much of his business was over. MSHA would ban him from performing bore hole tests in the future, and it might even seek to prosecute him. The question was whether he would rat out Paul.

Will had little doubt that Paul was perfectly aware of what Singleton was doing and had told him to do it. There was no way that Singleton, shy and uncertain as he was, had cooked up this scheme on his own.

How to get this out of Singleton?

The best method was probably to call Singleton into the office right away, have an FBI agent present and scare him.

But there was no way Will could arrange that right now. He'd have to spend days, maybe weeks, trying to persuade someone at MSHA to take him seriously. In the meantime, Paul would certainly get wind of the problem. That little item in the *Mountain Eagle* about the "Crawl and Puke" was bound to make him that much more careful.

Maybe Mrs. Hogg would say something. Maybe the neighbor he just helped to pack would say something to somebody.

It was bound to get out.

He had to get to Singleton. He started the truck back up and headed down the hollow. There was another pickup in the parking area of Singleton Drilling when Will arrived. He got out and once again knocked on the door. No answer. He knocked again. Still no answer. He turned to walk around the back and nearly ran into Singleton, who had somehow appeared by his side.

"Holy—" Will said.

"Sorry," Singleton said in his laconic drawl.

They both stood frozen for a moment—Will in shock and Singleton out of habit.

"Dee," Will said, gathering his wits.

"Yes, sir," Singleton said.

"It didn't look like anybody was around," Will said, stalling.

"Yeah. We're fixin' to move," Singleton said.

"Move? Why?" Will said.

"Lost our water," Singleton said, and his mouth twitched briefly into a frown.

"What?" Will said. "From the Red Fox inundation?"

Singleton gave a slight nod, his jaw muscles working strenuously.

"You got your water from the old works?"

More nods.

Will was stunned. Then he remembered that someone had mentioned that the inundation had affected more than just Hell-for-Certain. He pictured the topographical map in his car. Hell-for-Certain and Dead Indian creeks ran almost side by side near their beginnings.

"But," Will said, unable to help himself, "didn't you know this would happen?"

Singleton blinked.

"Pardon?" Singleton said, looking cagey.

"Dee, I just come from Missy Hogg's house. Virgil Hogg's house. The fella that shot himself?" Will said, and paused for effect. "I saw the well you dug for 'em last year. It's not twenty feet from a bore hole you were supposed to have dug for Blue Gem."

Singleton's giant Adam's apple began to bob up and down like a cork when a fish bites. He cocked his chin.

"Yuh?" Singleton said. "So?"

"So?" Will said. "You put a straw into the old works at about the same time and in about the same place that you supposedly dug a bore hole confirming that the old works were nowhere near?"

Singleton looked at the air beside Will, pursed his lips, and continued to blink while his Adam's apple bobbed.

Will made a quick decision.

"Paul trusted you, Dee, just like we all trusted you at Blue Dog. We trusted you and you got people killed. Both times. You drilled a gas well at Blue Dog? And here, you say you drilled bore holes and you didn't? You got a lot of blood on your hands, Dee," Will said, scorn dripping from his voice.

"Didn't kill nobody," Singleton said sullenly.

"No? Well, my kid brother died at Blue Dog. And nine men died at Red Fox, Dee. No, ten men, counting Virgil Hogg. Ten men who'd be alive today if you'd warned Paul that he was nearing the old works," Will said, pressing. "Your business is over, Dee. Nobody's gonna hire you now. Who's gonna trust you? And while I can't get you for Blue Dog, 'cause that's too many years ago, you'll be facing criminal negligence charges for Red Fox. Maybe even manslaughter. You're going to jail, Dee. Jail."

Will felt that he should storm away for added effect. But he was rooted to the spot, staring at the coordinated, two-way dance between Singleton's eyes and Adam's apple. One moved up and down, the other side to side.

The silence hung.

"I done what I's told," Singleton finally said.

Will smiled inwardly. Finally, he'd outlasted someone. Silence had worked!

"What do you mean?"

Singleton's eyes narrowed. He seemed to reconsider. His lips pressed into a tighter lock.

"Paul told you to drill that gas well for Blue Dog? Paul told you to fake those bore holes at Red Fox? Paul told you to kill people?" Will asked sarcastically. "I don't get along with my brother, but he ain't a monster."

Singleton crossed his arms in front of his chest. He seemed to have decided not to talk. Will's heart sank.

Will sighed.

"I know you can't be this stupid," Will said, deciding quite suddenly to drop the artifice. "I just can't believe you let Paul take your own water. Your own . . . damn . . . water."

It was just unbelievable how often people in eastern Kentucky seemed willing to sacrifice themselves, their families, and their homes to the interests of coal companies.

Coal operators seemed to have an almost mesmerizing quality. Or maybe they controlled so much that people just gave up.

"We's all working for the same people," Singleton finally said, nodding.

"Who, Paul? I don't work for him," Will said vehemently.

"Yeah, you do," Singleton said. "Coal shuts down, you be out of a job right quick. Same as me. Same as everbody else round here." Singleton pointed down the hollow.

"So people got to die to keep the coal runnin'?" Will asked, shaking his head.

"Them fellas knew the risk," Singleton said. "They had good jobs. Paid well. Mr. Murphy took care of 'em."

"Took care of 'em? Paul killed 'em," Will said. "How is that takin' care of 'em?"

Singleton was back to nodding and staring. He seemed to have tuned Will out.

"Just tell me one thing," Will snapped, and Singleton's eyes returned to Will's face. "Did you see the old mine map? The real one?"

There was a flicker of something in Singleton's eyes. Recognition? Fear? Will wasn't sure. And then it disappeared. The driller said nothing.

Suddenly, Will was tired. Tired of everyone he knew letting him down. He walked past Singleton to his truck and stood beside it for several minutes. He heard a door close behind him and looked around to see that Singleton had gone inside.

Probably calling Paul. Probably receiving instructions that would once again save Paul from any embarrassment or penalty.

It was all so predictable.

Will opened his truck door, got in, and nearly had a heart attack.

Sitting in the passenger seat was Amos Blevins, the formidable miner now missing and presumed by the state police to be a drug-dealing murderer.

# CHAPTER FORTY-FOUR

W ill froze. So did Amos. The miner sat staring ahead as if waiting for unseen traffic to clear. Will briefly thought he might
be dead until Amos blinked.

The blink called Will to his senses. He had no idea what to expect
from the man whom state police had assured him was a serious danger.
But Will realized that he had never felt afraid around Amos Blevins.
The last time Will had seen Amos, the miner had just come out of a
rapturous religious experience.

"Mr. Blevins," Will finally croaked.

Amos turned to look at Will and then raised his hand. Only then
did Will realize that Amos had been holding a sizable piece of paper in
his lap that the miner now held out to Will.

Will raised his eyebrows. He tore his eyes away from the miner and
took the paper. He unfolded it.

"Another map," Will said and smiled. "I got a few of these. Speaking of which, where's . . . ?"

The miner jerked his thumb behind him. Will turned to look into
the bed of the truck and saw the pile of maps that had been on his pas-

senger seat now in the back, a large backpack set on top to keep them from blowing away.

Will nodded and turned his attention back to the map before him.

"What is this?" Will finally said.

The miner didn't answer.

Will looked at the man curiously, feeling like he was being tested. He turned his attention to the map.

Much of it was shaded, but land contours were still clearly visible. Will realized that the shape of one of the lines was Hell-for-Certain Creek. He'd become familiar enough with it from staring at his other maps.

"Surface mine area" was written in the map's legend, as were "Deep mine entrance," "Containment pond," and "Fill."

"It's a strip mine map," Will said casually. "Of Hell-for-Certain, looks like. But I don't get it. There isn't a strip mine here."

"Not now there ain't," Amos said, his voice rumbling out from deep below his heavy beard.

Will peered back at the map.

"Wait," he said. "You're saying . . ."

Will pressed his lips together. He let out a long sigh.

"I think I get it. I gotta admit, it's taken me a while, but I think I finally get it," Will said.

The miner just looked at Will. He seemed to want Will to complete the test.

"That's why all this happened. He's fixin' to strip mine this whole area. That's why he let the deep mine get inundated. He doesn't need the old mine. Hell, he don't want it. And he had to get rid o' all those houses and those people," Will said, it all finally dawning on him.

"This'd be a huge strip mine," Will said. "Dig this whole mountain up, and you get twelve, fifteen seams of coal all at once, instead of just digging out one at a time like you do in deep mining. Paul'd make two hundred million dollars, three hundred million dollars on this thing— ten, twenty times what he makes on a deep mine."

Amos began to nod.

"And one hundred times the damage to the land," Amos said.

Will raised an eyebrow.

"Never heard a miner worry about the environment," Will said.

"I got religion," Amos said. "There's more. I heard this guy," Amos jerked his thumb back at Singleton's house, "talking to your brother about the bore holes so's they could get their stories straight."

"Well," Will said and breathed deeply again. "It was all just a real estate deal for a strip mine. Makes sense. If you want to strip a place, you can't have people livin' there. And now that Uncle El's helpin' people to move, Paul can come in and get this thing done for nothing. He's screwin' everybody."

Will looked closely at the miner. The cab now stank from a mixture of old sweat and recent fear. The man was covered in mud, dirt, and grease. He wore a black quilted jacket with a torn sleeve. Big stains on his pants and sleeves looked like blood.

"Where you been?" Will finally asked. "State police think you killed Mike and Carl. Say you're a drug dealer."

Amos looked down at his hands, which were resting on his knees. He turned his palms up, and Will could see deep gashes on the miner's fingers.

"They arrested my wife, put her in jail," Amos said, still looking down. "She ain't done nothin'. And all I done is try to support my family."

Amos looked back up at Will.

"What are you doing here?" Will asked.

Amos reached over and pointed to a portion of the map.

"Says 'Singleton Drilling.' Has an address. Thought I'd see what I could see," Amos said.

"So you decided to get in my truck?" Will said and laughed.

"I heard you asking the right questions. Thought I'd help with some answers," Amos said, returning a small smile.

They both looked at each other for a long moment.

"Well, thank you," Will finally said.

"No, thank you. I think you'll help with my mission."

"Mission?"

The big miner nodded his head but didn't say more.

Will motioned to the map in his lap.

"This is the second map you've helped me get," Will said.

Amos gave the inspector a quizzical look but didn't say more.

"How long you think they been planning this? Got any idea?" Will asked.

"Well, that I don't rightly know. I saw a survey crew up above here more 'n a year ago," Amos said. "My foreman was pretty bent outta shape when I said some'm 'bout it."

"I mean, it's pretty smart," Will said, and looked out the driver's side window. "Paul wants to do a mountaintop removal mine, but he's got to get rid of all the people first. So he uses the deep mine to ruin everybody's water and drive 'em out, which is totally legal, and then he can do it with no problem."

Amos nodded.

"I mean, you gotta give Paul some credit. He's no dummy," Will said and shook his head.

He looked back at the miner.

"D'ya think that's why he put in a deep mine in the first place?" Will asked. "He know all this that long ago?"

Amos shrugged.

"It's just a helluva thing," Will said. "I mean, I believe you. All makes sense now. Couldn't figure out before why he'd deliberately set about cutting into the old works. Now I know."

They both sat in silence.

"Jeez," Will said.

The door to the Singleton house opened. Dee Singleton stood in the entrance and stared at the two of them. He closed the door and disappeared.

Will noticed that Amos seemed to freeze.

"You decide what you're gonna do?" Will asked.

Amos shook his head.

"Well, I gotta call this'n in," Will said. "We got enough here to, well, make a helluva case. I might be able to pay Paul back for some-thin' that happened ten years ago. I can drive you back to my house if you like. You can decide there what you want to do. I don't have to tell 'em about you right away."

Amos looked at Will closely.

"All right," Amos finally said.

Will started the truck and began to back out. He stopped, got out of the truck, and retrieved the maps from the bed. He handed the stack to Amos, who carefully put them on his lap. They drove away.

"Lucius, I got about six maps here. They're all pieces of the puzzle," Will said into the phone. "But it all fits. Paul deliberately cut into the old works to get rid of all those houses on Hell-for-Certain—oh, and a few more up Dead Indian—because he wants to strip-mine it."

Will glanced over at his kitchen table. Amos was on his second bowl of cereal. Will wished he'd had something else to offer the man, who'd obviously not eaten a good meal in some time. But Amos had seemed satisfied with a midafternoon breakfast.

Will rolled his eyes and glanced back out his front window.

"It's not crazy," he said. "Look, I'm telling you the bore holes were bullshit. Dee Singleton sunk a well into the old works last year. He knew it was there, he knew it was filled with water and he told Blue Gem."

Will paused.

"No, I don't know that for sure, but Singleton all but admitted it." Another pause.

"Yeah, I talked to him."

Will bit his lip. His face fell.

"Lucius, who gives a damn about that now? We got a coal company that deliberately exposed its workers to lethal dangers. Killed nine, ten people. It's the worst damn thing I ever heard of."

Will glanced back at Amos and shook his head in disbelief.

"This is not about Paul," Will said deliberately. "I'm not gonna argue with you about this anymore. You need to get on the phone to Lexington and tell that lazy-ass assistant U.S. Attorney up there that he needs to send an FBI agent down here right away. I could call him on my own, but I'm doing you the courtesy. All right?"

Will began to nod.

"That's fine. But look, I'm not gonna come in until tomorrow. I got some things I gotta get done here on this thing."

Will ran his fingers through his hair. He needed a shower.

"Yeah, and we're gonna need to figure out what we tell the state police. There's two murders that's probably involved with this thing and a bunch of other shit we can talk about."

Will nodded.

"No, I'm well aware of how the FBI feels about other investigative agencies being involved," Will said. "Yeah, I promise not to call the state police today. We'll figure it out tomorrow. All right, see ya tomorrow."

Will hung up, sighed, and gave Amos a can-you-believe-it? look. Will was about to launch into an extended explanation of the call when he noticed that Amos's expression, tired and entirely neutral, hadn't changed at all.

Will realized that Amos probably had no interest in MSHA's internal politics.

"Lucius will do the right thing," Will summarized, as much for himself as for Amos.

Amos nodded and shoved another spoonful of cereal into his mouth.

Will smiled, pulled out another kitchen chair, and sat opposite the miner. He watched the big man eat for a moment. There was something deeply satisfying about watching someone eat food, your food, with relish.

Will conceded to himself that he'd had little to do with the meal's preparation. General Mills was to thank for that. Still, it felt good.

Amos finished his second bowl and put his spoon down. Will handed him a paper napkin from a stack that had remained untouched since Tessy's departure. Amos looked at it as if it were a French bauble. He smiled at Will, who realized that a man covered in grime might not be overly concerned about a drop of milk on his beard.

Will chuckled. Amos followed. Their stout-hearted laughter built like an Anvil chorus until both were nearly crying. Wiping his eyes, Will finally got up from the table.

"Lemme get you a towel," Will said and both men started to laugh again. Will returned with a fresh towel and put it on the table.

"Shower's just in back here. We can put those clothes in the laundry," Will said.

Amos looked up at Will with a thoughtful expression.

"You can stay here tonight. I got a couple extra rooms," Will said in what he thought was an answer to the miner's questioning look. "But tomorrow, we gotta work all this out."

Amos got up from the table and picked up the towel.

"I sure could use the shower, and it'd be nice to clean these clothes," Amos said, nodding. "But lemme think about whether I should stay here tonight. I ain't told you half a' what happened over the last few weeks, and I ain't too keen on seeing too many more police officers again."

Will frowned.

"All right," Will said. "One thing at a time. Just chuck the clothes out of the bathroom when you're out of 'em, and I'll start the washing machine."

Amos picked up his backpack, which had been leaning against a wall, and headed into the back of the house.

By the time Amos was showered, Will had retrieved the maps in his truck and had spread them out over the kitchen table. Amos walked back into the kitchen area holding his towel out in front of him.

"You might want to throw this here out," Amos said with a smile.

Will took the towel and threw it back toward the laundry area.

Amos's clothes were still not dry, but he had managed to dig a clean shirt and pair of pants out of his backpack. Will thought that there was something odd about the clothes but said nothing.

Will gestured to the maps on the table. "This is gonna be a lot easier to explain if you're around."

Amos nodded, a crooked smile on his face.

"You make a decision?" Will asked.

Amos looked at Will sideways.

"I feel like I done what I was supposed to do. What I was called to do," Amos said.

Will sensed that Amos was trying to say something important.

"How do you mean?" Will asked.

"I feel that I was called to stop this here strip mine," Amos said, putting his hand on the map he'd given Will. "I don't know if I done that, but I took it as far as I can. It's in your hands now."

Will nodded.

"Stoppin' strip mines isn't really my job, Amos," Will said. "But if what you're saying is that this investigation is gonna tie Paul up in knots, well, I can pretty much guarantee that."

Amos smiled.

"I think that'll do," Amos said.

Will looked down. He could see that Amos wasn't done, and Will was happy to wait.

"The thing about it is," Amos said, still struggling to come up with the right words, "I been on a mission ever since this whole mess started, but now my mission's pretty much done and I don't know what to do."

Will's expression didn't change. He had come to a decision in the truck that he wasn't going to turn Amos in. The man had put himself in Will's hands to further this investigation, and Will couldn't betray that trust.

But it was going to be difficult for Will to explain to the state police, the FBI, and any other investigators why he had failed to call them within minutes of running across a fugitive. Will thought he might even be open to a charge of aiding and abetting, a felony.

Will's life and investigation were going to go a lot smoother if Amos stuck around. But Amos probably knew that, so Will stayed quiet.

"The only thing left for me is Glenda, my wife," Amos said.

Will kept his eyes on the floor.

"We don't really know each other," Amos said. "But if somethin' happens, I'd appreciate it if you'd look in on her."

Will smiled and looked up at the miner.

"Startin' to sound like a funeral around here," Will said.

Amos looked away and both were silent for a moment.

"I got the Bethlehem map out in the garage," Will said. "Let's go look at it."

Amos nodded. Will got his jacket and headed toward the door. When he put his hand on the knob, Will looked out the window and saw a black Taurus sitting just beyond the end of his driveway.

"Shit," Will said.

"What?" Amos asked.

"There's a car at the end of my driveway. A guy's been watching me for a couple of weeks. He must be workin' for my brother. Maybe from the Kentucky Department of Mines and Minerals," Will said.

"You got a gun?" Amos asked.

"Yeah. Yeah, I do." Will walked back to his bedroom and took a pistol out of his sock drawer.

"There's a back door here. I'm gonna circle around and come up on his side," Will said.

"How long you figure that'll take?" Amos asked.

"Four, five minutes."

"All right. In five, six minutes, I'll go on out the door and give him some'm to look at 'sides you," Amos said.

"Sounds like a plan," Will said, shaking with nervousness. He went to the back door, opened it, looked back, grinned at Amos, and plunged into the brush. Amos went into the kitchen and searched the cabinets.

Will stayed low and jogged a wide path around his house and into the woods. He held the pistol in his right hand and let the weight pull his hand down. He tried to lighten his steps as he approached the road. The ground was dry, and the leaves beneath his feet sounded like a children's orchestra. He saw the car and crept the last dozen yards. He stopped about fifteen feet away.

A moment later, the door to Will's house opened and a large kitchen pot came crashing down the front steps followed by another and then a third. Will could see the man in the car look up at the noise. Will rose, jogged doubled over to the passenger door and prayed that it was unlocked. He tried the handle, and the door swung open. Will pointed his pistol at the same tall, skinny guy he'd seen in the bar a week before.

"Buddy, you move and you're dead," Will said.

"Jesus! Jesus!" the man said and raised his hands from the steering wheel.

"Get out!" Will ordered. "Do it slow."

The man nodded and, obviously shaking, opened his door. Will jogged around the front of the car, keeping his gun trained on the man as he exited. He stood beside the car, his hands up. Will kicked the car door closed and stood with his gun trained on the man's chest.

"You working for Paul?" Will asked.

"What?"

"You working for Paul Murphy? Blue Gem?"

The man looked confused.

"KHSAA," the man said.

"What?"

"I work for the KHSAA. Kentucky High School Athletic Association. I'm an investigator for 'em."

"High school athletics?" Will asked and lowered the gun a bit. "Are you serious?"

"Yeah."

"What the hell you doin' here?"

The man swallowed, looked around, and Will raised his gun again.

"I'm investigating your daughter's transfer to Hazard. Whether your divorce is real. Whether your daughter got recruited," the man said in a rush.

Will lowered his gun, put his hands on his knees, and started to laugh. The man gradually let his hands fall to his sides.

"Oh Lord, Lord, Lord," Will said.

"What?" the man said.

Will looked back and saw Amos peek his head out of the house.

"It's okay," Will called. "The man investigates high school sports!"

And with that, Will let out another peal of laughter. Amos came out on the porch, a bemused look on his face.

"Can I see some ID?" Will finally asked.

The man fumbled for his wallet, fished out a card, and handed it to Will, who shook his head.

"All right, but you gotta go now. You don't know how close you come to gettin' shot," Will said and wiped his forehead with the back of the hand holding the gun.

The man nodded, got back in his car, backed out, and drove down the hollow. Will could hear his tires squeal. Will came walking back up to the house, shaking his head. As he got to the stairs, he heard the phone ring. He jogged up the stairs, walked by Amos, and picked up the phone on the third ring.

"Hello?" Will said, a smile still in his voice.

"Ah, Will?" It was Uncle Elliott, clearly thrown to hear even a hint of happiness in Will's tone. The night before, Will had been nearly suicidal.

"Uncle Elliott!" Will said. "Listen, I got it figured out. This whole thing was about a strip mine. The mine inundation, Rob's death, the map. Everything. It all fits. Paul's fixin' to strip-mine Hell-for-Certain. And it's gonna be the biggest damn strip mine you ever seen. That's why he had to get rid of the houses up there. That's why he deliberately cut into the old works. It's all about money."

There was no response.

"Uncle Elliott? I'm tellin' you, I got the strip-mine map. Right here. Got it from the miner man at Red Fox."

"He's there? Isn't he a fugitive?" the old man asked.

"Yeah, well, he was. But he's no more dangerous than I am."

"Son, I called 'cause I thought we needed to have this here out with Paul once and for all. What you're tellin' me means that's even more important. I called Paul today, and he said he'd meet us at the old Blue Dog mine."

"The Blue Dog mine?" Will asked. He had not been back since the explosion, ten years earlier. "There's nothin' there no more, is there? Why there?"

"I don't know, son. But you need to come. You gotta have it out with him so you can put it behind you. 'Fore you file charges against your own brother, you need to tell him why. And then you can do your job. I'll meet you there in twenty minutes. Oh, and bring that miner man."

"Why?"

" 'Cause once Paul even sees that guy, he'll know it's over."

"All right, I'll ask if he'll come," Will said.

"Good, I'll see you soon. I'm proud of you, son."

"Okay. See you there," Will said and hung up the phone.

Amos didn't actually need much persuading. He seemed to want to confront, or maybe inspect, Paul as much as Will.

"I been camping out under his porch," Amos said.

"You what?" Will asked with a laugh.

"Yeah. Figured a while ago he was at the center of this thing."

Will shook his head. The man was impressive. There were no two ways about it.

"Well, let's get," Will said, and they walked down to his truck and drove away.

Will felt his anxiety mount the closer they got to the old mine. He had never been back. Never intended to go back. The old Blue Dog mine was the graveyard of his life's happiness. And if his younger brother were to haunt anyplace, it would be there. Knowing that Jeff's death had been a family conspiracy—with Paul, their father, and Will all playing some role—didn't make it all better. Bright and funny, Jeff had been the glue that held the family together.

And he was still dead.

Will felt his breathing constrict. When he turned onto the mine's gravel entry road, now choked with weeds, he briefly considered stopping the truck to catch his breath. But he didn't think putting on the brakes would do anything for his chest, so he kept driving.

The road rose steeply up the side of the mountain and ended in a small canyon bounded on both sides by mountain slopes. The office trailer was still there but barely recognizable. The explosion had scorched a corner of the trailer, and it had fallen in there. Insulation hung from the thin walls.

At the edge of the gravel was a grove of now leafless hackberry trees, several grown to a surprising height. Their bare, scawny limbs made the place look haunted, which it probably was.

Uncle Elliott's white Caddy was parked near the trailer, and as Will drove up, he saw Paul's Jaguar behind the trailer. But neither man was in sight. Could they actually be in that nasty trailer?

Will pulled up his truck and glanced at Amos with a puzzled expression. Will took several deep breaths and opened his door. Amos came around the truck, his expression blank. The mine site was dead silent.

"Uncle Elliott?" Will called. No answer.

"Uncle Elliott?" he yelled louder. Still no answer.

After more deep breaths, Will started toward the trailer. Amos followed a step behind. Will felt like a stray dog approaching the pound. Everything in him shouted that he should be running in the other direction.

They neared the door, and Will raised a hand to try the handle.

The shot exploded out of the collapsed part of the trailer. Will ducked, looked over to see Uncle Elliott holding a rifle, and then saw Amos fall backward.

"Jesus!" Will shouted.

Uncle Elliott stepped out of the ruined wall of the trailer, pushing aside tattered insulation as he went. He was wearing a heavy tan jacket, jeans, and hiking boots—dressed to hunt.

"Uncle Elliott? What the hell you doing? That man's helping my investigation."

"He's a fugitive, Will."

Uncle Elliott walked to Amos and stood over the big miner. Amos was still breathing, but his eyes were clouding over. Will came out of his frozen crouch and rushed toward Amos, whose eyelids fluttered and then closed.

"Jesus," Will said.

"Let's get this done. Come on," Uncle Elliott said and walked back toward Paul's Jaguar carrying the rifle as if about to use it again.

Will followed a few steps behind, mouthing the words "What the fuck?" as he went.

The old man rounded the car, stopped, and looked down. Will came around the front and saw Paul lying against the driver's door, blood splashed down his face and shirtfront. He was either unconscious or dead.

"Oh my God," Will said.

"I hit him in the head," Uncle Elliott said. "Wanted to give you the chance to kill him."

"What?"

"Will, this man ruined your whole life. He killed Jeff and pinned it on you. He turned your father and mother against you. He took every bit of the family company away from you. He's been worse to you than your daddy was to me, and if I coulda had the chance to kill your father, I'da taken it."

"Will." Paul barely whispered the word. His eyes were still closed, his head still slumped to one side.

Uncle Elliott raised the butt of his rifle.

"Stop, damnit," Will said and held out his hand.

"Will," Paul said louder. He opened his eyes but didn't otherwise move. "The flood. It was Uncle Elliott. Not me."

Slumped against the car, Paul fell the rest of the way to the ground and turned his head to the sky.

"Damn right it was," Uncle Elliott said, his eyes shining. "Will, we're talking two hundred, three hundred million dollars. More money than God's got."

"Oh hell. That's right. You own the land. You were the one choosing miners for the crews," Will said, blinking.

"Your brother ain't the sharpest tool in the shed, son. He just figured this out last night when he talked to the surveyor. You knew less than him, and you got to the answer. I had to tell my old friend Preacher Seymour to lead you to Joe and Gaynell's store, but you got there. I's hoping you could just arrest Paul, get him outta the way so's I could start strippin'. But now that he's got it figured, he'd only mess it up. Gotta kill him, son. Got to."

Before Uncle Elliott finished, Paul spoke again.

"What?" Will asked, refusing to approach his brother.

"Blue Dog, too. Gas well his idea," Paul mumbled.

"Paul, you lying sumbitch," Uncle Elliott said. He raised his rifle again.

"Whyn't you just shoot him?" Will asked.

The question seemed to please the old man.

"Can't. Wouldn't look good. We need the police to think Paul shot the miner over there, and the miner beat Paul. Then they'll pin everything—the flood, the other two murders, everything—on Paul."

"Why?"

" 'Cause this the gun that killed them other fellas."

"But it's your gun?" Will asked.

"They don't know that."

"So you killed those other fellas?" Will asked.

"Well, the foreman knew too much from the get-go, and Carl, well, he figured it out after a while," Uncle Elliott said, nodding. "Can't have that."

Will's mind raced. If Uncle Elliott planned all this out, set up the inundation, killed the miners, everything—that meant he must have been in league with the driller, Dee Singleton. It was Dee who put in that gas well at Blue Dog and caused the explosion. Uncle Elliott must have known about it.

"Whyn't you tell me about this, Uncle El?" Will demanded, and jerked his thumb toward the nearby mine entrance. "Why?"

"Son," the old man paused, his eyes narrowed. "You needed to get here yourself."

"But your kidneys are gone. You can't think you're gonna live long enough to spend all that money."

"This is the thing that's been keepin' me going, Will. Gettin' my piece."

Will nodded. He turned and took several steps toward the mountainside. Four narrow entryways, slots in the mountain, opened out into the mine area. There was just enough light to see a few feet into the nearest entryway. Gone was the limestone dust that coated the walls when Will worked there, but he could still envision the innards of the place: the dogleg at the twenty-ninth break, the complicated ventilation bridge at the fiftieth break, the endless conveyor.

It was probably all still there, along with the inevitable roof falls that came with years. Will could walk into the mine and let it take him, as it nearly did and probably should have done ten years earlier.

Still looking at the mine, Will asked, "And the miner man here? The rest of the crew? They just collateral damage, Uncle Elliott?"

"That man's a drug dealer, son. The whole crew was. That's why I hired 'em. Nobody'll miss 'em."

"And Rob?"

"The nigger?" Uncle Elliott asked.

Will smiled. It was the tipping point. Will was pretty sure that he would never have been able to kill his brother in cold blood, and he certainly wouldn't do it now. Rob was expendable to Uncle Elliott because he was black. Will suddenly wanted nothing to do with his uncle.

Will walked ten yards more toward the mine and, as he turned to face Uncle Elliott, put his hand in his jacket pocket.

Uncle Elliott had lowered the rifle and swung it so that it was almost pointing at Will.

"I always wanted to be a cowboy, Uncle El. Let's me and you shoot it out."

Uncle Elliott pursed his lips. "You're a dumb shit," the old man said and raised the rifle.

Will watched him move with a weird sense of detachment. Will was ready to die, sort of wanted to. But he was competitive enough to want to win this duel, if only to take his friend's murderer with him.

Uncle Elliott had the first shot, but at fifteen yards only managed to hit Will in the side. Twenty-two-caliber rifles were great when you hit someone head-on, but if they hit bone at a sharp angle, they tended to glance off. The bullet deflected off Will's ribcage.

Will's disinterest in the outcome meant that his hand was steady. The two guns exploded at the same moment. The old man's second shot went wide; Will's struck true. Will kept firing. He got off four shots before Uncle Elliott collapsed.

Will walked forward, curious. The old man had fallen forward, not backward or sideways as he and Rob had always imagined. Will stood over his uncle for a moment, squatted down and turned him on his side. Blood was pouring from a wound in his neck. He was gurgling. Will put his hand on the old man's cheek. Uncle Elliott's eyes opened briefly, and he looked at Will as if puzzled about something.

And then he died.

Will let the old man roll back on his face. He stood up.

Paul was looking at him sideways, obviously unable to move his head or neck. Will looked at his older brother and bit his lower lip. Neither said anything.

Will turned on his heel and walked back toward his truck, started it, and drove toward Paul's car. He swung around Uncle Elliott's body and stopped a few feet away.

He got out, opened the tailgate, and came to his brother's side.

"Paul, I'm gonna put you in the back of the pickup. I'm worried about moving ya, but I don't think we can wait for an ambulance," Will said.

Paul blinked.

Will put his arms under his brother and managed to lift him. He staggered to the pickup and put Paul as gently as he could in the bed. Will had to shove Paul to get him the rest of the way in, and in the shift Paul passed out. Oops, Will thought.

Will jogged around to the driver's door, got in, put the truck in gear and edged forward. He stopped, opened his door, and looked around. Amos's body was gone. He walked around to the front of his truck and then looked under the vehicle. No body. Will realized that he hadn't seen the body since before the shootout.

"Amos!" Will shouted. "Amos Blevins?"

The sound echoed around the canyon.

Will jogged toward the last mine entrance and looked inside. "Amos?" he shouted. Nothing. He jogged past the others and did the same thing. He made a circuit around the mine area and came back toward the trailer. He pulled aside some of the insulation at the ruined corner of the trailer and looked inside. Nothing.

He shook his head and returned to his truck. As he drove down the mine entrance, Will craned his neck forward and scanned the area. No Amos. He drove Paul to the hospital.

# CHAPTER FORTY-FIVE

W hy didn't you tell me?"
 Will asked the question softly, no anger in his voice. He was sitting in a chair beside his brother's hospital bed. Paul had bandages covering the top of his head. The right side of his face was paralyzed, so it was hard to judge his expression.

"Dad told me not to," Paul said, the words slurred.

"But Paul, Dad died three weeks ago. And he ain't been himself for two, three years," Will said and looked out the window. "I been thinkin' all these years that I killed Jeff, that I hurt Rob, that I destroyed the mine, that it was all my fault. Nearly killed me."

A frown tried to crease Paul's face. He closed his eyes for a moment.

"Too hard," he slurred with some effort. "Too hard to tell you."

Will looked at the floor and nodded. His brother had become a son of a bitch in recent years, and Will had assumed that it was because he blamed Will for the explosion. Will now realized that it was because he blamed himself.

There's nothing worse than knowing that you've wounded someone because of your own stupidity or greed. Guilt must have been eating away at Paul's insides for years. Will suddenly felt sorry for him.

Something metal banged against the door to the little bathroom in the corner of Paul's hospital room. The door opened only slightly. Will sprang to his feet and pulled the door all the way open. His mother came out, pushing an aluminum walker.

"Thank you, son," she said. She hesitated.

"Come on, sit here, Momma," Will said and motioned to the chair beside Paul. "I gotta get going anyways."

She pushed toward the chair, stopped beside Will, and put a frail hand to his cheek. She seemed ready to cry. Will put his own hand over hers, squeezed and then kissed it. She made it to the chair and sat.

"Caroline'll be back soon, Paul. Said she just had a few errands to run. I'll be back this evening to look in on you," Will said. "Momma," he said, nodding to his mother. He left the room and nearly ran headlong into Sergeant Detective Gene Freeman.

"Hey, what're you doing here?" Will asked.

"Oh, we got a prisoner got banged up," the policeman said. "This your brother's room?"

Will nodded.

"How's he doing?" Sergeant Freeman asked.

"Let's walk," Will said, and they both headed toward the exit.

After a few yards, Will said, "He's pretty banged up. Paralyzed on his right side: arm, leg, everything. Gonna have to learn how to walk and talk again. Even eat."

"That's rough."

"Yeah," Will said and nodded.

"You two getting along?"

Will shrugged. "It's complicated."

Paul's wife, Caroline, had asked Will to run the company while Paul recovered. Will would have to quit MSHA, but Paul might never come back anyways.

Will had refused. For ten years, all he'd wanted in life was to return to the company and his family's good graces. Now that both were within reach, he no longer wanted either. He'd finally realized that he wasn't the cause of the myriad problems in his family. They were.

"Family," the sergeant said and pursed his lips. "Speaking of which, I heard from the KHSAA yesterday afternoon. Sounds like they're gonna drop the investigation into Helen's transfer to Hazard. And they're no longer looking to prosecute you for scaring the living shit out of their investigator."

"I'm thinkin' you had some'm to do with that," Will said.

"Well, I told 'em about what happened and said there was no way we could get a grand jury to issue an indictment. They weren't too happy at first, but seems like they'll come around."

"I'll tell Tessy," Will said.

Will was due to see her that afternoon, and he knew she'd be glad to hear that the KHSAA was no longer interested in Helen. She'd hinted the day before that she would probably move back in with Will if the investigation closed.

Will had been thinking about the offer ever since. Again, it was something he'd been hoping for. Again, he decided he'd probably not take the offer. He needed to be on his own for a while and see what it felt like not to hate himself.

"You going back to MSHA?" the sergeant asked.

"Yeah. Feel like I just started doing the job for real. And I got a taste for it now," Will said.

"Could cause a ruckus there," the cop said.

"What else can they do to me?" Will answered with a sad smile.

"Kill you."

They both chuckled.

"Speaking of which, anyone find Amos Blevins yet?"

The sergeant shook his head.

"What in the world could have happened to him?" Will asked.

"You sure he got shot, right?" the cop asked.

"Pretty sure," Will said. "I thought he was dead."

The trooper shrugged. "And what about the strip mine? It gonna get done?"

"No," Will said. "Crazily enough, Uncle Elliott left his rights to me. And I'm not gonna do anything but help those folks leave. I'll have to sell most of the land to do it, but I'm not sellin' to nobody that wants to strip it."

Sergeant Freeman shook his head.

"See ya around," Will said.

"Give your wife my best. I'd like to meet her one of these days," the sergeant said.

"Sure."

Will smiled, waved, and they went to separate places in the parking lot.


Glenda had been up for hours, unable to sleep. She finally drove to the Lick Creek gas station just as dawn was starting to break. She sat in her car outside the station for several minutes, looking around and waiting. She'd been told that Amos was dead, but a part of her didn't believe it.

She got out and went into the station. There was a middle-aged, plump woman behind the counter, smoking. She nodded at Glenda.

Glenda walked slowly through the shelves to the bathroom, opened the door and went in. She stood with both hands on the sink and looked at herself in the mirror. She closed her eyes and sighed. She left the bathroom and was pushing her way out the door of the station when she stopped and turned around. She went to the shelves, got a Snickers bar and a Gatorade bottle, and brought them to the counter.

"Wait, I left my purse in the car," she said.

The woman behind the counter gave a curt nod, and Glenda trotted out the door.

She went around to the driver's side of the car when a light shone in her face, blinding her.

"Mrs. Blevins?"

"Yeah?" Glenda said, trying to shield her eyes. Between her fingers, Glenda saw a bearded man of average height wearing glasses and dressed in white. He was holding an old-style lantern that gave off a surprising amount of light.

"I am Jacob Fellinghausen," the man said, and glanced around. Glenda realized that the man seemed to be wearing an old-style night-gown with dark trousers underneath.

"I have come to take you to your husband," Fellinghausen said.

"Where?"

"In my barn."

"Is he alive?"

"Yes, only how he survived I do not know. He has asked for you."

"Oh Lord," Glenda said and began to cry.

"Come with me in my buggy. It will be slower but more sure than any directions I might give."

Only then did Glenda notice a horse-drawn black trap standing at the side of the road near the station.

"Okay," she said, and started walking toward the buggy.

"You should dispose of your car," Fellinghausen said without moving. "Leaving it in front of the station would lead to questions."

"Oh. Right," Glenda said. She walked quickly to her sister's car, got in, and because her hands were shaking badly, took a moment to start it. She circled around the station, drove to the other side of the road, and parked it under a tree. She left the keys under the front seat.

She trotted back to the trap, where Fellinghausen waited. He held the passenger door for her. She stepped in, the springs giving way. He walked around, got in beside her, and took up the reins. The horse started to walk.

There was no windshield. Glenda shivered.

"I have no coat or blanket. I am sorry," Fellinghausen said.

"What happened?" she asked. "How?"

"He came to us two nights ago. He had been shot. I wanted to take him to the hospital. He would not hear of it. I thought he would die."

Glenda put a hand to her mouth and sobbed again.

"He is exceptionally strong," Fellinghausen said. "That, or God has truly anointed him. By last night, it was obvious that he would live. He asked me to find you."

Glenda got a bad case of the hiccups, so she didn't speak for some time.

They turned off Daniel Boone Highway onto a road that soon became gravel. After another ten minutes of driving, Fellinghausen turned into a farm. He stopped the trap, and Glenda sprang out. He led her to a stone barn.

"He would not stay in the house. I think he feared what might happen if he died or was discovered there," Fellinghausen said as he opened a wide barn door. "He has made a bed in the tack room."

Fellinghausen pointed, and Glenda walked quickly to an inner door.

The sun was just rising, but the barn was still dark. Fellinghausen left his lantern inside the barn door and walked away. Glenda opened the tack room door.

Amos was lying on what appeared to be a pile of blankets. He was asleep. Glenda collapsed to her knees and then crawled forward. She hugged his feet, and Amos woke up. He smiled at her.

"Hey," he said.

"Hey yourself, cowboy," Glenda said and crawled to him.

Later, when he dropped her off at the Lick Creek station, Fellinghausen gave Glenda a wooden cross. She knew she'd wear it forever.

"But if there's no KHSAA investigation, then there's no reason for me and Helen to stay in Hazard," Tessy said.

"I know, baby. I just need a little time," Will said.

"For what?"

"Think things through."

"Since when have you wanted me living someplace else?" she asked. Will shrugged.

"Honey, this whole thing was never about you and me. It was about Helen," she said.

"Yeah," Will said, and looked back toward his truck. They were standing outside Paul's mansion. Helen was sitting in his passenger seat, waiting. Will held up a finger to signal a minute more. Helen nodded.

Will turned back to his wife.

"I need to figure out my place in the world, Tessy. You been propping me up for a long time, and that's probably one o' the reasons you cooked up this whole crazy scheme, even if you don't admit it to yourself. But I think I can stand on my own now, and I need to see what that feels like."

She blinked several times, tears gathering on her lashes.

"How long will that take?" she finally asked.

"I don't know."

She nodded and looked at the ground.

"I'm sorry," she said.

"Me, too, baby."

"I'll wait," she said.

Will gripped her arm, kissed her cheek, and turned back to his truck. He heard her sob and stopped for a moment with his hands on his hips. He started walking again without looking back.

He got into his truck and headed the vehicle down the hollow.

"Well, what do you want to do, Helen? Go play a little basketball?"

"Do we have to, Daddy? I am so sick of Mom obsessing with that game," his daughter said, her voice fierce.

"Really?" Will asked and laughed. "All right, how about if we go to the Wal-mart and then the diner?"

"Sure," Helen said and leaned her head against her father.


"'. . . Thomas answered him, "My Lord and my God!" Jesus said to him, "Have you believed because you have seen me? Blessed are those who have not seen and yet believe."'"

The minister closed the book and looked out upon the congregation.

"The word of the Lord," he said.

"Thanks be to Thee, oh Christ," the congregation answered.

He walked down from the beautifully carved lectern and stood in front of the congregation near the altar. A pale rose light from the stained-glass windows on the eastern side of the church washed over him.

"Just a reminder," said the minister, dressed in a beautifully colored cassock. "On Wednesday night, we're going to have a meeting to start planning our annual Easter pig roast. Please come. Are there any other announcements?"

He looked out to the congregation.

A bearded, broad-shouldered man wearing odd clothing stood up in one of the pews.

"A word," he said. "A word about saving these mountains God has given us dominion over."